BLOOD ON THE BAYOU

Bouchercon Anthology 2016

BLOOD ON THE BAYOU

Bouchercon Anthology 2016

EDITED BY
GREG HERREN

DOWN&OUT BOOKS

Down & Out Books
3959 Van Dyke Rd, Ste. 265
Lutz, FL 33558
www.DownAndOutBooks.com

Cover design by JT Lindroos

ISBN: 1-943402-34-5
ISBN-13: 978-1-943402-34-2

To Librarians,
who feed both the mind and the soul

CONTENTS

CONTENTS

Introduction
Heather Graham

There are few places on earth that offer as unique an aura of mystery as New Orleans, Louisiana. From moss-draped oaks on grassy banks to cemeteries known as "cities of the dead," the very air and architecture seem to whisper of the secrets kept and stolen, history hidden in the mist, and more—all within a realm of exquisite and often decaying elegance.

Naturally, from the city itself abounds with true tales of those who created murder and mayhem, to the cruelties of Madame de LaLaurie who, with her husband, tortured slaves with macabre medical experiments. When their house of horrors was discovered by the police due to a fire set by a desperate cook, the couple managed to ride off in a carriage into the streets of New Orleans—before disappearing from the ages. Too, there was the supposed sultan, viciously slaughtered in his "palace." The deserted mulatto beauty who froze to death upon a roof, the distained lover who threw herself from the roof—or not! Was it murder most foul?

The city is cloaked in the mysteries created and stirred up by brilliant voodoo priestess Marie Laveau, a woman with a remarkable talent for listening. Creating hair styles for the city's rich and esteemed, she often learned what she should say to those who came for advice. Her legacy is amazing—in fact, stop by St. Louis Number 1 and pay her visit. Let your imagination run as you travel the cemetery where so many dignitaries are interred in their magnificent tombs, mausoleums, or "ovens."

You'll be inspired yourself!

Beautiful, decadent, wicked, refined—all these things, and more! The high ground on the river hosted the French and the Spanish and American flags—and was torn here and there by years of brutality and war. Truly, unique from her founding upon the great Mississippi, there is nothing like the city of New Orleans.

Some of the world's greatest writers have been *haunted* by New Orleans themselves, from Anne Rice and Truman Capote back to Tennessee Williams and Eudora Welty, the list is a literary who's who. The Hotel Monteleone is—along with the Algonquin in New York City—one of country's greatest literary landmarks. You can still pop by and have "Dinner at Antoine's," as in the famous Frances Parkinson Keyes novel.

And, today, of course, the trend continues. Writers flock to New Orleans. It isn't just seeing NOLA, it's *feeling* NOLA. From the blaring music and risqué clubs and bars of Bourbon Street to the historic "spirit" of Lafitte's and the distinguished and circumspect tables of Arnaud's, there is a blend of the wild and the beautiful—from an anything goes attitude to centuries-old charm and dignity.

Come to New Orleans. See her incredibly atmospheric cemeteries, walk her streets, take a mule-driven carriage and hear tales of war, pestilence, and plague. You, too, will begin to feel the city, because, as in the best fiction, the city is not just a place—it is truly a character.

Now, please, sit back and enjoy these contemporary tales of mystery and intrigue, because there is no place for mystery like New Orleans, where the breeze off the Mississippi may run hot or cold, where the mists fall upon moss with such haunting beauty, and where, one can imagine, just about anything *mysterious* might occur.

Icon
Alison Gaylin

Icon has dressed for the occasion. Purple jeans and sparkly Converse high tops. Oversized T-shirt that hangs on her skinny frame, emblazoned with the logo for her mom's latest movie. Nice touch, the movie logo. *Inspired.* Her shining blonde hair is in Becky Thatcher braids and, feeding swans in Audubon Park, she looks almost impossibly young and innocent. Until she turns her face to me. "He's late," she says.

My fanny pack vibrates. I pluck my phone out and glance at the screen. The sun is very bright, hot on the back of my sweaty neck. I have to shield my eyes to read the text, which, sure enough, is from him.

BEHIND THE LIVE OAKS DUE NORTH. GET HER TO TURN.

I tug on my left earlobe—our signal—and Icon nods in that subtle way of hers, imperceptible to anyone but me. My heart starts to pound. *Showtime.*

"Look at the cute bunny!" I shout, gesturing at the row of live oaks due north, not twenty feet behind Icon. From where I'm standing, I can see an arm, a crouched knee and then his lens, glinting like the eyes of an animal.

Icon whirls around, aims her whole body at the line of live oaks, her face bursting into a smile. "Where?" she cries, and for a moment, I see her as he does: A beautiful, exuberant little girl. Cover-shot material. Big money.

But it's all over in an instant. Icon spins back around again, puts her back to the trees. "I don't see any bunny." She says it in a pouty voice, loud enough for him to hear.

3

Behind the live oaks is foresty brush—a good hiding place, convenient for him to retreat into if spotted. Convenient for us, too. Interesting how needs can intersect, no matter how at odds those needs may be. My phone vibrates with another text.

TOO FAST. DIDN'T GET THE SHOT.

I move closer to Icon, blocking her from his camera with my broad body in a way that I know appears unintentional. She looks up from her hands. I mouth the word, *It worked*. She smiles, then goes back into character—pouting, spoiled celebrity brat. I count to ten, then text him back.

I'LL BRING HER OVER.

Last night, as she was getting ready for bed, Icon told me that I'm her best friend. And strange as that was, I had no doubt it was true. She's my best friend as well. She is nine years old and internationally famous. I'm fifty-one and would probably be living on the street if I wasn't on her parents' payroll. But we do share something. To call it an understanding would be to simplify what it is.

A bicyclist speeds by on the path behind us, wheels clicking and humming. I wait for him to pass. Besides Icon, Mr. Live Oaks and me, there are very few people in the park. It is a stifling hot August day. Mosquitos buzz over the pond and a smell hangs in the air—algae and fish and ripe, rotting things. No one wants to be out in nature, not today. No one except for hunters.

Icon looks at me. I lay a finger to the right of my nose—another signal. She nods and, without warning, throws her head back. "I don't want to go home and you can't make me!" she shrieks. Following the script. She buries her head in her hands as I back away, doing my best to look flustered. I'm not much of an actress, but I don't need to be. "But...but..." I say. "But."

"I hate you, I hate you, you big fat meanie!"

I can't see him save for the lens, but I know he's eating it up. *You ain't seen nothing yet.* It's hard not to smile. When Icon raises her head again, I know, she will be sobbing.

I've been with Icon since she was six months old. Her parents—we'll call them Mr. and Mrs. X; their names get said enough—bought a house here right after Katrina, a fine old mansion in the French Quarter, rumored to be haunted by the ghost of a consumptive French prostitute.

Even though it had sustained very little damage in the flood, they gutted the place, renovated it top to bottom, threw in lots of chrome accents, white marble floors and white satin furniture, chrome and white everywhere like some sort of debauched surgical theater, only with the ugliest art you've ever seen hanging on the walls. It's embarrassing really, living here. I've never once felt the presence of that prostitute. I'm convinced she left out of pure disgust.

At any rate, the burst of empathy that led Mr. and Mrs. X to our ravaged town in the first place awakened in them feelings of permanence, of "building for the future," as Mr. X told *Rolling Stone.* Those feelings set the stage for the birth of their first child, Icon. Yes, that is her real name. She hates it. She'd use her middle name, as is customary for the children of narcissistic celebrities burdened with gimmicky monikers. But Icon's middle name is Katrina.

They hired me because I'm from the town that their hearts went out to. All of Icon's original team of nannies were from New Orleans as well, but I'm the only one who's lasted. I've lasted a long time, too. The average tenure for a nanny in this house is three to four months, but I've been with the X's employ for close to a decade. Mrs. X says it's because I'm the only responsible nanny she's been able to find. Icon tells me it's because she'd kill her parents if they ever fired me. But while I do believe that both of them are telling the truth, I'm also the only nanny Mr. X has never tried to have sex with, a strong reason for job security if there ever was one.

Slowly, Icon lifts her head from her hands. Her face is purplish red, drenched in tears. She opens her mouth wide, her face a tragedy mask. I wait for the scream and when it comes, it curdles the blood. It shakes the bones. You can feel it, deep in the crevices of your teeth.

For a moment, I forget to move. I am that in awe of Icon, of her talent. But I then I remember. *Must hit my mark.* I step out of the way, giving Mr. Live Oaks a clear bead on the temper tantrum. Strange, but in a way I'm jealous of him, the thrill that must be running through his veins, capturing this event. "No, no, no!!" She pounds the dirt with her fists, the swans hustling into the water, gliding out of her reach as fast as they can.

I've seen many temper tantrums over the years—most all of them chilling, some of them epic. But this one, this is a true tour de force. I know it's my imagination, but for a moment I swear I can hear him over there amongst the plant life, dropping his camera and applauding.

Icon was not always an only child. When she was four years old, Mrs. X gave birth to a son—a rosy-cheeked boy they named Buddha. Icon cooed over Buddha when her parents were around, asked to hold him and feed him and to help Mama pick out his clothes. But not when they weren't. I could see the coldness in her eyes when she looked at him—a coldness I recognized in myself. Mrs. X paid less attention to us, took us on fewer outings in the Escalade in favor of her chubby, Dior-clad baby son. It was hard not to feel left out and jealous, and so we did. We wallowed in it.

Icon's other two nannies had recently been fired—at the

same time; try and guess what happened—and so she and I were on our own a lot. Many days, I'd throw a baseball cap over her blonde curls and take her to District Donuts on Magazine Street and there we'd binge, unnoticed, to our hearts' content. It was during one of those visits that she said, very calmly. "I'm going to get rid of him."

"What do you mean?"

Icon gave me a withering look. I knew her well enough not to play dumb with her, even back then. Her eyes are pale blue and frosty as just-picked ice and when trained on you, they can make you feel as though you are about to lose your footing. "I guess I know what you mean," I said.

Was there nothing I could do? Shouldn't I have told her parents or consulted a child psychiatrist or even called the police—anything to prevent a tragedy I knew was about to happen? I've asked myself these questions dozens of times since that chilly February morning in District Donuts and either I don't know the answers or I don't want to know them. All I can remember is taking a huge bite of my donut (flavor of the day, Irish coffee), savoring the creamy mocha taste and feeling, not for the first time, as though I'd crossed over a line made of fire. The flames kept rising. I couldn't turn back. "Now, now," I said to the little girl sitting across from me. An adorable little girl with pink frosting on her nose, smiling wide enough to burst. "Now, now."

Buddha's death was described in the press as SIDS, though the actual cause was suffocation. Somehow, in the middle of the night when the rest of us were sound asleep, he'd managed to wedge his head under the big, furry SpongeBob pillow he loved so much, cutting off his air supply. Buddha's night nanny swore up and down she had taken SpongeBob out of the crib before putting him to sleep, but no one believed her. She was fired.

The Xs mourned for several weeks and gave an interview to *People*—shortly after which, Buddha's day nanny, a nasty, thin-lipped woman who once told Mrs. X, "Your daughter is not to be trusted," fell to her death from the widow's walk in the wee hours of the morning.

After her funeral, we went on a family vacation to Paris. Icon was an angel during the long trip on the private plane and so, to reward her, the Xs got them to close down Euro-Disney for a full day, just for us.

It was thrilling. We went on all the rides. I don't know that I've ever seen Icon so happy.

There were other strange deaths. The cat drowned in the koi pond out back. The dog euthanized after somehow falling down three flights of stairs. The elderly gardener chainsawed nearly in half in a gruesome apparent accident that sent Mrs. X to a number of psychics, convinced that the consumptive prostitute had put a curse on the house.

I knew better, though I couldn't admit it out loud, or even in my thoughts. The cat had scratched Icon's face. The dog had ripped apart one of her favorite dolls. The gardener had caught her disposing of the guinea pig in the azalea bush—days after he'd supposedly gone missing—and told me about it. (*"He's crazy,"* Icon had insisted. *"I would never. You have to believe me."*)

But the math tutor I couldn't ignore.

Icon had always hated math. As skilled as she was at memorizing Shakespeare passages and learning new languages, she couldn't seem to grasp the simplest concepts where numbers were concerned. Even multiplication tables were a struggle. So when her parents added Miss DuBois to the home-school staff to "get Icon up to speed," it was with the best of intentions. Miss DuBois was young and vibrant, a recent Tulane grad who no doubt saw employment with the Xs as both a stepping stone and a blessing, complete with free rent. She planned on getting her masters in economics, once she saved up enough money.

Miss DuBois wasn't like Icon's other math tutors had been. When Icon couldn't get a problem right, she didn't just throw up her hands, give her the answers and plant a gold star on her workbook. "If I tell you the answer," she would say, "you'll never learn."

The problem was, though, that Icon didn't *want* to learn. "She doesn't get it," she complained to me one night when I was reading her to sleep. "I'm paying *her*. It's not the other way around."

"Icon?"

"I hate her."

"*Icon?*"

"Yeah?"

"You aren't planning on...hurting Miss DuBois in any way, are you?"

She stared at me. "Why would you even *say* that?" she gasped. And then she smiled—that bright grin of hers that would have been infectious, had I not known it like I did, like I still do. She was eight and a half years old, but for a flash she was four again, across the table from me at District Donuts. I could almost see the frosting on her nose.

I said nothing to Miss DuBois, didn't voice my concerns to anyone. But I watched Icon very closely. I made sure her schedule was packed with outings, sometimes tipping off the paparazzi just to make sure she was seen. Keeping a safe distance, I followed her around the house. After her bedtime, when the guards had gone home for the night, I snuck into the surveillance room and watched her on the camera 'til I was certain she was asleep, popping caffeine tablets to stay alert.

And then, one night, it happened. It must have been four in

the morning and, after that many days without sleep, I was so close to delirious that for a few seconds I thought I was hallucinating and tried to blink the image away.

But no. There she was in her white nightgown, slipping out of bed, sliding her dresser drawer open and taking something out. When she opened the door to her room, I caught a flash of the object in her tiny hand. It glinted.

The surveillance room is in the basement, three floors away from the room Miss DuBois was sleeping in. I am a large woman and not in the best of shape. Icon is all of eighty pounds and fleet as a fox.

At least I knew where she was headed.

I tackled each flight of stairs, sweat pouring off of me, breath cutting through my lungs, to the point of where I worried my heart might give out. My feet thudded on the marble. I prayed Mr. and Mrs. X had taken their Ambien, prayed the other household staff wouldn't care enough to open their doors at this hour.

"Please, please, please," I whispered. "Please don't be too late…"

When I caught up with Icon, she had her hand on the doorknob. In her other hand, I could see the object now in three dimensions: a hunting knife, blade exposed, easily twelve inches long. *Where the hell did she get that?* "Stop," I breathed.

She took her hand off the doorknob and turned to me. "Oh," she said. "Hi, Maddy." I realized how rare it was she ever called me by name.

I laid a hand over hers. "Don't do it."

She froze. Stared at me with those eyes of ice. "Don't do what?"

I stared back. "Don't," I said again, "do it."

"But," she said. "But. But…." Icon's tiny fingers gripped the knife. Her eyes softened, glistened.

I held her gaze and said it quietly. "You'll have to kill me first."

A tear trickled down her cheek. Her lip started to tremble. I'd have thought she was acting, but I knew her acting well enough to understand that she wasn't. For the briefest of moments, Icon looked as ashamed and helpless as any other little girl her age, hand caught in the cookie jar but still wanting that cookie. "It's not fair!" she wailed.

That's when the door opened. Miss DuBois stood there in an oversized Saints T-shirt, her hair in a ponytail, sleepy and outraged at the same time. "What do you think you're..." she said. Then she noticed the knife. She swallowed. I watched her throat go up and down, wondering how I could explain this, what I could do...*This isn't what it looks like* wasn't going to work. That much I knew.

"Oh my God," Miss DuBois said.

I heard myself say, "Get out of here."

"What?"

"Pack your bags. Leave tonight." I took a breath. Cleared my throat. Puffed myself up as best I could and said it in the most official voice I could muster. "We are no longer in need of your services. Please leave."

"But..."

Icon raised the knife. I caught her wrist, surprised by the tension in it.

"Jesus," Miss DuBois said. Her face went white. She backed away, Icon shaking in my arms, wet cheek against my skin, saying it over and over again in a thin, baby voice. "Why won't you let me, Maddy? It won't take long. Why won't you let me cut her dead?"

Miss DuBois was packed and gone within the hour.

Over the next few weeks I began to understand Icon in a way I never had before. I had thought they were an extension of her temper tantrums, these killings of hers. But they weren't that at all, and I could only see it in their absence. I wasn't sure whether she was born with it, or if it was a symptom of the way she was raised—as an accessory more than a child, a cute little thing with a ridiculous first name and no control over what she wore or where she went or what she learned in homeschool, wandering around this chrome and white monstrosity with no one to hang out with but the nanny. She had never wanted a dog or a cat, but they'd been given to her regardless. Photo ops with bows around their necks, much like herself, both of them white-blonde to match her hair and her mother's.

No, it wasn't a temporary rage that made her seize control of lives and end them. It was need. I was the only one who noticed the change in her after Miss DuBois left, how sad she grew, listless in front of her Nickelodeon shows. I'd try to take her out, but she wasn't having it. And when she stood with her parents on the red carpet at that kids' charity event, when she endured staged, camera-friendly playdates with the cook's snot-nosed son, Icon covered her face. She never smiled.

"Are you okay?" I asked her one night, while watching a rerun of *iCarly*.

"No," she said.

"I know."

"Please help me, Maddy."

I looked at her. "All right," I said. How could I not? It was a need, after all. And needs linger. They grow. Needs must be filled, lest they consume us completely. Lest we die together in this awful house and haunt it forever.

One month later, an article came out in the world's sleaziest supermarket tabloid, *The Asteroid*: THE TUTOR TELLS ALL. Mrs. X brought it home with shaking hands, dropped it on the kitchen table. "Look at this!" she moaned at me, at Icon, at anyone who would listen. "*Look at it!*"

Icon didn't even glance up from her Frosted Flakes, but I did. It was five pages long and filled with tales of the "vain and selfish" Xs and their "spoiled-brat daughter." Details of temper tantrums and smashed toys, of dinners consisting only of junk food, of Mr. X's week-long Frenchman Street drinking binges and the hours Mrs. X would spend in front of the mirror, popping Xanax and fretting over her crow's feet and letting Icon run wild.

When I got to the last word, though, I was able to breathe again. Though the unnamed "tutor" was clearly Miss DuBois, there was no mention of the night with the knife. "She did need money for graduate school," I said.

"I feel sick," said Mrs. X. She was propped up against the chrome refrigerator, arms tight around her concave stomach. "I feel *violated.*"

"Oh, nobody reads those tabloids anymore," I tried. "It's not like it's TMZ."

She looked up at me, eyes red-rimmed and pleading. "That article," she said softly. "It said I indulge Icon. Do I, Maddy? Do I indulge her?"

"No," I said. "You don't." *You don't know her well enough to indulge her.*

From the kitchen table came a keening sound that made my stomach clench up. I spun around to see Icon, hunched over the tabloid, her finger pressed against a picture.

"What's wrong, sweetie?" Mrs. X didn't say it. I did. "What's wrong? Let me help."

Icon spoke in a strangled voice. "They're...they're so...so mean," she said. I moved next to her and stared at the picture—a shot of Icon, eyes wide, teeth bared, cheeks a deep, angry red. The caption read, *THE BAD SEED: Out-of-control Icon lashes out in public!*

Icon said, "Remember how mean they were?"

"Who?"

"Those...those men."

I remembered, now. Of course I did. It had been one of those days when I was keeping my eye on her, taking her out on dozens of errands and excursions and photo-friendly walks, all to make sure she was never alone with Miss DuBois. It was a humid day and the air was thick and hard to breathe. She was overtired and overheated and we were going on the world's most boring errand ever—to the post office to buy stamps. I'd forgotten to put her baseball cap on, and I think the postman must have tipped them off. Or maybe it was that teenage girl texting against the street lamp on St. Phillip, that pink-haired tart in the short-shorts.

But whoever called it in, there they were, three of them, buzzing around us outside the post office, cameras whirring, both of us trying to swat them away. And the things they said...

"Icon, is it true your mom is dying of cancer?"

"Icon, where's your daddy? Does he love other ladies besides Mommy?"

"Icon, have you gained weight? You look fat!"

"Turn around, you little brat. Look at the camera, you ugly little..."

Icon lost it, shrieking like a harpy, spit flying out of her mouth. "Go away! Go away from me!"

The cameras went wild. Even though I couldn't see their faces, I could sense them smiling, counting up the dollar signs. *Paydirt.* I hated them.

"I remember them," I said to her now, and as I put my arms around her narrow shoulders, as I held her close and told her to take deep breaths and said everything will be okay, said nasty men like those photographers always get what they deserve...it hit me. The way to fill Icon's need and still be able to sleep at night.

"Maddy?" Mrs. X said, pushing away from the fridge. "I'm a good mother, aren't I?"

I didn't answer right away. I was reading the tiny photo credit under the picture of Icon, writing down the name..."You are a good mother," I said finally. But not to her.

The first one went off without a hitch.

It's easy to get a paparazzo's phone number when you work for world-famous celebrities. And when you call that paparazzo and tip him off that you and said celebrities' controversial only child will be at a certain place at a certain time, he will be there with bells on—even if that place is a condemned building on an overgrown lot in Tremé. *Don't tell anyone else*, I'd warned him over the phone. *Do you think I'm crazy?* he had replied. And then he'd offered me money for the tip. Lots of it.

We like to put on a show first, Icon and me. Make them think they've hit the jackpot before we close in on them. That's what we did with that first one, Icon pitching a classic fit, screaming that I'm the worst nanny who ever walked the face of the earth as we stomped into the crumbling building, me warning her to *shut your piehole or else.* I couldn't see him in the darkness, but I could hear his camera. I could hear him giggling.

When it came time, I held him down. Again, it was easy. Most of these guys I outweigh by at least fifty pounds. And Icon really does know how to use that hunting knife.

Afterwards, we destroyed his camera, swiped his phone and left his body there in that abandoned building for the police to discover. Once we were home and all cleaned up and in our pajamas, we sat on Icon's canopy bed and went through the dead man's contact list, looking up his follow photographers. As it turned out, there were five listed. Not a lot, but enough to keep us busy for a while.

Mr. Live Oaks is our last. And, as we finish up our routine and start to move toward him, I can't help but feel a bit melancholy. "Don't worry," Icon says. "We'll find more."

"Huh?"

"There's tons of mean people out there, Maddy. We just have to figure out where to look."

I stare at her. "How is it you can do that?"

"Do what?"

"Read my mind."

She grins. "It's like I told you before. You're my best friend."

"What the hell are you talking about?" Mr. Live Oaks says as we approach. "Why isn't she screaming?" But he doesn't matter. Not anymore.

As Icon reaches under the hem of her movie T-shirt and grabs the hunting knife, it strikes me how lucky we are to have found each other in this big, cruel, crazy world. And how happy it makes me to provide for Icon, to give that sweet little girl all the things she truly needs.

The Blind Lagoon Misadventure
O'Neil De Noux

They barely had time to pull the small boat under the overhang and get the body off before the rain blew in. The two gray-clad coroner's assistants zipped up the body bag, lifted it on a gurney before rolling the gurney across a white shell parking lot to the coroner's van. The rain peppered the tin overhang, drowning out the crunch of van's wheels across the shells as it pulled away.

Detective Joe Savary stood just under the overhang on the raised walkway next to the water with his sergeant, who lifted her khaki purse—actually a 5.11 tactical bag—on her left shoulder. Jodie Kintyre, in another of her skirt-suits, this one pale green that brought out the color in her wide-set hazel eyes, turned back to Savary and said, "Finish up as soon as you can. See you at the post."

Lightning streaked overhead and a thunderclap reverberated so hard it shook the walkway.

"I know this is Bayou Sauvage National Wildlife Refuge," Savary said, waving at the water now. "So this *is* Lake Pontchartrain, right?"

"Blind Lagoon." Jodie pointed across the water to a line of cypress trees. "The lake is beyond that strip of land over there." The wind picked up her blonde hair, swirling it, but her pageboy just returned to its place with barely a strand out of place. Savary had no such problem with his close-cropped hair.

"Didn't know we had lagoons in Louisiana. Except the man-made ones in Audubon Park. City Park."

Jodie shifted her bag. "Technically this is Blind Lagoon

Lake." She ducked her head and headed for her car. She called over her shoulder, "See ya' in the morning." Past their knocking off time, Jodie still had to drop downtown to complete the shift daily report before going home.

Blind Lagoon Lake. That makes a lot of sense, thought Savary.

He turned to the crime lab technician climbing into the small boat with his flashlight. "Let's finish up, shall we?"

At six-four, Savary was too large to get into the small craft with the crime lab tech and stood next to it as the rain increased beyond the overhang, a damp breeze washing in, bringing the musty, rancid odors of the swamp. The Bayou Sauvage National Wildlife Refuge, at nearly twenty-three thousand acres, was the largest swamp within the city limits of any American city. Savary, like most New Orleanians, had never visited it. It was a *swamp.* If he wanted to see gators and cottonmouths, there was the Audubon Zoo where they couldn't just pop out at you. Here there were also golden silk spiders hanging in huge webs—fierce-looking spiders with longs legs striped in black and gold, tuffs of black hair at their leg joints, long golden bodies about six inches long.

He focused on the boat as the initial search had come up with little beyond dried blood next to the victim's head. It was a new boat, yellow and blue fiberglass, an outboard motor and three small lockers, a padded seat. An orange life preserver was fastened outside each locker. The victim had been in a dark green polo shirt, khaki Dockers, brown running shoes. Next to the body they'd found a silver digital Sony camera.

The tech was Victor Jones and his skin was a couple shades lighter than Savary's dark brown. Jones stood and stretched, eased to the side of the boat, said, "I can't find anything else."

"What's that gray spot?" Savary pointed to a small splotch on the other side of the boat and the tech moved over there. A similar gray splotch was on Savary's side of the rail as well and he took out his flashlight.

"Looks like some sorta goo," Jones said.

"Some over here too." Savary's light played across a two inch splotch of organic matter, picking up thin slivers of plastic or maybe glass.

"I need you to collect both samples."

A sudden gust of wind brought rain in on them and the tech reached for his bag.

"It's now or never," he said and photographed both samples before collecting them, putting each in a separate vial.

Savary turned to a white pickup truck pulling into the lot with a boat trailer attached. The truck wheeled around and backed the trailer to the walkway, the engine killed and a heavy-set man in his thirties climbed out. The man was about six feet, maybe two hundred eighty pounds, wearing a black Saints T-shirt two sizes too small, faded jeans, and well-worn brown cowboy boots.

"I'm the one called y'all." The man extended a hand to shake. "Luke Gathers. Luke's Boat and Kayak Rentals. We're over on Christmas Camp Lake. Crazy sumbitch musta cut across Flat Bay and through the swamp to end up here."

Savary had found the rental papers on the boat and was writing fast in his notebook. "He give you his name?"

"I made a copy of his driver's license."

The victim's driver's license along with his wallet were in a brown paper bag in the back of the crime scene SUV. Victor Lansing from Baton Rouge. White male, seventy-seven years old.

"When did he rent the boat?"

"Yesterday morning. July first."

That was the date on the rental papers. "What time?"

"Shortly after we opened at seven a.m. His car's still at the landing. New Cadillac. I was afraid to leave it overnight even with the gate locked when he didn't come back yesterday. He said he might be late."

"Was he alone?"

"Yes, he was."

"Fishing gear?"

"Nope. Just a camera."

Savary looked into the man's deep-set eyes, asked, "How'd you find out about this?"

"Man came and told me he found the boat and the guy looked dead inside."

"What man?"

"An Isleños. Canary Islander. You know, skin dark as yours but they ain't African. I don't think. Spanish or Portuguese with Canary Island blood."

Savary knew what he meant. The Isleños had the features of a white man but skin dark like Savary, who had classic African-American features.

The man scratched his belly. "Where are the Canary Islands, anyway?"

"Off the coast of Africa."

"Oh."

Savary knew of Los Isleños, a lost people from the Canary Islands who'd been in Louisiana as long as the French and Spanish.

"This Isleños have a name?"

"Condor Nuñez. He's always around. A fisherman."

"Where does he live?"

"I don't know."

"What does he look like?"

"Dark skinned. Straight black hair, wears it long. Short dude. Maybe five-six. Skinny. He's always on a bicycle or in an aluminum boat painted flat black."

"How old?"

Luke Gathers shrugged.

"Teenager or over forty?" Sometimes it was like pulling teeth.

"Between forty and sixty, I'd say."

Savary looked at the man's pickup again, noticed the logo. "I thought kayaking went with blue water rafting." The only blue water Savary had ever seen anywhere in Louisiana was in swimming pools.

"No. People kayak through the swamp."

Yeah, so they can pet the alligators. This gave support to the movement to re-design the license plate from *Louisiana—Sportsman's Paradise* to *Louisiana—a State of Confusion.*

"Did the old guy mention why he was out alone on the swamp with a camera?"

"Nope."

Savary heard his call letters on his radio. Jodie calling. "Thirty-one twenty-two to thirty-one sixty-eight."

"Go ahead, thirty-one twenty-two."

"Your cell working?"

"I think so." He pulled his cell from his pocket saw he'd missed a couple calls from Jodie. He punched her number and she answered after the first ring.

"Just got word our victim's a retired federal judge."

"Oh, no."

"Exactly. You might want to secure that boat in case the feds want in on this."

"Good idea."

She hung up and Savary turned to the tech, asked if he was finished.

"For now."

Savary told Luke Gathers of Luke's Boat and Kayak Rentals, "This boat's a crime scene. Any place we can secure it until tomorrow?"

"I got it rented out in the morning."

"Not anymore. A crime scene's a crime scene until we release it."

"This is private property."

The crime lab tech cut in. "We'll call, get a tow truck with a trailer over here. Bring it to the police garage."

Gathers thought about it a second. "You guys take it. When will I get it back?"

Savary gave him a cold smile.

"Okay. I got a tarp to cover it," Luke said. "I watch *CSI* all the time. I'll protect your evidence. I'll bring the boat to my yard and hold it for you." The man went to his pickup and backed the trailer up to the edge of the walkway. He brought a large tarp to cover the boat, hooked a rope to the front of the boat.

"Know what happens if the FBI comes out here tomorrow and you don't have the boat secured?"

"Yeah. Yeah. Yeah."

Savary waited until he and the crime lab tech were alone. "I want you to get out here at seven when he opens with your evidence vacuum and suck up everything on the boat and dust the boat for prints. All of the boat."

"You're serious?"

"Serious as murder."

When the order came out online—everything was via email these days—instructing female plainclothes officers to wear pants rather than skirts or dresses, Jodie Kintyre filed an immediate grievance to the civil service board and the order morphed into a suggestion. This morning she stepped into the morgue in a slimming dark blue skirt-suit. Savary stood in the hall with a confused look on his face. He wore his light gray suit today.

"Don't see our victim here," he said, nodding to the seven body bags lining the hall outside the poorly-ventilated autopsy room known to homicide detectives as "The Chamber of Horrors."

"You sure?"

A coroner's assistant stepped out of the autopsy room and Savary asked about their victim.

"That the one the FBI took?"

Coroner's investigator Sam Ruttles, NOPD-retired, came into the hall with the body-count clipboard, said, "Yeah. Couldn't believe it. Damn FBI rolled me outta bed at four a.m. with a federal writ of some sort. They had tech guys in plutonium suits. Put the body in a silver van and took off."

"So our pathologist didn't see the body."

"No, but the coroner did. Dr. Ousten himself. You know he don't come around much but he knew the victim so he came in early and was examining the body, had the clothes off, was examining the wound when the feebees showed up."

Dr. Alvin Ousten, the long-time coroner of Orleans Parish, was more politician than pathologist but every once in a while he put on his doctor's smock and did some postmortem work on a body. He had been all over the news right after Katrina. Like most politicians, he didn't miss a chance to put his face on TV.

Ruttles reached into his lab coat and pulled out a small, brown paper bag. "FBI was in such a hurry, they forgot this. I was waiting to give it to your crime lab tech."

"What is it?"

"Vial inside with gray organic substance found in the head wound. Some sort of slivers, maybe glass or plastic."

Jodie took the bag, asked, "Did Dr. Ousten say anything about the wound?"

"He was mad as hell when the feds came in and commandeered the body. He reminded them he's the coroner and outranked them." Ruttles chuckled. "Imagine reminding the Lords of the Washington the local coroner was in charge of all bodies. They ignored him."

Jodie tapped the big investigator's shoulder. "What did he say about the wound?"

"Blunt force trauma. Skull fractured. He'd be positive if he'd been able to X-ray it or crack open the skull, but Ousten's seen enough blunt trauma to recognize it." Ruttles pointed to his own right eye-brow. "Got smashed right over the eye and old people, well, their bones are brittle."

As Savary and Jodie were settling at their gray metal, government-issue desks, Lieutenant Dennis Merten leaned out of his office and waved Jodie over. Merten's wide face, as dark as Savary's, only more shaded brown, like burned wood, carried a perpetual scowl which was in full effect that morning. Just within Merten's office sat two men in expensive suits. Had to be feds. The one nearest the door checked out Jodie as she stepped in, closed the door.

Savary went down to the crime lab to ask about the evidence they'd secured from the boat and to give them the vial from the coroner.

"Nope," Lt. Smithers said, slamming a file cabinet door. "Don't want it. FBI took all the evidence we collected. Came with a search warrant from federal court." Smithers was taller than Savary, but much thinner with a lean face and beady eyes. "I gave them everything. Good riddance."

Savary wished getting rid of cases was always this easy. As he started out, it occurred to him to ask, "What about the camera?"

Smithers waved his arms. "Took it all."

Savary shrugged. "Would have liked to know what the old guy was photographing."

"Oh, we downloaded the jpegs to our master computer. I could email them to you. Weren't that many."

"Yeah. Send them to me."

Back in the bureau nobody bothered to clean out the Mr. Coffee pot so Savary got to it and since he was making it, he made the coffee and chicory as strong as he liked it. He opened a fresh can of Pet Milk and poured in a big slurp to go along with his two sugars and was just sitting down when the lieutenant's door opened and Jodie came out. He raised his cup and nodded to the pot. She fixed herself a mug before plopping in her desk chair.

"There's going to be a task force and I'm on it. The FBI has suspects already, people with grudges against this retired federal judge." She took a hit of coffee. "It includes three former state politicians and a jealous husband. Apparently Judge Lansing had an illicit affair with a former beauty queen who was married to a Baton Rouge real estate agent who didn't appreciate his wife's dalliance."

Lt. Merten's door opened.

Jodie added, "You better get out of here before he tags you to join the task force."

Too late to duck out as Merten came right for them, nodding at Savary before saying, "I'll need your notes to give to the feds."

Savary dug his notebook from his briefcase. "You want my sketches too?"

"You made sketches?"

"Of my sergeant's legs. I sketch them when I'm stressed. Calms me down."

Marten's eyes went so narrow they nearly disappeared and Jodie started laughing.

"You really sketch?" Merten asked.

Savary tapped his temple with a finger. "Only in here." He tore the note pages out and handed them to his lieutenant, who wheeled and headed back to his office.

"Uh, Lou."

"Shut up!"

Savary smiled at Jodie and held up the vial from the coroner's office, told her about it as Merten slammed his door.

Jodie leaned back in her chair and closed her eyes. She did

that when she needed to decompress, relax, float away to wherever her mind took her. She would sometimes doze off and her face seemed so tranquil.

Savary checked his email and found one from the crime lab. He clicked on the attachment icon and the iMac automatically downloaded the attachments. It only took four seconds. One of the few niceties after Katrina were so many companies eager to assist the city. Apple donated fifty computers directly to NOPD, some making their way to the Homicide Division.

Victor Lansing had taken nineteen photos, mostly trees dripping Spanish moss and brown water shots. There was an egret in one picture. The last three pictures showed a fish jumping out of the water. At first he thought it was a little fish until the last picture which showed the fish up close, leaping from the water, right up to the camera. A big fish. A good picture, showing the long snout, elongated body. It wasn't a gar, no gar jumped, and it wasn't a tarpon, not with that snout.

More men in nice suits filed into the squad room and Savary hurriedly packed up his briefcase, tossing the evidence bag inside. He stood and finished off his coffee.

"You coming?"

Jodie shook her head disgustedly.

It wasn't until Savary was in the "police-only" elevator did it occur to him what he could do with the vial.

Sitting on a concrete bench in the Loyola University quad, Savary watched the students scurry past on their way to classes. Must be the summer semester. When he was in college, the students looked a lot different. He had trouble telling the girls from the boys today. They all wore jeans or light sweat pants or gym shorts and flip-flops. Not one of the females wore any make-up. *So this is what unisex means?*

As the noon bell rang on the medieval Gothic-looking church with its towering spires at the front of the university along St. Charles Avenue, a woman came out of one of the red brick buildings and headed toward Savary who immediately recognized her and thought, *now that's a dress.*

Dr. Lizette Louvier wore her dark brown hair long, parted down the center, flowing in the breeze past her shoulders, barrettes on either side of her head. Her pale yellow dress was snug and short but not overly. She wore low heels. As she came up, smiling at him now, he saw she wore less make-up than usual but the crimson lipstick sure stood out. He knew she was almost thirty now, but looked much younger.

Savary stood as she came up, nodded over his shoulder. "What's the name of that church?"

"Holy Name of Jesus."

He'd been inside once. Place was prettier than St. Louis Cathedral.

Lizette squinted up at him as the sun hit her eyes, "So, what's this favor you need?"

"I know you're a literature professor. I need some sorta science professor."

She chuckled, "I teach History. What 'sorta science' are we talking about?"

Lizette stood a good foot short than Savary, her chin raised to look him in the eye. Her eyes were dark gold, no, topaz-colored. Married to a former NOPD homicide detective, she was part of the blue brotherhood as a cop's wife. Lizette was a woman who always looked Savary in the eye and always with a hint of mischief, like a little sister ready to pull a prank on her big brother.

Savary dug the vial from the paper bag and held it up to the sun.

"Some sort of organic matter. Maybe a chemistry professor?"

Lizette looked at the vial shook her head. "Organic. You

need Zoology, Entomology. Let's see who's around."

Most of Loyola's buildings were red brick and old. The Science Building was new and made of concrete. An ugly monstrosity the architect tried to make pretty with multi-colored railings. Faculty offices lined the bottom floor with classrooms and labs above.

"So, how's your husband?"

"In court testifying against the former insurance commissioner. He helped bring the jerk down with some special investigating." She shrugged. Her husband was now a private eye.

Lizette managed to locate Professor Carlos Seville in a lab along the second floor. The man's face was thin and lined with deep furrows and his hair was what Savary expected of a science professor—white-gray, standing straight out as if he'd just pulled his finger from an electrical socket.

"Yes. Yes, Dr. Louvier. What can I do for you on this bright morning?"

"It's afternoon," Lizette said, reaching for the bag in Savary's hand as she introduced the big detective. Seville stood shorter than Lizette but was much heavier. He blinked up at Savary, then at the vial.

"Evidence," Savary said. "From a murder scene. It was from the victim's wound. On his head. There was also some on the boat."

Seville unscrewed the vial and looked inside.

"The man was on a boat in a swamp." Savary glanced at Lizette, added, "Bayou Sauvage."

"I will need to take it out and put it on a slide."

"Sure."

It took Seville a minute to swab out the specimen, put it on a slide and slip the slide under a microscope. He nodded as he looked thorough the lenses. "It's organic. From a fish, I'd say."

"That plastic-looking..."

"Fish scale but no ordinary fish scale. More of a bony material from a scute." Seville looked up, smiled at Lizette, said, "I'll need more time to figure what type of fish we're talking about. Couple days."

Savary asked, "What's a scute?"

"Bony plate. Some fish have it rather than scales."

"Could it be a gar fish?"

Seville tapped the detective on the shoulder. "Couple days." He turned to Lizette now and said, "Does this mean you owe me a favor?"

She smiled. "It does." She turned and left and the old man's eyebrows went up and down as she walked away. Savary took out a business card and hurriedly wrote his cell number on the back, gave it to Seville and had to catch up with Lizette to thank her.

"Let me know what kind fish we're talking about," she said. "Was the man fishing?"

"Nope. No fishing gear. Just a camera." Savary smiled. "How'd you know the victim was a man?"

She laughed at him. "Morning news. Dead guy found in a boat at Bayou Sauvage."

He didn't make it to his car before his cell rang. Jodie sounded harried, "Remember I told you to take a couple days off?"

"Yeah. You were serious?" He could tell she was in no mood to joke, but couldn't resist.

"Don't come back here," her voice lower now. "Take the rest of the day and tomorrow off. See you Thursday."

"What's up?"

"The FBI have three suspects. They're assembling search warrants. We'll be here forever."

"Search warrants for what?"

"That's on a need-to-know basis and we don't need to know." He heard her huff. "Profilers are flying in from Quantico. They think it's white supremacists."

"Aw. I'll miss all the fun."

"This ain't fun." She hung up.

Joseph Savary learned early that fathers came last in a divorce case, even if he had joint custody of Emily and Carla.

"Whaddya mean, I can't have the girls? I'm off tomorrow. Completely off."

"Yeah," his ex-wife said. "Remember telling me that the last time I let you have the girls when it wasn't your turn? Remember taking them out of *Happy Feet* and dropping them off to me at work because some jackass got himself murdered?"

"It was *Happy Feet 2*."

"Kids don't forgive or forget that they only saw half a movie because your work's more important. Weren't you paying attention during the divorce hearing? Your job's always more important than me and the girls." She hung up.

So Savary found himself washing his car Thursday, vacuuming his apartment, watching *Inside Man* on cable TV. Cool opening music and Denzel at his finest. Clive Owen was smooth and the twist at the end nicely done. His favorite part was when Denzel needed someone to interpret what turned out to be a speech in Albanian and told the other cops to just ask around outside. Someone in New York City had to understand the language and sure enough, there was a woman with parking tickets who needed a favor.

The call from Professor Seville caught Savary on the Pontchartrain Expressway.

"Did you say the goo was from a surgeon?"

"No. A sturgeon. Big fish. Can get as long as eighteen feet along the Amazon, although the biggest around here runs about twelve feet."

Twelve feet? That's pretty big.

"Sturgeon, huh?"

"Yes," the professor said. "Jumpers. They leap from the water for no reason. Been known to jump into small boats, injure fisherman. One killed a fisherman in Florida just last year.

No. No way.

"Doc, can I email you some pictures? Maybe you can tell me if the fish in the pictures is a sturgeon."

"Sure. Can you copy my email address?"

Savary swerved to the side of the elevated expressway, put on his flashers and dug out his pen and pad and said, "Go ahead."

Five minutes after the email and attachments were sent, Professor Seville called Savary.

"That's a sturgeon, all right. Jumping from the water. Can't be positive, but I'm ninety percent sure it's a sturgeon. Where was the picture taken?"

"Blind Lagoon."

"What?"

"In Bayou Sauvage National Wildlife Refuge out by the Chef Pass. Would sturgeon be around swamps?"

"Wherever there's fresh water, brackish water. Those bayous, small lakes and lagoons out there have all sorts of fish."

Savary grabbed his briefcase and almost made a clean getaway only to run into Jodie at the "police only" elevator.

"What's the rush?"

"Got to check on something."

He moved toward the stairs, Jodie calling out, "On one of your unsolved?"

"Yeah." Savary had two unsolved cases he refused to close and periodically worked on them but not today.

He found Luke Gathers, owner and operator of Luke's Boat and Kayak Rentals, at his dock on Christmas Camp

Lake. Luke stood washing off a flat bottom air boat, one of those with a huge fan at the stern that propels it over a swamp—water, marsh, land.

The man was not happy to see Savary, turned his back to the detective who went over and turned off the hose.

"Real funny. Damn FBI took my boat, my computer and files. What you want now?"

"I need to locate the Isleños. Condor Nuñez."

Luke shook his head. "You just missed him. Not five minutes ago. You musta drove right past him. He's on a red bicycle."

Damn. Savary had driven right past an older man on a red bike. He hurried back to his car, turned it around and took the gravel road back up to Highway 90. He looked up and down the four-lane black top, and turned away from the city and headed for Chef Menteur Pass. It took him five minutes to catch up to the man on the red bike just as he was turning off the highway.

Savary pulled in front of the man, parked and got out with his dark sunglasses, loosened tie, short-sleeved white dress shirt, Glock 17 semi-automatic resting in its Kydex plastic holster on his left hip, next to the gold star-and-crescent NOPD badge clipped to his belt. He leaned against the trunk.

"You must be Condor Nuñez." Savary smiled.

"Yes. I am Condor." The man pulled up the bike but didn't get off.

"I'm Detective Joseph Savary. NOPD Homicide Division. You're the man who found the body in the boat aren't you?"

Condor looked around, nodded.

"You live around here?"

"Is there something wrong?"

"What did you do with the fish?"

"Fish?" The man looked at his feet a moment.

"The big sturgeon. It was still in the boat, wasn't it?"

"I did not steal—"

Savary let out a long breath. "Mr. Nuñez. You took something from a crime scene." He reached over, grabbed the handle bars and Nuñez climbed off. The man's bicycle went into the trunk of Savary's car before Savary pulled out his digital recorder.

"I'm not going to read you your rights because you're a witness, not a suspect. You understand?"

Condor shrugged.

"You tell me the truth and nothing will happen to you. You lie to me and I'm arresting you. Simple as that."

"The man was dead."

"But the fish wasn't, was it?"

Condor stared at the sunglasses and Savary slowly removed them, let him see his eyes as he smiled. "You found a dead man in a boat. No law against that. You found a fish. No law against that. I just need to know what you did with the fish."

Condor looked down again. Savary wiped the sweat from the side of his face.

"There was a fish in the boat and the man, well, he couldn't do nothing with it, could he?"

"So, what did you do with the fish?" Savary raised the tape recorder. "I'm going to take your statement and you can have your bike back and you can go if you tell me what happened to the fish. You know what a sturgeon is, don't you?"

Condor looked at the ground, took in a deep breath.

"What did you do with the fish?"

"I ate it." Condor squinted at him in the bright sunlight. "I got the head back at my camp."

FBI Special Agent C. C. Chadwick, agent-in-charge of the Lansing Case Task Force, stood outside Lt. Merten's Office with papers in his hands. The lieutenant's door was shut. In his fifties, Chadwick wore a silver suit that matched the color of his hair. Savary counted nine other agents standing or sitting at desks. Jodie had her back to him as she sat at her desk. She wore a black tactical jumpsuit with "Police" in gray letters on back. When she glanced back at him, he saw she had only minimal amount of make-up, no eyeliner. This was her way of objecting to this.

"...and suspect number one," Chadwick said as Savary sat at his desk and turned on his iMac. By the time he finished his daily report, checked it for spelling errors, Chadwick was finished with suspect number four. Savary hit the "send" button and zipped his daily report to his sergeant and lieutenant, per department protocol.

Savary called Dr. Lizette Louvier and in a soft voice left a voice mail message telling her about the fish and his daily report, which her husband would get a kick out of. It took longer than he thought it would before his lieutenant's door opened slowly and Merten came out with a piece of paper in hand. He moved past Chadwick, momentarily interrupting the man's speech. Merten got about halfway to Savary's desk and roared, "You're pinning it on a fish?!"

"Suspect number five!" Savary called back. "Sturgeon. Nine and a half feet long, weighing about a hundred pounds. Got a picture of it about to slam into our victim. I dropped the fishes head off at the crime lab on the way up."

He waited for Chadwick to look at him.

"I saw this on *CSI*." Savary grinned. "Your lab can put it all together." He held up the envelope with the slide, smiled, and put his sunglasses back on.

Jodie laughed so hard she almost fell out of her chair.

And Down We Go
BV Lawson

So this was what it felt like to drown. Or as good as. The water was up to the brake pedals, and I was surprised it wasn't coming in faster. Then, with a shudder, the car sank deeper in the tea-colored water—not up to the windows, but soon. We had fifteen minutes tops before we hit the bottom.

Next to me in the passenger seat, Joe stopped moaning long enough to do his best impression of a fox-in-heat-wail. No, that wasn't the right metaphor. I was seriously going to have to work on my metaphors. Guess I could blame it on the drowning and all.

Joe whipped off his seatbelt and jabbed his finger at the door lock button. When that didn't work, he pounded the car door, but it wasn't budging. "Oh, God, we're going to die, we're fucking going to die!"

He fumbled in his pocket, yanked out his cellphone and dialed. "Not getting a thing, not one bloody bar." Then he threw the phone onto the floor where it made a "splish."

"Can't get cell service out here, Joe. No towers."

"For fuck's sake, how can you be so calm? Do something except sit there like you was waiting around for a bus."

I opened the console and fished around inside until I found what I was after and held up the tool. "See this? Now here's what's going to happen. When the water gets up near the top of the windows, the pressure will equalize. We should be able to open the doors. But if we can't, I'll use this baby. One quick tap on the window, and it'll shatter to smithereens. Then we just slide out the window and swim up to the surface."

"I can't swim that good. You know I can't swim that good, Frank."

I knew. I wasn't some Olympics wannabe myself, but I felt pretty sure I could make it. Pretty sure. I didn't want to point out the bayou's murky waters would complicate things. We might turn upside down and then how'd you tell which way was up?

The water was at the tops of my socks now. I hated wet socks. Dorothy always made sure my socks were extra dry before she put them in my sock drawer. I glanced in the rearview mirror at the urn strapped into the backseat.

Dorothy had loved metaphors—or was it similes? Never could tell them apart—as if they were soul food. Even wrote them down in a journal. To put in her book someday, she'd said. I had them cremate that journal along with her, and bits of it were probably back in that urn right now.

Dorothy also loved this place, the Barbue Bayou. Loved the calls of the chorus frogs and the egrets, the smell of the salty marsh air in the morning, the way the light cast shadows through the oak trees covered in ghostly Spanish moss.

I said to Joe, "Sheila sure did a nice eulogy, don't you think? Dorothy would have got a kick out of it."

Joe turned to me, his pupils as wide as black marbles. No, make that black coals with bits of fire in them. Then he grabbed the lapel of my suit. "Don't you start planning our wakes already, you hear me? We'll use that hammer thing of yours, just like you said."

I brushed off his hand and turned on the radio. Still worked, at least for now. "Wonder how many bodies are buried down here. You ever wonder that, Joe?"

"'Course not. What the hell makes you say that?"

"Just wondering. I mean, you've heard the rumors. That time we sold a load of smack to the Cohens, and they disappeared a week later. Remember?"

"We ain't murderers. We sell things, people buy things.

That's it. What happens after we sell shit to 'em ain't none of our business." Joe looked at the floor and his breathing got more shallow. "It's up to my shins, Frank. You see that?"

The water wasn't as cold as I'd imagined it would be. Dorothy used to wade at the edges along the shore, dipping her feet in. Splashing the water up at me, laughing about it being as cold as an Arctic summer day.

She'd loved metaphors and she'd loved the bayou, but she never learned to love the business. Told everyone I was a "regional sales manager," then got all vague on the details.

Joe banged against the door again and punched the door lock button over and over. "The water's coming in faster. Don't you think it's coming in faster?"

Seemed that way to me, too, but I didn't want Joe hyperventilating and using up all the air. "We got plenty of time left, Joe."

"Plenty of time? For what? Are you going bonkers, Frank? 'Cause if you're bonkers, I want to be the one with that hammer thing." He lunged over and tried to grab the tool out of my hand, but I shifted it to my left hand where he couldn't get at it.

"Plenty of time to reminisce. About the good old days. Like when you and I made our first big score on that shipment of stolen Rolexes. Remember that?"

"Yeah, yeah, it was great, we made a lot of money. So?"

"And the time we almost got caught by Carroll County's finest with a load of Air Jordans. But we escaped through a trap door in the warehouse. Afterwards we got as drunk as a lone Baptist in a fishing boat and did that whole blood brother thing. Still got my scar." I lifted up my shirt sleeve an inch to expose my wrist.

Joe didn't look, his eyes glued to the hammer. "And we'll get drunk again when this is all over. Just stop with the stories, huh? I'm not in the mood."

"Why is that, Joe? You always used to love my stories."

"Guess I never had to listen to them while drowning before."

"Is that the only reason?"

The water was up to his groin now, but I wasn't sure if his pants were wet on account of the bayou seeping in. He practically snarled as he said, "That and the fact you're an idiot, Frank. Why the hell was you in such a hurry driving back from the funeral? Why'd you take that corner so fast? We been down that road hundreds of times before. I know you was upset with Dorothy's death and the funeral and all..."

"It wasn't the funeral." I turned up the radio when it started to sputter. "Hear that?"

"So the radio ain't working right. Tell me something I don't know."

"That was Dorothy's favorite song. Fate's kind of funny that way, don't you think?"

"You know what I think? I think you're going daft. Stark. Raving. Bonkers. Stress, that's what it is. Gimme that hammer thing, Frank." Joe's voice was turning into a soprano.

I didn't have to look down to tell the water was level with my navel. Level with my navel—not exactly a metaphor, but kind of a rhyme. *Write that one down in your journal for me, Dorothy.*

I must have said that aloud because I caught Joe staring at me. "You're fucking losing it."

I turned up the radio as loud as it would go, trying to catch the last snippets of the fractured song before they were snuffed out. "Why'd you do it, Joe?"

Joe mumbled to himself, but I could hear him. "Good God, I'm trapped with a madman." Joe tried to turn in his seat, but with all that water, it was getting hard to move. "Whatdja mean? Why'd I do what?"

"You know what I mean."

"Sleeping with that underage kid who said she was eighteen? Watering down the smack I sold to Nino? I ain't no saint, Frank."

"Why'd you kill her, Joe?"

"Kill her? Kill who?" I could've swore I saw water on Joe's brow. From sweat and not any bayou brine.

"Dorothy never did anything to you. She liked you."

He moaned again, less like that fox-in-heat and more like a wolf with his paw stuck in a steel trap. "Still don't know what you're going on about."

The water reached my armpits. The smell was a lot stronger now, a mix of rotting fish and moldy compost. "I know it was you. I know you hit her on the head with a rock, then pushed her down the stairs."

"You don't know nothing, Frank."

"The examiner guy made a point of telling me about the unusual pattern on the back of her skull. Like a dog, he said. Or maybe a wolf. Kinda like that wolf-shaped rock you carry around in your car. Good luck charm, you called it. Only, last time I was in your car, I didn't see it. Funny thing, that."

Joe started floating in his seat and grabbed onto the hangar bar above the door to pull himself up toward the ceiling, toward the remaining pocket of air. He gulped in several breaths. "It's nothing. Must've fallen out. And you just keep that hammer ready, you hear me?" Definitely a soprano now.

"Oh, I'll keep it ready. And I'll use it soon, don't you worry none about that. But you gotta tell me, Joe. Confession's good for the soul. Just in case we don't make it and all. Why'd you kill her? Why'd you kill my Dorothy?"

The water crept up the outside doors. It'd only be a few minutes now. *And down we go.*

Joe started hyperventilating for real. He panted out, in-between those shallow breaths, "She double-crossed me. But I didn't mean to do it, Frank. Just wanted her to tell me what she'd done with my money."

"Dorothy would never double-cross you, Joe. She didn't want any part of the business."

"She overheard me when we was discussing the particulars of the Ralston heist. That was my baby, my idea. It was going to be my big score until someone got there first. It had to be her. And you ain't never double-crossed me, not once. Who else woulda known?"

"Corey Ralston, that's who. Wanted to get back at his brother. I got him to confess, thanks to a little coaxing from Mr. Smith and Mr. Wesson."

Joe was breathing so fast, I didn't think he could speak, but he did. "Didn't. Know. Not. Right."

I wasn't sure if he was calling me a liar or if it was some kind of last-ditch apology. Didn't matter either way. The water was far enough up the door for me to use the hammer. So I moved it to my right hand in preparation and wiggled out of my shoes.

But before I did, I pulled something else out of my suit pocket. A handy little gizmo I paid cash for at a dive shop in North Carolina. I'd seen wreck divers use it as a backup breathing device if their main tank failed.

I put it in my mouth, cupped both hands over the hammer and whacked it at the top of the window. Once the glass shattered into a thousand pieces, the remaining water rushed into the car, and I felt the car start to tip over. No time to lose. I pushed upward, kicking with my legs like one of Dorothy's chorus frogs, aiming for the faint sheen of light I prayed was the surface of the water.

One stroke, ten, twenty. And then I broke through and swam to the shore. I hauled myself out and stood there, looking. Looking and watching a few bubbles percolating up fifteen yards from shore—the only sign of the car that now lay on the floor of Barbue Bayou.

No signs of Joe. He really wasn't a good swimmer.

I almost felt sorry for the guy. Almost. Poor, dumb Joe. He

didn't even realize I coulda used that hammer when we first went into the water, long before we went down to the bottom.

I reached into my pants pocket and pulled out the rock I'd hid there, the one shaped like a wolf. The same one I'd found in Joe's tackle box, with traces of Dorothy's blood still on it. I tied my scuba breather to it with some vines and hurled that rock as far as I could and watched it sink into the black stew.

Dorothy had said she wanted her ashes scattered over the bayou, this bayou, the one she loved so much. I guess this was close enough. I turned my head, listening. And I almost thought I could still hear that radio playing her song.

Wayward Soul
Eric Beetner

I never thought I'd be the type of guy to go visit a whorehouse, let alone end up smuggling a girl out of that same house under cover of night. But there I was, knee deep in swamp water and worrying about water moccasins and leeches and getting shot in the back if we got found out. I think the snakes worried me most of all.

Now I ain't a bad looking guy if you don't view me straight on, but I found myself in a three-year dry spell. I'd had girlfriends in the wake of the one who got away—Deena. Christ, eighteen years ago now. I was set to marry her and then she put an end to it when I was only three payments away from owning that damn ring.

None of the other girls quite measured up, I guess. Bad relations just soured me on women in general so I stopped trying. Then I looked up and I was buying my third calendar since the last time I got laid.

So someone told me about the house in the swamp. A big plantation style, two-story mansion with a wraparound porch and dormers on the second floor where the girls lived, the house was way off the beaten path in a patch of land best suited to the mosquitoes, swamp rats, gators and those damn snakes who called it home. But it did great business and being so far afield, the law never bothered nobody there.

Place didn't have a name, or if it did I never learned it. Wasn't exactly a neon sign out front, just a few rusty kerosene lanterns hanging off soft porch pillars covered with moss. Kerosene was supposed to keep the skeeters at bay for Reggie the bouncer. Not that any man or insect would be fool enough to try to take even a drop of Reggie's blood without his express written permission. That man could scare a crocodile so bad it'd turn itself into a damn handbag.

It was a long walk from the parking lot down a muddy path under Spanish moss hanging over a long plank footbridge to the house. It smelled a little like I remembered sex—musty, humid, earthy and a little ripe.

Inside were about a dozen girls on any given night. Name your poison and they had her. An Asian, a black, a Mexican, big tits, small tits, redheads, brunettes. Then I saw a pair of eyes through the crowd and I was hooked.

First time I found Kristal—with a K—I never looked back. She was young. They all were. Not much call for a forty-year-old whore, unless someone comes in with that particular desire in which case I guess Miss Ruthie who runs the pay counter would step out of retirement for a night and service a client her own self. She certainly acted like she could still play the game. Kept her legs shaved and everything. I always got the impression she was waiting on the call.

Kristal was blonde, medium chest but firm. Great behind. Mostly she was kind in her eyes and her smile. She was a real girl-next-door so long as you didn't mind living next to a whorehouse in a swamp.

She led me back into the world of lovemaking and I went to visit her about once a month for the next year and a half. Don't get me wrong—I never assumed I was anything more than two hundred bucks on the nightstand to her. I didn't go falling for a whore, though you could call what I felt for her love, no doubt about it.

So when she asked me to help her, well, I couldn't say no.

She was in debt and couldn't pay it back or some such problem. She explained in detail but it didn't matter. She wanted my help and I was eager to give it, even if I didn't quite know how. A criminal type, I am not.

It got so's we'd make love and then spend the rest of the

time on the clock discussing how to get her out. She got real good at making me finish fast. Then we'd sit there in the heat and plan, her still naked without a care and me shirtless and self-conscious, slapping at mosquitoes who felt like they came armed with mini-pneumatic drills.

When it came time, we kept it simple.

I crossed the footbridge knowing this was the night I'd bring Kristal out of there. It was always humid there so my panic sweat didn't look suspicious to anyone. Down below in the water I saw those damn snakes. And not only one. A tangle of three, maybe four big ol' water moccasins tussled in either a fight or an orgy. It did not strike me as a good omen, either way.

I nodded to Reggie who sat, stone-faced as usual, and waved me inside. If I got caught trying to bring Kristal out, I think I might have taken my chances down among them snakes.

"You know how much I appreciate this, don't you, Eldin?"

Kristal did her best to show me her appreciation, but my heart wasn't in it and neither was anything below the belt. The frogs and such outside were so loud I felt like they were laughing at me.

When it was clear the lovemaking portion of the evening wasn't happening, she tried to explain more, but I didn't need it.

"It's just that I can't pay back what I owe them because they take such a large percentage, and not everyone who comes here wants a girl like me. Hardly any. They all want Mona with her giant tits, or the Japanese girl to be exotic. Did you know you're my most regular customer, Eldin?" She must have realized she'd been complaining and ruining the fantasy. She stopped, smiled, laid a hand on my arm. "And my favorite."

I gave her a weak smile. Even my mouth couldn't get it up. I was too damn nervous.

After our time together I left out the front door. The way my shirt stuck to my body made me look like just another satisfied customer. If they only knew.

Ruthie smiled at me, figuring I'd been taken to Heaven's gates and back again in Kristal's boudoir. "See you soon, Eldin."

But, on my way back to the car I snuck around the back of the house along the big wraparound porch and waited for Kristal while she ducked out when everyone thought she was in the bathroom cleaning up for the next john.

I hadn't planned well at all. I'd have brought hip waders or some other means to protect my legs from the swamp water. Way the house was, it sat up on poles sunk deep in the muck so if you wanted in or out by any other means than the front walkway—well-lit and watched by Reggie at the front door— you had to go by water.

Kristal slipped out back door and we went over the railing into the swamp. It was cold and the footing was awful. Your feet sank in and it wouldn't let go. Took about three steps before I lost my shoes to the sucking mud.

We made our way into the swamp and away from the house. Wouldn't do any good to come slopping around and pass by under Reggie's nose. We had to get a little lost out there and take a wide crescent back to land. Good news was, as far out as you went, the water never got no deeper. Only creepier.

Every tree branch in the moonlight was another water moccasin coming to fang me. Every brush of dead leaves in the water another leech sucking my blood. Every sound that wasn't my own feet was a gator come to make me his midnight snack. It got so Kristal took the lead and pulled me along out of the swamp to where my car was waiting.

But damned if we didn't make it unnoticed and reached my car without seeing a snake at all. After a quick leech check we drove on out of there and she was free.

She thanked me and hung her head out the window and let her hair blow in the night air. She smiled big and howled at the moon once we were on the highway. I felt like I'd really done something good, even if I had lost my favorite girl at the house.

Like I said, I had no illusions. We weren't running away together. I was supposed to take her to her mom's house and that's where we were headed.

It was the middle of the damn night though and I'd gotten us a hotel room, as was the plan. We stopped there and Kristal said she wanted to show me her appreciation for what I'd done. She started kissing on me and I really wanted us both to take a shower after that damn swamp water, but I went along with it knowing it would be the last time I'd get to make love to her.

Everything worked this time.

She didn't do any of her tricks to speed things up. It was slow and tender and it gave me a false hope that maybe we could make a go of it, her and me. But the feeling didn't last.

I had worries of my own. I'd been a regular customer for so long surely they knew my car. Nobody had seen us leave together, but wouldn't they assume?

I figured I had to brave it and go back next month on my same schedule and act all surprised that Kristal wasn't there. I'd have to make a show of considering other girls, but I knew I couldn't pick anyone else. It'd be like cheating on her.

Shit. Maybe I did have it bad for her.

Cold light of morning would cure that.

"Mama's sure gonna be surprised to see me," she said.

She had the window down like she needed all the oxygen

in the world. Like she'd been buried alive and I'd dug her out.

"I'm sure she's gonna be thrilled," I said. What I really wondered was if her mom had known what her little girl had been up to for the past two years. And if she did, what would she think of me? Man who rescued her, sure, but also the man who defiled her for money. My plan was to leave her there as quick as possible. Maybe even drop her at the curb.

Three hours and one gas fill up later, we stopped in front of her mama's house.

"Well..." I said.

"Well, come on. I want you to meet Mama."

Kristal tugged at my arm and I followed her. I figured the way she was bounding up the walkway of the little ranch-style house like an excited puppy fresh from the kennel, her mom must not've had any idea what she'd been up to.

Kristal knocked quickly and called out, "Mama, it's me!"

I took a small step back, tried to swallow what felt like a wad of cotton in the back of my throat and hoped this would be a nice howdy-do and I'd be on my way. I had some serious grieving to begin over Kristal. It was a feeling I hadn't had since Deena cut out without even leaving a note. At least this time I was there to watch the girl I loved go.

The door opened and the woman there looked shocked, then pleased, then tearful. They embraced in a cloud of squeals and sobs.

"Krissy!" her mama called her.

I watched for a minute, touched by the scene and also wondering if I should just back away and get to the car while they were occupied. Kristal finally broke their embrace and stepped aside to introduce me.

"Mama, this is—"

"Eldin," her mama said.

It was my turn to be shocked. I was looking at Deena—the one who got away.

We stood in slack-jawed silence like it wasn't just a man

from her past but Jesus Christ himself who showed up on her porch to sell her vacuums.

"Deena...my goodness."

"You two know each other?" Kristal said, as confused as the rest of us.

"A long time ago," Deena said.

"A long time," I agreed.

Deena's face went tight. "How did you find her?"

Odd question and one I wasn't sure how to answer. Do you admit she was in a whorehouse? I guessed Deena thought Kristal had run off and now I was here to bring her back.

"How long have you known?" Deena worried her hands into knots.

Again I was speechless. How long had I known her daughter was a whore?

"Mama?" Kristal said.

I felt like I should explain even if Deena wouldn't. "Your mom and I, turns out we dated many years back. About eighteen or so if I recall. We were...pretty serious and then—" I wasn't sure how to phrase it. "Then she left."

"I got pregnant," Deena said.

News to me. News that about knocked me on my ass. But the real shocker came a few seconds later. I ain't never been good in math, but once the rusty gears in my head caught up I turned to Kristal. About eighteen.

My body wanted to pass out, throw up and shit itself all at once. Kristal was my daughter.

I turned around and started saying, "No, no, no, no," as I spun circles in the grass. I grabbed my head to keep it from whirling off.

"Eldin?" Kristal said. She didn't know, thank God. Hadn't put the two together. And if Deena didn't know where Kristal had been working she didn't know yet either.

But I knew, and that was bad enough for all three of us.

I stopped spinning and threw up into a bush. Every time I

looked and saw Kristal there her eyes were still the same gentle eyes I'd stared into while we—*don't think about that*—her skin the same soft skin I'd caressed. She was that girl, but now she was also my child.

I heaved again.

"My God, are you okay?"

"No, no, no, no."

Throw me to the snakes. Lay me down at Reggie's feet and have him carve me up for gator bait. I was scum. The worst kind of man. The worst man who'd ever lived in sin on this earth.

I turned and ran. I left the two loves of my life on the porch watching and wondering after me, hoping they would never talk it through enough to fit the pieces together. I had to live with it, but they shouldn't have to.

Then again, maybe I didn't have to live with it. Maybe I shouldn't.

I stopped at the hardware store to get my supplies on my way back to the motel. Suicide was out. I'm too much of a coward. And besides, that's getting off too easy for my sins.

I'd taken down all the mirrors. Couldn't stand the sight of me. I had my duct tape, my hatchet and the motel phone with nine-one already pressed. I took a deep breath and pressed the final one. I told the ambulance what had happened and where to come, then hung up and got ready.

If I'd waited until after I did it to call, it would have been too late. This way, I time it right and I won't bleed out.

I took my pants down. Peeled off a long strip of duct tape, reached down and got the meat out of the way, taped it to my stomach. I made a full loop around my waist to hold it in place. Then I stepped over to the little side table, laid my junk out and felt the cold of the veneer tabletop shrink my scrotum.

I ripped another strip of tape and grabbed my sack, stretched it out as far as I could without too much pain, then rolled the strip of tape across and stuck myself to the table. I doubled up with another strip and had to work to get the right bend in my knees to keep the skin flat on the table without pulling up too much, which hurt.

I realized my mistake one step too late. The door. I hadn't unlocked it. If the ambulance came and had to fight a dead bolted door, I might be out of luck. Shit.

I got a thumbnail under the edge of the silver duct tape and worked a corner free. No other way but to do it. I pulled up sharply.

No two ways about it, that was unpleasant. I had the strip of hair stuck to the underside of that duct tape as proof. Tiny beads of blood rose to the surface of the delicate skin. But it was about to get much, much worse.

I unlocked the door, let it sit open a crack, then waited for the sirens. About seven minutes later I heard them. I was damn glad I'd waited to call. Seven minutes and I'd have been bloodless.

I raised the hatchet in my hand, listened to the ambulance bump into the parking lot of the motel. I heard the siren wind down and doors open. I took a look to get my aim set, then closed my eyes, leaned my head back and swung.

The hatchet split hard through the tape and cracked the veneer of the table as I fell away. My knees gave and my eyes sprang open, but all I saw was the ceiling as I tipped back. Then I passed out.

Now I preach to wayward souls. I try to help people before they sin. Avoidance is what I preach. Some sins are too great to ever recover from. You can't say prayers, Hail Marys, do good deeds, preach the word. Some things can't be undone.

Had a guy in here last week confessing to all sorts of things. Petty bullshit, but I didn't tell him that. I almost bust out laughing when he said, "I'd give my left nut if I could take it all back now."

It won't help, buddy. Not even if you take 'em both.

Good and Dead
Elaine Viets

Landlady Margery Flax was getting gently sozzled on a poolside chaise at the Coronado Tropic Apartments in Fort Lauderdale, Florida. Private eye Helen Hawthorne was one glass of wine behind her.

Margery was a stylish seventy-six, with a springy gray bob, a chunky amethyst necklace, and a purple pantsuit. Her tangerine nails were the same color as her glowing cigarette. She wore her wrinkles as marks of achievement. Helen was forty-one, a leggy brunette married to her private eye partner, Phil Sagemont. The PI pair lived in the two-story building and ran Coronado Investigations out of Apartment 2C.

The two women were munching popcorn by the pool. A light breeze ruffled the turquoise water, sending purple bougainvillea blossoms sailing across the rippled surface. The evening sun painted the old art moderne apartment building pale pink.

Helen yawned.

"Bored?" Margery asked.

Helen nodded. "Phil's working nights and I haven't had a case in a month."

"I have the cure," Margery said. "But you'd have to go to New Orleans today."

Helen sat up, her boredom banished. "Why didn't you say so sooner? New Orleans," she said. "Mmm. I'd love to investigate jambalaya, shrimp remoulade, and po' boys."

"Not to mention hurricanes," Margery said.

"Katrina was awful, but the city has made an amazing recovery."

"I meant the drink," Margery said, and took a long drag on her Marlboro. "Passion fruit, lime juice, one-hundred-fifty-one-proof rum."

"You can have the hangover," Helen said. "I'm thinking beignets at the Café Du Monde. I can almost taste the powdered sugar. So what's the job?"

"A missing person who made off with a hundred grand," Margery said. "I know the missing person—and the woman who wants to hire you. It's quite a tale."

Margery fired up another cigarette and soon fell into her soothing, once-upon-a-time voice.

"Rosalee Alop was a good woman—and she looked it. Her flat shoes and lumpy, colorless clothes announced she was a church lady, a faithful wife, and a hardworking office manager. No lover would dare touch her iron-gray waves."

She absently patted her own gray hair, gently tousled by the breeze, and more than a few men.

"Rosalee lived a life of virtue until last week," Margery said. "Halfway through Holy Week, all hell broke loose. It was Wednesday. Some Christians call the Wednesday before Christ's crucifixion, Spy Wednesday."

"Right," Helen said.

"Tradition says that's when Judas conspired to betray Jesus for thirty pieces of silver. Last Wednesday, Rosalee suffered her own betrayal and when she went home, her world turned to ashes. There would be no resurrection. At about eight forty-five on a steamy Wednesday morning, Rosalee unlocked the turquoise door to Consolidated Worthy Causes."

"Never heard of that charity," Helen said.

"Most people haven't," Margery said. "Tight-assed bunch. Tight-fisted, too. Their motto says it all: 'Helping the deserving poor without making them dependent on handouts.'"

"Oh, right. CWC is near here in downtown Fort

Lauderdale. The pink-and-turquoise building on Andrews Avenue."

"That's it," Margery said. "Rosalee thought the building's bright colors were too frivolous for their serious work. Her grim suits more than compensated for the tropical party colors. She was the charity's only full-time employee. Her job description went on for two pages. That morning she was expecting Junie Bea, the shiftless mother of a toddler, KK— Kimmie Kardashian Dillard—to wander in for her child's milk allowance."

"With a mother like that, why did CWC give KK milk money?" Helen asked.

"CWC said it wasn't the child's fault her parents hadn't made it to the altar. Instead of the tube-topped Junie Bea, in stepped Drusilla Cheney, CWC director, sleek as a panther in pink Armani.

"Rosalee blurted, 'Why are you here? The board meeting isn't until next Wednesday.'

"'We've had an emergency, Rosalee,' Dru said. 'I had to call a board meeting by phone late yesterday. Sit down, dear. I'm afraid the news concerns you. We didn't get the Weems-Wells Foundation grant. The one that pays for our office and your salary.'

"'But they always give us that grant,' Rosalee said.

"'Sad, isn't it?' Dru said, but I doubt she sounded sympathetic. 'Fortunately, the board has come up with a super new plan to save CWC. We own this building, and Roger, a director, is a real estate agent. He believes we can get scads for this site.'

"'Where will we be located?' Rosalee asked.

"'Roger says we can use a room at his Plantation office,' Dru said.

"'Plantation! Out in the burbs! I walk to the office now.'

"'That's okay,' Dru said. 'We're hiring Roger's daughter Audrey as a temp to take your place.'

"'A temp! Do you know how much I do?'

"'A lot, sweetie,' Dru said. 'We've all seen your job description. Audrey is young and enthusiastic and the office is near her parents' home. Plus, donating that space is a nice business deduction for Roger.'

"'But what about me?' Rosalee wailed. 'I'm fifty years old.'

"'You'll do fine,' Dru said. 'We'll write you a glowing recommendation and give you a nice severance package.'"

"Those cheapskates," Helen said. "Real estate in that part of town is sizzling. Roger will make a bundle on that sale. How much severance is Rosalee getting? Thirty thou?"

"Twenty," Margery said. "Rosalee didn't even make minimum wage. She worked for that piddling salary because she had a husband and she believed in CWC. Rosalee started crying and Dru told her to buck up."

"Buck up!" Helen said. "After that poor woman lost her job?"

"Dru told Rosalee she only had one more chore: the next morning, when she came in to pick up her severance, a manila envelope would be on Rosalee's desk. 'Just hand that envelope to Mr. Rodriguez, the bank officer we always use, and get a receipt. Now you go for a nice lunch, dear, then take the rest of the afternoon off. Tomorrow, pick up your severance check, perform one little chore, and you're free.'"

"Dru is one cold-hearted bitch," Helen said.

"That's no way to talk about your future employer," Margery said.

"I haven't taken the case yet," Helen said.

"You will. Rosalee was shell-shocked. She called me. I invited her over for a screwdriver. I said the orange juice was good for her."

"What orange juice?" Helen said. "Your screwdrivers are six parts vodka to one part OJ."

"Whatever. It was just what she needed," Margery said. "Rosalee let down her hair and told me she wasn't always a drudge. When she was twenty-nine, before she married Dennison and started at CWC, she had an unforgettable Labor Day weekend at the Royalton Hotel in the French Quarter with Bobby, a local she met at a bar. It was a long weekend—accent on long. She said she still thinks about Bobby, even though they're both married to other people."

"That must have been some weekend," Helen said.

"I suspect it got better in retrospect," Margery said. "Rosalee said her husband Dennison was a dependable, faithful man. I translated that to mean he wasn't much fun in the sack. Ol' Bobby must have been some stud. She said he was a trainer, and she was sore for a week from his gymnast-tics. He was all muscle: broad shoulders, six-pack abs, good legs."

"She remember anything about his face?" Helen said.

"He had thick blond hair, green eyes, a noble nose, and a dimple in his chin.

"Rosalee was a match for him. She showed me a faded photo of herself from that wild September weekend in 1994. She was a stunner—long blonde hair, stylish clothes, high heels. Even now, at age fifty, she could still be good-looking. Some makeup and the right clothes and she'd be quite the cougar.

"Too bad when she turned thirty, Rosalee found God and Dennison and lost her looks. Check out her current photo."

Margery handed Helen Rosalee's CWC employee photo. "She worked to make herself unattractive," Helen said. "That gray hair in an old-lady cut added ten years. Her jaw is clenched and her mouth is a thin line. She could be the cover girl for *Prison Matrons Monthly*. Any photos of her frisky fling?"

"None. Bobby didn't want to be photographed. He swore he wasn't married, but he wouldn't even take her out for food. He had room service send up their meals for four days. Rosalee thought that was romantic."

"I'd be suspicious," Helen said.

"Rosalee said she didn't need photos: She'll always remember Bobby."

"What's his last name?"

"Charbonnet, a common NOLA name. When he was in the bathroom, Rosalee checked his driver's license. He's definitely Bobby Charbonnet.

"Whatever Bobby and Rosalee did that weekend seems to have started her on the path to godly living, but Rosalee didn't go into details. She'd downed two screwdrivers in a hurry, so I made her eat lunch and drink coffee. She decided she wanted to use her twenty thou severance to move to Costa Rica after Dennison retired this November.

"Suddenly, she looked at her watch and said, 'It's three o'clock. I have to fix a nice dinner for Dennison and tell him the good news.' When she left, Rosalee was sober enough to make it home. Once she got there, she went off the rails.

"Before she could tell Dennison they would be enjoying their golden years in the tropics, he asked Rosalee for a divorce."

"What? Her husband ditched her after twenty years?" Helen said. "She have any idea he was stepping out?"

"None. Dennison said he was going to marry a choir singer he met at organ practice—and don't you dare make the joke I think you're going to." The red eye of Margery's cigarette glared at Helen.

She kept silent, thinking of numerous punch lines.

"Dennison said Rosalee spent the night in the guest room. Early the next morning, she packed a suitcase and took his car. She stopped at their bank, but Dennison had already cleaned out their joint account."

"The rat!" Helen said.

"The rest I got from Drusilla. Rosalee drove to CWC later that morning. 'She must have opened the envelope I left for her. I didn't seal it. We trusted Rosalee. The envelope was closed with brass prongs. Rosalee saw my note to Mr. Rodriguez, the bank officer, instructing him to cash in our hundred thousand dollar CD. Two board members had signed the paperwork and the cash was to be deposited in the CWC account.

"'It was a terrible breach of trust for Rosalee to open that envelope,' Dru said."

"And firing Rosalee without notice wasn't?" Helen said.

Margery snorted. "Rosalee must have seen red—then green—when she read that note. That hundred thousand dollar CD was proof CWC had enough money to run the office and pay her salary for at least a year or two. Instead, the greedy director grabbed that hot property, hired his daughter, and Rosalee was out on the street.

"Rosalee cleverly altered the form so the CD's cash was deposited into her personal checking account."

"And the bank never questioned that?" Helen asked.

"Mr. Rodriguez had dealt with faithful Rosalee for years. Next, Rosalee transferred the hundred thousand, plus her twenty thou severance, to a different bank."

"With branches in New Orleans?" Helen asked.

"You guessed it. Then Rosalee moved the money again, maybe to another account under a different name. Her husband's car was found at the airport on Good Friday. She bought a plane ticket to New Orleans, and no one has seen her since she boarded the flight. CWC knew Rosalee had skipped town, but didn't realize their money was gone until their regular board meeting today.

"That's when Dru Cheney called. She wants to avoid the police and the embarrassing publicity and hire you to find Rosalee and the missing money. I quoted her double your usual fee, plus our expenses. I hope you don't mind that I'm going along as an operative."

"I like your company," Helen said, "but why do I need an operative?"

Margery grinned. "I'm the only one who can recognize both versions of Rosalee—hot and cold. I'm guessing she's in NOLA for a hot weekend with Bobby. She may even try to get him to run off with her. I think she'll get new ID, if she doesn't have it already, then head for Costa Rica, with or without Bobby."

"Where do you think she is in NOLA?"

"The Royalton," Margery said. "It's still in business. That's where her life changed twenty years ago. I booked us a nonsmoking room with two beds. Dru is standing by to sign the contract and write you a check. A nonstop flight leaves at five-forty."

"You're awfully organized for someone half in the bag," Helen said.

"I can hold my liquor," Margery said. "I've made our travel arrangements online. Text Phil the news. He can take care of your furbag. Throw some clothes in a suitcase. I'm already packed. We can be in NOLA by dinnertime."

And so they were. Helen was used to South Florida humidity, but when she stepped out of the NOLA airport, she was wrapped in a warm, steamy sponge. Margery fired up a quick cigarette while they waited for the hotel shuttle.

"How will you survive in a nonsmoking room?" Helen asked.

"I'll find a cancer stick crowd outside the hotel. I can locate them by their hacking coughs."

By the time they arrived at the hotel, Helen's hair was limp and frizzy and her clothes were wrinkled. "This is the Royalton?" Helen asked the driver as he stopped under the hotel's sagging canopy. Broken neon buzzed over Royalton's Superb Steaks next to the lobby.

"Yes, miss," said the driver, in his soft Big Easy accent. "I do recommend the steakhouse. It lives up to its name: Superb."

Helen and Margery followed a herd of gray-haired tourists

into the lobby. The dingy walls were the color of yellowed teeth, the dark wood paneling was scuffed and dinged, and the marble floor was cracked and dirty. Helen and Margery checked in, then waited in a long line for the only working elevator.

Their room looked exhausted: two sagging beds with moss green spreads, dusty velvet curtains and pictures no one would ever steal bolted to the walls.

"Let's ask the front desk staff if Rosalee is staying here," Helen said.

The twenty-something desk clerk looked like he was born to be an old man. He was skinny, stoop-shouldered, and balding.

He shook his head when he saw Rosalee's photo. "I'd like to help, ma'am. But all the women here look like her." Helen surveyed the flocks of gray-haired tourists, chattering in French, German, and British English and waving brochures, cell phones and maps.

"How about this one?" Margery asked, producing Rosalee's fling photo.

The clerk shook his head. "Believe me, I'd notice someone that hot."

But the lobby was so crowded, Helen wondered if he would. "Let's try dinner at the hotel restaurant. Maybe we'll spot her."

Royalton's Superb Steaks hadn't been renovated since its nineties heyday, but Helen and Margery liked its slightly down-at-heels atmosphere. They slid into a generous booth flanking the velvet-draped windows.

"Big Brother is watching," Margery said. "I see three security cameras."

Sophie, their red-haired server in a crisp white shirt and black bow tie, asked, "Would you ladies like to join our Superb Steaks Club?" She held up a purple card. "Buy ten steak dinners and get one free."

"Thanks," Helen said. "But we're just visiting." She ordered jambalaya. Margery wanted a strip steak. "Rare. Walk it through a warm kitchen."

Sophie laughed and brought Margery a sharp, heavy silver steak knife monogrammed RSS.

"Do I have to cut the steak off the cow myself?" Margery asked.

"No, we'll do that for you," Sophie said. "As soon as we wave the steak over the grill, your dinner will be ready. Enjoy your French bread."

"I need a cigarette," Margery said to Helen. "Text me when my dinner arrives."

While Helen slathered her warm bread with soft butter, Sophie settled a couple into the next booth. Helen thought the beefy fifty-something man seemed rigid with anger. Pads of fat hid a once-muscular frame and his expensive blue-checked shirt strained at the seams. His large, fleshy nose shadowed a cratered chin dimple. His brassy hair was badly dyed, but Helen was sure his deep green eyes were real, not contacts.

The woman with him was a babe. A little mileage, but her makeup was expertly applied and shoulder-length blonde hair framed her face. Her stylish black dress showed off her curvy figure.

The couple both ordered steaks. "We're in a bit of a hurry," the man said. "Could you get our dinners quickly?"

"You belong to our Superb Steaks Club," Sophie said. "Do you have your card?"

"Look, I'm in a hurry," he said. "Just get our dinners."

"Yes, thank you, sir," Sophie said, and Helen guessed she'd been tipped. "I'll tell the chef."

As soon as Sophie left, the man snarled at the blonde, "I'm only having dinner with you because I have to eat. Then I want my money and I'm outta here."

This is interesting, Helen thought, leaning back to eavesdrop better.

"You'll get your money, baby," the blonde said.

"I'm not your baby," he said. "And you didn't have a baby. There is no Amy Rose. You've been lying to me for twenty years. Twenty freaking years. I paid you a thousand a month in child support, plus tuition so Amy Rose could become a radiation tech. You got a quarter of a million. I want it back."

"I don't have it, Bobby," she said. "I bought a house. I'm divorcing my husband and he'll get it. But I have a hundred twenty thousand. We can share it. We'll go off together to the Caribbean. Live somewhere cheap."

She was begging. He wasn't buying it.

"Listen, Rosalee," he said.

Rosalee. A woman who wouldn't get her half of the house in the divorce because she was on the run. Rosalee had had a wild weekend with Bobby, a hunk with green eyes, a noble nose and dimpled chin. Helen texted Margery: ROSALEE & BOBBY IN THE NEXT BOOTH? CHECK THRU WINDOW.

As Helen reached for more bread, a lone brunette with a flowered silk scarf on her head slid into the cramped table behind Bobby and Rosalee's booth. She was slender, average height, and wore a tailored beige pantsuit with a four-pocket blazer. Scarf Woman could barely wedge herself into the curtained recess. She handed Sophie a purple card and said, "The usual, medium rare."

Helen, who'd spent time in upscale retail, recognized the scarf and suit as Gucci and the brown hair peeking out from the scarf as expertly styled. *Who wears a silk scarf on her head in this heat?* she wondered.

Bobby and Rosalee's conversation had turned snarly, and Helen tuned back in. "We had some fun twenty years ago," he said, "but that's all. When you said you were knocked up, I did the right thing and supported your so-called baby. I should have asked for a blood test."

"But you didn't, Bobby," she said, her voice soft and syrupy. "Why?"

"Because I'm honorable."

"Or because you didn't want your rich fiancée to find out," Rosalee said. "You married Marie in December and took over her daddy's construction business. What if she knew you were doing the wild thing at the Royalton while she was planning her big society wedding?"

Helen heard a *ding!* and fumbled for her phone. Margery had texted: IT'S HER. BEST MAKEOVER SINCE CINDERELLA. I'LL STAY HERE. U LISTEN.

The server bustled out with Bobby and Rosalee's steaks, then stopped by Helen's table. "Your meal will be out shortly," she said. "May I get you and your friend a drink on the house?"

"No, thanks," Helen said. "My friend had to leave. Could you pack up her dinner to go?"

Now Bobby and Rosalee's booth sounded like a snake pit. "Who did you get to pose as my so-called daughter?" Bobby hissed. "You must have used at least two blondes. I didn't tumble to your scheme until dear little Amy Rose was in tech school. You sent me a cell phone photo of her at your home. It was so blurry I couldn't see her face, but I definitely saw her tattoo in that tacky tube top: a crescent moon and stars on her left breast. Then six months later, she was going to a dance in a strapless dress. Guess what? She'd lost the tattoo. You'd played me for a fool and I quit sending checks. I want my money back."

"You can have some of your money," Rosalee said. "We'll go away together and share it."

"I don't know you. I spent a weekend with you twenty years ago and forgot about it—except I paid through the nose for a little fun."

"Here's your jambalaya," the server said, setting a steaming plate in front of Helen. She jumped. She'd been listening to the drama in the next booth. Helen inhaled the perfume of spicy chicken, shrimp and Andouille sausage.

"I'll bring your friend's to-go dinner in a minute," Sophie said.

"And the check," Helen said. She dug into her jambalaya and listened to Rosalee pleading. "Bobby, I love you. All those lonely years in Florida, you were the only man I thought about. Even when I was with my husband, I was really thinking of you."

"You scammed me, lady," he said. "Give me my money and get out of my life."

"Scammed! What about your wife, Marie? Does she know those payments you made to keep your Great Aunt Emily Bridwell Peyton in a Fort Lauderdale nursing home were really to me? How's she going to feel when she discovers there was no Aunt Emily? Is that worth two hundred fifty thousand to you? It should be!"

"Give me my money," he said, his voice dangerously low.

"No!"

"Then you'll regret it!"

"No, you will."

Rosalee stood up and rushed out of the restaurant. Bobby threw some money on the table and followed.

Helen texted: B&R LEAVING. FOLLOW R. She looked around wildly for the server. Where was Sophie?

"Here's your steak to go," the server said. "And the check." Helen glanced at the seventy-dollar check. Bobby and Rosalee were getting away. She handed Sophie a hundred-dollar bill and said, "There's more when I get back. Wrap up the rest of my dinner, please."

She sprinted for the exit next to the hotel's sagging canopy and was caught in chaos.

A Majestic Minneapolis Tours bus was unloading flowered suitcases the size of steamer trunks. Pale, pleasant people milled about, talking about the humidity. A mud-brown beater blocked the ramp to the hotel parking garage, its radiator leaking green lizard blood. A harried tow truck driver struggled to load the battered car onto his flatbed. A bellman tried—and failed—to clear the crowd.

Where was Margery? Helen saw her fighting her way through the crowd to the parking garage ramp.

"Margery!" Helen shouted, and nearly fell over a yellow striped suitcase. She dodged two more suitcases and a weary, sweating bellman before she popped out of the confusion, next to Margery. "Where's Rosalee?"

"She ran up the garage ramp," Margery said. "He followed about same time that tour bus arrived with half of Minneapolis. Bobby just took off like the devil was chasing him, driving a black Cadillac Escalade. I photographed him." She held up her cell phone.

"And Rosalee?"

"She hasn't come down yet," Margery said. "That dead car has blocked the ramp and they're having a hell of a time loading it on the flatbed. There! Finally."

The tow truck lurched into the narrow French Quarter street and Helen and Margery ran up the crumbling concrete ramp, breathing in the stink of mold and exhaust, as impatient drivers honked their horns.

"No sign of Rosalee," Margery said, sweat running down her wrinkles.

The line of cars stopped at the third level. Helen saw a scattering of parked cars. Two rows from the exit, high-heeled feet stuck out between a white Chevy Malibu and the concrete wall. Helen touched Margery's shoulder, pointed to the feet, and put her finger to her lips. Margery nodded. Helen reached into her purse for her pepper spray, which had made it through the TSA check. The women crept toward the car until they were hidden behind a pillar.

Rosalee was lying next to the Malibu, a thick silver knife in her chest. Death scenes are rarely beautiful, but Rosalee's was an eerie study in black and red. She lay in a dark pool of blood, the white Malibu and the mold-streaked concrete wall spattered with blood. At the edge of the gory pool, a twenty-something man, scrawny as an alley cat, was riffling a small black patent leather purse. He tossed out a lipstick and a room key. His overgrown soul patch gave him a goatish look. He grabbed a fat roll of bills from Rosalee's purse.

Helen shouted, "You! Don't move!"

Margery snapped his photo. He dropped the purse and started to run, but Helen stepped in front of him, pointing the pepper spray at his eyes. "This will hurt," she said. "A lot." He stopped.

"I didn't do it," he said, sweat exploding on his forehead.

"Scum! Robbing this woman after you killed her," Helen said.

"No!" he said. "She was already dead. I took the money. She's not going to need it."

"You let her bleed out and stole her cash," Helen said. "We saw you."

"You saw me taking her money. I found her with the knife in her chest. She wasn't bleeding any more. I watch *CSI*. I know dead bodies don't bleed. Her heart wasn't pumping any blood."

"What's your name?" Helen asked.

"Squirrel."

"That's what your mother calls you?"

"No, I'm Russell Reed Squires."

"And you didn't call nine-one-one?" Margery asked.

"I can't. Because of...uh, my business."

"Murder and robbery?" Helen said, grabbing his greasy brown hair with one hand, pepper spray still aimed at his face. He tried to move, but her fingers were too tightly wound in his hair.

"No! I sell a little weed and blow. This is my territory. There are no cameras in this garage. I hang around out until someone calls me and then I deliver. I got a call from a customer up on three, parked in spot sixteen. I made the delivery and he drove off. I saw the dead lady and took her money. But that's all."

He pointed at Margery. "Ask her. She saw me get the call."

Margery nodded. "He took a call and sprinted up the ramp. I bet his cargo pants are loaded with product."

Helen pulled a taco-sized plastic bag of whitish powder out of the cargo pocket closest to her, and chucked it over the side of the open garage into the alley below. It exploded like a flour bomb.

"Hey!" the dealer said.

"Shut up," Margery said. She liberated a bag of dried plant material from another pocket and tossed it. Helen and Margery quickly emptied his inventory into the alley, then Margery helped herself to a cabbage-size ball of bills.

"Margery, did you see Mr. Squires head upstairs before or after Bobby left?"

"After," Margery said. "This specimen slithers, but he couldn't have killed her. He doesn't have any blood on him. Look at the blood spatter on the Malibu. He doesn't have any blood on that disgusting muscle shirt. He doesn't have any muscle, either."

"Hey!"

"How old are you?" Helen asked.

"Twenty-three."

"Ever been arrested and convicted?"

He tried to stone-face her, but Helen menaced him with the spray. "I did eighteen months for possession," he said.

"Adult or juvie?" she asked.

"I just got out."

"Put that woman's cash back in her purse," Helen said, and he did. "Take his picture again, Margery. The cops will be able to identify him and his sweaty prints will be on

Rosalee's shiny patent leather purse. Get out of here."

The dealer disappeared. Margery stepped closer to the blood pool to examine the body. "That's a monogrammed Royalton's Superb Steaks knife. I bet Bobby killed her."

"What's that white thing by the Malibu?" Helen asked.

Margery got closer and photographed it. "A napkin monogrammed RSS with a lipstick smear and a grease spot."

"Bobby hid the knife in the napkin to get it out of the restaurant," Helen said.

"Did you see him running out with the knife?"

"No, I was trying to flag down the server," Helen said. "Let's ask Sophie if she's missing a knife. We need to find out where Bobby lives. She'll know. He belongs to the Superb Steaks Club."

Helen saw a checkbook sticking out Rosalee's purse, and used her shirt tail and a pen to ease it out and open it. The account was for Emily Bridwell Peyton at a Fort Lauderdale address. The balance was one hundred fifteen thousand dollars. Stuffed in the checkbook was a driver's license with the same name and address and the glam Rosalee's photo. "I've found the missing money," Helen said, carefully sliding the checkbook back.

Margery was counting Squires's drug money. "Eight hundred twenty bucks here," she said. "Should we call nine-one-one and report the murder?"

"Later," Helen said. "We have a killer to catch."

As the two women ran for Superb Steaks, Helen told Margery about the shadowy woman in the Gucci scarf who sat behind Bobby and Rosalee. Once inside the restaurant, they were grateful it was nearly empty. Sophie greeted them with a smile. "Ladies, you've come back for your dinners."

"We were hoping you could feed us some information," Helen said. "Bobby, who was sitting with the blonde in that middle booth, he's a regular, right?"

"Yes," Sophie said.

"Did he swipe his steak knife?" Helen said.

"How did you know? He's never done that before. Those knives are expensive. The manager counts them every night. I'll be docked a hundred dollars out of my paycheck for that missing knife. The owner can't afford to replace them. And I'll lose twenty-five bucks for the monogrammed napkin the lady with the flowered scarf took. That means I'll make almost nothing this week."

Margery peeled eight twenties out of Squires's stash. "Would that help?" she said. A relieved smile lit Sophia's face. She started to reach for the money, but Margery held onto it.

"We need their names and addresses," she said. "Bobby and the scarf lady. We know they belong to the Superb Steaks Club. Who are they?"

"The scarf lady is Marie. She's married to Bobby," Sophie said. "But they never come here for dinner together. Bobby is a player and brings in so many women, I never acknowledge them and he tips me well. Marie, his wife, has a steady boyfriend named Parker who meets her here. She sees Parker on Tuesdays and Saturdays. Bobby brings his women on Mondays, Wednesdays and Fridays. I think they must have some kind of agreement. I know she can't divorce Bobby. I heard her tell Parker she'd lose her family home if she did. Parker wants to marry her. She told him that Bobby is ruining her family's construction business.

"I expected fireworks when Marie showed up tonight, but she kept her face was hidden by the scarf and sat in the alcove. Bobby never knew she was here."

Margery handed her the money and put down two more twenties. "When did Marie leave?"

"As soon as her husband and that blonde he was with ran out. Her dinner was thirty dollars. She left exactly that much—no tip—and then stole the napkin."

"Do Bobby and Marie live together?" Helen asked.

"Yes. Not too far away. Big white two-story on Prytania Street in the Garden District." She looked up the address on the restaurant computer, then added a phone number. "That's Bobby's cell." Margery gave her another twenty and she and Helen ran outside.

The hotel doorman flagged a cab and soon Helen and Margery were at Bobby's house on Prytania, a graceful white brick with black shutters and an airy gallery. Lacy wrought iron protected the palm trees, magnolias and bougainvillea in the manicured yard.

Helen called Bobby's cell and was relieved when he answered.

"Mr. Charbonnet?" Her voice quick and urgent. "I heard you talking to Rosalee about the payments you've been making to her for twenty years. If you don't want your wife to find out, talk to me. I'm right outside your house."

"Who are you?" Bobby demanded, but Helen saw a lace curtain twitch and then the front door opened. Bobby met Helen and Margery on the sidewalk.

Helen said she was a private detective, introduced Margery as her associate, and they were tracing Rosalee and the hundred thousand dollars she'd stolen.

"She took it from a charity?" he said. "I'm not surprised. That woman is a cheat and a liar."

"She's also dead," Helen said.

"What? How? Where?" Bobby was bug-eyed with shock.

"Where do you think, Mr. Charbonnet?"

He was hyperventilating now. "No! I don't know. I parked on the first floor of the garage and saw her walking up the ramp. She was alive when I left her."

"She was stabbed on the third floor of the garage," Helen said.

"That's not possible."

"I saw her," Helen said.

"My wife must have hired someone to kill her," he said.

"Marie's been going over the books for our business. I think she noticed when I quit making payments to Rosalee. She hates me."

"What's your wife look like?" Helen asked.

"Skinny brunette, dresses nice in designer stuff. About that high." He held up his hand at about five feet six.

"Does she own a flowered Gucci scarf?" Helen asked.

"I don't know Gucci from Pucci," he said.

"Really?" Helen said. "You're wearing an expensive Thomas Pink shirt."

"Wife bought it," he said. "Bought this watch, too."

"You're on the outs with your wife and she bought you a nine thousand dollar TAG Heuer?

"We were still getting along then. She says I dress like a homeless person and embarrass her. Parker, the man she's been seeing, gave her a designer scarf for Christmas with flowers all over it. I thought it was ugly as homemade sin, but she raved about it."

"I think your wife was at the steakhouse wearing that scarf," Helen said.

Suddenly, Prytania Street was alive with police cars. One jerked to a stop next to Bobby, and a tall, fit cop with buzzed hair got out. His name tag said RUBELLE.

"Mr. Charbonnet?"

Bobby managed a nod.

"Do you know a Rosalee Alop?" Officer Rubelle asked.

Bobby's eyes were wide with fear, his voice low and desperate. "You've got to help me, Ms. Hawthorne," he said. "I've been set up. My wife killed Rosalee."

Officer Rubelle swaggered over to them. "Mr. Charbonnet, I asked if you knew a Rosalee Alop. We got an anonymous nine-one-one tip that you stabbed a woman to death in the parking garage of the Royalton Hotel tonight. Were you at the Royalton tonight, Mr. Charbonnet?"

"Tell the truth, Bobby," Helen said.

"Excuse me, miss," Officer Rubelle said. "I wasn't speaking to you."

"She's representing me," Bobby said.

Helen felt like she'd been punched. She hadn't agreed to take on Bobby as a client. He hadn't signed a contract. She glared at him, and he clasped his hands in prayer and mouthed, *I'll pay.*

"Are you a lawyer, miss?" the police officer said.

"I'm a private detective from Fort Lauderdale." Helen presented her ID.

"Florida, huh?" the cop said. "I believe Florida is one of the states that has mutually agreed to recognize the right of private investigators to conduct interstate business, but I don't believe that includes representing murder suspects."

"But she found the body," Bobby said, his face white and greasy as steak fat. Helen vowed to take her payment out of his fat hide, strip by bloody strip.

"Did you find the victim, Ms. Hawthorne?" Officer Rubelle said. "Tell the truth now, like you said to Mr. Charbonnet."

"I found her," Helen said. She was relieved her contract with CWC allowed her to disclose that information. Florida law prohibited her from discussing a case without the client's permission.

"The victim's name is Rosalee Alop. She embezzled a hundred thousand dollars from a Fort Lauderdale charity, Consolidated Worthy Causes. I was hired by CWC to find Ms. Alop and the missing money. I tracked her to New Orleans, where she met with Mr. Charbonnet at Royalton's Superb Steaks tonight. They argued and she ran out to the parking garage. Mr. Charbonnet followed her. I ran after them. By the time I left the restaurant, Mr. Charbonnet had driven out of the hotel parking garage. I went up in to find Ms. Alop. I discovered her body on the third floor."

"I discovered the body, too," Margery said.

"And who might you be, ma'am?" Officer Rubelle asked.

Margery was eager to announce she was an operative, but Helen cut her off. Margery would be no help sharing Helen's cell in the NOLA jail.

"She's my landlady, Margery Flax," Helen said. "She wanted to see New Orleans and came along with me."

Margery must have realized she'd be more help out of jail. She quickly softened her expression and did fair impersonation of a sweet, Marlboro-smoking senior.

"So this lady in purple is a tourist," Officer Rubelle said, "and you're a professional investigator, Ms. Hawthorne. And you didn't call nine-one-one?"

"I was in a hurry, officer," Helen said. "I believe the killer is at this house."

"You *believe? Believe?* I believe I just might file a complaint against you, Ms. Hawthorne. You could have called nine-one-one anonymously from a free public phone."

"There wasn't one," Helen said. She figured that was true. Working public phones were as rare as south Florida ski resorts.

"Then you should have used your cell phone," he said. "This is professional negligence on your part. Which department in Florida oversees private investigators?"

"The Department of Agriculture and Consumer Services," Helen said, and waited for the inevitable laugh.

"Agriculture?" the cop said. "Then you've stepped into a big pile of fertilizer, Ms. Hawthorne. If you'd called us, we would have arrested Mr. Charbonnet ourselves."

"He didn't do it," Helen said, her voice shaking.

"The waitress in Superb Steaks said Mr. Charbonnet stole a steak knife from the restaurant," the cop said. "A similar knife was found in Ms. Alop's chest with fingerprints on it. We're running those prints now, but we're sure they're gonna belong to Mr. Charbonnet."

"I'm sure they will, too," Helen said. Bobby looked like he might pass out.

"That same public-spirited waitress said Mr. Charbonnet and Ms. Alop were fighting over money," Officer Rubelle said. "Mr. Charbonnet was furious because the victim had bilked him out of a quarter of a million dollars. He wanted his money back and she said she didn't have it. He said she'd be sorry and the next thing you know, she's dead and he hightails it back home here.

"Fortunately, some responsible citizen did what you should have done, Ms. Hawthorne, and called the police. Now we're going to arrest Mr. Charbonnet and throw you in jail for obstruction of justice."

"Bobby didn't kill Rosalee," Helen repeated. "His wife Marie did. She was at the restaurant. Check the monogrammed napkin that was dropped near the Malibu's tire and you'll find her lipstick and DNA on it."

"Already bagged and tagged," the cop said. "We know how to do our job. Lipstick and DNA are supposed to be on napkins. Anyone could have grabbed her napkin off the table and dropped it near the car."

"Except Bobby Charbonnet," Helen said. "He left while Marie was still eating at the restaurant. She meets her boyfriend Parker for dinner there twice a week. Ask the server, Sophie. Check Marie's and Parker's Superb Steaks Club cards. That same server will tell you that Parker wants to marry Marie, but she doesn't want to lose her fabulous Prytania Street house when she divorces Bobby.

"He's been mismanaging her family business and skimming money to send to the victim. His wife made that anonymous call to nine-one-one. A voice print will prove that. Marie set him up. If Bobby was in jail, she could divorce him and keep her showcase house."

"Nice theory, Ms. Hawthorne, but there's no proof."

"I think there is," Margery interrupted. "That steakhouse is loaded with security cameras. Check them, and you'll see a woman in a flowered scarf and fancy suit using her napkin to swipe Bobby's knife off his empty table. That woman is Marie. She followed Rosalee up to the third floor of the parking garage, stabbed her and then drove home. Check the tapes yourself.

"You should also check the data on the Superb Steaks Club cards for Bobby, Marie and her boyfriend Parker and find out how often they ate there. And when you're in this house, look for the clothes Marie wore to dinner tonight. She had on an expensive suit and scarf and they're sure to have blood on them. Is she going to throw away several thousand dollars in clothes?"

"That goes for Mr. Charbonnet's clothes, too," the officer said.

"Absolutely," Helen said. "But he's wearing a checked shirt and khakis, and that's what he wore to dinner. The security camera will back me up. So will the server. There's no blood spatter on Bobby's clothes, though he does have a grease stain on his pants."

"Well, I suppose I can call homicide at the restaurant," the cop said. "They're still working the scene."

"That would be ever so kind of you, Officer Rubelle," Margery said, batting her eyelashes. Helen stared at her irascible landlady doing a southern belle act. It was like seeing an alligator in a ruffled bonnet.

"It's so exciting to watch a police professional at work," Margery purred. "Almost worth missing the Super City Tour, though I did want to see the French Quarter."

The cop preened, then made the call to the homicide detective working the crime scene. "You all stay here while we verify this," he said. "I'll go see if Mrs. Charbonnet is home."

"She is," Bobby said. "She's in the upstairs sitting room, last I knew."

Officer Rubelle and another uniform rang the doorbell and disappeared into the air-conditioned showcase. Margery, Helen, Bobby and two uniforms sweated outside for more than an hour. It was past ten o'clock when Officer Rubelle came out and announced, "We'll take statements from each of you. The search warrant for these premises is on the way."

"You have my permission to search my house," Bobby said.

"We're doing this by the book, sir," the officer said. "Mrs. Charbonnet is now a person of interest."

As Marie Charbonnet was escorted out of her showcase home, eyes glittering with hate, Helen went inside to give her statement in a red velvet parlor furnished with antebellum antiques. Margery was next. Afterward, she and Helen sat outside on the veranda, Margery smoking one cigarette after another.

"I can't believe your Scarlett O'Hara act," Helen said. She mimicked a fake southern belle accent, *That would be ever so kind of you, Officer Rubelle. It's so exciting to watch a police professional at work. Almost worth missing the Super City Tour, though I did want to see the French Quarter.*

"Hey, I kept you out of a New Orleans jail," Margery said. "Be grateful."

"I am," Helen said. "But I feel sorry for poor Rosalee. She really loved Bobby."

"The hell she did," Margery said. "You don't blackmail the man you love for twenty years. What are you going to do with the money in her checkbook?"

"Let the police handle it," Helen said. "It's part of a crime scene. I'll write a report letting our client know where it is. But Rosalee is still married to Dennison, so that hundred and fifteen thousand is part of her estate. CWC can fight it out with him."

Margery was tapping on her cell phone. "I'm booking us a flight home for tomorrow," she said. "Two o'clock work for you?"

"That will give me time for a beignet at Café Du Monde," Helen said.

At midnight, a badly shaken Bobby tottered out, his checked shirt a wrinkled mess and his hair coated with thirty-weight oil.

He sat down next to them on the front steps. "It's over," he said. "The cops found Marie's bloody clothes and some towels hidden in the dryer. The video of her taking the knife, along with the waitress's testimony are enough to arrest Marie. They're charging her with Rosalee's murder."

"When they prove that's Rosalee's blood on the clothes and towels and Marie's lipstick and DNA on the napkin," Helen said, "they'll have enough for a conviction."

"Don't forget the server's testimony," Margery added.

"Thank you," Bobby said. "You ladies saved me."

"Best way to thank us is to pay us," Margery said. "Nothing says 'I'm grateful' like a stack of cash."

"I'm not sure Bobby can hire me," Helen said. "I don't know if I'm licensed to take a case in New Orleans. I'd have to check the law."

"Well, you can pay me, Bobby," Margery said. "No law against me sharing my good fortune with a friend."

"How much?" Bobby asked.

"Five thousand," Margery said. Helen's eyes bulged.

"For one night's work?" Bobby said.

"We saved your bacon," she said. "Also, I had a thousand dollars' in expenses. Sophie the server was taking a big risk telling us what happened. Thanks to her, we were here when you needed us. I had to pay her for that information."

With two hundred twenty dollars of the drug dealer's money, Helen thought. The crafty Margery had already snagged a profit of nearly eight hundred bucks.

"That's a little steep," Bobby said.

"Hey, we were here when the police were going to haul you off to jail," Margery said. "How much would a lawyer have cost if you were arrested? What would an arrest do to your business's reputation? Not to mention a trial?"

Bobby knew when he was beaten. "All good points. May I write you a check, Margery?"

"You may, but you don't have the best financial record. How about you give me that fancy watch as collateral until the check clears? There's a branch of my bank on Canal Street. If your check passes muster, you can stop by the hotel at eleven tomorrow and I'll give you your watch before we leave for the airport."

While Bobby wrote the check and handed his TAG Heuer to Margery, she asked, "Where can I get a good hurricane at this hour? What do you recommend?"

"I don't recommend a hurricane for anyone. They're killers: a hundred and fifty-one rum and fruit juice is a lethal combination."

"I can handle it," Margery said.

"Well, Pat O'Brien's is supposed to be the home of the hurricane. But any bartender in New Orleans can make one. The Carousel Bar in the Monteleone Hotel in the French Quarter is fun. The bar looks like a real carousel. It even spins."

"After a drink or two, they all spin," Margery said. "Let's go, Helen."

The Mayor and the Midwife
Edith Maxwell

A stylishly dressed young woman let herself out of the modest home where I, midwife Rose Carroll, was headed. As I approached my pregnant client's abode, the girl turned and we nearly collided.

"Pardon me, miss," she exclaimed before sweeping past. Her day gown, of a lawn fabric sprigged with tiny pink and red flowers, was cut in the new narrower style, with wide lace added at the neck and waist. Her flamboyant scarlet hat, worn at a jaunty angle nearly hiding her face, looked like one of the designs from Mrs. Hallowell's Millinery.

Amused by this devotion to fashion, one which I neither shared by nature nor was allowed to indulge in by my Quaker faith, I knocked at the door, above which hung a small brass Jesus on a cross. A maid showed me in.

The mother-to-be, Venice Shakspeare Currier, sat in her bedroom cradling her well-rounded belly. A white candle flickered on a low table in the corner, where a small brocade rug invited kneeling to pray to a gilded image of the Virgin Mary.

After I greeted Venice, I said, "I passed thy caller in the lane just now." I unpacked a tape measure and Pinard horn from my birthing satchel.

"That was Addie Daigle," Venice replied. "She recently married my cousin Anton, who's my husband's business partner. It was sweet of her to stop in, since I'm certainly not going out these days."

I proceeded to measure her belly from top to bottom. I pressed the flared end of the horn against her taut skin and listened to a strong, rapid fetal heartbeat. "It's fine for thee to take some air in the lane."

"It's mild now. But, Miss Rose, I don't know how I'll care for my little fellow when winter comes. It's going to be awfully cold here in Massachusetts, isn't it?" This was the young wife's first year away from her family in New Orleans. She'd expressed to me on several occasions her apprehensions about having married Zachary Currier and moving all the way from Louisiana to Amesbury. She didn't question her love for her husband, but she worried about the weather.

"Indeed, it will be quite cold this winter." I took her pulse.

"Zachary tells me he's going to have to halt his steamboat excursions when the Merrimack River freezes over. I've never seen a river go solid." Her honey-colored eyes widened.

"Thee shouldn't worry. Thee will bundle thy child properly and thyself, as well."

"I'll try. Zachary wants to name the baby Joseph after my papa. He's the mayor of New Orleans, you know," she boasted in a gentle tone, pronouncing the name of the city something like "Nah-linz."

"Thee knows we cannot discern before the birth if the child will be male or female." I pushed my spectacles back up the bridge of my nose.

"*Mais oui,* of course." She smiled, then cast me a look. "You know, my grandfather speaks Quaker talk like you do."

"Really? Thy grandfather is a Quaker?"

"He is. *Grandpere* came to Louisiana all the way from Delaware," Venice said. "My papa doesn't talk the way you do, but he's a reformer because of what *Grandpere* taught him. Trying to fix politics in New Orleans isn't easy." Venice let out a long yawn.

"I'm going to let thee rest now. All seems well."

I let myself out. Zachary Currier hadn't made an appearance, but he was no doubt at work in his steamboat office a mile away on the Merrimack. A native of Amesbury, he'd been apprenticing on a steam paddleboat on the Mississippi when he'd met and fallen in love with Venice.

I stepped out onto the lane. The afternoon sun on this lovely autumn day illuminated the red and golden leaves like a gilt-edged painting.

A fine Hollander rockaway carriage pulled up to the house, its high graceful wheels crunching on the paving stones. After the uniformed driver pulled the glossy brown Morgan to a halt, a man in a handsome suit and top hat stepped out of the coach, his dark mustache well oiled, his midsection well fed.

"Good afternoon, miss," he said, tipping his hat. "I'd be much obliged if you would show me into this fine abode." He widened the vowels like Venice did, with the middle of "obliged" and "fine" stretching into "ah" sounds. "If it is the home of a Mister Zachary Currier, that is."

I extended my hand. "I'm Rose Carroll. This is indeed Zachary's home, and that of his wife, Venice. But I'm not employed in the household. Thee will have to ask the maid for admittance."

The man stared at me for a moment, then threw his head back and laughed before shaking my slender hand with his meaty one.

"A Quaker, are you?" he exclaimed. "*Mon Dieu,* just like my dear *Papere.*"

"I am, and a midwife, as well." I cocked my head. "Would thee happen to be Venice's father, come from New Orleans?"

"That's the truth, young lady. I'm Joseph Shakspeare. Has my grandson arrived yet?"

"Not yet. It could be another six weeks, although the baby will likely arrive in about a month's time."

"And how fares my girl?"

"Thy daughter is quite healthy."

"*Tres bien.* Her mother sent me to check on Venice's welfare, as the missus is involved with her own nursling. Our youngest of six is only a year-old and quite attached yet to his meals of mother's milk."

"As he should be," I said. "Farewell, then. Enjoy thy stay."

He twirled one end of his mustache and regarded me. "*Mais*, I've just come from a visit with the selectmen of this fair town. Thought we could exchange some honest words about city government and all that, seeing as how I'm a mayor looking to reverse a terrible situation of corruption. But those fellows were *pas vaillant*. You know, standoffish."

"It is New England, land of the Puritans." I tried to suppress my smile. "And I know the term. I speak some French with my French-Canadian clients."

"Well, what's a man got to do to buy his colleagues a drink in this town?"

I thought for a moment. "I can introduce thee tomorrow to our town's police detective. Kevin Donovan is a competent and forthcoming officer. He'd be willing to talk with thee about government. He also enjoys a spot of drink."

"Splendid, my dear Quaker, splendid. Send word as to the time and I shall appear."

"I will, Joseph."

"*Merci*. Now I must find my Venice."

I was surprised to see tears well up in his eyes. He may have been a metropolitan mayor fighting corruption, but he was a tender one.

At nine o'clock the next morning I sat in Kevin's office with Joseph. He'd picked me up in the hired carriage and now we waited for Kevin to appear.

"Venice was happy to see thee yesterday, I'd guess," I said.

"Indeed she was." Joseph beamed. "We're going out on the river later today on Zachary's pleasure boat, since the weather is so fine. We're going to pass a good time."

"It'll be a pleasant ride."

Kevin burst into the room mopping his high rounded brow with a handkerchief. "Pardon my tardiness, sir." He pumped Joseph's hand, then greeted me. "Hello, Miss Rose."

"Joseph, I'd like you to meet Detective Kevin Donovan," I said. "Kevin, Joseph Shakspeare, mayor of New Orleans."

"Excellent to meet you, Detective. Miss Carroll here says you run a tight ship."

"We do our best." Kevin sat behind his messy desk. "But don't you mean Shakespeare, Miss Rose?" He cocked his head.

Joseph laughed. "Everyone thinks I can't spell my own name. No, Miss Carroll was correct. I share the bard's name minus one letter."

"I see." Kevin nodded. "Now, what can I help you with, Mayor?"

"My mission is to reduce corruption in city government. We have a group called the Ring down there, and they oppose me at every turn. I'm here visiting my daughter, Mrs. Currier, and thought I'd see what the fine town of Amesbury had to offer."

"I will leave you gentlemen to it." I rose. "I'm off to see clients."

Both men also stood. Kevin opened his mouth to speak when a young officer appeared in the doorway. "Excuse me, sir, but there's been a death near the Merrimack, a Zachary Currier. The death might be suspicious."

I gasped. Not Venice's husband.

Joseph's eyes widened. "*Maudit!*" he whispered.

"Currier. That's your daughter's married name, you said?" A frowning Kevin asked Joseph.

"Her husband's Christian name is Zachary." Joseph, his face pale, turned to the young officer. "He's a paddleboat owner. That the one?"

"Yes, sir."

I brought my hand to my mouth. Another suspicious death in our quiet town.

"This is a disturbing turn of events." Kevin shook his head.

"Has his wife been informed?" I asked. This kind of shock could easily bring on labor. Her baby might be mature enough by now to survive the birth, or might not.

"Not yet, ma'am," the officer said.

"I must go to her. My *pauvre fille*," Joseph said. "You'll come along, Miss Carroll?"

"Of course. Let me quickly pen a note to my next client saying I need to cancel. I can hail a boy outside to deliver it."

I looked at the detective. I'd assisted him in several cases by keeping my eyes and ears open in the community, especially in the bedchambers of my birthing women, where secrets were often revealed during their travails. The detective had reluctantly grown to accept my participation.

"If it's murder, I'd like to help by listening, watching, and reporting to thee as I have done in the past."

Kevin nodded. "Then meet me at the Currier steamboat dock after you see to the wife, will you?"

I climbed out of Joseph's carriage in front of the dock an hour later. He'd instructed the driver to take me down to the river. Before I'd left Venice's side I ascertained that, so far at least, the distraught young woman had not started her labor. I left her father to console her and said I'd be back.

The dock bustled with police. A coroner's wagon was parked nearby, its gray horse waiting patiently in the traces. The open upper deck of the long white steamboat, a deck I'd seen full of weekend frolickers recently, now sat empty and forlorn.

The door to a small building opened. Kevin and another officer walked out grasping a struggling young man between them.

"*Moi*, I never did!" the fellow exclaimed. "I wouldn't kill Zach. We're in business together." His speech lilted in the southern way like Venice's.

"Yes, but you're also employed sewing sails as a side business, I hear," Kevin said. "That puncture wound in the victim's neck could've come only from a needle, and I very much doubt it was self-inflicted." He caught sight of me. "Ah, Miss Rose. We're taking Anton Daigle in for questioning."

Anton's eyes pleaded with me. "I didn't kill *mon cousin*, miss. I didn't."

"Come along, now." Kevin and the other officer bundled Anton into the back of the police wagon parked behind the ambulance. As the door shut, Kevin turned back toward me, dusting off his hands.

"What reason would Anton have to kill his partner?" I asked.

"He probably had a deal where he'd inherit the victim's half of the business. Sometimes they write up contracts like that."

"Did thee find the murder weapon?"

"Not yet. I'll show you the body."

"Very well." As a midwife, I was acquainted with death, beyond the several murder victims I'd had the misfortune to encounter. I did my best to bring women and babies safely through the normal but dangerous journey of birth. But sometimes I lost a mother or a newborn, or an infant succumbed to disease in its first weeks. I'd seen lifeless bodies before.

I followed Kevin into the office building, barely more than a shack with a window where tickets were sold. A wooden desk faced the door and another lined the back wall.

Zachary Currier lay half on his side behind the front desk. One hand grasped a tipped-over chair as if he'd reached for it as he fell. A dark pool soaked the floor under his neck and red marks slashed the side wall. An officer guarded the body.

"Watch the door from outside," Kevin instructed him. After the man left, Kevin moved the victim's head slightly and pointed. "See here? Stabbed in the neck. Daigle there knew exactly how to hit the vital vein."

I gathered my skirts in my hands to keep them away from the blood and leaned down to examine the neck. Indeed, a small round puncture wound pierced the skin above where Zachary's right carotid artery would be. The spray on the wall would be from the pressure of the heart continuing to pump out blood until the poor man had lost enough to die.

"Looks like a needle wound, wouldn't you say?" Kevin asked.

"Certainly a thin sharp object. Thee hasn't found it?"

"Not yet, but we will."

"Who reported the death this morning?"

"It was Daigle himself." Kevin's mouth turned down in disgust. "A fellow reported that Daigle had just arrived when he dashed back out and raised the alarm. Probably killed Currier earlier, went home for breakfast, and came back all calm and easy like."

"Of course thy officers will closely question the neighbors and other businesses here on the river." I stared at him over my spectacles. "Thee has a penchant for jumping to conclusions a bit too hastily, Kevin."

He cleared his throat. "Of course we will. And we'll find the bloody needle, too."

After they carried out Zachary's body, and with Kevin's permission, I made my own search of the office. I pulled out desk drawers, knelt to peer under the furniture, and checked the dusty corners. I examined the ticket counter, with its used tickets stuck on a spike.

I didn't locate the weapon, however. I peered closely at the spike. While its tip was certainly sharp enough, the rest of it was too thick to have caused the small wound. The carotid rested about an inch and half in from the skin of the neck, if I remembered my anatomy studies correctly. No, a long sharp needle or pin was going to be the culprit. Unfortunately, it could be deep in the river by now.

I did find one small item that seemed out of place in an office. I pocketed the slim white feather, thinking to pass it along to Kevin. Perhaps it wasn't suspicious. There were gulls and other birds aplenty along the wide river, still tidal here ten miles inland from the Atlantic. But the detective might want to take a look.

When I went outside, though, Kevin had left. The officer on guard said he'd gone back to the station. I began my walk back toward the grieving young widow. Could Kevin's posited motive possibly be true?

"Boil water," I directed Venice's maid as a clock chimed noon. "And I'll need a stack of clean cloths and two basins." As I'd feared, Venice was experiencing regular and increasingly frequent pains of labor when I arrived. I was glad I'd left my birthing satchel here this morning before departing for the dock. Joseph paced in the back of the room.

He hurried to where I stood. "Did the detective figure out how Zachary died?" he whispered.

"He appears to have been murdered," I murmured. "Kevin thinks it was your nephew Anton."

"*Quoi?*" Venice screeched. "Anton wouldn't kill my Zach."

"Anton said as much," I told her. "But the detective took him in for questioning, regardless."

Venice groaned as another contraction set in. "Thee must wait in another room," I said to Joseph. "I need to examine the baby's progress. And we can't be having a man in the birthing chamber."

He nodded. "Just one moment."

He knelt in the prayer corner, crossed himself as he bowed his head, then folded his hands in front of his chest. He murmured prayers for a minute, then crossed himself again.

"*Fait du mal*! It hurts, *Papere*," Venice wailed, her eyes squeezed shut and her face crunched in pain.

"*Cher*, you'll be all right." Joseph stood and stroked his daughter's forehead with a gentle hand, but he wore one of the most anguished faces I'd ever seen on a man. "I look forward to meeting *le petit*, and we're going to bring you and him home to *Maman* as soon as we can. Don't you worry about a little thing. Miss Rose here is going to take good care of you."

He left and the young maid returned, eyes wide. She placed the kettle on a dresser, setting the folded linens and basins next to it. "Do you need me to help, miss?"

I let out a breath. I very much wished to have an apprentice at my side, but the one I was training was away. "I should be fine. But please don't be far in case I call for thee."

She nodded and scurried out as Venice lay curled on the bed, moaning through another pain.

When her contraction ended, I said, "I need thee to sit up." I propped pillows at the head of the bed and boosted her up until she was sitting almost straight. "Bend thy knees. I'm going to check the opening to thy womb."

"I want my *defunt* Zach." She gazed at me, tears streaming down her face. "My baby won't have a *Papere*, Rose. Whatever will I do?"

"Thee has a caring father and family back home. But let's get this baby out first."

I washed my hands, wishing I could also wash away this dire situation. A baby coming too early, a murdered father, and a mother far from anything familiar.

I pushed up the sleeve of my gray work dress and slid my hand inside her. Only a half-knuckle's worth of dilation remained. I slid my hand out as I held her and the baby in a moment of silent prayer, that they would both make it through the next hour in good health.

With her next pain, Venice grabbed her knees, emitting a guttural sound. When the contraction subsided, she collapsed back on the pillows. "Rose, I'm afraid. Some *bon de rien* killed my husband. Am I next?"

It was my turn to stroke her sweaty brow. "There, there. No bad person's coming to kill thee."

"Anton never would've hurt Zach. His wife, Addie? She's a different story."

But I didn't get to hear that story. With the next pain Venice grabbed her knees again. Her scrunched face reddened with exertion. I grabbed the top couple of cloths off the stack and spread one under her buttocks. I drew the cord scissors out of my satchel even as a tiny dark-haired head appeared at the opening. Such an early baby was likely to be small and present little difficulty in birthing. Whether its lungs would be mature enough to sustain life was a different question.

A blessed hour later the swaddled babe was in his mother's arms, with his grandfather in a chair at the bedside. The birth had been as easy as they come. Venice's passageway had not torn, the afterbirth had been intact, the little fellow had breathed well, and he'd already suckled his first meal. He now regarded Venice with the calm dark-eyed gaze of all newborns.

Venice glanced at her father. "*Papere*, I was going to name him Joseph. But now I must call him Zachary. You understand, *n'est ce pas?*"

He nodded, tears again in his eyes.

"I have something I must do," I said, patting my pocket. "I'll return before nightfall to check on thee, Venice. And I'll bring an herb to help thy milk production."

"You're a *traiteure*, Rose. What we call a healer back home." Venice smiled, just a little.

I smiled back.

I hurried along the lower edge of Main Street back to the river, the mid-afternoon sun glinting off the water. After I chatted with several neighbors of the steamboat office, as well as with a man running a fish shop next door to the dock, I hailed the horse-drawn trolley that ran from the bridge into town. I'd put together two and two and I urgently needed to convey the sum to a certain detective. But first I had a bit of research to do.

Twenty minutes after alighting downtown, I laid out my idea to Kevin in his office.

"This is quite a stretch, Miss Rose."

"I believe thee holds an innocent man, Kevin. Doesn't thee wish to see justice served?"

He stared at me, finally letting out a long sigh. "All right. I'll check that one fact, and then let's be off."

Half an hour later we stood in the clean but somewhat shabby parlor of the Daigle home, a small house near the rail depot. Addie again wore the pink and red-sprigged day dress I'd seen her in yesterday.

"What do you want?" she asked. "You already have my husband."

Kevin nodded to me.

"Thee knows thy husband is suspected of killing Zachary Currier this morning."

She kneaded one hand with the other. "I was just on my way to the jail to visit him. My poor Anton was under such pressure."

"What kind of pressure?" Kevin asked, pulling out a small notebook and a stub of pencil.

"Working the two businesses up here. He'd escaped the

Ring down there in New Orleans where he's from. But the work was just about killing him. I'm not surprised he cracked."

"Did he?" I asked. "Where was thee this morning a few minutes before dawn?"

"Asleep here in my bed, of course."

I gave a brief nod to Kevin, who went into the hall and returned with Addie's fanciful red hat.

"Sure enough, it's from Mrs. Hallowell's," he said after examining the tag inside.

"What d'you want with my hat?" Addie tried to grab it but Kevin was too fast for her.

I pulled out the feather from my pocket and held it up next to the three small white feathers that were part of the hat's decoration.

"A perfect match," I said. "Mrs. Hallowell herself told me these are most rare, feathers from a nearly extinct African miniature heron. She had only the four."

"And what of it?" Addie scoffed. "I've gone into the steamship office many times wearing that hat."

I glanced at Kevin. I hadn't said the office was where I'd found the feather.

Kevin drew out a handkerchief and carefully extracted a long hat pin from the bow at the back of the hat, a pin with rust-colored stains. "I daresay our microscope will discover traces of Mr. Currier's blood on your hat pin, ma'am."

"And I believe we'll find spots of blood mixing in with the red flowers on thy dress," I added. "A neighbor saw thee enter the office early this morning. Thy own husband said thee was not in the marital bed when he arose." I wondered how she knew to find the carotid, but perhaps it had been luck, not skill.

Addie turned to look out the window.

"Why did you kill him, Mrs. Daigle?" Kevin stood tall, official, stern.

She faced us, head held high. "I deserve a better life than this. We never have enough money." With a curled lip she gestured around the room. "I didn't think Anton would be stupid enough to get himself arrested. I thought we'd get the whole business for ourselves."

"Thee seemed willing to let us think Anton was the murderer a moment ago."

"Well, *I* certainly didn't want to be hauled off to jail." She tossed her blonde curls. "And if he's guilty, then the business is mine, isn't it?"

"I guess you never read their business contract," Kevin said in a soft voice. "In case of one partner's death, his half of the enterprise goes to his wife."

"No!" Her eyes went wide. She lunged for Kevin, her fingernails aiming for his neck. Kevin neatly sidestepped and caught her hands behind her. He gave a whistle, and another officer hurried in from the hall to cuff Addie's hands behind her back. He turned her toward the door.

She twisted back to glare at Kevin and me. "You'll regret this."

"I doubt it," he murmured.

I approached the Currier home as dusk fell to find Joseph and Anton leaving the house. I supposed Anton might be angry with me for my role in Addie's arrest, but I greeted them, regardless.

"How is Venice?" I asked. "I brought her the herb I'd promised."

"She is grieving terribly," Joseph said. "But at least she has her baby." He clapped a hand on Anton's shoulder. "And we're putting up my nephew for the time being."

"It's generous of you, *Nonc* Joseph." He looked at me. "I have to sell my house now, to pay for my wife's lawyer."

"I see," I said. "Perhaps you heard of the assistance I provided the detective. I'm sorry—"

Anton held up a hand. "Addie did a terrible thing, and you made sure justice was served. Please don't apologize." His eyes sagged but he kept his chin up and shoulders back.

I nodded in silence.

"We're off to church to say a prayer for both Zachary and his baby son." Joseph tipped his hat.

The two climbed into the waiting carriage. I knocked at the house, relieved to leave detecting behind. I had a new mother and baby to see to.

Blowhards on the Bayou
Deborah Lacy

Simone Duplanter was the kind of woman that men loved, and women hated. Her hair was always perfectly in place. Her makeup impeccable. Her expensive clothes always flattered her generous curves. Beyond her physical beauty and a truly mesmerizing Southern drawl, Simone's other gifts included advanced flirting, creative backhanded compliments and large quantities of unwanted advice.

She was the whole package. And after four hours of being trapped in this woman's company, Lisa Desmond wished she could leave that package on the doorstep and call someone to haul it all away.

"I love Mardi Gras! Wooo hooo!" Simone yelled raising a bottle of champagne in the air. She sounded more than a little boozy. "*Laissez les bon temps roulez*! Let the good times roll!" She drank straight from the bottle and then offered to share. But there were no takers. They all had their own.

"Did I ever tell y'all about the time that I dated Brad Pitt?" Simone said. Anyone within a hundred mile radius had heard the story, but that didn't stop Simone from telling it.

Lisa supposed her mood might have been better if she had been drinking since noon like everyone else, but she couldn't drink and take her meds, so the meds won. She pulled a few strands of plastic beads out of the bag and hung them on one of the nails by her place on the float. She wasn't sure where to put her cellphone, but she had been taking photos all day and didn't want to stop now.

"Baby girl! It's Mardi Gras!" Lisa's old college roommate Jenna squealed, even perkier than usual. "You've been mopey all afternoon. You have to turn that frown upside down."

"You didn't really just say that?" asked Lisa.

"I plead the fifth," Jenna said taking another swig of Jack and Diet Coke. "Where is your drink?"

Lisa held up her plastic cup filled with plain old orange juice.

"Come on, baby girl, get happy! We are riding in a Mardi Gras parade today. With the Valkyries Krewe. I mean look at this float. Twenty full feet of fake bayou on wheels."

The float was a papier-mâché wonderland. The sides of the float featured painted marsh grass and muddy water. Faux fireflies danced just over the water. But the focus of the float was the man-made cypress trees dripping with real Spanish moss. Nestled in the branches of each tree there was a floating cartoon head of a famous Louisiana windbag politician, and let's be honest, they're all windbags, which is where the float got its name: *Blowhards on the Bayou*. It was perfect, and Lisa couldn't stop taking photos.

"Things might get a little rough today," Jenna said putting her drink down.

"I know, I will hold onto the rail when the float is moving," Lisa said, practicing to grip the railing. "I will lean back towards the float a little when I am throwing beads, and I will not lean over the side."

"Oh, that's not what I meant. I'm not worried about you falling off the float. I'm worried about the fireworks. Simone has been in high form lately. At least when she totaled your car last month, it was an accident. Mary Beth Ralston found Simone with her husband last week."

"In bed?"

"I don't know the details, but they were having sex, wherever it was. It's bad enough that Mary Beth lost her job to Simone last year, but now this. Bless her heart."

Lisa knew what it was like to be on the wrong end of Simone's machinations, but that didn't explain why Mary

Beth had accepted Simone's invitation, "We'll just keep them on opposite sides of the float."

"Louisiana ain't big enough for the two of them, much less this itty bitty float. And that's not the only thing," Jenna said, "but hush. Here comes Mary Beth."

Lisa hadn't seen Mary Beth in years, but the petite woman still wore her brown hair in a classic pixie cut. Some things would never change.

She carried three enormous bags of stuff to throw off the float at the crowds—beads, stuffed animals, and cups. The bags were bigger than Mary Beth. Lisa helped her get her bounty on board.

"I still have three more bags in the car," Mary Beth said, "I made thirty-five hats."

"Thirty-five hats?" Jenna said. "Are you crazy, baby girl? You must have been making those things all year."

"Why do you need all of those hats?" said a redheaded woman that Lisa didn't recognize.

"The women of the Valkyrie Krewe decorate hats to throw to the crowd during the parade," said Jenna. "It's so much more exclusive than the beads. You know it's like the decorated shoes Muses throws, the purses Nyx throws, Tucks throws decorated toilet plungers—so tacky, and Zulu, they decorate coconuts, but they just hand them to people, so they don't take anyone's head off."

"Oh well, I'm not from around here, and I didn't decorate any hats," said the redhead. "My name is Rosie, by the way. I'm a friend of Simone's."

"Baby girl, Simone Duplanter does not have friends," Jenna said as she touched the girl's shoulder. "Just kidding. I'm only kidding. We need to get you a drink."

Jenna reached into a cooler and handed the girl a bottle of champagne.

Five women Lisa didn't know got on and went to the other side of the float.

"Who the hell are they?" Rosie the redhead asked.

"They're in from Baton Rouge," said Jenna. "They donated ten grand a piece to the Sunshine Kids charity for their spots on the float. The money will go to help those kids with cancer."

"Woo wee," Rosie said popping open the champagne. "Great for the kids but that's a lotta dough. Makes me feel less stupid for spending so much money on all of these trinkets."

Lisa knew how she felt. She'd spent over a thousand dollars on plastic beads alone. She tried not to think of her money being swept up by the clean-up crews at the end of the night. Riding in a Mardi Gras parade was a dream come true and she was only going to do it once in her life.

"The float rolls in thirty minutes," Simone yelled with excitement from the other side of the fake bayou. "Thirty minutes! Yee Haw!"

Lisa took some time to finish hanging all of her beads on the nails, and made sure her first stuffed animal bag was open. She had a special bag of swag for her little sister, and she put that on a nail all by itself.

"Here," said Mary Beth handing Lisa a gold necklace with a pouch as a pendant. "Wear this around your neck and slip your cell phone into the pocket. That way, you won't lose it."

"That's awesome. Thank you."

"Better go potty and put your outfits on. Twenty minutes, woo hoo!" Simone yelled again.

"Good God. Now she's telling us when to pee," Jenna said, as she stepped into the green and yellow polyester pantsuit they all would wear over their clothes for the night. Mary Beth handed everyone a necklace with a cell phone pouch.

"Simone had better stop drinking," Mary Beth said, "or she's going to fall over the side."

Jenna laughed nervously.

Lisa slid her own jump suit on over her jeans. Between the diesel engines in the floats and the flying food and drinks, the costume was an added layer of protection. She put on her wig made with phony Spanish moss, helping her to blend in with the fake bayou. She would wait until later to put on her mask.

"We have got to take photos before we get started," Jenna announced pulling out her camera phone.

She, Lisa and Mary Beth took a selfie, which Simone photo bombed. Lisa took photos of the beads hanging next to the Spanish moss. They all put their heads in a cypress tree next to their favorite blowhard politician.

What a sight they must be in their Spanish moss wigs posting photos to Facebook. Rosie declined to have her photo taken.

"Jenna! Delivery!" a man with a Saints visor yelled, "I've got your po'boys and muffelettas here."

"Max!" Jenna yelled. She handed him an envelope and took the bags of sandwiches from the man. "Thank God. We're starving. Dig in, girls. Koz's has *the* best sandwiches in New Orleans. Better get a layer of food in your stomach so you can last the night."

Lisa found a roast beef po'boy sandwich, and dug in. The gravy was heaven on bread. Thank goodness there were plenty of napkins.

"Seriously, y'all look like you've never eaten before," Simone said slurring her words just a bit. "Slow down. Chew your food, y'all."

Lisa thought Simone was the one who needed to slow down. Jenna offered her a sandwich but Simone wasn't interested in food. She was too busy regaling Rosie the Red-head about the time she met Nicolas Cage eating beignets at Café Du Monde.

She had just finished her sandwich when she heard a woman squeal, "Lisa Desmond!" She recognized the voice immediately. It was her high school nemesis, Gwen "Blue

Eyes" Saint. Lisa spent four years being number two to Gwen's number one—spelling bees, yearbook editor, and pining after Jack Wilson. She came in second to her so often that Gwen used to call her "Number Two." But that was more than a decade ago. Lisa was over it.

"What are you doing here, Gwen?" Lisa said. She hoped her tone didn't sound too insincere.

"The float is leaving in three minutes!" shouted Simone. "Lisa, Jenna, Rosie, Gwen and me, y'all, we're on the sidewalk side. The rest of y'all are facing neutral ground. That's the other side of the float if you're not from around here. Woo hoo!"

Gwen said, "Simone told me where you were standing, so I laid out my beads next to you so we could catch up. She says you're an optometrist. Looking into people's eyes all day, that sounds exciting."

It wasn't exciting, but it was a good way to make a living. Lisa didn't dare ask Gwen what she did for work. She didn't want to hear the answer.

The rest of the women put their masks on and claimed their places on the sidewalk side of the float. Gwen was at the front, then came Lisa, Jenna, Mary Beth, Rosie the Redhead and at the end of the row was Simone.

A whistle blew, and the float's diesel engine roared. The smoke made Lisa cough. She had wanted to ride in this parade her entire life. She decided that as soon as they started rolling, she was going to have fun. It would just be her and the people of the city she loved most in the entire world: New Orleans.

She braced herself on the rail and grabbed a strand of purple beads. The parade float started to move forward.

People in the crowd started waving their arms and yelling, "Throw me something! Hey! Hey!"

Lisa scanned the crowd for a deserving recipient for her first strand of beads. She saw a little blonde girl on the shoulders of Max, the guy who owned the sandwich shop. She threw the strand of beads softly as she could, and the little girl caught the beads and laughed. Her daddy waved thank you. Lisa could get used to this.

"I want to hear some noise," yelled Simone over the din. "Woo hoo!" Still holding the champagne bottle in one hand, she grabbed a handful of beads with the other and hurled them into the crowd. The first pile landed straight in the mud, missing all of the people ready to catch them. Her next pile of beads hit a man square in the face. She didn't even notice.

Since this was not Jenna's first parade ride, she carefully handed stuffed animals to any child or parent close enough to the float. Many kids sat in wooden boxes attached to the tops of ladders, so it was easy to toss them the plush animals. If a toy hit the ground, even for a second, it would be so dirty and disgusting that it would be useless forever, so Lisa started handing out her stuffed animals this way, too.

Mary Beth focused on throwing her hats, and every time she pulled one out the crowd yelled, "Hats! Hats! Hats!" If Lisa ever did this again, she promised herself that she would decorate the hats.

Gwen gracefully threw out the expensive lighted necklaces and Rosie just sat there and drank, taking in the whole scene.

Simone threw an entire bag of stuffed animals into the crowd and was about to throw her champagne bottle when Rosie stopped her and made her sit down.

Simone reached for another bag of stuffed animals and used them as a pillow before she passed out. Once she was safely laid out on the wooden floor, Rosie started throwing her beads, one or two strands at a time. And boy, did Rosie have an arm on her. She could throw those beads all the way to Mississippi and back.

The crowd was so noisy that Lisa almost missed her little sister, but saw her in time to get her special bag gently thrown down to her. Their mom snapped photos and e-mailed them to Lisa immediately.

Lisa took a short video of the crowd waving and yelling for beads. She quickly posted it online. That's when she noticed that Simone had just posted a selfie looking very drunk. Lisa looked down the float at Simone. She was still lying on the floor passed out. So how was she posting photos?

Lisa looked at Gwen, "My throat is so raw from the diesel smoke," Lisa said. "Does anyone have any water?"

"There's a whole case over by Simone," said Jenna.

Lisa walked back to the end of the float where Simone lay. Simone clearly wasn't in any shape to be posting photos. Her necklace with the cellphone pouch was missing and her skin was sickly pale. Lisa reached down to feel for Simone's pulse. Maybe it was because of the noise of the crowd, or the movement of the float, but Lisa couldn't find a pulse.

She pushed open one of Simone's eyelids. Her pupils were huge. It looked like they had been dilated with belladonna, like she would do in the office to get a better look inside an eye. But too much champagne doesn't do that to pupils.

"Rosie," Lisa yelled over the noise of the crowd. Rosie was too busy throwing a T-shirt into the throngs. "Rosie!" Lisa yelled again. "Is Simone taking any medication?" But Rosie didn't hear her.

If Simone had overdosed on belladonna, either on purpose or accidentally, Lisa would need to wash her stomach with activated charcoal. But she didn't have any, and there was no way to do that on a Mardi Gras float. Lisa couldn't be sure what was wrong with Simone, but she dialed 911 anyway. The call failed. Network overload.

Lisa waved Jenna over, "Can you get a phone signal? I think Simone is in trouble." She had to talk loudly to be heard over the crowd.

Gwen came over with her phone and the two of them both tried dialing the police.

"I can't get a signal," Gwen said. She bent down next to Simone and pushed open her eyelids. "She's been poisoned. It's belladonna."

"You can't know that," said Jenna.

"And it is belladonna," Gwen stood up. "Ask Lisa. She's an optometrist."

Gwen was still an insufferable know-it-all.

"Jenna," Lisa said, "Go check the other side of the float and see if any of those Baton Rouge girls have any medical experience. Simone needs help."

Jenna put down her drink and went to the other side of the float.

"Those Baton Rouge girls can't help her," Gwen said. "Simone is dead."

"Oh my God, she can't be dead," said Lisa. "This is Mardi Gras. How can she be dead? We have to get help." Lisa's throat was hurting more now, from all the yelling and the diesel smoke.

Rosie started throwing Simone's beads over the side of the float to the roaring crowd.

"We need to stop this float now and get the police," said Lisa.

Jenna came back from the other side of the float, "Those Baton Rouge girls are about as much help as an alligator at a bridal shower. They don't know shit about shit." Jenna had one of those Southern accents that made cussing sound almost like poetry.

Mary Beth joined Gwen and Lisa in front of Simone's body. She fell to her knees and started crying. "I wished she was dead, but I didn't really mean it. I'm going to hell for sure now."

"Let's get the float stopped," Lisa said looking for Simone's empty champagne bottle. "Call the cops." The police would want to test the bottle for poison.

"If we stop the float, the whole parade stops," said Gwen.

"Then we're stuck in the crowds until the police fight their way through. We only have an hour more. We're better off getting to the end."

A bunch of beads came flying over the side of the float, pelting Jenna in the face, "What?"

"The crowd is mad that y'all are talking instead of throwing," Rosie said. "I'm trying to keep them happy, but it's near impossible. One of you, help me."

"Rosie, you realize your friend is dead?" Lisa said.

"You can't help her now. She only invited me here because she felt guilty. We might as well enjoy the night."

"That's cold," Jenna said. "That is just super cold."

"I'm sure that all of us had a reason to kill Simone," Gwen said.

"No we don't," said Lisa.

"Look," Gwen said. "There are five of us: me, Lisa, Mary Beth, Jenna and Rosie. Simone screwed all of us in some way. She invites us here and one of us kills her. The big question is which one of us is guilty. All we know for sure is that Simone was killed with belladonna taken from Lisa's optometry office."

"We don't know that," Jenna said. "How could we know that?"

"It could be one of the Baton Rouge ladies, or the sandwich guy," Mary Beth said.

Someone from the crowd chucked a bunch of trash over the side of the float and it fell to the floor.

"Simone refused to eat a po'boy," Jenna said, "and the Baton Rouge crowd doesn't know her from Charmaine Neville."

"She's dead," Gwen said, "And one of you four poisoned her."

The women looked at one another while Rosie threw little Saints footballs out into the roaring crowd.

"Mary Beth's husband was sleeping with Simone," Jenna said.

"Simone was blackmailing you," Gwen said.

"How the hell did you know that?"

"What are we going to do, accuse each other until the parade was over?" Lisa said.

Lisa's phone beeped and she was glad for the distraction. Her mother's photos of her on the float had come in, but she still couldn't get a phone signal. She scanned the photos from this afternoon and the ones from the float. In one of the pictures she saw a pixie-sized Valkyrie stealing Simone's cell phone necklace.

"Ah ha!" said Lisa. "Mary Beth killed her. Look at this photo. Mary Beth is stealing Simone's cellphone so she could keep posting photos and we'd think she was still alive."

Gwen looked at the photo, "A short woman is definitely stealing the phone."

"But I didn't need to kill her," Mary Beth said. "I just needed evidence for my divorce trial. Simone said she had photos of them having sex. I thought I'd snag her cell phone when she was too drunk to notice. I saw the photo of her drunk, and posted it to make her look bad."

"So Mary Beth is innocent," Gwen said. "She wouldn't have stolen the phone if she knew Simone was going to die. I'm going to rule out Mary Beth."

"Why do you get to decide anything?" Rosie asked.

"Yeah, maybe you killed her, Gwen," Jenna said. "What was she blackmailing you about?"

"She wasn't blackmailing me. And besides, I wasn't even with y'all this afternoon," Gwen said, her voice getting a little higher with each word. "The killer had to have given her the belladonna this afternoon."

"How can you possibly know this shit?" asked Jenna. "How did you become the world's leading expert on belladonna?"

"That's a very good question," said Mary Beth.

Lisa went back through her photos and found one of Simone from this afternoon. Gwen was clearly in the background of the photo.

"Ah ha!" Lisa yelled. "You were there this afternoon when we were eating oysters at Bourbon House" She held up the phone for them to see.

"That doesn't prove anything," Gwen said. "So I was at Bourbon House. It doesn't mean I poisoned Simone."

"But you did poison Simone," Rosie said, holding a necklace of rubber ducks. "You knew she was dying, but you didn't want Lisa to get her help."

"At least I didn't spend the whole time throwing Mardi Gras beads."

"Simone didn't die from the belladonna from this afternoon, so you tried to give her another dose here on the float, after you pronounced her dead."

Lisa backed away from Gwen and from Rosie, "But if you knew that, why didn't you stop her? Why didn't you save Simone?"

"She didn't need to," Simone said, "because I'm not dead."

Startled, Lisa jerked back into a papier-mâché cypress tree and nearly knocked it down. Her wig got caught on a branch and it came right off.

Rosie pulled out a pair of handcuffs and put them on Gwen.

"I'm sorry for the charade y'all," Simone said, "but someone's been trying to kill me. Rosie here, she's an investigator."

For once in her life, Jenna was speechless.

"Gwen thought I was dead because she was doing the killing," Simone said. "Rosie put the belladonna in my eyes so Lisa would think I had been poisoned."

"I'm so glad you're alive," Lisa said. "And I've never been

so glad to be Number Two. Oh. That didn't come out right."

Jenna laughed, but she was the only one.

"But how did you know that you were going to be poisoned with the belladonna tonight?" Mary Beth asked.

"Rosie made an educated guess that with Lisa here, the killer would try to use that poison, so she'd get the blame. That's probably why Gwen kept making a big deal about the belladonna. She's not as smart as she thinks she is."

"I searched Gwen's bag and swapped out the belladonna she brought with her for sugar water when she wasn't looking," said Rosie.

"But why did Gwen want to kill you?" Lisa asked.

"Let's just say that my nose went a little too far into her business," Simone said. "I know that happens a lot, but Lent is almost here, and I am fixing to be a better person, least good enough so no one wants to kill me."

"I'm not sure that's a reasonable goal," Jenna said with a little smirk. "Now where's my Jack and Diet Coke?"

Simone smiled, "We'll I'm gonna try anyway. Starting with Mary Beth. I'm sorry I slept with Johnny. I'm happy to give you the photos, and the video. You can keep the phone. I'll even testify in divorce court if it helps. Now, Jenna, I'll give those papers back to you and no one else need ever know what you did that night on Bourbon Street. And, Lisa, my dear friend Lisa. You get anything you want darling because you were the only one of all y'all who even tried to save me.

"Now come on, I know it's been a weird night, but it's still Carnival. And 'cept for Gwen, we've all got a lot of stuff to throw. So let's forget about it and let the good times roll!"

Crescent City Blues
Michael Penn

In my opinion there is nothing, and I do mean *nothing,* more annoying, more infuriating, than a flickering light. Unquestionably, one of the simplest things to repair—I've found that most people are just too damn lazy to do it.

Located off Royal Street, Lou's Fish and Steakhouse was just one of those places. Though the building was barely two stories tall, its marquee went straight up the side thirty feet high in bright, bold, gaudy, red letters.

And since they skimped on proper wiring, the blasted thing flickered all...night...long.

My office was on the third floor, directly across from Lou's. Though I had installed blinds over the windows, red streaks still penetrated in, turning clients who visited my office into red-striped zebras. I positioned my desk so that my back was to the windows, thereby preventing me from being perpetually blinded.

My only consolation was that the building was far enough from Bourbon Street to prevent me having to hear the furor that went on there. Still, about once a week, a refugee from Bourbon Street would manage to stumble over to my part of town and begin singing and yelling until they were either removed by a policeman or simply passed out.

It was evening as I leaned back in my chair, the springs squeaking in protest. I let out a long, tired sigh for it had been a long, tiring day. Earlier, the temperature had reached into the upper nineties. Adding the humidity, it felt more like a hundred and twenty. Now evening, it was beginning to cool off into the low eighties. The humidity, still remained somewhere between intolerable and unbearable.

A good rain was what the city needed to get the temperature under control. A good rain to wash away the grime, the humidity, and the ripe odor that permeated the air. There had been sprinkles of rain, but they were only flirtations and served only to make conditions worse.

As I sat back, my shoes kicked up onto my desk, I was having trouble recalling the last time it had precipitated, which was surprising due to the usually lengthy the rainy season.

I had lost count of how many shirts I had worn during the day. As soon as I would sleeve a fresh one on, it instantly became fouled with sweat.

The fan overhead was no help—only to mix the room's humidity like a ladle in a soup pot. Fortunately I knew a good cleaner—Nicky Bienville, down the street. He charged the standard rate of five cents a shirt, but for me, he pressed three for a dime because he liked me.

The smell of spicy Creole food from both Lou's and other nearby establishments had been waffling into my office since dinnertime and my stomach was grumbling something fierce.

Hang in there. I pulled out a pack of Luckies from my shirt pocket. Lighting a smoke, I took a deep drag. It tasted harsh, but it withdrew the hunger pains. At least it was legal, which was more than could be said for the booze.

A gunshot sounded in the distance. The shot wasn't too faint—meaning that the gun was probably fired around Bourbon Street.

Cigarette in mouth, I began the chore of developing photos in my darkroom that I had taken for a client. A blonde had hired me to trail her husband to see if he was two-timing her. I had a feeling that after she saw the pictures, especially the bedroom ones, that hubby was going to find himself in a world of trouble. I wondered if the phrase "four-timing" was ever used.

Hanging my last photo on the clothesline, I heard a knocking on the front door to my office. Since my secretary, Connie, had left for the day, I wiped my hands with a semi-clean towel and scooted over to answer it. A second rapping sounded, this time louder and more hurried.

"I'm coming!" I snuffed out my Lucky into a nearby ashtray. "Hold your horses." Through the door I made out a figure in the hallway trying to peer in through the glass. Guessing it was my client, Trish White, being over anxious to get her photos, I opened the door.

And, brother, was I ever wrong.

A man hurried into my office and slammed the door behind him. He was wearing a designer suit that must cost him more than most people earned in a month. It was a pinstripe affair, with a silk handkerchief protruding neatly out of his left breast pocket ready for use, but never to be touched. Since only an overhead light illuminated the room, the contours of his face were kept in the shadows. A derby was jammed over his eyes, making it the difficult for me to see him clearly.

"Darcy Hamilton?" he asked in a frantic voice. "Darcy Hamilton, the investigator?"

"That's what the sign says," I replied, walking to a nearby lamp.

"No!" he objected, raising his arm. "Please...leave it off."

I lifted my fingers from the switch and turned to him, hesitating for a moment before reaching back and flipping it on. "Relax. No one can see you from outside."

The lamp illuminated the room, and he looked up from the floor. *Dressed to the nines,* as one of my other clients would have said. The suit was impeccable, without a crease or speck of dirt to be seen. How he was pulling that off in this weather was an accomplishment. His shoes were so polished that I could see my unkempt hair in the reflection. "I'm sorry," he interrupted as he cleared his throat. "I was expecting...when I saw the sign..."

"Mister," I said, reaching for another cigarette. I knew where this conversation was going and it was time to cut him off. "I've got no time for games. As you can plainly see, I am a woman, the only one in the city in this profession. Now were you looking for someone to help with your problem or someone to compare genitals with? If it's the latter, I can give you the business card of a colleague of mine over on Canal Street."

"Ten blocks...! No...you've got to help me!" Pacing the room, he stopped at the far window. Peering through the blinds, his face turned a dark crimson. "Someone is trying to kill me!"

"Whoa. Slow down. Why don't you have a seat and start from the beginning."

He sighed and sat down.

"Smoke?" I asked, pulling out my pack of Luckies.

"Women smoke those?"

"Smoke?" I repeated.

"No thanks." He pulled out a pack of his own. Malls. "Those things can kill you."

I couldn't help but notice that as my visitor lit his cigarette that I was dealing with one refined fellow. The way he sat in the chair, held the cigarette, his wardrobe—all drew the same conclusion. This guy had been to private school, taken Etiquette 101 and had gotten an A. "So...let's start with your name."

"Oh," he replied, sitting up. "Where *have* my manners gone to?" He extended his hand to me in a gentlemanly fashion. "Mr. Marcus Givaconte. My friends call me Mark."

"Okay." I sat down near him. "Givaconte...what is that, Italian?"

"Sicilian."

114

"Whatever. Why don't you tell me what has happened that makes you believe someone wants you in a cedar box?"

Mark removed his hat. His straight, black hair was slicked back to his collar. His eyes matched his hair and his moustache was groomed in a way that made him resemble an actor.

"It's my wife." Mark said. "We're currently separated. I'm sure you are aware of the difficulties in getting a divorce. My wife is involved in some questionable business practices. It consisted mostly of bootlegging, but she had a hand in other activities—such as the horses."

"Your wife did this...?" I was finding this hard to believe. "What's her maiden name?"

"Esposito."

I let out a whistle.

"I take it you've heard of that name?"

"Yes, Mr. Givaconte. I've heard of that name. So have most people in this city—especially the police." I took a long drag.

Mark stayed silent for a moment before continuing. "Last month there was a robbery in our home. Her family was using the house as a refuge for some laundered money. Twenty thousand dollars was stolen."

"That's a lot of bread. You catch the thief?"

"No." Mark put out his cigarette. "For obvious reasons, my wife refused to contact the police. Instead, she chose to have the matter handled *internally*. Her father and several other *relatives* came over to investigate. They concluded that none of the locks in the house had been tampered with and someone who knew the combination had opened the safe. All this pointed to me. Her father asked to speak to her in private in the study. I went upstairs into the guest bedroom, which is directly over the study, and placed my ear to the floor. What did I overhear them discussing? Killing me! Taking whatever cash I could get my hands on—which did not amount to much, I snuck out of the house. I wandered through the French Quarter staying at different hotels under assumed names. I couldn't go to the police because I had no way of knowing if any of them were on the take. I was referred to you."

Mark fell silent. I looked at him for a moment as I finished my smoke. "Did you do it?"

"What?"

"Did you take the money?"

"Why no! Of course not!" He shifted slightly in his chair.

"Any ideas?"

"If I did, I would not be requiring your services, now, would I?" he said with an annoyed tone.

"If you are having difficulties with these questions, then you're going to have a hell of a time explaining yourself to the police—or your *in-laws* when they catch up to you."

He rose up. "I think that I have made a mistake in coming..."

"Sit down."

He glared at me for a moment.

"*Sit down.*"

He sat.

I stared at him for a moment, trying to determine if his story was a line of bullshit. I was betting at least some of it was, but I was willing to give him a little more of my time. "Have you eaten?" I asked him.

"No."

I reached for my keys on my desk. "I know a place that has the best Southern cooking in town."

"I don't think I should be seen in public."

"Don't worry. No one will care who you are. Unless of course, you've been followed."

Mark paused for a moment. "All right."

Bob called it inherent beauty for that as much as I *cross-dressed*—as he called it, and the little makeup I wore that I still outclassed any other female wherever I went. Not that I preferred to dress masculine but if I were to wear a skirt and heels, how much respect would I get from my clientele? Usually I wore dress pants, a loose shirt, and suspenders—or some variation. Instead of being dismissed as a blonde floozy, I was judged by reputation, instead of body parts—unlike many of the other females living in this part of town.

Some men told me I dressed sexy.

Go figure.

Walking into Lou's, I was immediately assaulted by a familiar array of heavy spices, bitter herbs, and foul-smelling cheap cigars. Though I'd grown accustom to that mix, I thought that Mark was going to pass out.

"You eat here?" he asked, looking around the smoke-infested restaurant. All eyes immediately turned to us and the place became silent. Even the Joes, consisting mainly of dock workers, were staring at the Suit that had come through the door, looking like a fish out of water. Some of them sported a look that he would make an easy target.

Then they saw me, knew better, and went back to eating.

The stories about me circulated quickly in this part of the Crescent City.

Catfish Bob, the restaurant's owner, walked over and greeted us. "Crumbs!" he bellowed. "Been so long since I've seen you that I was wondering if you forgotten where the restaurant was!"

Catfish Bob was his American nickname. His real name was Robert Nuvell. He had moved from Reading, England right after the War. I had asked him why he wanted to live in The Big Easy instead of somewhere more cosmopolitan. He longed for the heat and humidity. That the cold, rainy London days was something that he could do without. Being a Jazz fanatic made New Orleans the logical choice. So he opened a Creole restaurant. A Brit running a Creole restaurant. He located two excellent cooks and the restaurant thrived. Certainly, it wasn't an establishment that required reservations, but if someone walked in during the dinner hour, they would be hard pressed to find an empty table. Considering it was one of the town's larger restaurants, that was something that Bob took great pride in.

Crazy Brit. But he had a good heart and was one of my dearest friends—even if he had an annoying habit of asking me out.

We sat in a booth in the rear of the restaurant to ensure privacy. A waiter took our orders—jambalaya with a side of gumbo.

Mark, was uneasy about being here. "Do you want something to *drink*?" I asked.

Mark looked back at me incredulously. "We *are* in the midst of Prohibition?"

"This place doubles as a speakeasy."

He looked around. "Why...I don't see anything..."

"If you did, the cops would have shut this place down." I stood up. "I'll be right back."

Walking to the bar, I was greeted by its tender, Leonard. "What'll it be, Darcy?"

"Two special sodas, Lenny."

He nodded and went to the Soda Jerk. I kept my eye on him but never saw him slip in the rum.

Bob leaned up against the bar as Lenny handed me the drinks. "You've got quite a stiff over there, Darcy. Date? You know, it's been a while..."

"You know that I only have eyes for you, Bob. Besides, he's a possible client."

"What's his trouble?"

"The wife."

"Cheating?"

"More than that."

"Hmm...it usually is." Bob glanced at Mark and turned back to me with the worried, paternal look when he felt I was getting in over my head. "He's trouble. I could tell from the moment he walked in. It's written all over his face. Be careful with him, Darcy. He looks like a snake. A well-groomed snake."

"Nothing new, Bob."

Again with the look. "Are you daft? Why are you still in his company?"

"Let's just say I'm curious."

He leaned over, whispering. "Remember what I said."

"Don't worry, Bob. It's under control."

"I'll remember to have that inscribed on your tombstone."

I sat back down with the drinks. "So, you have no thoughts as to who wants to frame you?"

Mark shrugged. He took a sip from his glass. "I don't know. Maybe an associate of hers."

"Who was she in business with?"

"I've heard her mention two names constantly."

"Who?"

"Joseph Maretti and Tony Tovalino."

I let out a whistle. "Your wife is mixed up with some bad company. She sure picked two of the most dangerous people in town to play in the sandbox with. Even the police stay away from them. Each is a major player in the New Orleans underworld." I paused as our waiter arrived with dinner, water, and bread. "What's so dangerous is that they hate each other. If either learned your wife was even talking to the other, your wife would have found herself in some serious trouble. Mob ties or not."

Mark forked up a piece of catfish and began chewing. Instantly his face turned crimson and he began to cough. I handed him a glass of water.

"What *is* this?" he gasped, his face turning red.

"Catfish, just like I said. This ain't no sissy food like pizza."

"My mouth is on fire!"

"You should be glad that I didn't order you the crawdads!" I slid the bread closer to him along with a small bowl of dip. "Dunk a piece of bread into this before you eat your next piece. It will make the catfish taste more mild."

"A little late!"

I smiled. "How have you lived here and not eaten this type of food?"

Mark shrugged as he chewed on a piece of bread.

It was at that point things changed.

Or, more specifically, got bad.

Real bad.

Real fast.

Three men stepped through the front door, each of them were wearing brimmed hats and long trench coats. No one wore those things—unless you were trying to act inconspicuous. It was a ruse that might work in the winter—as if this town actually had a winter.

It was apparent we were dealing with some dull bulbs.

I got a good look at the men and groaned. The one with the tweed hat standing in the middle, looked very familiar.

Mark's back was to them and had no idea what was happening.

"Do you recall ever meeting a man with a large birth mark on his face?"

He thought for a moment. "Yes. Ugly bastard. He stopped at the house. Nora said he worked in retail. The man was a brute...no manners at all." He paused. "I kicked him out on account of that." Mark saw the worried look on my face. "Why do you ask?"

"Never mind. Slide into the bench more. You'll be less visible."

"Is something wrong?"

Ignoring him, I looked to Lenny and nodded. He left and disappeared into the kitchen.

I turned back to Mark who was becoming alarmed. "That

man just walked in. His name is Henry Swavado, a bully-boy for Maretti. You might have been followed after all. Stay calm, everything's under control—this could all be just a coincidence."

But I was sure it wasn't.

A horrified looked appeared on his face. Mark was starting to panic.

"Goddamit! Stay calm!" I hissed. "We can handle this! Lose your cool and I'll shoot you myself!" I pulled out my pistol and placed it onto my lap.

Henry and his partners began walking through the restaurant.

They stopped at ours.

"Darcy Hamilton." The three surrounded the booth. "Why am I not surprised to see your pretty face here? Though I was hoping to see you on one of Bourbon Street balconies."

This elicited a chuckle from the other two.

"What do you want, Henry?"

Henry's eyebrows lifted. "Cutting the chit-chat? That's fine." He smirked. "We're here for lover boy, and I'm sure he's told you why."

Mark became paler than the ivory tablecloth.

"I can't let you do that, Henry."

"Oh, really." He brushed back his coat to reveal the handle of a Tommy Gun. "I think you will. Make no mistake, sugar. I have no qualms about cutting you down if you feel like getting in my way."

That annoyed me. I hated being called *sugar*.

"Henry, are you still bitter?"

"What?"

"It would seem that you are."

"What are you talking about?"

"Oh, you've never told your little friends, have you?"

Sweat formed on his brow. He realized what I was talking about.

"I guess you threw out the slacks, didn't you, Henry?"

"What pants?" He started playing stupid.

"The ones that you soiled."

He responded with a snarl. Knowing Henry's temper I should have stopped there.

I really should have.

"You see, Henry...when was it? A year ago? " I turned to Mark. "Henry was given the task of offing one of my clients. Now, being the smart guy that Henry was, he waited on the rooftop across from my client's apartment waiting for him to emerge so that he could take him out with a rifle shot."

Henry shifted uneasily.

"Let's just say that Henry here wasn't doing a good job at staying hidden. I confronted him and Henry found himself hanging out over the ledge. Henry, wasn't it then your brown slacks got a little more brown?"

His fingernails dug into his hands as he balled them up into fists "You let me fall."

"The fire escape was under you."

"Two stories down."

"You're still alive, aren't you?"

"I cracked three ribs and busted my right leg."

"Poor baby. Beaten by a woman."

It was that comment which probably put him over his tolerance level.

Like a movie screen, his face displayed everything and I could tell he was going to make his move. What was about to transpire could have been avoided, but I had pushed Henry too far and his super-ego could only take so much punishment. The gun inside his coat was literally screaming to be used.

One of us was going down.

And it sure as hell wasn't going to be me.

I really hate killing people.

I really do.

In one fluid motion, my hand whipped out from beneath the table.

A lone shot went off.

It was all I needed.

Though the bullet was above my mark, it did the job. Like a wax statue staring out into space with glazed eyes, Henry stood standing for a moment and then crashed backwards onto the table behind him—much to the dismay of the diners there.

His two cronies raised their Tommys in response but that's as far as they got. Lenny had come through, as he and another waiter took out each of them with a well-placed bullet.

It was messy.

The smoke cleared. Several diners scrambled out the exit—those who were still green to this part of town.

I tucked the gun under my shirt.

Mark turned green. Brain bits from Thug #1 were on his dinner plate. A moment later, dinner made a bee-line out of his mouth as did lunch. Steak and eggs from the looks of it.

The bodies were being wrapped up in table-clothes by the busboys.

Catfish walked over to me and tossed a napkin at Mark. "Clean yourself up there, lad."

"Thanks for the help, Bob. You and Lenny got me out of a tough spot. Sorry about the mess though. I tried to be as neat as I could."

Bob put his hand on my shoulder in a reassuring way. "Not to worry. We'll have these blokes carted off, the floor mopped, and the place back together in a jiff."

"What about the police?" Mark asked.

"Don't worry about them. If they choose to show up, they aren't going to find anything. We're going to haul these corpses over to River Street and dump them in with the fishes. A couple of days in the brine, even their own mother won't be able to recognize them." He let out a hearty laugh and walked over to assist the busboys.

Mark watched as they cleaned the last remnants of the firefight. "You must be good friends with Robert for him to do all of this."

"If you want to stay alive in this neighborhood you need to have friends you can trust."

"Aren't they afraid of getting arrested?"

"Henry and his goons were low-lifes. We did everyone a favor. The people eating here will never report any of this to the police. They know it's Mob-related and that's reason enough to stay quiet."

Mark sat silent.

I lit another Lucky and walked over to the bar. I came back a minute later with two more of Lenny's sodas, hoping it would settle his nerves.

Mark drank them both.

We sat for several minutes in silence as we watched the employees scrub the floor. The bodies were taken out the back."

"So, Ms. Hamilton...have I been dropped as a client?"

Looking at Mark, I was certain that he was holding back choice, selective bits of his story. Bob's warning kept rolling around in my head. I should have gotten up and told him that he wasn't worth the risk.

I should have told him to go find another sucker.

I really should have.

But I didn't.

"Not yet."

"Splendid," he answered, lighting up a cigarette. A grin appeared on his face—the alcohol was taking effect. "You will not regret this. That, I can assure you."

The Dark Places
Sheila Connolly

A lot of people wanted to kill me. So far I'd been lucky, and they hadn't gotten close enough to do any damage. But they kept coming.

I'm smart. I know how to hide. I know where the dark corners are, and how to slip from one to another without being noticed. That's how I've managed to stay alive this long. New Orleans has plenty of dark corners, warm and damp. Most of the time the people following me get tired of chasing me and give up. They know I'll be somewhere nearby. I know they'll keep trying. Pretty much a stalemate.

In New Orleans I'm the new kid in town—I haven't been here long and don't know anybody. I'd snagged a ride on a train—yeah, I know, old fashioned, but I like trains—and gotten off here, and I'd spent the last few days exploring the place. Like most tourists I was drawn to the shiny, sparkly parts of town, like Bourbon Street. But that got old kinda fast. Too many people, too much happening all the time, day and night. After I'd checked that out, I headed for the quieter neighborhoods, the ones where I wouldn't be noticed. I'm good at making myself invisible.

There was nowhere else I wanted to go. I hung around. I made some friends—well, more like acquaintances. We'd nod at each other on the street, but we didn't exactly party together. Heck, nobody had any money. At least the fancy restaurants tossed out a lot of food that was really fine, and we did a lot of dumpster-diving for dinner. The weather's warm, so it's easy enough to find someplace to sleep, mostly hiding during the day so nobody would hassle me to move on.

That's okay with me—I'm happier prowling around at night.

And then I saw something I shouldn't have. I kinda have a knack for that, although it's not good for my health, if you know what I mean. I'd be hanging out somewhere, minding my own business, and something would happen in front of me—a drug deal, a shake-down, somebody beating on somebody else. It wasn't like I went looking for stuff like that. I just happen to be in the wrong place at the wrong time, and nobody even notices me. I thought heading south would help, but no, it just keeps happening. What can I do?

This time wasn't any different. I was chilling behind a dumpster, not bothering anybody. Then I see a couple of guys come out the back door of some kinda bar or club, dragging someone with them. One sorta hung back, keeping watch, like, while the other one started working over the third guy, who looked like he was either drunk or stoned or he'd already taken a few punches. Still, he was doing a pretty good job of fighting back, until guy number two pulls out a gun, bang, and the spaced-out guy goes down and quits moving. I made myself as small as possible behind the dumpster, but Lookout Guy, who'd been keeping an eye on things, jumps about a foot in the air and yells, "Why the hell did you do that?" Then he must've caught my movement out of the corner of his eye. "Hey, what's that?"

Gun Guy was going through the pockets of the guy on the ground—the one who now had a pool of blood creeping across the pavement under him. "Damn, where is it?" he muttered. Then he turned to Lookout Guy. "Huh?"

"Over there," Lookout Guy pointed. "Behind the garbage."

Gun Guy looked over in my direction, then shook his head. "You're getting' jumpy. There's nobody there. But somebody mighta heard the shot, so we'd better get him outta sight, quick."

Lookout Guy checked out my direction one last time, and I

made sure not to twitch. Then he turned back to his pal and together they hoisted up the dead guy and carried him down to the other end of the building. I could hear them grunting and swearing under their breath. When they were a safe distance away, I scuttled out from my hiding place and peered after them, in time to see them dump the guy into the trunk of a car, then get in and speed away. All that was left was the puddle of blood. And the thing that had flown out from Dead Guy's jacket when he went down, and had skidded over by the dumpster where I was hiding. The other two were too busy strong-arming the guy to notice.

I noticed, but I'd make a lousy witness. I hadn't been around long enough to recognize anybody. Nobody would listen to me. And who was I going to tell?

I didn't know what to do. I was scared somebody would come out the back of the building and see me, but if I moved somebody might notice—the sun was coming up, and it was getting lighter fast. In the end I hid behind the dumpster and chewed on a piece of bread I found. I might have fallen asleep, bothered only by somebody opening the dumpster. He didn't notice me. It was full light when I heard voices and looked out from my hiding place. Two uniform cops, it looked like, and a guy in a suit.

"Where'd he go?" one of the cops asked.

Suit Guy shrugged. "He was in the bar. He left. I can't watch everybody who comes and goes. I've got a business to run."

"Which door he leave by?"

Suit Guy shrugged again. I guess he didn't like to waste words.

The two cops exchanged a glance, and it looked to me like they'd gotten that answer before. "What time did he show up?" one asked.

"I dunno. Nine, maybe?"

"How long did he stay?"

"A coupla hours, at least."

"Did you see him talking to anybody in the bar?"

Suit Guy raised an eyebrow and snickered. "Well, he was talking to one of the girls, if you get my drift."

"Did they leave together?"

Suit Guy shrugged. "Like I said, I can't keep an eye on everyone. I'm nobody's baby sitter. Why you think he was back here, anyway?"

"We watched him come in. We didn't seen him come out, at least, not out the front. We're standing by the only back door. Right?"

"Yeah, okay."

"And then there's that." One of the cops pointed at the blood pool, only now it looked like old red paint. It was beginning to smell funky as the morning heat got to it.

Suit Guy protested, "You're sayin' that's his blood? Heck, lots of guys come out here and exchange a few words, and maybe some blood gets spilled. Doesn't mean anybody's dead. You gonna take DNA samples and all that stuff, like on TV?"

The two cops exchanged another glance, only now they looked frustrated. "Nah. Department won't waste the money on fancy tests, not without a victim and a damn good reason."

"So, we done here?" Suit Guy demanded. "I could use some sleep before I re-open today."

The two cops looked at each other. "Yeah, I guess," the first one said. "We know where to find you." Suit Guy turned and hurried back into the building before they could change their minds.

The cops weren't hurrying to leave. "That's a lot of blood," the second one said.

"Yeah," his pal answered. "Looks pretty fresh, too."

"Anybody report any gunfire last night?"

"In this neighborhood? Nah."

"So we don't know if it's Costello's blood or not."

"Nope. Not without a test. But nobody's seen him since he went into this hole last night, and we searched the place pretty good. Even took a look in the dumpster. He's not here."

I thought about that thing that Dead Guy—Costello—had lost, that was now sitting under the dumpster. It was metal, shiny, in a plastic cover. Not a wallet—I knew what those looked like. Problem was, I couldn't read the metal thing—I don't read too good. And I was scared to move it, or even touch it. But I knew it was Costello's. The cops would probably like to know it was Costello's too. How could I tell them without getting myself into trouble?

I peered around the edge of the dumpster. The cops looked really mad, and who could blame them? It was one of their own who'd gone missing—and worse, but they didn't know that yet, and maybe they'd never find out if I didn't do something. But what? I glanced under the dumpster again. The shiny metal thing wouldn't be here for long, though, since it sounded to me like the dumpster was pretty full, so some big truck was going to come empty it soon, maybe even this morning, and they'd never notice the thing lying on the ground in its battered plastic cover. I had to decide: could I try to draw the cops' attention to what I'd found—which meant to me, which was always risky? Or did I just forget it and disappear?

After you've knocked around as much as I have in my life, you kind of get a sense of what's fair and what's right. Maybe I didn't have a lot of friends, but plenty of us who met on the road, just in passing, exchanged a nod, just to be polite. If we knew where there was food or a safe place to crash, we'd share, because I guess we hoped that somebody would return the favor down the line. I figured it was a better way to live than distrusting everybody I met. So trying to help poor Costello, or at least, help the friends who were looking for him, seemed to be the decent thing to do, even if it wasn't easy.

I started to dart out from my safe corner behind the dumpster but stopped, quivering with fear. I'd spent a lot of time in my life avoiding cops, so it was going to take a lot for me to draw their attention. One of the guys glanced my way, probably noticing my movement out of the corner of his eye, but then an expression of disgust crossed his face and he looked away. I get that a lot. I gathered up my courage and crept a little closer, then closer again, until I was next to the blood pool. That got the cops' notice.

"Hey, get away from there, you," one of them yelled. I backed off fast, but he didn't follow me. "That's disgusting," he muttered.

Well, that hadn't worked, so I crept closer again, until my feet touched the edge of the blood. "Damn it, get away!" the first cop said, and finally moved toward me.

"Ah, don't pay him no mind—he's not the only one..."

The other cop didn't pay any attention to him. "He's got Costello's blood on him. That's contaminating the crime scene. I'm not gonna let him get away with that."

"Aw, come on, that's ridiculous. We don't even know if it's Costello's blood. You're just pissed off."

"You bet I am. You really don't think it's his?" First cop wasn't about to give it up. He looked at me, where I watched and waited. Then he rushed at me.

Luckily I was faster than he was, and I had a head start. I went straight back to the dumpster and wormed my way behind it. He followed, enraged now.

"Come out of there, you little piece of crap!" He knelt down to see where I'd gotten to—and that's when he saw the metal thing. His anger disappeared in an instant. "Hey, come here," he called out to his partner.

"What, you need my help to take him down?" the other guy said, laughing.

"No, you jerk. Take a look." He gestured under the dumpster.

His partner grudgingly knelt down beside him. "Well, I'll be damned. That's a badge. Wanna bet it's Costello's?"

"One way to find out," the first cop said. He fished out a handkerchief and reached carefully for the thing, then pulled it out into the daylight. "Yup, it's Costello's. He was back here, all right. And that guy inside was lying to us from the start. What say we go talk to him again?"

"I'm right behind you. Say, you gonna put it in your report that a cockroach led you to the evidence?"

Survivor's Guilt
Greg Herren

I'm going to die on this stupid roof.

It wasn't the first time the thought had run through his mind in the—how long had it been, anyway? Days? Weeks?—however long it had been since he'd climbed up there. It didn't matter how long it really had been, all that mattered was it felt like it had been an eternity. He'd run out of bottled water—when? Yesterday? Two days ago? It didn't matter. All that mattered was he was thirsty and hot and he now knew how a lobster felt when dropped in boiling water, how it felt to be boiled or scalded or burned to death.

He was out of water.

Not that the last bottles of water had been much help anyway.

In the hot oven that used to be the attic of the single shot-gun house he'd called home for almost twenty years, the water inside the bottles had gotten so damned hot he could have made coffee with it and it tasted like melted plastic, was probably toxic, poisonous in some way. Wasn't plastic bad for you? He seemed to remember reading that somewhere or hearing it on the television a million years ago when his house wasn't underwater and there was still air conditioning and cold beer in the fridge instead of this...this purgatory of hot sun and stagnant water and sweat-soaked clothes.

But drinking hot water that tasted like plastic and was probably, maybe, poisonous—that was better than dying of thirst on the hot tiles of this stupid stinking roof. He'd tried to conserve it, space it out, save it, trying to make it last as long as possible because he had no idea when rescue was coming.

If it ever came at all.

He'd been on the roof so long already—how long *had* it been?

Days? Weeks? Months?

Should have left, should have listened to her, should have put everything we could in the truck and headed west.

But they'd never gone before, never fled before an oncoming storm, laughed at those who panicked and packed up and ran away, paying hotels and motels way too much money for days on end.

Hadn't the storms had always turned to the east at the last minute, coming ashore somewhere to the east, and New Orleans breathed another sigh of relief at dodging another bullet while saying a prayer at the same time for those getting hammered by high winds and storm surges and power outages and downed trees?

Hell, that last time the storm had gone up into Mississippi and the highways south had been damaged and blocked, keeping people who'd gone that way marooned for well over a week.

So, no, there wasn't no need to go this time, either, because Katrina would surely turn east like so many before her had.

Stupid, so damned stupid.

He could be in a hotel room in Houston at this very moment, basking in the air conditioning, drinking lots of ice-cold water, waiting for the water to recede and come home, see what survived, see what could be saved and what couldn't.

Ice.

He'd sell his soul for an ice cube.

But when rescue came, he'd have to explain...

No, no need to think about that now.

If—no, *when*—rescue came, he'd deal with it then.

The sun, oh God, the sun.

He'd never been this hot in his life before, at least not that he could remember.

The closest was at the beach in summertime, but there was always something cold to drink, the warm gulf waters to plunge into for some relief.

He felt like he was broiling inside his own skin.

Sometimes when it became too much he'd slip back down inside the attic. The oven. The air down there so thick and humid and hot and dusty he could barely breathe, but at least he was out of the sun. The air was barely breathable, clinging to his skin, so thick and wet he felt sometimes like he was drowning,

Every so often the wind would come, blowing through the vents at either end of the attic, and it felt so good he felt like crying.

But he couldn't stay down there for long. He had to stay out on the roof, in case rescuers came. He couldn't take a chance on missing them.

If someone came for him.

Don't think that. Someone had to come, rescuers will come. If I don't believe that I'll lose my damned mind.

Maybe it's divine punishment for—

Yet another helicopter flew past overhead, the latest of many. He'd stopped waving and yelling and jumping up and down when they passed overhead, like he wasn't even there. His throat was so sore from yelling he could barely make a sound anyway. They never stopped, but he knew—he *knew* they were rescuing people. They had to be. What else was the point to the big basket hanging from the underside of the helicopter, if not for lowering down to people stranded up on roofs like he was?

He just had to be patient. It would be his turn eventually.

He just had to stay alive until it was his turn.

The whole city was probably underwater for all he knew.

At least it was for as far as he could see, shimmering filthy water everywhere.

Should have left, should have listened.

One of them would—had to—stop for him, before he died.

Meantime, roasting, baking, frying, dying in the late August sun, or was it September now?

Every once in a while he heard a boat motor passing close by. He didn't bother making noise anymore when he heard those, either. There wasn't any point. They hadn't heard him when he could still yell. Back when he could still yell, whenever that was. However long it had been.

They never heard him. They never came.

His throat hurt so badly from all the yelling he'd done when his throat could still make a sound other than a hoarse rasp he might have damaged his vocal chords. He might never be able to talk again.

Which wouldn't matter, anyway.

If I never get off this roof.

He picked up the wine bottle again, poured the last swallow of hot red wine into his mouth. Alcohol dehydrated the body, he knew that, remembered that from somewhere. But some liquid was better than no liquid.

The sour hot wine hit his empty stomach. He hadn't eaten, hadn't had anything to eat in—it felt like an eternity. He'd passed the point of being hungry.

But he worried that since all that was left was hot wine, he might make himself sick.

If he started throwing up he might just throw himself off the roof and drown himself.

It was tempting to think about. The thought came now and then, when he was so hot he could barely stand it, when his skin hurt so bad, blistered from sunburn that he climbed down into the stiflingly hot attic and wept, but was too dehydrated for tears to form. That was when he thought about drowning himself, diving through the trap door into the water and drowning himself.

Joining her down there.

Then he would get back to his right mind and open another bottle of wine and sip it slowly.

He looked at the empty bottle in his hands, and tossed it off the end of the roof.

It splashed when it hit the water.

It was the last of the wine. All that was left now was hard liquor—a bottle of hot gin and a bottle of hot cheap tequila.

He hadn't wanted to touch the liquor, so he saved it for when there was nothing else left. Every time he took a swig of the wine he got light-headed, so there was no telling what the liquor would do, on his empty stomach and dehydrated body.

He wasn't even hydrated enough to sweat anymore. He hadn't had to relieve himself since—weeks ago? It didn't matter. Nothing mattered. Time didn't matter anymore, it was all one endless nightmare of heat and humidity and the sun, oh God, the sun.

Water, water, everywhere—but not a drop to drink.

No one was ever going to come.

I can't believe I'm going to die on this stupid roof. I should just kill myself and get it over with.

No, someone will come.

Someone had to come.

Should have left, should have listened.

The sun was setting in the west in an explosion of oranges and reds reflecting off the stagnant, dark, oily water. The roof of his truck was still slightly visible when he looked down over the side of the roof, its white roof almost glowing through the filthy water. Paid for, finally, years of paying off that damned loan finally came to an end just a month ago, the pink slip arriving in the mail last week. And now it was drowned, just like the city and God knows how many people. Ruined, gone, the money he put into it wasted. He'd babied it, too—oil change every three months without fail, servicing it before it was needed, the fucking thing so well taken care of it would have lasted easily another five to ten years if he kept babying it.

It doesn't matter anyway. Everything's ruined. The city's dead. We'll never come back from this.

Thank God the old house had an attic—yes, thank God for that—the kind with a trap door with a long dangling chord that hung down in a corner of the bedroom. You pulled the chord, the door came down, and a wooden ladder unfolded. He'd left the door open when he came up, when the water came, as the house filled up, left it open thinking it might help when rescue came.

If rescue ever came.

Even though she was down there.

Someone will come, he told himself again, someone will come for me.

Someone has to.

If he didn't believe rescue would come, he would lose his mind.

If he didn't believe someone would come, there wasn't any point in going on, to this suffering, to this agony of broiled skin and dehydration and starvation and air so thick he could barely breathe it, the stink of the wet wood rotting down below.

And despite the delirium, despite the agony, somehow— somehow he wasn't ready to give up.

If he gave up now, the suffering of the days? Weeks? Months? Was for nothing.

Nothing.

But it would be so much easier to give up. Then I wouldn't be thirsty anymore. Then I wouldn't be hungry anymore.

If he stopped believing one of the helicopters would lower a basket for him, or a boat might come by to take him to safety, to whatever might still be out there, away from the water, he might as well kill himself now.

There was a rope coiled in a corner of the attic. He could

tie a noose and find something, somewhere, on the roof or in the attic, to loop it around and just let his weight fall, his neck snapping, death coming quickly and easily.

That would be so much better than this slow, horrible death from heat exhaustion and dehydration on the roof.

But the sun was going down at last, and night was coming.

He'd survived another day.

It would still be hot, and humid, and the smell of the water wouldn't go away, but the night was better.

Now he had to just survive another night.

He could still see the skyline of the business district in the distance in the darkening sky. There were no lights anywhere. Thick black plumes of smoke billowed in several places he could see, but there hadn't been an explosion in a while.

Or gunfire. He hadn't heard gunfire in a while.

Night wouldn't relieve the relentless humidity, but at least being out of direct sunlight would be better, give his blistering and salt-crusted skin some relief.

There might even be a breeze.

And he could stay out on the roof, not have to climb down inside to get away from the vicious rays of the sun.

No air moved in the attic, the heavy wet air almost suffocating in its thickness.

He could smell his own stink, and sometimes imagined he could even smell his flesh frying in the hot sun. His skin was burned, red, raw, but he couldn't breathe the fetid stale dead air in the hot attic all day. A cold shower to bring his skin temperature down was all he could think about, or packing himself in a tub of ice. That wasn't going to happen any time soon.

Ice. The thought of it made him want to weep.

Should have left. Should have listened.

She'd been right.

"We need to go," she'd said on Saturday, whenever that had been, however long ago that had been. She'd never been afraid of storms before, never wanted to leave. This unease, this nervousness, was something new, something he'd never seen before in her. There had been storms before when he'd wanted to go, and she'd laughed in his face, mocked him, and they hadn't gone. She'd been right those times.

He had liked that she was afraid of this one, that it made her nervous. She seemed off-balance, for once, not sure of herself.

"It won't come this way, you know they always turn east before land fall," he'd replied, dismissing and laughing at her, shutting her down every time she watched another emergency news conference, or when The Weather Channel ran another worst-case scenario for the city, as everyone began packing up and heading west for Houston, north for Jackson, and the city began to empty out. He had mocked her panic, her nervousness, enjoying this new side of her he'd never seen before, and was determined to take advantage of it as long as it lasted. He'd sent her to the store for supplies. Batteries and bread and bottled water and peanut butter and protein bars and hell, might as well get some liquor, too.

Liquor never went to waste, after all, and it didn't spoil.

She'd came home hours later, complaining about how crazy the Walmart had been, everyone talking about evacuating and the city being destroyed, whining the way she always did when she didn't get her way.

"You know they say that every time," he'd replied, sure of himself, smug he'd held firm and not given in, cracking open a beer and flipping away from The Weather Channel with its constant predictions of doom and aerial views of the traffic snarl on the highways out of town. He had found a baseball game and relaxed in his easy chair.

Probably no work on Monday, he'd thought as she clattered around in the kitchen angrily, muttering to herself, *so might as well kick back and have a nice little mini-vacation.*

Some mini-vacation this had turned out to be.

The sun usually set around nine in the late summer, didn't it?

His watch was down on the first floor, under the water. The power had been off before the nasty filthy dirty murdering water had started filling up the house, drowning everything as far as the eye could see. Days, time, had all lost all meaning for him. The only thing that mattered was night or day. He didn't sleep well—could anyone under the heavy hot wet blanket of humidity?

He didn't really care anymore. Nothing really mattered other than the sun was going down and his skin would have some blessed relief.

And he would hear her again, whispering.

We need to go, Mike. We can't stay here.

Every time the sun went down. Every time it got dark.

It's a big storm. At least the power will go out and do you want to be here without the A/C?

Sometimes he thought he might just be going insane.

If he wasn't already, that was.

He wasn't sure of anything anymore.

We can stay with my sister in Houston, we don't even have to pay for a motel, Mike, can't we go, please?

The water lapped against the side of the house.

Water, water, everywhere.

Through the attic door into the downstairs, he could see things floating when he looked. Furniture, books, cushions, once even the dresser was there.

He hadn't seen her down there in a while.

He was always afraid he'd look down and see her face, floating just below the surface, her eyes staring at him.

Should have closed her eyes.

He wasn't sure where she was and he didn't care.

Sometimes he would see her, walking on the surface of the oily water, pointing her finger at him, complaining, whispering, *we should have left, I wanted to go, this is all your fault, you know, like everything is always your fault you can never do anything right this is why I never listened to you...*

And he would wake from his fevered sleep, shivering even though it was so hot, even though the air was so damp and heavy and warm it just pressed down on him until he thought his bones might break.

His lips were so damned chapped. His skin was red and hurt, blisters here and there on the peeling baked skin. He wanted water to drink, something to eat besides chips and crackers and peanut butter and bread. He wanted off the roof. He wanted a bed. He wanted to be away from New Orleans, it didn't matter where as long as it was far away from the drowned city. Sometimes he wondered if the entire world was under water, that it wasn't just New Orleans that drowned.

Someone would come, he knew it. He just had to hold on, stay alive no matter how horrible it got. He wouldn't die on the damned roof of the house he'd never liked in the first fucking place.

She'd wanted the house. Once she saw it when they were driving around looking, this was the house she wanted, even though it was on the wrong side of the Industrial Canal, even though it was in the 9th Ward. "It spoke to me," she'd insisted, "and it's cheap! We can fix it up ourselves. It'll be perfect!"

He'd given into her, even though he didn't want to live down here. She was right about the price—it was less than they'd been thinking they'd spend, and the monthly mortgage payments were a lot more affordable than any of the other houses they'd looked at. It wasn't until later, when they'd moved in, that it even occurred to him that it was the only place they'd looked at in the 9th Ward. When he brought it up to her, she'd admitted she'd found it on her own and fell in love with it, colluded with the real estate agent to get him to see it.

They'd worked on him until he'd given in.

It wasn't the last time she'd gotten her way.

We need to go, Mike. It won't be safe here. I'm scared.

She always got her way, didn't she?

Not this last time.

Which was why he was up on the roof. Because just once he didn't want her to get her way, wanted to stand up for himself and not give in for once, put his foot down for good and *mean* it.

So, really, in a way, it was her fault.

And if someone did finally come, if someone ever did come to rescue him, he was never coming back to this godforsaken place.

Because she would be here, waiting for him. She would never leave him alone, not as long as he was here, even if the house was bulldozed and he built a new one.

Mike, we have to go, it's scary, it's a big storm, we've got to go.

He lowered himself back down through the hole in the roof, carefully avoiding the jagged edges of the beams he'd hacked through with the ax to make the hole in the roof, so he could get out there, out of that suffocating attic, away from the rising water. He switched on the flashlight, looking for the liquor, and saw there was actually another bottle of the red wine after all—it had rolled off to the side, and he hadn't noticed before. There was no need to switch to tequila just yet. He fought with the corkscrew, chewing the cork up, little flakes floating down into the wine but he didn't care, he could always spit them out, and took a slug out from it. The sourness made him wince but it was wet, and that was all that mattered.

He heard a splash.

That wasn't from outside.

The trapdoor to the lower level was open, a large rectangle of dark with the long shadows creeping across the floor.

He took a deep breath and backed away, not losing his sweaty grip on the green bottle. He'd closed it before he went back out on the roof, hadn't he?

He couldn't remember.

Hadn't he decided to close it, in case he saw her down there in the water again?

He could hear his heart beating.

He focused on keeping his breathing even, taking deep breaths, ignoring the rising fear creeping up his spine.

I just forgot to close it, is all, I meant to close it but maybe it didn't latch, that's all there is to it, just close it now. She couldn't have gotten up here. I'd have heard her.

She's dead, you idiot.

But that wouldn't stop her, would it?

Just close the damned door. All that's down there is water. You're making yourself crazy. She's dead, dead, dead. Just close the door and you won't have to worry about her.

But he couldn't move, wouldn't move, he kept standing there and staring and trying to remember if he'd closed it or not. He would swear that he did, but he wasn't sure of anything anymore. The heat, the humidity, the damned bugs and the sun and the monotony, the way everything kept changing in his mind, the way he couldn't remember how long he'd been up on the damned roof, how long it had been since the water rose, since he'd climbed up the damned ladder to the attic, since he'd taken the hatchet and chopped his way out to the roof.

The shadows were getting longer. Soon it would be completely dark.

Mike, we have to go really, it's a big storm and what will happen to us if the levees fail?

"Shut up shut up shut up!" he yelled, or tried to, but all that came out of his sore and parched throat was a croak.

He took a step forward, swallowed, and took another.

One after another until he was standing next to the dark

opening, looking down into the flooded house.

She wasn't there.

Shaking now, he reached for the flashlight and flicked it on, pointing it with trembling hands into the darkness.

The oily dark water reflected the light back up at him, the filthy water swirling around in what used to be his bedroom.

Their bedroom.

He closed his eyes and said a prayer before opening his eyes again.

No, she still wasn't there.

The last time he'd looked down and seen her—when was that? It didn't matter, it was after the water came and he'd gone up to the roof—she was still there, face up floating in the water, her dark hair fanned out in the filthy water, eyes wide open and staring up at him accusingly.

You killed me. We should have left, but we stayed and you killed me.

He knew he couldn't really hear her, she was just in his head, but still—he kept the light shining down there, swinging back and forth. He heard another splash somewhere down there—maybe it was a gator? There wasn't any telling what was down in that water.

During the day, he could see the river levee in the distance—maybe it had held, but there was no telling where the water had come from. That didn't matter anyway. All that mattered was that it was there.

So maybe...if the bayous and canals or even the swamps had filled with water, it wasn't out of the question there could be gators in the water-filled city.

But wouldn't he have heard something if a gator had gotten her? Some loud splashing or something?

She's dead so she couldn't fight it but still a gator wouldn't have been able to get her underwater without making some noise?

He'd seen snakes a couple of times, making S-curves to

move forward in the water outside, but not inside the house.

The house.

What was left of the house?

The plasterboard was probably dissolving from the wet, and there was no mistaking the smell of wet, rotting wood. Hell, black mold was an issue even when the house wasn't underwater—how many times had he had to climb a ladder to wipe down the ceiling around the air conditioning vents with bleach to kill it?

Yeah, this house had been a good investment.

Even if the water somehow got pumped out—and it didn't look like that was going to happen any time soon—the house was ruined. It would take a lot of money to make it habitable again.

Maybe this time New Orleans would be left to drown.

He turned off the flashlight and backed away from the hole. He took another slug of the hot, cloyingly sweet wine.

She'd wanted to evacuate Sunday morning when The Weather Channel and all the weather broadcasters had gone into full-scale panic mode. "The mother of all storms," the mayor had called it. He just shook his head at her fears, her complaints, his mind was made up and that was that. "They say this every time," he'd scoffed at her. "Remember Ivan? Jorges? I can't even remember how many times they said it was the end. If you're so damned scared, *you* go. I'm staying put."

She wouldn't go by herself. He knew that.

And why get in the damned truck and be stuck in stop-and-go traffic, eight hours to go the seventy stinking miles to Baton Rouge just to hole up in a hotel somewhere that jacked up their room rates to gouge the evacuees only to have the stupid storm turn east like they always did at the last minute and New Orleans would be fine.

Yeah, no way.

They weren't going anywhere.

They'd lost power sometime in the early morning before the full fury of the storm came, and when it did come, it wasn't that bad. Howling winds and crashes outside, sometimes the house itself shook, but then, after what seemed like an eternity, it was over.

It was over and they'd survived.

He'd gone outside. Some tree branches were down, debris everywhere he looked, a big live oak down the street had been uprooted and smashed through a house. Everyone else was gone, evacuated, holed up in a hotel or shelter somewhere west on I-10.

They had a few hours before the house started filling up with water.

He'd lost his temper when she started panicking. He just meant to slap her but he hadn't meant to slap her so hard, it was an accident, she slipped in the water and hit her head on the table and went limp, and before he knew it the house was filling up with water and she was dead and he had to get up into the attic, had to make sure food and liquid was up there...

He reached over and looked down into the darkness. He shone the light down, his heart pumping, as he waved the beam of light around.

Nothing but floating furniture.

No sign of her.

He heard something.

Was that an outboard motor?

Bottle of hot wine still in one hand, he tucked the flashlight into the waistband of his shorts and climbed back out onto the roof.

It was definitely an outboard motor, and getting closer from the sound of it.

The flashlight dimmed in his hand and went out.

Swearing, he shook it as he tried to yell, but his vocal chords were too fried, his throat too raw.

Miracle of miracles, the flashlight came back on, and he started waving it in the direction the motor sound was coming from.

Oh please, God, oh please, God, oh please, God.

He was almost blinded as a strong spotlight shone in his eyes.

"Hey, there," a voice called as the motor idled, close by, near enough for him to see if not for the damned spots in front of his eyes. But as the bright red shapes began to fade, he could see someone swinging up onto the roof, and heard footsteps, and something cold and icy and wet was put in his hands. He almost wept, it felt so good, the cold against his hot skin. "Have some water, man. My name is Pete LaPierre, me and some buddies came down from Breaux Bridge to rescue some people—they told us we couldn't and we thought, damned if we don't have our own boat all we need is some water to put it in and here we are."

He twisted the cap off the water and poured some of it down, the coldness stinging his throat. He dropped the wine bottle he'd forgotten, heard it hit the roof and roll down the side and splash when it hit the water. He didn't care, this cold water was like he'd died and gone to heaven, he just wanted to cry—

"Are you the only one here? No one else around here, down in the attic? You must have been pretty lonesome."

He took another drink of the water, slow and steady, and felt a cramp forming in his stomach—*too much cold too fast*—and he breathed in and out for a moment, waiting for the cramp to pass, pressing the cold plastic bottle against the hot skin of his forehead.

He shook his head no.

"Come on, then, let's get you out of here." Pete LaPierre clapped him on the back, and he followed him down the side of the roof, and dropped down over the side into the boat. It wasn't much, just a fishing boat with an outboard motor and a large cooler filled with ice and water and beer and—

"You need you a hot shower," Pete said, and he revved the motor, steering the boat away from the little house and away through the dark night, using the spotlight to make sure there was nothing beneath the surface.

He looked back at the house.

He might never ever see it again.

He slumped down in the boat and took another drink of water.

Someone was pressing a sandwich on him, one of Pete's buddies, but he just waved it away.

They might not ever find her.

He exhaled, and watched the stars pass by overhead.

Way Down We Go
Barbara Ferrer

The French Quarter, New Orleans
November, 2005

Mike rapidly opened and closed his fist, slapping his other hand against the inside of the arm, pausing only to feel for the telltale rise of the vein. Praying for it to come up.

Oh God, yeah...there—*there* it was.

He loosened his jaw, the filled syringe he'd held clenched between his teeth dropping into his palm like a baby bird coming home to roost. With practiced ease, he shifted his grip and plunged the needle into the raised vein, his head dropping back against the weathered brick wall of the alley as the rush burned through his bloodstream and the familiar euphoria washed over him, ebbing and flowing in time with the rowdy strains of "Iko Iko" that drifted from some nearby club.

"*I bet you five dollars he'll kill you dead,*" he sang along in his head—he thought—until he heard the cheer and answering chant of "Jockomo feena nay!" from the group weaving through the lights glowing at the far end of the alley, pointing the way toward the noise and rowdiness of Bourbon Street. A little more subdued, maybe, but signs of life were evident, the parties of the Quarter staging a return. Celebrating survival. Shooting a big, civic middle finger at that fucking storm. That mean-assed bitch had blown into town, done her damage, then left them scrabbling in her left-behind shit like the god-damned Lord of the Flies. But she could just go fuck herself—she'd been banished and they were still here. Still here and not going anywhere. Not anytime soon, no, sir.

Sweat trailed along his scalp and around his ear, cold and

151

sinuous as a snake. No...*no*...He fucking hated snakes. Blinking rapidly, he tried to dispel the image, rubbing his back against the rough bricks to get rid of the feeling of something dark slithering down his neck and along his arm, leaving a dank, clammy trail in its wake, like it'd just come slithering up from the bayou, fangs bared and dripping venom.

The syringe dropped from suddenly nerveless fingers to join the rest of the crap littering the narrow alley—this sliver between two ancient buildings just wide enough to trap the shadows. Perfect for a quickie, whether it was with someone—or something—you wouldn't normally be caught dead with out there, even if *there* was the hedonistic surroundings of the Quarter where any and everything went. The remains of all those illicit trysts lay underfoot: a mélange of cigarette butts and crushed go-cups, used syringes and condoms that had a way of tripping up tourists stupid enough to try to use the alley as a shortcut.

Too often, those stupid tourists ended up as part of the remains.

The storm had brought with it a respite, if one cared call it that. He didn't. To him, all it'd really been was replacing one flavor of bad for another—stupid ass tourists replaced with natives who'd been too fucking arrogant or idiotic to get the hell out when they could.

Why was he thinking of all this shit? He was trying to forget the bad. Forget the sting of cold water against his face—cold that was alien to New Orleans in August. Trying to forget fighting against the wind and rain, trying to convince folks to leave, that he'd drive them to the Dome, to the Convention Center, to anywhere that wasn't where the storm was trying to beat her way into their house...the House of the Rising Sun, the Crescent City, the Big Easy...

So easy...It had once been so easy. It needed to be easy again.

Mike never used to trust easy. Easy was for suckers and

the lazy. He'd believed in busting ass, going out every day to protect the downtrodden and the innocent because, believe or not, there were still innocents 'round these parts. One might argue he'd even once been one himself, seriously as he'd taken his oath. He'd been upstanding and dedicated and suffered the slings and arrows of being an idealist in a city where idealism and five dollars would get you an order of coffee and beignets and not much else.

Live long enough in New Orleans, however, and a body eventually succumbed. Easy was their way of life after all. Even when working hard, there was a sugar-sweet ease that drenched everything in a way unique to them.

A trumpet, its melody both mournful and defiant, wailed through the heavy, humid air. So warm, even late, late at night, with the shadows and ghosts and anonymity as his only company. Just like he liked it.

The familiar lethargy began to claim him, sweet and relaxing, from his fingertips through his muscles and all the way down to his bones, making him feel loose and malleable, as if he was sinking right into the weathered bricks, merging with the building, all grit and time-worn but standing proud and strong, even after centuries of duty, quietly observing the years as they went by. Like...a sentry.

Yeah...he liked the idea of that. He'd served sweet NOLA most of his life anyhow—felt the weight of his commitment pressing hard against the base of his spine. If this alley swallowed him whole, like it was threatening to, he could carry on his existence as an eternal sentry, stand guard and watch everyone go about their business...doing the things they did, good and bad, that gave the city richness and patina. This city, man—she was like a lady past her prime, ragged round the edges but still damned fine enough to attract all the boys and knowing it.

He smiled, rubbing his palms over the rough surface beneath them, caressing life back into the old girl, letting her know he thought she was still hot. He'd never leave her for any of those sleeker, bigger cities with their promise of shiny and new. Hell, why would he leave? All that sleek shininess, it was bullshit—a smokescreen hiding all the same sorts of darkness that the Bible-thumpers derided about his beloved girl. Usually before going out and scoring a blowjob, the hypocritical fuckers. And New Orleans would give it to 'em, with a smile curving the edges of her lush, painted mouth and a finger up the ass for good measure. No bullshit about his city, no, sir.

Rolling his head to the side, he peered down the tunnel-like expanse of the alley, the dark length lithe and supple, his beautiful girl reaching out to embrace him to include him in the revels. Slowly, he began making his way toward the movement—so fucking beautiful, bodies moving together, then apart then together again. Out of the darkness a graceful arm reached out, long fingers curling, glints of brightness winking at him from their tips as if weaving a spell made of stardust and neon.

"Please—"

He blinked again, smiled at her request, tried to move a few steps closer, stumbling as muscle and bone rebelled, wanting to stay, the weathered bricks tightening their embrace as if wanting him to sink into every pore and crack.

"Help me, *please*—"

It was the darkest part of the alley and he was still too far away. Too far and getting further, as the disembodied arm reached out once more then fell away, the once-graceful fingers grasping at thin air, searching for purchase, their diamond bright tips glinting rapidly with increased desperation. Adrenaline surged through his system, fighting through the junk holding his body hostage.

He blinked furiously trying to separate reality and the fantasy—what if it was all a fantasy? What if it was all real?

What the hell was real?

"*Please*—"

He groped at the small of his back for his piece with one hand—reached into his pocket with the other. Braced his legs. Lifted the gun in what should've been a practiced grip.

Sweated as it trembled.

"Police—" He flashed his badge. "Step away and show me your hands. Now!"

Except there was nothing there. Nothing more than the stink of piss and illicit sex and the distant wail of a trumpet that sounded like laughter on the night air.

The slap of the folder landing on Mike's desk reverberated through his skull as forcefully as if a legion of sadistic hamsters with baseball bats had just swung for the fences.

"Jesus *fuck*—"

"Wake up, son."

"Wasn't asleep," he grumbled as he straightened in his chair, wincing as his muscles protested even that small movement. It was getting harder and harder to recover the mornings after. Or maybe it was just there were more mornings requiring recovery.

The ache from last night's shot chose that exact moment to throb extra hard, as if in agreement.

Or request.

He shoved the thought and the dry-mouthed desire it brought with it to the back of his mind. The desire had no place here. Not now. Its only place was nighttime and the shadows. Not a bright, blue-skied day, no matter how much the sun streaming through the windows made his eyeballs itch and throb with a want for those soothing shadows.

"Yo—Mike."

"Yeah—I got it, I got it." He shifted again, pulling his head from out his ass and attempted to focus on the folder Helo had slapped on the desk.

"Fuck the folder—I just used that to get your attention."

"Sadistic bastard."

"Tell me something I don't know." Helo grinned. "And enjoy."

"Dude—not enough fucking coffee." It was a half-hearted bitch, though, because after a lifetime in NOLA—hell, after the fucking storm—nothing had the capacity to shock him any longer. Besides—whatever Helo did to blow off steam was no more Mike's business than it was Helo's what he did. Each was aware the other had secrets—what those were wasn't important. Until the day they had to be.

"You're such a pussy, Pavlović."

Mike threw him a one-fingered salute with one hand and with the other, he reached for his mug.

"Finish your mother's milk—we've got a call."

Mike stood, drained the dregs of his long-cold coffee, and grabbed his jacket and keys in a smooth, practiced motion. If he thought about it too hard, it would bug the hell out of him, how easily he performed the maneuver. In his dark humor moments, he put it down to practice made perfect—and he'd practiced this move a lot. Especially the last three months. But wasn't that why he'd wanted to become a detective in the first place? Get the hell off the beat—do some real good on the streets with the people instead of strut around like some useless asshat in a light blue shirt? He couldn't deny wearing civvies made a difference these days, considering how most people in the city looked at cops. Not that he could blame them. As a whole, they'd fucked up good and proper.

"Where we off to?" he asked as they made their way out of the station and to Mike's pickup since it was his day to drive. With the department still out so many cars, the detectives were reduced to using their personal vehicles. At least Mike had gotten rid of his Harley the year before. He and Helo were tight but not *that* tight.

"St. Jeanne d'Arc."

Mike stared at Helo as he rounded the truck's bed. "A cemetery? You shitting me?"

Helo shrugged as he got into the cab. "I'm sure there's a really sick joke in there somewhere."

A frisson of unease slithered down Mike's back. "Yeah, save it."

"You don't have to tell me twice. I make jokes about finding the dead in a cemetery, my bubbe's liable to slap me six ways to Sunday."

"Your grandma's currently in Atlanta with your sister."

Helo's brows rose over his aviators. "You think a minor detail like that'd stop her?"

"Point." He headed toward Bayou St. John, dodging storm debris still littering the streets and keeping a careful eye on the lights. Not all had been restored yet and those that had weren't what one could call reliable. Not that there was a lot of traffic to deal with right now. Couldn't help but wonder if there ever would be again. New Orleans had pulled a Phoenix routine more than once in her merrily depraved past, rising from the ashes time and again, but this time things'd been different. This time, the goddamned storm had plowed head-long into them with a hellbent wrath that roared and howled with unholy glee as if attempting its damnedest to sweep them clean off the face of the earth.

There were plenty who deeply regretted that the storm hadn't succeeded.

The ache chose that moment to resurface and throb with especially painful intensity, as if to remind him that yeah, they were still there—but at what cost?

"Coop been called?" he asked as he fished a cigarette and his silver lighter from his shirt pocket with a hand that shook only slightly.

"According to the uni who called it in, he was actually there first."

More unease—stronger still—tightened its coils around his

spine. He shifted, the chafing of the seat's upholstery weirdly reassuring, obliterating the cold sweat dampening his neck. He drew deep on the cigarette, holding the acrid smoke in his lungs for a long, calming second before blowing it out the cracked window in a thin, practiced stream.

A few more drags and he even managed to convince himself he was being a paranoid son of a bitch for no good reason. A feeling he managed to hold onto until he pulled up to the stone wall marking the outskirts of St. Jeanne d'Arc, a faded grande dame of a cemetery in that uniquely decrepit New Orleans sort of way.

He drove the perimeter of the old graveyard, still miraculously rimmed with an unbroken stand of oak trees— several missing big chunks of branches and all of them stripped bare of their lacy curtains of silver green Spanish moss, but still standing, by God—until he came to a break in the wall from which a single twisted iron gate still hung. In the gap left by the missing half of the gate, stood Dr. Cooper McNamara, Orleans Parish coroner, deep in conversation with a tall, dark-haired woman Mike didn't recognize. At the sound of the truck, Coop didn't bother looking up, merely waving a hand in acknowledgment as he continued talking. The woman, however, turned her head toward them, her brief glance grave and assessing and immediately setting Mike's teeth on edge.

"Who's the dame?"

Mike groaned. "Dame? You've been reading Hammett again, haven't you?" He parked behind the white coroner's van and climbed out.

Helo met him at the front of the truck. "Cable's still out— what the hell else am I supposed to do?"

"Find new writers." After a final drag on his cigarette, he dropped it to the dirt, grinding it out beneath his boot. "I'm sure there've been a few in the last eighty years. As for the chick, I have no idea who she is."

158

"Chick? Seriously?" Helo snorted. "And you're giving *me* shit?"

"Better than dame."

Which this woman was definitely *not*. Her type went by a different moniker—sure the Saints T-shirt and jeans were appropriately faded, the hiking boots battered and worn, but the ramrod straight posture, porcelain skin, and diamond studs exposed by her sleek ponytail told the actual truth if not the reason *why* an Uptown beauty queen was hanging around a cemetery chatting to the coroner like she was at some fucking tea party.

"'Bout damn time, y'all."

"Who twisted your panties up your crack?" He turned toward the woman. "Ma'am."

Just that quick Helo shifted between shooting his mouth off at Coop and politely greeting the unknown woman. Mike had always envied the ease with which his partner could shift gears. He was like a German Shepherd that way: equal parts charming, goofy, and ferocious while Mike was more bloodhound—dogged and plodding and not giving an inch until he'd tracked down the source of the scent.

Right now, just beneath the dust and mold and decay one associated with cemeteries and the sweet-spicy scent of the climbing roses that had somehow escaped the storm's wrath and were blooming with riotous defiance along the stone wall, he could scent a definite unease.

"Now you know how we usually feel, waitin' on your sorry ass," Mike said, ignoring both the pounding at his temples and the raised-eyebrow expression on the strange woman's face.

"Don't mind either of them," Coop drawled. "I've known 'em both longer than I'd care to admit."

"I see," she said her tone neutral and annoying as fuck. He'd pegged her right, for sure. So what in the hell *was* she doing at his crime scene?

"Dr. Fournier, she's the one who called it in," Coop said, a faint smile playing about the edges of his mouth as if he knew exactly what Mike was thinking. Probably did, smug bastard. "Lilly, these are two of New Orleans' finest—Detectives Mike Pavlović and He—"

"Helo Lowestein."

Despite the unease and faint antagonism still niggling at him, Mike couldn't help but chuckle at Helo's rush to cut Coop off before he could utter his full name. A name Coop damn well knew Helo loathed and answered to on only the most formal of occasions—or to his bubbe. Coop, of course, was bound and determined to attempt to use it at every possible opportunity.

"Lillian Fournier." The woman shook each of their hands in turn—her grip cool and surprisingly firm. More surprising still was the slight rasp of calloses, especially given the title by which Coop had introduced her.

"I was working at the FEMA camp over at the park when a few of the regular kids alerted me to..." she hesitated before finally settling on, "the body."

"Which is down this way," Coop said as he turned and started walking.

"Didn't know this camp had a clinic," Helo said as they followed Coop down the main path, between a row of crypts lined up like drunken sentries.

"They don't," she replied.

So what in the hell was she doing there?

Not that it was important to the matter at hand—not really—so Mike filed it away for later, choosing to focus instead on their surroundings. He made mental note of the storm debris littering the grounds, the dark brown waterlines marking most of the crypts, the dates carved on their fronts, the latest of which was more than a century before.

Hell of a place to die.

Or rather—hell of a place to be dumped.

"Jesus take the wheel," he muttered under his breath while Helo let loose with a long, low whistle.

Propped up against an actual mausoleum, which compared to its neighbors was in relatively decent condition, was the body. Reclined against the marble wall, clothes, shoes, and jewelry intact, hell, she was even wearing lipstick, she would have looked perfectly normal—peaceful, even—except for the fact she'd been scalped clean. Nothing but bone, immaculate and gleaming white in the late fall sun like a halo above what even in death was a very pretty face.

"The kids who found her—they okay?" Helo asked hoarsely.

"With what they've lived through the past few months, who the hell knows," Coop answered, the same strain in his voice as had been in Helo's. As what Mike felt.

"We're gonna need to question them," he said.

"They're back at the FEMA kitchen trailer—" Dr. Fournier's voice was cool and clinical and set Mike's teeth on edge as much as her initial appearance. "I left them helping to make biscuits for Thanksgiving dinner. Makes them feel useful."

For the first time since they'd been introduced, Mike met her gaze head on. Dark, inscrutable, and faintly challenging, it wasn't anything he hadn't seen a thousand times before, so it was no shock when she broke, casting a quick glance up at the angel perched serenely on the mausoleum's roof before meeting his gaze again.

"I work as a researcher at the NIH but I grew up here. Came back to help out any way I could."

"That so."

Nothing changed outwardly, but the air around her practically vibrated. "You have a problem with that?"

"Me?" He shrugged. "Absolutely not. I have no problem with charity. Especially of the Uptown variety. Just warms the cockles of my heart, it does."

"Oh."

"What?"

"Nothing." Expression shuttered, she turned away, effectively blocking him out. "The kids swear they didn't touch her. Considering her state, I'm inclined to believe them."

"She looks pristine," Helo muttered as he crouched down, pulling a pair of latex gloves from his back pocket as he did. "No way she was killed in these clothes—they look like they just came off the rack."

"Not only that—the skull is immaculate. To get it that way, especially while leaving the rest of her so intact would have required time and a great deal of care."

Dr. Fournier hesitated, long enough for Coop to interject, "What's on your mind, Lilly?"

She hesitated another moment before answering. "The kids who found her—they've got it in their heads that she was some sort of sacrifice for Mama Guaya."

Helo snorted. "Thank God for the power of conjure women and local myths."

"Think there's any truth to their theory?" Mike asked as he pulled on his own gloves and crouched alongside Helo. And if the look Dr. Fournier was currently shooting him wasn't exactly of the "could kill" variety, it was at least scathing enough to have flayed off a few strips of skin. That is, if he wasn't already immune to that sort of thing. Benefit of growing up with four sisters, as was the impulse to take a poke at the bear.

"Just some of us have lived here long enough to have respect for—"

He stared at the hand he'd lifted for examination. Soft, with long slender fingers ending in perfectly manicured nails. Acrylics, he noted faintly, memories of his sisters' weekly rituals washing over him. Comparing colors and designs and decorations, each trying to outdo the other. The ones before him were fancy like that—bright pink and studded with rhinestones that sparkled in the sunlight. That might have caught the light from neon that trickled into an otherwise dim and shadowed French Quarter alley.

Glints of brightness winking at him from their tips as if weaving a spell made of stardust and neon.

But it was the ragged edges on three of the nails that made his stomach heave and had him lurching to his feet, breathing heavily through the cotton wool suddenly coating the inside of his mouth. Sunlight and the scent of roses and chipped, dirt-stained marble tunneled away in a euphoric rush, leaving him in a stinking brick-lined alley, a sharp prick of beautiful pain in his arm, the sounds of a city coming back to life seeping into his skin as the tar coursed through his blood-stream, allowing him to fly and see it all even as it held his muscles locked up tight.

"Please."

Once-graceful fingers grasping at thin air, searching for purchase, their diamond bright tips glinting rapidly with increased desperation...

The rigidness holding his body tight went slack, so fast, he felt a warm trickle go down his leg beneath his jeans. "Hitch a ride with Coop," he managed around the dry thickness of his tongue.

"What the hell?"

"Mike—?"

Coop and Helo's combined voices came at him, tinny and faint, while Lillian Fournier's dark gaze zoomed in, uncomfortably close and uncomfortably aware.

She knew.

She knew about him.

He didn't give a shit.

He just needed to get the hell out of there.

Needed to know.

He drove blind—completely unaware of lights or storm

trash or people or any other damned thing beyond his need to know.

It took him a while, pawing through the shit, human and animal alike, and the go cups and paper fliers and used condoms and needles, but eventually, he found what he was looking for. He'd known—the instant he saw those ragged, torn edges on the hand of that pretty, pretty girl, he'd find at least one. Painted bright pink, rhinestone glinting on its tip.

With a gloved hand, he picked up the torn, sparkling nail, placed it in a small evidence bag, slipped it in his pocket, and puked his guts up, adding to the detritus littering the alley.

Standing, he wiped his mouth, reached into another pocket, full daylight be damned, and pulled the syringe he'd had the forethought to prep in his truck before he began his desperate search.

Shoving the waist of his jeans just far enough out of the way, he plunged the needle into his hip, not giving a damn about finding a vein or feeling the immediate rush. None of that mattered. Right now—right this goddamned second—his only objective was to quell the insistent ache and silence the frantic "*Help me, please*—" echoing in his head.

Gumbo Weather
Thomas Pluck

The daily sun shower speckled the windshield with diamonds.

"Know what you're thinking," Russ said from up front, perched like a stork in a motorcycle jacket.

"Reckon you do," Jay replied. He lounged in back, cracking his knuckles. Squinting his steely, sunken eyes and turning the diamonds into stars. He ran a hand through his shock of black hair.

"You stomp this dumb shit's hands with your work boots, he'll just kick the kid around instead."

"Maybe I'll back the car over his ankles, then."

"Man can't work, he can't pay. Sally Jiggs'll want his twenty large from your pocket."

Three points on twenty grand meant six yards a week. Steep price to pay, Jay thought.

Their man's name was George Fells. Back when the Saints were the Ain'ts, George had bet against them hard. They won the big one, and he'd been paying for it since. Russ called it penance for disloyalty to the home team.

The man drank at Sally's bar on Napoleon, near the port. If they busted George in there they'd scare off the gamblers, bring too much heat. So they waited a few spots behind his car in their banged-up cab, listening to summer rain hit the roof.

Last time George Fells was late, they found him at home. A little green house off Tchoupitoulas. It was windy and cold;

gumbo weather. Jay rapped on the door.

"Get the damn door," George said from inside.

"I'm making roux." A woman's voice.

George sank as he recognized them at the door. He was a swarthy bayou boy like Jay. He wore a Ragin' Cajuns sweatshirt with the sleeves ripped off, and showed them his back after he turned the lock.

A little blond blue-eyed boy worked Crayolas at the kitchen table, and a woman in sweats and a ponytail stirred a pot of chocolate-colored roux at the stove. Gumbo starter; flour and oil. She had her trinity—celery, bell pepper, and onions—diced in a bowl and ready to go. The heady scent filled the kitchen.

The woman rolled her eyes as the two men came in from the cold.

"Ma'am," Jay said, nodded. Russ smirked.

George bumped his wife's bony hips aside as he stomped past. His son looked up, hopped off his chair, went to hug his daddy's leg.

"Outta my way, ya little shit." He walked right through the kid. The boy fell on his behind, little eyes went wet. He started to wail.

The boy's momma sighed, turned off the heat. "Ruined," she said, avoiding Jay's eyes. As she picked the boy up, his shirt lifted, revealing leopard-spot bruises.

Jay watched the room fill with red mist. Took a step, then Russ squeezed his shoulder hard. Brought him back to the acrid odor of burning roux.

George returned with a roll of bills and a frown carved above his stubbled coal chunk of a chin.

Russ counted. "You're a yard short."

"You're taking it out my boy's mouth, you vultures."

"That boy you use as a punching bag, you piece of shit?" Jay grabbed George's pinky and twisted. George shrieked, fell to his knees.

"Jay," Russ said.

"You son of a bitch," George said.

"Yep. A twenty-two carat bitch she was," Jay said. "Not half as mean as the dog who fucked her."

Jay dragged George by the hair to the stove.

George's eyes went wide as Jay tilted the pot toward his face. "Roux gets hot as napalm. I made the bitch stop stirring, once. Can't remember why. Still got the scars down my back."

"Jay, c'mon now," Russ said.

Jay shoved George away. "Now, Georgie, you go kiss the little girls and make 'em cry. But next time you're short on the puddin' and pie, I'm bringing the tin snips. And if that boy's got a mark on him—"

"How'm I gonna work? I work with my hands!"

"We know all you do is type and talk," Jay said. "You can hunt 'n peck with nine." He pushed him onto the floor, gave a dead-eyed stare. "Tell your wife I'm sorry we ruined supper." He set the pot on the stove, and they left to make their next collection.

When they cleared the book best they could, they left the day's envelope at the bar drop. Parked the work car at Sally's taxi stand, and headed out in Jay's purple Challenger for steaks at Charlie's. Charlie had needed a loan to restore after Katrina. Sally anted up, so his boys ate free.

"You can't beat the sick out of a man like that," Russ said.

"Sure feels good trying."

"Just saying, our job's to collect, not save the world. Most of 'em are degenerate gamblers. Some worse."

"You can sit there, knowing he's taking it out on her and that boy?"

"I took a whipping almost every day, growing up."

"Me too. Don't mean we liked it."

"It ain't our business."

They worked on their steaks a while.

"You take the belt to your kids?"

"Hell no. But it ain't your business if I do."

"Okay, then. So you think it ain't right."

"I don't kick back with Early Times every night like my old man did, neither."

Jay pointed with his fork. "What if someone made it their business? Busted up your old man?"

Russ shook his head, poked at his potatoes. "I'd have to side with my pop. He's my blood. What about you?"

"I told you about that. Still looking for him."

"You gotta let that go. It's not like he named you Sue."

Jay laughed, took a slug of Wild Turkey.

"You got the right," Russ said. "What he did? It was me, I'd say he needed killin' too." He'd seen the constellation of cigarette burns on his partner's belly. "But the rest of us, who just came up getting knocked around? It's more complicated."

"Reckon so," Jay said.

"They didn't know better," Russ said. "Their folks whaled on 'em too. That's all they knew. Don't make it right. Not one bit. Makes it harder to hate 'em, that's all. Once they're old and weak."

Jay nodded, staring into the amber of his glass.

"Your stepfolks, they ever slap you around?"

"Not a hair on my head."

"I know, butter wouldn't melt in their mouth."

"Nope," Jay said. "Slide right off like it was the Virgin Mary's left tit."

They shared a laugh, and bourbon too.

"Just ain't that simple," Russ said. "You hate what they did, but you love 'em. So you find a good woman who holds you all night, tells you the sun shines outta your ass. She shits out a few beautiful kids for you. And you love 'em the best you can."

"I'll drink to that," Jay said. And they did. "You think George'll whup 'em harder, after what I done?"

"Who's to say? You didn't make him start. You ain't gonna make him stop. Comes down to it, a man's gonna do what he wants."

That was three months back. Now there was another cold snap, and George Fells was a week late once more. He'd come in to Sally's to bet on the Tigers game. Russ got a text from Clyde the bartender when he showed.

Jay stared into his own eyes in the rearview, then down at his hands. His stepdad Poppa Andre had been good with his hands. Made a tidy living, working the beauty out of wood, making furniture. He and Aunt Angeline had fled Louisiana with him, saving Jay from that pit of hell. And they'd paid hard for it later.

Andre had told Jay to go school, to use his head, not his hands. But that hadn't worked out. Jay had to take care of a bully at school who beat on his friends, and raped one. A mean son of a bitch who needed killing. Jay had paid for that with a quarter century in prison.

Now he tallied how much he was willing to pay for George Fells.

He could sell the Challenger. It might cover the principal, and whatever bullshit payoff fee Sally charged. A Shylock never made it easy to quit. They'd bleed you forever, to get that weekly juice. Maybe Jay could buy a shitbox like this cab, and buy George's loan.

Then he could slam George's hands in the back door, and drive his wife and the boy to her kin, wherever they were. He could tell George the new vig was letting them go.

It felt about as real as the diamonds on the windshield.

George huddled against the rain in a gray hoodie. Russ rolled the window down and whistled for him. Instead, he took off.

Jay shouldered the back door open and ran. When he

169

caught up, he yanked the strings of George's hood closed, kneed him in the gut. Russ came up the curb to cut them off. Jay threw him in back, jumped on top, elbow first.

"Rent was due Friday, and you're betting like a free man? Sally don't like that."

George coughed. "Gotta be so rough?"

"I'd rather be sitting at the bar eating oysters," Jay said, and slapped him through the hood. "You make me run, I'm liable to be ornery."

"Ain't got it on me."

"Pick a finger. Russ, get me the tin snips."

"I got it at home," George said. "No need for that kind of talk."

Russ double-parked in front of the green little house. Was getting to know the way by heart.

Same small kitchen with the steel-legged table and white peeled floor. Gumbo simmered on the stove. George's wife looked up with a yellow ring round her eye, as they shuffled in from the rain. Boy was on her knee, reading from a Little Golden Book. He eyed his father quick, then went back to his book.

"Two weeks' juice, now," Russ said.

George limped in back for the cash.

Jay whispered to the woman. "You got kin, ma'am? This ain't right."

"Mind your business," she hissed, and didn't look up.

George came out with an ugly little pistol.

"Easy now," Russ said, and raised his hands.

"George, what are you—"

He cracked the butt down on her head. "Shut the hell up!"

She moaned and low-walked out the room with her wailing son in tow.

Jay kept quiet. Hands up. Stepped away, felt the heat of the gumbo pot at his back.

"You do this, you're bringing hell down on your whole family."

"This how it's gonna be, boys. Russ, I know you got children. You stay." George aimed the gun at him. Kept his distance. "Jay? You're gonna hit the money drop."

"You crazy? What you think that's gonna do? That's Sally's money. You're good as dead."

"If you catch up to me."

"It won't be us, George. They'll be worse. Don't think they won't shoot that boy of yours."

"Jay, get goin' now."

"Russ has the piece, Georgie."

"You think it's real funny, callin' me that?" He stepped forward, stuck the little revolver into Jay's eye socket. "Maybe you come back, we'll all be dead. Ain't no other way out from under this rock!"

Russ's hand drifted into the coat for his pistol. Jay saw it with his good eye. He wondered if George saw him look, if that was why he turned and shot Russ in the throat.

Jay dumped the soup pot on him. George screamed, firing into the ceiling as he clawed his bubbling face. Jay swung the pot back and forth by the handle, clanging off the man's skull. When George collapsed, Jay hammered his face until it resembled a rotten cantaloupe.

Russ stared at the ceiling, haloed in a widening ruby pool. He mouthed a few silent words before his eyes went blank.

"I'm sorry, partner."

Jay slipped the .45 and the payment book from Russ's jacket.

He left the woman moaning in her parlor. Dumped the cab in Gert Town with the keys in the ignition, and took a streetcar back to the Challenger.

* * *

"Clyde, send him in."

Jay shuffled in with his head down, hands in the pockets of his pea coat.

Salvatore Gingerelli held court in back of his bar, hunkered over a poker table littered with empty oyster shells and fat envelopes. He looked like a track-suited linebacker gone to seed, well-tanned, a fat cigar in his jeweled hand. His two favorite earners, Philly Lasardo and Lee Walker, flanked him.

Philly had a thick mane dyed black and wore glasses on a chain around his neck. He counted bills, and didn't look up. Lee turned his pinched face toward Jay without a word. The iceman never said much. His eyes said enough.

"What's on your mind, Jay?" Sally exhaled a dragon plume of Montecristo smoke.

"Russ is dead, Sal. George Fells shot him. I took care of him."

Jay took the book out of his jacket, let the dog-eared pages flop among the seashells.

Sally nodded. "Sit down, Jay. Let's talk about this."

Jay hunched into his seat, chewing his lip. They already knew, that he was sure.

Sally took a decanter of scotch from the private bar behind him, poured it into two cut crystal rocks glasses. He nudged one toward Jay, who took a gulp.

"Anyone see you?"

"No. Wife and kid were in the other room."

"So she knows. Lee, why don't you call our friend at the Second Precinct. Have him send someone friendly over."

Lee nodded, flipped open a black phone, and walked to the back.

Sally dipped the chewed end of his cigar into his scotch. Scratched at his leg.

"George worked at the port, didn't he?"

"Yes, sir."

"Good life insurance. Let her slide a few weeks. Get the funeral taken care of."

Jay rocked in his chair, nodded. Fingered his keys in his pocket.

"Sal, she was asking. What would it take to pay off the principal?"

The big man laughed. "Whatever she's got and twenty large more. Her husband killed a good soldier."

Jay nodded. "He was a good man." He stared at the shucked oyster shells a moment, then slid an envelope from his pocket. "Today's bag." He handed it to Philly, then stuck his hands in his pockets again.

"He was," Sally said. "It's our life. It is what it is."

Philly opened the envelope, and frowned at the newsprint inside.

Jay fired the .45 under the table twice. Sal's cigar dropped, the rest of him froze solid.

Dirty bills flew like feathers as Philly fell backward in his chair. Lee, a wiry old lion, leaped across the table at Jay and they tumbled to the checkered floor. He straddled him and wrenched Jay's gun hand, the meat of his thumb against the hammer.

Jay reached up and stuck two fingers in Lee's mouth. Yanked hard, gave the dour man a bloody smile. When Lee clutched his ruined face, Jay shot him through the hands. Philly wailed at the back door, pawing the bolt. Jay pushed himself up, Lee's limp body rolling off him.

A shotgun barrel broke the outline of the doorway to the bar.

"Clyde," Jay hollered. "Drop that thing, you dumb shit. Before I shoot you through the damn plaster."

"You gonna shoot me anyway!"

Jay shot twice through the wall. The shotgun dropped. He never learned if he hit Clyde or not. Sally's head hit the oyster shells, thick lips bubbling red. Snubby .38 in his hand. Jay put another round in his bald spot.

Out back, he shot Philly between the shoulder blades. Took the keys to his Cadillac from his pocket.

Cruising over Lake Pontchartrain, Jay boomeranged the gun toward the dirty water. He'd miss the Challenger's muscle.

His father would get to live out his days whoring and stubbing out cigarettes in some backwater saloon. But Jay would leave the fat envelope with Russ's wife, and whoever took over Sally's book would find George Fell's number marked paid in full.

ebgdea
G. J. Brown

The banjo would be found, one day, lying on a floor, smashed—dried blood caking the strings. It would be last played, just after Joe Martyn received a kiss courtesy of Elizabeth Stringer. The kiss would take place in a grubby back alley, next to the service door of the Lucky Star restaurant. Joe dreamed of marrying Elizabeth. Elizabeth dreamed of holding hands with Donny Osmond and David Cassidy. She was too young to know what three in a bed meant. Her older sister, Tricia, wasn't. She thought the idea of a threesome with Donny and David was just fine. Just fine indeed.

As Elizabeth rubbed the spit from her lips while straightening her hair, Joe stood bemused, unsure what to do after the kiss. He thought about asking for a second helping. He would still be thinking about it when Elizabeth was shot by a bullet from a World War II pistol.

The bullet would have missed Elizabeth, striking off the peeling cinder block wall behind her, if she hadn't stopped to smooth out her blonde locks. Elizabeth was proud of her hair. Her mother told her it shone like a film star's mane on a moonlit set. She loved those words. The bullet entered the back of her head, before blowing out, through her forehead, spraying Joe with brain, blood and bone.

The banjo lay, warm, in the hands of a small boy called Dilly Witcha. Dilly had been sneaking a peak on Joe and Elizabeth. Dilly was frequenting, as he often did, the space behind the Luck Star's garbage cans. A good place to hide. Everyone from pre-pubescent school kids to golden years lovers used the alley behind the Lucky Star to make out, but none of them ventured close to the smell of the garbage cans. The metal walls of the cans, baked solid with decaying Chinese food that had fermented in the southern heat of that summer, stank. And that suited Dilly's purposes just fine. Anyway the stench wasn't too bad, if, as Dilly did, you stuffed a dollop of Rembrandt up each nostril.

When Elizabeth's gray matter hosed down Joe, Dilly had been ghosting chords on his banjo. He liked to think he was a whizz with the instrument but, deep down, he knew he didn't have the patience to get past the half-dozen tunes his grand-pappy said were all you needed to impress the girls. His favorite was 'Dueling Banjos.' He could play it well enough until it sped up. Then he was screwed. But playing the opening was more than good enough for *good* enough.

Over the years Dilly would be asked why he had played the chords. Why touch the thing? What possessed him? After watching a young girl die, what welled up inside him that demanded his fingers pull out the six chords? Dilly would commit suicide thirty years later, blood dripping on the banjo below his swinging feet; shards of the DVD of *Deliverance* he had tried to eat, stuck in his throat. He wouldn't be found until after the five young girls had died.

Detective Sarah Tracy pushed the mug of iced coffee across the desk. She could feel sweat oozing from every pore, even with the police station A/C wound up to the max. New Orleans wasn't her home turf. She was used to the dry heat of Los Angeles. She wanted back to her own world. Yet, in many ways, this was her own world. With a serial killer in the wind, a *child* serial killer, she was assisting the FBI. After all she had been the one that had caught 'One Eye' (seven boys under eight dead), so called because of the one eyed teddy he left at the scenes, and she was the one that had tracked down Mark

Topp (five girls, aged six to eleven). Both were on death row and, now that the Banjo Killer was responsible for four innocent girls lying in the morgue, Tracy had been parachuted in to another child killer storm.

She stood up. 'Okay.' Everyone in the room turned to her. She scanned the officers, a mix of feds and NOPD. 'So what do we know? Profiling says late forties, early fifties, white and male. Could be a smart bastard, likely to be a loner. Might or might not be local. No fixed modus operandi. Ellie was hit by a car. Barbara was stabbed. Gina was found hung from her school swing and Diane was drowned in her aunt's bathtub.'

New Orleans was in meltdown over the killings. All four victims were twelve years old. All four had shoulder-length blonde hair and, even in a reasonable light, you could have lined them all up next to each other and sworn they were from the same gene pool.

In the wake of all four murders, multiple witnesses had heard the first six chords of 'Dueling Banjos' being played. Everyone knew that E was the next chord in the sequence and now you couldn't book a hairdresser for the lines of twelve-year-old Emmas, Ellas and Ellies having their straw-colored hair shorn.

The officers looked at Sarah. The reality was they had squat. Squat wasn't good. Sarah wasn't there to deliver squat. And something was all wrong with the profile they had. In her gut it was way, way wrong.

ebgdea

'Another one.'

Sarah stood up, a lightning rod feeding her spine. 'Tell me.'

John Stein, a two-decade veteran of the force, spoke. 'Blonde, twelve years old, by the name of Chrissy Martyn.'

'Not an E.'

'No, we checked. Chrissy. No E.'

Fuck, a new wrinkle, not the next chord in the song.

ebgdea

'Mrs. Martyn, I'm so sorry for your loss.'

Lea Martyn didn't move, didn't lift her eyes, didn't even breathe. Sarah went on. 'We need to ask some questions.'

Lea was a granite rock devoid of life.

'Was Chrissy your daughter's real name?'

A small nod.

The rest of the questioning went badly. It rarely went well. Lea had last seen her daughter playing with her friends in the back yard. They had all rushed in when Lea had shouted that lemonade was on the menu. The other kids swore Chrissy had been playing right up to the second Lea called them but, in the chaos of kids rushing for sugar, she had vanished. Now that the evil son of a bitch had gone off-piste on the chord thing the city would implode. All twelve-year-old girls were up for grabs.

ebgdea

'Shit. Why didn't we know this?' Sarah's right hand flew to the phone. In her left was a photocopy of Chrissy's birth certificate. Only it didn't say Chrissy. It said Elizabeth.

'My husband called her that.' The voice was weak as diluted rainwater. Less than a year from now Lea would step in front of a semi. She would be holding a picture of Chrissy. 'I thought it was sick, so I always called her after my grandmother.'

'Sick. Why?'

'Why name your daughter after a dead girlfriend.'

ebgdea

'Okay. So the game's changed,' Sarah was addressing the team again. 'We have a name. Joe Martyn. Age forty-two. Separated from Lea Martyn, mother of Chrissy. Joe's the father. Left home a year ago. Heavy user of anti-depressants and booze. Chrissy's birth name is Elizabeth which puts us right back on track for the next victim's name to start with A.'

'Always a fucking relative in it somewhere.'

Sarah looked at the young officer who had spoken. He was wrong. Most serial killers didn't know their victims, but today was the exception day.

Sarah continued. 'Joe Martyn witnessed the murder of Elizabeth Stringer thirty years ago. He was twelve. They were making out in a back alley near Charles St. A guy called Ted Robertson was doing a number on a pawn shop. Ted got in a fire-fight in the alley and a stray bullet killed Elizabeth.'

'Don't tell me,' said the young officer, 'Elizabeth was twelve years old, shoulder length blonde hair.'

Sarah passed out the decades old photo. Elizabeth could have been the twin sister of any of the victims.

ebgdea

'We've got the bastard.'

Sarah, head in hands, forty-nine hours out from her last shut-eye, looked up. The voice from across the room rattled on. 'He just made three withdrawals from three cash machines in Gentilly Woods. I'm getting the CCTV footage emailed over.'

ebgdea

Joe Martyn was trembling. 'It's all I can get.'

The woman held the young blonde-haired girl tight, a carving knife across her throat. Alice was shaking, but cried out. She just wanted her mother.

The woman shuffled. 'A thousand bucks. What the fuck am I going to do with a lousy thousand bucks. Where can I go on that?'

Joe winced. 'It's all the machines will let me have. I can't go into the bank. They're looking for me. Just let her go. Please.'

'Fuck you. It's all your fucking fault. You let my sister fucking die. Stood there in that fucking alley, pecker in one hand, waiting for a quick tug. I fucking saw you. You could've saved her.'

Joe sobbed. 'Christ, you've killed my daughter and all the others. I couldn't have saved Elizabeth. I was twelve. He had a gun. It was an accident. It was...' Joe choked.

Tricia, Elizabeth's older sister, had found Joe in a ten-dollar flophouse. He didn't know how but she had. He was full of Tennessee White Whiskey—barely conscious. She had told him what she had done. How many she had killed, and why. She had described how Chrissy had pleaded. Just before she had garroted her with piano wire. Then Tricia told him there was one more to go. One more girl and he could stop it—but it would take money. A lot of money.

'Drop the weapon.'

For the second time in his life Joe Martyn was coated in the brains of another human being.

Sarah was sitting with Joe. The interview room was hellish but process was process. Joe needed to be debriefed.

'I didn't know she had a gun in the other hand.' Sarah wiped some sweat off her forehead. 'When she turned I had no choice but to shoot. If the guy at the Quick Stop hadn't recognized your face from the news we would have been too late.'

Joe sipped at a plastic cup, half full of warming water. 'She killed Chrissy.'

'I know. I know. But you saved Alice. You saved her and Tricia is dead.'

'She said it was all my fault. That I could have saved Elizabeth back then. I couldn't. Don't you think I've not pulled that whole thing apart a million different ways.'

'You couldn't have done anything. I read the report. She needed to blame someone else.'

Joe slumped a little lower. 'Then why not blame the bastard that shot her sister.'

'He died of lung cancer three weeks ago. It's what set her off. That and the thirtieth anniversary of Elizabeth's death. She wrote the whole story in her diary. Every single word and more. Her head was in another world. The last entries are a work of art—in a bad, bad way.'

'Jesus. If the shooter died, wouldn't...'

He didn't know how to finish the sentence. So Sarah obliged. 'Wouldn't she have let it go? She couldn't.'

'Couldn't or wouldn't?'

'Both. The shooter was her boyfriend.'

'Her boyfriend?'

'Been going out in secret for a year. No one knew. That's why she was there that night. She was the lookout for Ted.'

Joe shook his head. 'The lookout'

'She put Ted up to it. He needed to get money for their engagement ring. But not any old ring, it had to be an exTremély expensive one. Tricia had insisted. That was why Ted was robbing the pawn shop. If Tricia hadn't been so greedy, Elizabeth would have lived.'

Voodoo at the Jitterbug
Kaye Wilkinson Barley

Hélène opened the door, leaned a hip against it, took the cigarette from her mouth and looked her sister up and down.

"What the hell are you doing here?"

"Hello to you too, *soeur*," said Chloé.

"*Soeur*? Hell, honey, we ain't never really been sisters. What do you want?"

"I'm here to see *Grand-mère* Cécile."

Hélène looked Chloé up and down one more time. "What? You think we don't both remember this is an anniversary? A date that marks the saddest day of our lives? The day our husbands died defending your honor outside that ridiculous shop you left your home to run? What the hell kinda name is Jitterbug, any damn way?"

"I lost my husband that day a year ago too, Hélène." Chloé replied.

Hélène looked at her sister for a few long seconds before saying, "I'll see if she's receiving."

And slammed the door in Chloé's face.

Chloé dropped her head, shook it from side to side. "Oh, Hélène," she whispered. "You haven't changed a whit, *chère*. Who can hold a grudge longer than you?"

Chloé smoothed her cotton dress under her as she sat on the rough unpainted porch steps with her feet on the dirt. *How many times over the years did I sit in this very spot, looking out over this same view wishing I could be anywhere else but here? Careful what you wish for. That's what Grand-*

père Abélard always told me. How was I ever supposed to know that getting one dream could cost so much? One with the sweet silly name of Jitterbug?

It had been twenty-eight years since Josette Cormier dropped her two young daughters off at her parents' home one hot August afternoon saying she was going to pick up some boudin at the little store down the road and would be back in two shakes.

"I believe dat be the last we sees a her now," said Cécile.

Her husband Abélard looked at her with his eyes wide. "You tink?"

She nodded.

"Cho! I got an ahnvee for some boudin."

Cécile looked at her husband in astonishment. "Fool! Boudin! That's all you care about when I jus' tol' you your girl pro'ly on her way gone for good an we got des two yong'ns to look after?"

"Well, beb, ain't like we ain't been 'spectin' it."

They looked over at the two little girls squatting at the edge of the shallow bayou water, poking around in it with sticks, stirring up mud and tadpoles while zirondelles flitted between them.

"Dos two," said Abelard. "Dey gonna be okay. Better here den wit dey mama."

Cécile nodded. "But will dey be happy? Or will dey want more? Like dey mama?"

Hélène and Chloé were happy.

Until they weren't.

There was a lot of growing up years during which the girls roamed free as the white-tailed deer they watched graze peacefully in the area surrounding their home on the bayou.

They filled their days fishing with *Grand-père* Abélard or helping *Grand-mère* Cécile tend the garden or standing next to her at the stove learning the magic of roux used in the many soups and stews their grandmother served up.

As Hélène became as good a cook as her *grand-mère*, Chloé became more intrigued with another side of Cécile's talents.

While Hélène perfected her maque chou and pain perdu, Chloé was spending time in a small room off her grand-parents' bedroom studying old and elaborate bottles containing roots, powders and herbs Cécile used in making potions she sold to bayou residents. Potions for healing, she said.

Following the halcyon childhood years came the time-honored and not unexpected years of teenage rebellion when the bayou was no longer enough. The music from the big cities seemed to waft across the bayou on a whisper, calling their names.

Abélard and Cécile could hear the whispers too. They were the same ones that tempted and finally won their daughter Josette. Would it take Josette's daughters away from them too?

They decided it was time for a party. A fais do-do like this bayou hadn't seen in years. A party to bring in some of the young folks for Hélène and Chloé to catch up on local gossip, many of whom would never consider leaving the bayou and a lifestyle they loved. Maybe help remind the girls what they loved about their bayou home.

What started out as a party for the girls ended up being a huge source of pleasure for Abélard and Cécile as well. As the cooking and plans for music and dancing progressed, so did the clearing out of an old barn that hadn't been used for a party in a long, long time.

By the time neighbors and far-flung friends started arriving, there were tables spread around for food and drinks, chairs scattered around outside and in the barn. More tables set up for eating and the ever-present, never-ending games of bouree.

There was a stage for the musicians which would include probably half the people showing up. The band was an always changing group of people, but the music was a constant.

The dance floor was set and poles for stringing lights were erected.

This was, indeed, going to be a fais do-do to outshine past and future fais do-dos, without a doubt.

When all was ready and the time came, yee-haws and cat calls signaled the first wave of pickup trucks as they approached the house.

Abélard and Cécile stood smiling on the front porch as Hélène and Chloé ran out into the yard to see who was arriving, welcoming their guests with hugs and laughter.

Hélène gave out a squeal as a group of handsome young men began jumping out of the back of one of the trucks with more piling out of the cab. "Hey, how many coonass Cajuns can this truck hold, anyways?" she hollered.

"Cho, Beb!" asked Matthieu Ducet as he swung Hélène wrapped in a bear hug. "Who you callin' coonass Cajun? Don' it take one to know one? Even if she is one gorgeous Cajun woman!" When he put her feet back on the ground, she kept her arms around his neck, smiling up at him. He couldn't seem to let go and grinned back down into her face, lost in those green eyes of hers.

"I have missed you, you ol' fool."

"And I you, you evil witchy woman. You dun put a gris-gris on me, girl."

They laughed with one another and walked off arm in arm. They had a lot of catching up to do. Matthieu had grown up just down the road, but had moved to The Island and had found steady work with a group of guys he'd met up with and formed a band. They played a regular weekly gig at one of the fancy downtown hotels and had made a name for themselves.

Chloé walked shyly towards Justin Moreau, hanging back watching while he carefully removed his fiddle case from the cab of the truck. She watched him sit on the running board, open the case, take his fiddle out and start strumming it, stopping to tune it a little as he played.

"That always was your favorite thing to do, strum that ol' fiddle of yours," Chloé said.

Justin looked up. "Chloé," he said softly.

They looked at one another for what seemed like forever before Justin finally stood and opened his arms. Chloé walked into them and felt like she had come home.

He held her and kissed the top of her head gently. "I have missed you, *bebe*."

"I was afraid you wouldn't come."

"I tried not to. You underestimate your hold on me, *mon petit*. Always."

They were still standing that way when they heard a few whispers and harumphs behind them.

"Are you going to stand there holding that wee gal all day, or are we going to make us some zydeco, *beau*?"

Justin threw back his head, laughed loudly, and yelled, "*Laissez les bon temps rouler!*"

And, so it began.

Over the next three days, people constantly came and went, most bringing food and beverages of every sort. There was cooking over an open pit, bouree games being played at more than one table, and raucous laughter from every corner. And the music never stopped.

Even as people slipped into tents at night, the music continued. Someone might be sitting off alone at the edge of the bayou playing a sad and lonely tune, making a trumpet sound so forlorn a body just wanted to die.

Hélène and Chloé loved sitting on the front porch at dawn

so they could watch their world come alive as the sun came up. As all the swamp creatures began to stir and the birds began their morning songs, so did the boys lift their heads from their pickup trucks, brushing aside mosquito netting, wiping the sleep from their eyes.

"I wish they'd stay forever," said Hélène.

Chloé nodded.

"Justin is just as smitten with you now as he was before he left for New Orleans. Think he'll move back?"

Chloé bent her head to drink her *café au lait*. She didn't want Hélène to see the tears in her eyes. "He says he's going back today."

Hélène put her arm around Chloé's shoulders. "I'm sorry, *soeur*."

"And Matthieu? Is he going back?" Chloé asked.

"He is, but we both know it's only going to be temporary. The bayou is in his blood. He knows he won't be able to stay away. He wants to make some money, put it away, then come back and open a place. A restaurant. A bar. Someplace for music and dancing."

"Here?"

"Not here, but close. Closer to town."

The girls sat quietly drinking their coffee, watching and listening to the morning sounds. Each wrapped in thoughts of their future.

After her sister slammed the door on her, Chloé sat on the cold steps for so long she drifted into a half-sleep before she felt a tap on her shoulder. A little harder than necessary. She looked up and Hélène was looking at her with a strange expression in her eyes. "Chloé? Are you okay, girl?"

"I guess. Who knows? Right?" Chloé held a half-hearted smile as she got up from the steps. "Just drifted off to a long time ago, is all."

"And a land far away, as we used to say?" asked Hélène.

"Ha. So you do remember some of the good times?"

"Oh, yes. I remember. I remember when you were only dreaming about that little shop in New Orleans you always wanted. You always said you'd name it Jitterbug after that crazy book you loved so much. And it just makes the hard times harder. You know?"

"I do." Chloé walked over and took Hélène in her arms. "I have missed you."

After hesitating, Hélène hugged her sister close. "I have missed you, *soeur*." When she stepped back, Chloé saw the tears in her eyes.

As they stood looking at one another, searching for words to say to ease past hurts, they heard Cécile's voice.

"Ah, chil'ren, chil'ren—come in da house. Do not be ignoring your ol' *grand-mère*."

Holding hands, the women walked into the living room where Cécile sat like a queen in the old chair Chloé always pictured her sitting in. The chair that had been there even before they were dropped off to spend the rest of their growing years in this house with their grandparents. The chair from which Cécile ruled her small kingdom and where she held both her girls in her lap as she read to them, taught them and sang to them.

Chloé ran to her grandmother, fell to her knees, dropped her head into her lap, and sobbed as though her heart was breaking into a million little shards of past hurts and mistakes.

"Shhh. Shhh, *bebe*. We gawn make it all right," Cécile whispered as she rocked her girl as though she were the youngster she had once been. "Shhh, now."

Once Chloé had cried all the tears she'd been holding in her heart for so long and fallen into an exhausted sleep, her sister eased her off Cécile's lap onto a pallet she'd made up of soft feather pillows on the floor, slipped a pillow under her head and covered her with one of the faded and threadbare quilts that were scattered about the house.

When Chloé woke up several hours later, the house was in darkness except for the dim light from a single old lamp sitting on a table in the front window. The same lamp that had been sitting on that same table in that same spot since before Chloé was born. There was comfort in knowing that some things could be counted on to stay the same. This house wrapped its comfort of sameness around Chloé, and she felt safe for the first time in quite some time. Since the sudden brutal death of her husband, love of her life, and best friend since childhood, Justin Moreau.

"Oh, Justin," she whispered. "We should have stayed here. Right here. You'd still be with me, and we would have all the years we thought we would have still ahead of us."

Chloé bowed her head and cried. Again. No amount of tears were ever going to ease her broken heart.

When she woke again, the sun shone through the windows and she heard Cécile and Hélène in the kitchen.

She wrapped the quilt around her shoulders and walked into the kitchen, following the smells of *café au lait* brewing and beignets cooking.

Her grandmother hugged her close. "Good morning, *chère*."

Hélène ignored her until she walked over to wrap her in a hug. "Good morning, sweetie. Please don't stay mad at me. Life is too hard to have to live with you mad at me too."

Hélène hugged her back.

"I am so sad about your Matthieu," Chloe said. "And *Grand-père*. And my Justin. We should not be missing our men like this, and I would give everything I am, everything I have ever been, to have them back. Alive. Sitting around that table making music like they did so many times. Is it my fault they're dead?" She looked at her sister and her grandmother. "Dear God, is it?"

Cécile moved toward her granddaughter and looked her in the eyes. "No. No, *bebe*. And you must stop tinkin' like dat."

Chloé looked at Hélène with a question in her eyes.

Hélène shook her head. "No. But I needed to be angry at someone. How else can I stand this? How else can I live? I do not want life without him."

Then Hélène looked at both her sister and her grandmother. Her eyes hardened and her face set like stone. "It may not have been your fault, *soeur*, but you two knew you were playing at something dangerous. I tried to tell you, but no—you insisted it would be all right. Well. It wasn't. You both need to own and take responsibility for playing with fire. Selling 'pretend' spells and potions in the city at that ridiculous shop, Jitterbug, to tourists may have been a good way to make money, but look at the price. Look at the price!" Her breath caught, she put her hands in front of her face and ran out the back door.

Later that evening after a day of all three women going about their separate business quietly and alone, they joined around the kitchen table with *café au lait* and left-over red beans and rice.

Chloé straightened her back. "Hélène is right. And now, we need to do something to make it right. I'm here so you can help me figure out what that is."

Hélène snorted. "You gawn work one a your spells, girl, and bring back our husbands?" She asked with derision as she lit a cigarette and walked away from the table. She stood with her back to them in the doorway staring into the distance.

Cécile spoke quietly. "We cain't bring dem back, but I sho

can work a spell. Not a pretend one neither. I get dese bad people botherin' Chloé to back off. Dey wish dey hadn't ever heared a' New Orleans voodoo. Wish they hadn't spent all dey mama's money on pretend spells and den be mad 'cause dey didn't work. Fools! What dey tinkin'? Dat you can buy ready-made gris-gris at the cahner sto' like bread and milk? Chloé dun tol' dose peeshwanks she won't sellin' de real ting. Jus' for fun stuff to take home. Souvenirs. Like da glass beads, little voodoo dolls wit' pins, all dat junk, jus' bags a' swamp dirt was alla was. She tol' dem dat!"

"She might have told them that," said Helene. "It might even have been on that sign hanging on the wall. It might even have been printed on the bag the stuff was packaged in. Don't matter. They were still upset enough 'bout it not doing what they say it was supposed to do that they felt the need to come back and raise a little hell. A little hell that got out of control and ended up with people dead. One of those coonass fools and all three of our husbands. Drunks and guns. What have we come to that every redneck boy in the south can't go out anymore without his gun? Give him a gun and a beer and he loses every bit of sense he might have had. A good man trying to talk sense turns into the enemy and ends up dead. Lying in a New Orleans street in a puddle of blood with a fiddle still in his hand."

"What do you want to do, *Grand-mère*?" asked Chloé.

"This," said Cecile.

The three women sat around that table drinking coffee and talking all night.

Cécile did indeed have a plan.

For a woman who had done nothing but good with her knowledge of voodoo and magic her whole life, her plan was dark and it was evil. The women started tasting vengeance sitting around that table, and it began tasting sweet.

By the time the sun came up, they each had a list in front of them of their individual tasks they needed to take care of before the plan would be complete.

Hélène and Chloé were instructed to go their separate ways. Chloé into the woods and into the swamp. Hélène to an old cemetery a few miles on the other side of town. They were told not to come back until they found every item Cécile needed, and to bring her everything as soon as they had collected each item on their lists.

When Chloé returned late that night, she found Hélène and Cécile in the little room off her grandparents' bedroom. The same little room where she had learned so much from her grandmother so long ago. A room which she now saw through different eyes. She now realized how much power was contained in the boxes and the bottles. How much those written words in the old books could actually do. Hélène was right, she had played with fire. Stupidly. It had ended in a way she never could have dreamed. Three good men dead just so she could 'play' and make some money in a funky little shop in New Orleans selling doo-dads and gee-gaws. Harmless junk sold with what she thought was just a fun air of magic and mystery. Just another harmless Crescent City tourist trap. Pretend voodoo.

"You found everything, *chère?*" asked Cécile.

Chloé nodded and placed the filled burlap sacks on the floor.

"Good. Now, you bot go cleanup and gawn to bed. Leave me to my work."

Both women, tired to their bones, did so without argument.

Hours later, Cécile woke both women with a gruff, "Up. We gots work to do. No needs to git dressed. Nobody gawn sees you where we goin'."

Hélène and Chloé followed Cécile out to her old truck and climbed in still barefoot and wearing only their nightgowns.

They snuggled against one another and went back to sleep. Neither of them surprised when they saw where Cécile had brought them. They were in Saint Louis Cemetery No. 1.

Climbing down from the truck, they followed their grandmother to an old crypt in the far corner, the oldest part of the cemetery where stately old live oaks dripping with Spanish moss towered over the crypt. Without speaking, Chloé and Hélène sat on an ornate concrete bench a ways from the crypt while Cécile stood close to it, whispering words they didn't even want to hear. They watched her pace and whisper and wave her hands. They watched her stoop down and leave a gris-gris bag and a bottle of whiskey. Watched when she stood, marked an "X" on the side of the tomb, knocked on it with her fist, made three turns and yelled for help to do the right thing. When she turned and walked away they followed her, went home and back to bed, sure there must have been a reason why their presence was needed, but they didn't ask. They knew they had just paid a visit to The Queen. Voodoo Priestess Marie Laveau.

When they woke up, Cécile and the truck were gone. There were scraps of fabric and string, organic debris that looked like tree bark and dirt and a few half-empty bottles they recognized from Cécile's little room off the bedroom on the kitchen table. Chloé and Hélène exchanged glances, silently deciding they'd have their *café au lait* and cold couche-couche on the front porch this morning rather than at the kitchen table.

"Should we be worried?" asked Chloé.

"Probably," replied Hélène.

It was after midnight when Cécile returned. The sound of the front door opening awakened Chloé and Hélène. Their grandmother ignored them and went straight to her room. When she didn't return, Chloé and Hélène went to bed.

The next morning when Chloé and Hélène entered the kitchen, the table had been cleared and cleaned, two steaming cups of *café au lait* were on the table but there was no sign of Cécile. They looked to see if the truck was gone and it was.

Again, Cécile returned after midnight, and once again went to bed ignoring her granddaughters.

The next morning when the young women went into the kitchen, Cécile was at the stove making beignets and greeted them with a cheerful good morning.

It wasn't until they were settled around the table that she told them they would be going into New Orleans when they finished. To go put on their "goin' to da city" clothes.

When the three women pulled up in front of the closed and locked door to the little shop Chloé had been running for the past several years, the first thing they each noticed were all the flowers piled on the old wooden stoop. Then they noticed pictures of *Grand-père* Abélard, Matthieu and Justin taped to the storefront windows. Then they heard the music. The street was soon filled with second-line parade folks made up of old friends. They played their instruments, they shook their tambourines and they hollered and waved to Cécile, Chloé and Hélène as they passed, wishing them all well, marking the anniversary of walking their husbands back home in finest New Orleans fashion.

"Did you plan this?" asked Helene. "Is this what you've been doing the couple days you've been missing?"

"No, *chère*. I only hear 'bout dis early dis morning," Cécile answered. She took her granddaughters' hands. "Les walk. Get a bite at some café."

Hélène and Chloé both noticed their grandmother seemed to be looking for someone as they passed one café after another. Chloé heard Hélène's stomach growl and giggled. "We should stop at one of these places, say, rather than walking by them all till we're back home again."

Hélène put a hand against her noisy stomach. "Good idea, yes."

Cécile ignored them and continued walking until suddenly stopping with a strange look on her face. A tall man walked out of the café towards them, took Cécile's hand, kissed her on both cheeks and whispered in her ear. She squeezed his hand as he led them towards the café and pulled out chairs for each of them. A waiter showed up with *café au lait* for each of them, another showed up with a basket of hot beignets. Each kissed Cécile's cheeks and smiled at her lovingly as she introduced each of them to her "girls."

Once they were left alone, Cécile pulled out a bag and took a deep breath. She reached in and handed each of them a small doll, and placed a third one on the table next to her coffee.

Hélène and Chloé studied the dolls, which were dressed as young men. But as they looked closer they saw details which made them uncomfortable. They were mean-looking, dressed in scraps of dirty clothing, and they had stains on them that looked like blood.

"Shush, now!" said Cécile. And she pointed.

At a table at the end of the patio were three young men.

Chloé and Hélène looked at them, looked at their dolls and looked at the men again.

"Oh, no," whispered Chloé.

Hélène shook her head. "Are those...?"

"Yes," said Chloé. "Those are the men who killed our husbands. Shot them dead in front of me. Because they said I sold them 'cheap shit.' Cheap shit that didn't do what it was supposed to do. They came in drunk and rowdy and dirty after trying to murder their own father with 'pretend' gris-gris they bought for fifty dollars. And then spent hundreds more on other stuff. Stuff I told them was just souvenir junk. Not the real thing, and pretended I thought there was no such thing as the real thing. That voodoo was just made up and not to believed. They said their mother said I was a liar and she wanted them to get her money back. That she didn't get the kind of return on her investment she was looking for. But there was a fourth one with them. When he tried to calm his brothers down, one of them shot him. It was an accident, but dead he was as I was opening the cash box to return their money. Then all hell broke loose and our men ended up dead in the dirt beside the boy. Right where they were just sitting on the stoop playing their fiddles and singing. Shot dead by drunk fools while making music."

By now all three women had tears rolling down their faces as they watched the three men at the end of the patio. Watched them eating beignets and drinking *café au lait* as though everything was still right in the world. They didn't seem the least bit saddened by the loss of their brother and probably had given no thought to the men they had killed.

The police had arrested them, but their rich mommy and a crooked lawyer had them out on bail in no time. In time, a jury would decide their fate.

In the meantime, Cécile wanted them to suffer.

Hélène wanted to go get a gun and shoot them on the spot.

Cécile said no.

"We make dem suffer. If dey end up in jail fo da rest of dey lives, we still make dem suffer. It's da right ting."

With those words, she put a pin in the stomach of the doll she was holding. The meanest, dirtiest of the three dolls. As they watched, one of the men at the table they were watching grabbed his stomach and bent forward. As Cécile pushed the pin a little harder, the man screamed a bloodcurdling scream. Others on the patio looked up and watched as the man fell out of his chair and began writhing in pain. They watched and never moved.

Hélène, Chloé and Cécile watched also.

They finished their coffee, put their dolls into their purses and walked back to their truck.

They drove by the café on their way home. There was an ambulance parked in front and the young man was being placed inside it. Just as that was happening, Hélène and Chloé pushed little pins into their dolls. One of the men grabbed his head and fell to the ground screaming. The third man grabbed his neck. He also fell to the ground screaming. Hélène and Chloé waved to the other patrons on the patio, who waved back, nodding and smiling.

"Hear me now, girls. By all dat is holy in da name of The Queen, we is fini wid dat 'pretend voodoo' stuff. Dat Jitterbug place? It now be da real ting."

Chloé shook her head. "No..."

Cécile raised her hand and looked at her granddaughter sharply. "Shush, you. I have made a promise. A promise not to be broke. A promise made to the spirit of Madame Laveau. We gawn keep dat promise. You had no bidnes playing dose games you played. Dat's over now. Y'all hear me? Over!"

"Yes, ma'am," whispered Chloé.

Hélène and Chloé both suppressed shivers as they turned into the gates of Saint Louis Cemetery No. 1. They were here to draw a circle around the "X" they had left on Marie Laveau's crypt earlier. Drawing the circle signified their favor had been granted, and they now had a deal. That deal was binding. Anyone not believing it so was a fool.

Leaving the crypt Hélène stopped suddenly and grabbed Chloé's arm. "Did you hear..."

Chloé paled. "I heard. But surely to God, Marie Laveau did not just say to us from the grave *'Pretend voodoo, my wrinkled old ass.'* Did she?"

The Blue Delta
John Floyd

It was quiet at the edge of the woods.

Leonard Drago crouched in the underbrush and stared out at the flatlands stretching away beyond the last of the forest. He had hoped to cross those treeless fields under the cover of darkness, but the sun was already peeking over another patch of woods to the east. And he couldn't go east. His destination was straight ahead, north past this bone-dry farmland and on into the sad outskirts of his hometown, Bayou LeBlanc, where his dimwitted but loyal third cousin might be convinced to hide him until all this blew over.

Which might take a while. Leonard Drago wasn't your common criminal, and what they'd be sending after him wasn't your usual pursuit. Drago knew this would be a full-blown, multi-agency manhunt, and for good reason: he had escaped last night from the state prison seven miles from here, murdering a guard in the process and a civilian two hours later. It was this second killing that irked him. He'd encountered a drunk staggering down a gravel road in the middle of the night (how unlucky was *that*?), and in his distinctive orange jumpsuit Drago had had no choice but to kill him. Even more frustrating was that after strangling the idiot and going through his pockets, Drago had come up with almost nothing useful. No gun, no money, no cell phone. He did discover a fifth of bourbon and a hunting knife, though, both of which might come in handy. He'd also taken the guy's baseball cap and jeans (the shirt was too gaudy and eye-catching). The body Drago had thrown into a ditch beside the road, along with his prison outfit. Orange might *be* the new black on TV; in real life, a jailbird jumpsuit was a liability.

He desperately wished that that dirt road had produced a driver instead of a pedestrian. With wheels, there was a chance he could've been out of here, maybe out of the state, before the roadblocks went up—but now here he was, still afoot in an area only a short distance from the town where a bungled bank robbery fifteen years ago had ended a promising career in drug trafficking and petty theft. A young and stoned Drago had happily shot three people in that heist—two bank employees and a policeman. As a result, one of the ladies had died, and he'd later heard the cop had lost an arm. But the really bad thing, at least in Drago's view, was that all those sins lumped together had sent him up the river (literally, since the prison was located on the north bank of the mighty Blue) to serve a life sentence.

Until last night. He was no lifer now. He was free, and he didn't plan to get sent back.

For the tenth time, Albert Leonard "Skinny Lenny" Drago took a swallow of his latest victim's booze and checked his immediate surroundings, looking for snakes. He hated snakes. Satisfied on that score, he capped the bottle, took a deep breath, searched the horizon, and focused on a lone house about a mile away across the fields, the only sign of civilization anywhere in this stretch of the pancake-flat Blue River delta. A small barn and several outbuildings surrounded the house: a struggling farm, probably. But even a struggling farmer might have some cash tucked away, and a gun that Drago could steal.

He left the cover of the trees and headed north.

Jake Greenwood was using strips of cloth to tie his tomato plants to a row of upright poles in the garden that bordered his side yard when he looked behind him and saw the man approaching. A short, pale guy in a white T-shirt and baggy jeans, trudging toward him from the distant woods. On his lowered head was a dark blue baseball cap with something written on the front, still too far away to read.

Jake should probably have been more surprised to see someone out here alone and on foot—and certainly more suspicious. But right now he was thinking mostly about his dry and droopy garden and the dead battery in his truck, the one that was keeping him from running errands and fetching supplies from town. And about the fact that his best friend, Virgil Woodson, had promised he'd buy a new battery and bring it out this morning. Virgil was supposed to arrive any minute now, and Jake wanted to get these tomato vines squared away first.

He had managed to tie half a dozen more plants to their poles by the time the stranger reached the garden. "Mornin'," a voice said, from behind him. "Sad-looking tomatoes."

"They need rain," Jake replied.

He tucked the remaining ties into his pocket, wiped his hands on his overalls, and turned.

Drago stood there a moment, facing the tall black farmer, thinking hard.

He figured he had two options, one of which was to threaten this guy with his knife, force him into the house, find a gun (in Drago's experience, everybody in the South owned a gun), take him or a member of his family as a hostage, and drive out of here in the car or truck or whatever occupied the little garage he'd seen on the far side of the house. He felt sure there *was* a family. A swing set with a slide stood in the dusty yard, and a girl's bike leaned against a side porch. Drago thought he'd even spotted a small face in one of the back windows, watching him as he crossed the field, but he was so tired he wasn't certain.

The problem was, this fellow didn't look easy to threaten. He was big, and appeared to be strong as an ox. The better option, Drago decided, was to kill him quick—strong wouldn't matter if Drago got in close enough with the knife. Then he could try to locate a firearm and a vehicle and get going. As for taking a family member along as a hostage, that was probably a bad idea. Leonard Drago's policy was to travel alone and leave no witnesses.

With those things in mind, he relaxed his expression and said, "I need your help."

For a long time they stood there looking at each other.

Finally the farmer said, "You on the run?"

Drago studied the man's face. There was no friendliness in those eyes, no softening of the solemn features. But something about that face, and that no-nonsense voice, made Drago wonder if the guy might have run afoul of the law too, at some point, and if so, maybe he wasn't a big fan of what he would probably call the po-leece. Maybe the enemy of my enemy is my friend.

Still, it was better to take no chances. As he inched his way closer, Drago slowly reached behind him, lifted the tail of his T-shirt, and gripped the handle of the knife in his belt. "Nothing like that," he said. "I'm just lost. Got separated from my survey team south of here, near Blue River, and when I got through the woods—well, I saw your house, and..." He kept approaching as he talked, and at last he was standing there beside the row of tomato poles, right in front of the guy, an arm's length away.

Drago tightened his fingers on the knife, began easing it out—

And heard the distant rumble of a car motor.

Both of them turned to look at the dirt road bordering the property. A mile away, across the flats, a vehicle was headed slowly toward them, pulling a white cloud of dust behind it.

Even at that distance Drago could see the rack of lights across the top of the car. A police cruiser.

When he turned again, he found the man staring at him.

"I'll ask you again," the farmer said. "Somebody after you?"

Drago glanced once more at the approaching car, and realized he had to change his plan. He swallowed, let his shoulders sag, lowered the tail of his shirt. "Yeah. The truth is, I been growing some weed, me and my daddy. They arrested him yesterday, but I snuck away. I got relatives in Bayou LeBlanc—if I can get there I'll be safe." He stepped back behind the corner of the nearest outbuilding. "Help me, mister. Please. At least hide me for a few minutes."

The farmer hesitated a moment more, then nodded toward two slanted wooden doors set into the base of the shed beside them, out of view of the driveway. A storm cellar, Drago figured. In the grass next to the doors lay a pair of gloves and high-topped boots.

"In there," the man said. "It's the one place they won't search."

"Why?"

"Because it's locked. Barred." He pointed to the two-by-four wedged through the two handles of the cellar doors.

"So?"

"So I'll lock it again after you're inside. You can't very well do it yourself, right?"

"What if they figure out you did it *for* me?"

"Think about it," the farmer said. "Why would I hide a white man?"

That made sense.

Without another word the farmer walked to the cellar, bent down, slid the board free of the handles, and swung one of the doors open on its hinges. It *thunked* backward against the wooden side of the shed.

Drago followed him, stepping over the boots and gloves.

He looked for a long moment at the cellar, at the steps leading down into the darkness under the building. Being locked up— locked up *down there*—gave him goosebumps. But the patrol car was here now; he heard it crunch to a stop at the head of the driveway.

He knew he had no choice.

"Get in," the farmer said.

Minutes later Leonard Drago stood on tiptoe on the second step inside the cellar, squinting out through the tiny spaces between the slats of one of the closed and barred doors. The cop's car was parked out of sight, and the farmer had strolled out to meet his visitor. A moment later Drago saw them move into view, walking out across the side yard. The cop, a black guy in a uniform and a cowboy hat—was *everybody* black in this state now?—was holding an unlit cigar in one hand and a notepad in the other. As Drago watched, the cop put the cigar between his teeth, opened the pad, and flipped pages. He seemed to be asking questions, and pointing to the south; the farmer replied with frowns and thoughtful shakes of his head.

Drago felt his heart speeding up. He felt sure the conversation was related to him and his whereabouts. What if the policeman was explaining that the man they were searching for was not a dope grower but was in fact a thief and a murderer and an escaped convict? Drago waited, holding his breath, watching for a raised head and a pointing finger and a drawn gun.

It didn't happen. After a couple more minutes, the cop put his notepad away. He and the farmer wandered back toward the driveway, out of Drago's field of vision, chatting like old friends (so much for the hope that this guy hated cops, Drago thought), and after a moment he heard them pass beside his shed. On the way to the house, presumably.

Time ticked away. At one point Drago again thought he heard footsteps behind his hiding place, going away from the house this time, but he heard no voices.

Then he heard a car cranking, and the crunch of its tires on gravel, and the unmistakable sound of its motor receding in the distance. The cop must have left.

But nothing else happened. Drago waited, sweating, for his unlikely benefactor to return, to open the doors and let him out—after which he planned to repay the farmer by slitting his throat, and anyone else's who happened to be on the premises. But no one showed up.

Five minutes passed. Ten. Drago stepped down and moved to the right, trying to see his surroundings in the almost-darkness, and felt his foot hit something hard. He knelt, probed about, and found a huge rectangular pan containing a couple inches of water. Why was *that* here? No matter—at least he wouldn't die of thirst. As that thought occurred to him, he moved up the steps once more, raised his fists, and pounded on the doors. "Let me out!" he shouted.

Still he saw nothing outside the cellar, and heard nothing. He stepped down again.

And then he did hear something. Something *inside*. A movement, off to his left.

He felt his stomach turn over. *Something was in here with him.*

Drago pulled out his knife, held his breath. Tiny bands of light sliced in through the narrow cracks in the doors, but not enough to allow him to see the rest of the room.

He heard another sound, from the right this time. Quiet, whispery, like something brushing across wood. Then more sounds, behind him.

He felt bile rising in his throat, panic arrowing through him. Leonard Drago had been through hard times and scary situations, but he'd never felt fear like this before. He shouted again, wordless this time, a cry of pure terror.

Now there were more sounds, hissing sounds, sliding sounds, and a dusty, whirring buzz that he couldn't pin down. His knees went weak; he shifted position, and stepped on something thick and soft—he felt it move underneath his foot. Off balance, Drago fell to the floor.

Then everything happened at once. Something heavy and sharp hit him just below his ear, like a club with spikes on it. Something else slammed into his cheek, his forehead, his throat.

By now he knew what was it was.

He started screaming again.

At that moment, eight miles away, Deputy Sheriff Virgil Woodson stood on the front steps of the local library with his friend Jake Greenwood, looking through a window at the meeting room. Inside, Jake's wife Dee and his eleven-year-old daughter Kendra were taking their seats. On a makeshift stage in front of them stood a knight, a lady, and a giant frog.

Watching his family, Jake said, "Thanks for giving us a ride, Virge. And for not asking any questions in front of Dee."

"That's me—protect and serve," the deputy said. He looked around to make sure they were alone. "But I'm asking now. You gonna tell me what's going on?"

"In a minute. I'm just lucky there was a performance here today."

Virgil Woodson looked through the window again at Jake's wife and daughter. "It's the only thing I could think of to get them away from the house. And since I *am* finally asking questions—why did you all of a sudden *need* to get them away from the house?"

Jake gave him a strange look. "Because I didn't want to have to explain the sounds they might hear coming from the storm cellar."

"Say what?"

Jake checked his watch. "But I'm thinking that might be over with, by now. Let's give it a while longer—then I'll fill you in on the way back."

"Back where?"

"To my house. I told Dee I'd come back here and pick her and Kendra up later. I need you to help me with something." He looked idly toward Virgil's cruiser, parked at the curb.

"You're taking this 'serve' thing a long way," Virgil said. "You mean you need help with the new battery I brought you for your pickup? The one you didn't want me to take time to unload when we were *at* your house?"

"Yeah," Jake said. "That, too."

Half an hour later, after the short ride back home and after telling a stunned Virgil about this morning's unexpected visitor, Jake Greenwood dropped a coil of rope onto the ground beside his storm cellar, then knelt and removed the bar from the double doors for the second time that day. He pulled one of the doors open and let it fall against the base of the shed. In the harsh light he and Virgil saw a body lying on its back, still as a stone, at the bottom of the cellar steps.

Virgil whistled. "You were right. That's him."

"You think I'd have done this if there was any doubt?"

They stayed silent a moment, studying the corpse. That it was a corpse was obvious: the upturned face was swollen and bloody and pale as marble, the eyes open and staring as if wondering who was suddenly letting in all that light. The white T-shirt was speckled with red. Lying on the floorboards beside the body was a hunting knife and an Atlanta Braves ball cap.

"Hard to believe," Virgil said quietly. "What are the odds?"

"What?"

"The odds. That this particular guy, out of all the places he could've gone, would come to this particular farm."

"What are the odds that you'd show up in that patrol car just before he killed me?"

Virgil turned to his friend. "Was it that close?"

"He had his hand behind him, probably on that knife you see there. I'd be dead if you hadn't blundered in to bring me my battery. So would my family." Jake stayed silent a minute, deep in thought. "Divine intervention, maybe."

"Could be," Virgil said. "Funny thing is, I wasn't just coming to help get your car going—in case you don't remember, before you took me inside I asked you some questions the sheriff told me to ask. Questions you wouldn't answer, about this dude and his escape last night."

"Well, he won't be escaping again. Or killing anybody else."

Virgil wiped a hand over his face and glanced at the road to town. "You sure Dee and Kendra won't leave early, find another way home from the library, and catch us at this?"

"I told you, I'm supposed to pick 'em up. Then I'm taking Dee over to visit her dad."

Virgil was still frowning. "Them LSU folks ain't coming today, are they?"

"Next week," Jake said. "Are you done?"

"Done with what?"

"Are you finished trying to think up reasons we can't do this?"

Virgil blew out a sigh. "I guess."

Jake grabbed the gloves and tall boots sitting beside the cellar doors, pulled them on, threw the coil of rope over his shoulder, and walked straight down the steps. He checked carefully to make sure there was nothing lurking inside the dead man's clothes, then picked him up long enough to work a loop of the rope underneath the body's armpits and lash it tight. Moments later, he and Virgil heaved the limp body out of the cellar and onto the brittle grass outside. Jake wrapped it in a bedsheet and bound it with rope at the neck and knees.

It took five minutes to carry the body the two hundred yards west to an abandoned well. They dumped it, sheet and rope and all, into the well and tossed the knife and baseball cap in on top. Then they shoveled in several feet of dirt. Afterward, breathing hard, Virgil said, "Why don't I feel worse about this?"

"Because we were soldiers once," Jake said. "Kill or be killed. This isn't that different."

Virgil thought about that awhile, then nodded sadly. "Yeah, it is. You know it is."

"You saying I shouldn't have done it?"

"No." Virgil picked up his shovel, balanced it on his shoulder like a ditchdigger at quitting time, and stared worriedly up at the sky. "I just wish we'd be given a sign, that's all."

"A what?"

"A sign of some kind. An earthquake, a pillar of pink clouds, a James Earl Jones voice from above." He was still squinting into the clear blue heavens. "Or rain, maybe. That could be our sign, you know? A message, that everything's okay."

"There's no rain in the forecast, Virge. Get hold of yourself."

"All right, all right," he growled, and started toward the house. "Let's go tend to your automotive needs. I'm better at that than this."

"Sounds good to me."

"But I wish we'd get a sign."

At two o'clock that afternoon, yet another patrol car arrived at the Greenwood farm. This one was marked BAYOU LEBLANC POLICE DEPARTMENT. Two white men climbed out. Jake, who had been kneeling on the porch beside an upturned rocking chair, rose to his feet, put down his screwdriver, and invited them in. His daughter Kendra was sitting in the kitchen eating a cookie; her eyes widened when the three men trooped in and joined her at the table.

Police Chief Louis Terrell smiled and said, "Afternoon, young lady." He sat and looked around. "Where's your mother?"

"She stayed in town a while, helping Grandpa," Kendra said.

"Give her my best." Without waiting for a reply, Terrell placed both his hands flat on the tabletop and looked at Jake. "Guess you've heard Lenny Drago escaped last night."

Jake nodded. "One of the sheriff's deputies has already been out here, asking about it."

"They're the parish," Terrell said. "I'm the city."

"Actually, Lou, this *is* the parish."

"Well, I'm just a chauffeur today, so it don't matter anyhow. By the way—Officer Heisley, meet Jacob Greenwood. And this little beauty is Kendra. Y'all, this is Charles Heisley, of the state police."

Jake shook hands, then said, "'Fraid I've already told Deputy Woodson everything I know. Which isn't much."

"Mainly we're just wondering if you might've seen anyone around last night or earlier today," Heisley said. "Especially this guy." He took a photo of Drago from his pocket and showed it to Jake and Kendra. "Thing is, we found a dead body in a ditch this morning near Blue River, about four miles south of here, next to a pile of prison clothes. It occurred to us Mr. Drago might've headed through this area to try to make it to Bayou LeBlanc."

"If you're on the run," Jake said, examining the photo, "why head for a town?"

"It's where he grew up, still has some kinfolks around. You might remember a bank robbery there, years ago. Delta National."

Jake looked sharply at Terrell, but saw nothing in his face. "I've heard about it," Jake said to Heisley.

"Then I take it you haven't seen anyone strange lately?"

"Just my friend—the deputy I mentioned. He likes to mooch a meal now and then."

"Well," Heisley said, tucking the photo back into his pocket, "this visit was more to inform you than to question you." He stood up, prompting everyone except Kendra to stand also. "We'll let you folks get back to whatever you were doing."

"Praying for rain, mostly."

"All farmers do that." He shook hands again with Jake. "But I understand you at least have another source of income."

"The snakes, you mean? It's more of a hobby than a job."

"Jake gets friends and neighbors to bring them to him," Terrell said, "and then zoos and medical centers come get 'em and pay him for 'em."

"Interesting. Where do you keep them?"

"A converted storm cellar," Jake said. "Only in warm weather—but that's most of the year. Feed 'em mice once a week, plenty of those around."

"What kind of snakes?"

"Cottonmouths, mostly. A few copperheads and rattlers. My biggest customers are medical labs at Tulane and LSU, which use them to develop anti-venom."

"Interesting," Heisley said again.

As they turned to leave, Chief Terrell lagged behind. "Can I use your facilities, Jake?" he said, pointing to the bathroom down the hall.

Jake nodded. "We'll be outside." He pointed to Kendra to stay put at the table, then followed Heisley through the living room and out the front door.

On the porch, Officer Heisley took a toothpick from a shirt pocket and put it in the corner of his mouth. Wiggling it up and down, he said, "I didn't want to say this in there, in front of your daughter, Mr. Greenwood, but this man Drago—he's a killer. One dead in that bank robbery I mentioned, years ago, and two more in drug deals before that. Not counting a prison guard and the guy we told you they found this morning. He was choked to death."

"I understand," Jake said.

"Make sure you do. Keep doors and windows locked, and be watchful." Heisley paused and seemed to soften a bit. "Terrell says you're a good man. Says he knew your parents."

"Everybody around here knows everybody," Jake said. "Or used to."

"Different world, now," Heisley agreed. He removed the toothpick and flicked it over the porch rail like a cigarette butt. "And that's a shame."

"My friend says we need a sign of some kind."

Heisley turned to look at him. "A sign?"

"You know. A miracle, an act of God. Something to show us we're on the right path."

"Maybe's he's right."

They fell silent. When Chief Terrell came out to join them, the two cops thanked Jake again and stepped down off the porch. Jake watched them walk to their cruiser as Kendra eased out the door and stood beside him. Just before Terrell climbed in behind the wheel, he gave Jake a pleased look, and a solemn little nod. And drove off.

Jake frowned at the dust cloud, thought a moment, and studied his daughter's face. "Did Lou Terrell say anything to you, in there?" Before she could answer, Jake added, "He asked to go to the bathroom. Did he go?"

"No." Kendra suddenly looked older than her years. "Soon as y'all went out onto the porch, he sat back down with me, at the table."

Jake felt a chill go up his spine. "What'd he say to you?"

"He asked me if I'd seen the guy in their picture. Drago."

"What'd you say?"

Kendra shifted from one foot to the other. "I said I did."

"What!?"

"I did, Daddy. I saw him through my window early this morning, coming across the back field from the trees, while you were outside working. He had on a cap and a white T-shirt."

"Why didn't you say something earlier? To me or Virgil?"

"Nobody asked me. I figured it was just somebody out hiking or something, until I saw that picture the Heisley man showed you. And then I was scared to say anything."

"You mention anything about this to your mother, this morning?"

"No, sir."

"What else did you tell the chief?"

She frowned, remembering. "I said I'd heard somebody talking, outside. Then I'd heard the storm-cellar door slam."

Jake lowered his head, rubbed his eyes with his thumbs. "What did Chief Terrell do?"

"He sort of nodded, to himself. Like all of a sudden he understood. Then he patted my head and got up and walked out to where y'all were."

Jake drew a long, shaky breath.

"Did I do something wrong, Daddy?"

"No, honey. I'm just glad it was Lou you told, and not the other guy."

Kendra went quiet. She seemed to think that over. "Can I ask a question?"

"Sure."

"What happened to his hand?"

"What?"

"The Chief. His left hand is—well, it's like plastic. What's it called..."

"A prosthetic. You never noticed it before?"

"I never thought to ask before. I know he always wears

long sleeves." She paused and said again, "What happened?"

This time it was Jake who hesitated. He stood there leaning against the porch rail, staring out over the delta.

"He got hurt, a long time ago," Jake said. "The day my mother died."

Kendra frowned. "The bank robbery, you mean?"

"Yes. Lou Terrell was there. He was shot." Jake looked his daughter in the eye. "He lost his arm, trying to save your grandma."

Kendra swallowed. He could see her mulling that over.

"But...Grandma died."

"Yes, she did. I wish you could've known her." He lifted a hand, touched his palm to her cheek. "Take a lesson, honey: Sometimes things don't work out the way they're supposed to."

For several minutes, neither of them spoke. Somewhere in the distance, a train whistle blew. A crow cawed.

At last she said, "The Chief—Mr. Terrell. He's a good friend?"

"He's a very good friend."

The silence dragged out. Jake turned to look at her. "What?" he said.

"Well...he's white."

Jake couldn't help smiling. "Friends are friends, Kendra. Another lesson."

He watched her think that over.

"Better get to your chores, kiddo. We need to go pick up your mom soon."

"Okay."

Jake had knelt again beside the broken chair, screwdriver in hand, when he realized his daughter hadn't moved. She was still staring at him, her eyes narrow and focused and—somehow—*knowing*.

"What is it, Kendra?"

"That man. Drago." She paused. "We won't have to worry about him anymore. Will we?"

"No."

She walked to the door and stopped, her hand on the knob. After a long wait she said, "Sometimes they do."

He looked at her. "What?"

"Sometimes things *do* work out."

Jake just nodded.

He watched her go inside, then went back to his work. He was tightening the last screw on the mended rocker when he heard something, a soft pattering like the tap of fingertips on a drum. The sound grew, first to a trembling rumble, then to a roar. He turned to look out at the darkening yard, the driveway, the suddenly dripping eaves of the barn roof—and smiled.

It was raining.

Never Tell Red
Paula Pumphrey

It was a summer day like any other but something reminded him of how his daddy would squint his right eye at the bayou and say it was the calm before the storm and, for sure, those southern winds would whip up later. The old man's warning came back to him now about seven years after he died.

Captain Allain Broussard stood at the rail of his houseboat feeling it sway from side to side beneath him. Green water lapped against the yellow paint under the boat's name, *Night on the Bayou*, as eight passengers boarded for a Louisiana bayou tour. A man in a Pirates baseball cap pointed to the water saying maybe they'd spot "Old Monk," a snappy, eleven-foot alligator he read about in a guide book back at the hotel in New Orleans. Old Monk hid in the waters and had a fine reputation for lunging at tourists.

Some passengers posed for selfies in front of trees dangling with moss like Mardi Gras beads. A woman pulled a note-book and pencil from her backpack and began sketching a rusty bridge pasted to the blue sky.

They chatted and laughed a lot as they scrambled inside the boat and dropped down one by one on the first wooden bench.

"*Bonjour mes amis*, good day, my friends," the captain said turning to them. He adjusted his new sunglasses under the brim of a white officer's hat bearing a U.S. Navy silver and gold insignia. As he rested his right arm on the helm, three initials stitched in navy blue by his wife, Emilie, stood out on the pocket of his white shirt. His white slacks were lined with stiff creases and straight cuffs that met the laces of his running shoes. When Emilie steam-ironed his pants this morning she told him the creases were so sharp they could slice through cold water in the bayou...or a body. He noticed a slight smile on her red lips when she picked up her embroidery and walked to the chair.

They were waiting for two more passengers.

Seems like a good group, the captain thought as he studied their shiny silver cameras, designer bags and Oakwood Country Club crests on some of the men's shirts. When his wife handed him the list at the office she said all eight were from Pittsburgh, Pennsylvania, and had flown to New Orleans to attend a wedding. One more couple from Maryland made an online reservation late this morning.

As they waited for the couple to arrive, the captain slid a pair of binoculars from a black monogrammed leather case and scanned the backwaters. He knew Old Monk was lurking out there and might try to ambush them.

Where was Lily? He tossed the long strap on the binoculars over his head and spun around to see his sixteen-year-old daughter leaning against the side of the boat trying to unknot the rope from the dock post.

"Skipper!" the captain shouted to her followed by a short whistle.

The girl tilted her head and gazed in his direction as her long ponytail caught the breeze.

He nodded to her when he saw a couple walking toward the boat.

She tossed the freed rope into the hull and jumped on deck after they boarded.

"Ready!" she called back, her eyes fastened on her father. She rushed to the helm, flipped on the audio speaker and handed him the microphone as he worked the controls to pilot the boat away from shore.

"You might want to put your hats on," the captain drawled while spinning the wheel with his left hand. "Southern spiders like to drop down on y'all without an invite."

"Spiders?" several women said. They reached for their hats or their husband's to wear.

Several seconds later, the passengers settled down and started twisting in their seats for views of the bayou. Camera clicks competed with the swish of the water as the boat churned through the stream. Loud grinds from the engine interrupted the sounds of geese honking overhead. He lowered the boat's speed so the grating was less distracting as the bow ploughed through green algae that looked like frayed carpeting. The noise seemed to fade when the microphone crackled and the captain welcomed everyone aboard and introduced himself and his daughter.

"Folks, as we begin our tour on the bayou I'd like to give you a little Cajun history," he said. "Although Louisiana was originally a French colony, it belonged to Spain after the Seven Years War ended in 1763. On February 27, 1765, about two hundred French Acadians, including my ancestors, the Broussards, were forced out of Acadie, now called Nova Scotia, by the British and arrived in New Orleans. They sailed on an old, small and overcrowded cargo ship. When they came ashore, they were given grain, a gun, tools and land. Weak from poor conditions on the ship and living in a different environment, many of them died from malaria and yellow fever the first year. As years passed, the survivors became rooted to a new way of life for themselves and their families and adapted to their surroundings like the Red Oak tree. More Acadians came and joined them from different places. You folks might be interested in learnin' that many Acadians from Pennsylvania and Maryland sailed in ships from the Chesapeake Bay and traveled here. Maybe there's some of your folks livin' in these parts. We might be distant cousins."

As the boat cut wide wakes through the duck weed, the captain praised the early Cajuns for settling the land he knew and loved so well while tapping his right foot to a fiddle and accordion harmonizing on outdoor speakers. But it was the nostalgic smell of onions, celery and bell peppers cooking in Maw-Maw's "Holy Trinity" that made his eyes water.

"Maw-Maw was the best cook on the bayou," he said steering the wheel. "The best. There was nothin' my grandmother couldn't fix and ain't nothin' tasted better for breakfast than her grillades and grits, for sure."

"Look!" he said standing up to point to a small brown bird flitting between trees that were wading in the bayou. "A pop chock just landed on a bald cypress—our state tree. Over there stands a great blue heron beside a water tupelo just waiting to stab its prey when it walks past. There's another one getting ready to fly," he predicted. "Take a look at that wingspan."

He reached for his binoculars. "Those woods are home to ibises, ducks, snapping turtles, snakes, spoonbills, raccoons, deer and...folks, it looks like a bobcat." He adjusted the lens on his binoculars.

"Livin' on the bayou you learn to respect every living creature, even when you don't understand their behaviors. Animals do what their instincts tell them to do. That's how the Almighty created them.

"Wait a minute, folks, that isn't a bobcat," he said. "No, my mistake, that's a little black bear." He clanged the ship's bell three times. "Well, I'll be. Haven't seen none of them critters all summer." Then he let go a laugh that rocked the boat when everyone started laughing with him.

Story after story rolled off the captain's tongue, spiced with a Cajun accent and peppered with folk music as the battered boat glided through the bayou with a green and white awning flapping in the air and the sun peeking through torn seams on the canvas. No one interrupted as he spun his adventurous tales.

"He's a cool, Cajun captain," a woman said clapping to the music.

But when they passed a small, rundown shack in the woods with yellow and black police tapes marking the property lines, the captain was silent. While the passengers were surveying their surroundings, he idled the engine and walked to the far side of the boat away from their sight. Hunched over the rail he lowered his head and removed his hat as he remembered the morning headlines in the *Times-Picayune*. Last night André Gautreaux, eighteen, was found dead from a stab wound in the back in the run-down house they just passed. He replaced his hat and shook his head in disbelief. Returning to the helm he lifted the microphone and began describing various snakes living in the bayou.

Lily was watching her father. She already heard about André's murder when her best buddy, Bernadette, texted her early this morning. Less than a minute after reading it she ran into the bathroom and threw up. When Momma came in after her she told her she didn't want to go on the cruise today with Daddy. But Momma had that mean look on her face and said her daddy needed her.

"Well, he's gone," Momma had said to her like she was putting dirty clothes in the washing machine. She handed Lily a wet washcloth to wipe her mouth. "That's what happens to white trash." She wondered how Momma knew about André.

The captain kicked the speed of the boat a notch higher. The engine droned louder for a few seconds then dropped back to first speed. He pointed out a male heron sitting on a nest of eggs with the female and a nest of sticks in a tree. Seeing the nests reminded him of the day his shipmate, Louie, slapped him on the back to tell him about André's birth. They were two young sailors on a cruiser headed to Guam when Louie got word André was born back home in New Orleans.

To the captain, it seemed like yesterday. He sighed. He felt real bad André was dead, but he could see it coming. Louie didn't listen when he told him over and over that if he didn't act like a father his boy would wind up in Angola from drinking Southern Comfort, getting in bar fights or foolin' around with those prostitutes. Only he didn't call them prostitutes when they talked. May God have mercy on André and those sinners.

He looked back at André's house thinking maybe Louie should have spent more time fishing with his boy. They could have had father and son talks while waiting for the fish to bite. The captain knew it was hard to tell someone what you think is right...or wrong, but sometimes you have to do it if you love them.

"When my granddaddy and me went fishin'," the captain said, "Maw-Maw always packed us a black cast-iron skillet to fry catfish fingers. And since you're such friendly folks," he added, "I'll give you her favorite recipe to fry catfish so it's crunchy on..."

A loud rumble and clunk interrupted him before the engine cut out. He restarted it and the boat lunged forward then sputtered and stopped.

"Did you hear that?" A young woman asked the captain. "Is that growling?"

"It ain't this engine turnin' over," he said trying to make a joke.

"That's an alligator, for sure," he said when he heard it a second time. He walked to the stern of the boat but didn't see anything. Then he spotted Old Monk tucked between tall, green shoots of Bayou grass chomping on a turtle shell.

He tried to call Emilie but the connection broke up. There was no phone coverage.

Rubbing his brow with the back of his hand, he turned to

the passengers and said, "The engine is flooded. I idled the dang thing too long. It should start in a few minutes.

"While we're waiting, who knows where the word 'bayou' comes from?" his voice echoed into the microphone.

A man wearing a blue turquoise ring and a tattoo of a helicopter on his arm said, "The French?"

"No, it's a Choctaw word and they pronounced it 'bayuk.' It means 'small stream.'"

He could tell from their expressions he had their attention.

"Let me tell you about the Choctaw tribe," he continued. "At one time they were spread out over Louisiana and were neighbors to the Cajuns around here." He outlined an imaginary boundary with a sweep of his hand. "The government tried to get them to leave and relocate to Oklahoma but they didn't want to go. No, for sure, they did not want to go. They liked it right here livin' along the bayou with us. So they started making things from nature to earn money to take care of themselves. My grandmother bought baskets from the women and liked them real well. She said they were right friendly Indians and some spoke a little French. But then Maw-Maw never had difficulty talking to anyone, for sure. I don't know how she did it, but she understood you from the get-go and could speak English, French and some Spanish."

He paced back and forth in front of them as he talked. "Some days the Choctaw went to New Orleans with their little tiny babies on their backs to sell medicinal herbs they picked around here." He pointed to parts of his body where they said the plants relieved all sorts of ailments like backaches, fevers and an upset stomach.

"They made a little money sellin' plants and were hard workers trying ways to make a living on the land to support their families—although most of them barely got by.

"When the government tried to send them to Oklahoma to live, Chief Tuscahoma stood his ground and refused to..."

To the captain, croaking frogs meant dusk was settling on

the bayou and he heard them. He said he'd finish the history lesson, but he had to bring up some lanterns right now. Lily was in the galley fixing a real New Orleans dinner for them. He sighed. The sun was setting.

Minutes became an hour and then another hour. Every time he started the engine, it idled and shook the boat for less than a minute before it cut out. He forced a smile and assured the passengers that he was not out of gasoline. He told them his wife would send help if they weren't back soon.

A man in a Ravens T-shirt was taking photos of the sunset that looked like a giant tangerine melting into the black horizon. Lily went past carrying a plate stacked with warm biscuits, butter and honey. He took a biscuit and walked across the deck to the captain.

"Did you know the guy who died back there?" he said.

The captain tried to restart the engine. He laughed and said the grinding motor sounded like a beagle hunting ducks. The engine whined and stopped. He sat down and pulled out a side drawer and started organizing booklets and maps.

The man stepped closer to him. "How'd he die?"

"Sir, I have no idea what you're talking about."

"The guy in the house back there—the one they found dead this morning." He pointed with his left thumb in the direction of the house.

The captain shook his head.

"You don't know?"

"No. Just what I read in the paper."

"Maybe we read the same paper. Young guy. Wonder how he died."

"Can't tell you."

"Can't tell me or don't want to tell me?"

"You figure it out."

The man turned and walked away.

When Lily began passing blankets and pillows around, the captain clicked on the microphone and said, "Folks, there's something I should tell you." He waited.

"Let me elaborate. There was a murder on the bayou last night. The police discovered the body of a young man, eighteen, fatally stabbed inside his house. They haven't found and arrested whoever did it yet," he said. "We just passed the house. If you look behind you to the left, it's a small frame house with a front porch and red roof with police tapes around the property. It might be hard to see because of the trees." He added, "More than likely it was someone he knew."

For a few seconds the only sounds were the chatter of birds and rustling in the woods. "Listen, folks," he said as he lifted the brim of his hat and pushed it back on his head. "I grew up on this bayou and there are generations of good people who have lived all their lives on this land and raised their families here. I know many of them real well and I know every tree and twist and turn on the land and in these waters," he said pointing to the landscape. "I can't explain it, but I can sure feel it when evil is around. I don't feel there is anyone on this bayou right now that would harm us."

"But you thought it was someone he knew," a woman spoke up.

"That boy knew other people who don't live around here," the captain said.

"How much longer do we have to wait?" a man said crossing his arms. "We need to get back to the hotel and pack. We check out tomorrow morning."

"I understand and apologize to you folks for the inconvenience. You will receive refunds," the captain said. "My wife has probably figured out that we're stranded and will arrive soon. In the meantime, we kinda' just need to *tenir bon* or hold steady, mates."

"In the meantime..." a man muttered and looked at his watch.

Several people glanced down the bayou to see the victim's house as iridescent colors danced on the water.

The man who spoke to the captain earlier stepped beside him.

"Think there's a murderer hiding out there?" he asked.

"A murderer? Maybe Old Monk," he said. "I already told you, I don't know any more than what I read in this morning's paper. Got it?" He felt his face getting warm.

"I mean the one who murdered André Gautreaux," he persisted. He had a flat voice and spoke between rows of even white teeth without moving his lips.

The captain shrugged and pushed himself away from the rail. "I know who you mean. Don't know anybody who would want to kill that boy. I mostly knew his daddy but he hasn't been around here in years."

"Oh?" the man asked and turned to face him. "That's right, you said you grew up on this bayou. How did you know it was someone the victim knew? They found a mono-grammed lipstick case with blood on it near the house." He looked at him without blinking.

"I didn't say I knew who did it," the captain said glaring back at him. "How did you know about a...silver lipstick case with blood on it? I didn't read that in the paper. Are you a reporter...or a police detective?"

The man looked straight ahead for a few seconds. "I didn't say it was silver," he said. "First time on the bayou. Myste-rious place you got out here." He walked away.

The captain reached for his cup of ice water and took a long sip. Those damn cat and mouse questions annoyed him, he thought. Like hell, give him information. He would never tell him a thing. He put the cup down and turned the music off. Holding the side of the helm he coiled his body and descended the narrow steps to the galley.

* * *

226

When he walked in the galley he smelled red beans and rice cooking on the stove. He heard Lily in the bathroom crying and coughing.

"Lily?"

She did not answer him.

"Lily, what's the matter?"

The lock on the bathroom door clicked and Lily stepped out gathering her hair in a barrette.

"I heard you crying."

"I'm okay."

The girl walked to the counter top and began to place plastic bowls on a tray.

"Lily...I know."

Silence stood between them. She reached for a tissue.

A gray-haired woman poked her head in the doorway. "Sorry to hurry you guys along, but we're hungry up there," she said in a raspy voice. "Teddy is threatening to throw a fishing line over the side of the boat to try and catch a catfish if we don't get something to eat." Thin lines on her face crinkled as she laughed.

He watched Lily ladle rice and beans into four bowls on a tray, grab bottled water from the cabinet and start up the steps.

On deck, camping lanterns hung on high hooks around the inside of the boat casting a dim, yellow haze. Some of the passengers searched to find a place to lie down and rest. The boat rocked back and forth on the water like a worried mother trying to comfort her restless baby.

Below, the captain peered through the galley window at the dark, murky waters of the bayou. He gave up the thought of anyone coming to their rescue tonight. Better to wait it out until dawn.

Being rescued wasn't the only thing on his mind—Lily was pregnant and her baby's daddy was found stabbed in the back.

He rubbed his neck. Everything was humming along fine in their lives until this happened, he thought. Didn't Lily know her momma and daddy loved her? From the day she was a little baby she was everything right and good in their lives when sometimes it seemed confused and crazy.

He told himself he wasn't a good father or this would not have happened. André's dead and his daughter was having his baby. Father Xavier would say God was testing him like gold in fire. He thirsted for a couple shots of bourbon but he never stored liquor on the boat.

He pulled a chair out and sat down at the wooden table. His fingers pressed against his temples as he closed his eyes. Was this the 'dark night of the soul' his daddy often talked about when he was drinking? Daddy would laugh and slap his thigh if he saw him cry like a woman. But he hurt inside. Lily was too young to be a mother.

His chest heaved and his heart ached. "Don't test me, Lord, please don't," he whispered as he choked with tears. He grieved for his daughter who would never dance at her first prom. Now she's having a baby—a baby, he thought. Not long ago she told him she wanted to go to Tulane to become a botanist and he agreed to help her research plants.

That damn André. It was that *couillon's* fault. The boy had no common sense. He tried to tell her André was fooling around with the wrong people in New Orleans and to stay clear of him. The boy defied him after he told him not to come to their home to visit her when they weren't there. If he wasn't old friends with Louie he would have...

Suddenly, he heard stomping and shuffling and stumbling up on the deck and a woman shouted, "Where's the captain? It's his daughter!"

He shoved his chair back, ran up the steps two at a time and saw people propped on the rail looking in the water.

"What is going on?" he demanded rushing toward them.

"Your daughter jumped in the water," several people hollered at the same time. "Carmela tried to hold her back and lost her balance when she saw that alligator," a woman said as she sat on the bench fanning a paper over her friend's face.

"Old Monk," a man muttered.

"Old Monk," the captain repeated to himself.

Someone screamed at him, "Go, go, get your daughter!"

"Old Monk? Hurry up and get her!" another person ordered. "That alligator is hissing down there!"

The captain strode to the rail and shoved passengers out of his way. He looked down in the brackish water but didn't see Lily or an alligator. Where was she? He kicked off his shoes and socks and jumped in the water. Then he saw a snout and two big eyes about thirty-five feet away and moving closer to him—Old Monk. The alligator bellowed and started to open its jaws. The water was splashing higher around them as the jaws were unhinging wider. He thought Old Monk was getting ready to lunge at him when a shot was fired in the water. Then another shot. Both shots missed the alligator. Old Monk snapped his jaw shut and lowered his head under the water. The captain looked back at the boat and saw the man who kept asking him questions holding the twelve-gauge shotgun he kept hidden in a compartment under the helm. Old Monk was gone. He hurried to swim away and called out for Lily. He noticed her swimming not far from shore and went in the same direction.

Search lights beamed on the water from an approaching shrimp boat.

"*Comment Ca Va?*"

He recognized Emilie's voice. "How's it going?" he repeated.

The captain and his daughter waited on the shore until Emilie's boat arrived.

Passengers helped them inside his boat and wrapped blankets around them. The man who fired at Old Monk told him he thought he would have a gun on the boat and had searched for it.

When they were sitting alone the captain asked Lily why she did something so risky, especially when Old Monk might be waiting in the water.

The girl kept twirling and twisting her wet hair avoiding his eyes. "I saw you sitting at the table. I wanted to die because I disappointed you so much."

"You will never disappoint me," he said. He looked at the bayou and then back at her.

"Been thinkin' about whittlin' my grandbaby a fishin' pole."

Emilie nudged between them.

He asked what took her so long to get there.

"The police came to the office and told me I had to go with them to be questioned about André's murder," she said. They kept asking me the same questions over and over in different ways with different investigators and showing me photos to identify a suspect until I had a headache. I had no idea you were still on the bayou until I got home and you weren't there. I came right away to look for you."

"You did what you had to do," he said. He held her hand and asked her in French if the police told her a lipstick case was found outside André's house.

She looked at her hand in his. "Yes, before the police let me go they wanted to know if I recognized the initials on it...I didn't," she said.

When they arrived at the dock the passengers said goodbye and thanked them.

As they left, a voice called back in the darkness, "Mysterious place you got out here."

"For sure," said the captain. "Good night."

Stalker
Dino Parenti

You're gonna talk about Liza now.

Because you're following her, and it's easier expressing your thoughts to her back than to her front.

There she goes now, a sprite gliding through a parking lot with all the slack-jawed grace of a murmuration, sidestepping puddles of streetlights and bounding K-rails before plunging into shadows.

To keep up with her takes all your muscle-memory from quiet-humping hills in deep Cong countryside—proof that this part of you will never die no matter how hard you try to snuff it out.

You catch up to her again as she waits for a car to drift past before tearing across the street on coltish legs towards the south wall of Leland's Bar. The wall farthest from its crazy-bright sign that keeps you up most nights with its irregular flicker and yawning buzz that gives the cicada a run for their money, even at the edge of a marsh.

She tiptoes against the mottled tin siding to the back corner, and you decide to squat between parked El Caminos to catch your breath. In truth, there's no need for you to match her pace. You've done this fruitless dance many times. You know she's going to the garage. Its glow seeps from behind Leland's, a frosty effulgence slithering around corners and peering through the mesh of Spanish beard with the warmth of coroner's lights.

Will you look this time?

You'll probably get as far as the back of the bar before retreating to your apartment, as usual. In the stifling heat of your narrow room, where the plumbing shudders and the floorboards groan lurid secrets with every contraction, it'll be your old man's oft-stated credo that'll squire you to sleep: the worst sin you can commit upon your heroes is to unmask them.

In a blink she rounds the corner and melds into the light, and the same predictable breath scrambles up and grapples to the roof of your throat. Thus her namesake. Her invented self. Even removed from the glory of the trapeze, the moniker suits her just as well on the ground.

Within the majesty of the big-top, under a patina of makeup, she's known as *The Golden Starling*. But her real name is Liza. Mother of three. You might love her, and she might love you.

It's complicated.

You cross the street.

You remember the first time you saw Liza the way you remember the first time you fired a rifle. Both shocked you to the core with their power. Even the simple act of her hanging a poster in the bar for the forthcoming three-week run of Coolidge & Sons Circus was enough to put that same whammy into you.

You'd just started living in the apartment above Leland's where you worked four days a week. Because of your appearance, they relegated you to the back loading stock, filing inventory, bookkeeping, and generally maintaining a wall between you and the patrons. Whenever the barkeep called for a new case of Wild Turkey or a refilled keg of Stroh's, you shoved it through the canvas curtain between the bar and storeroom with your boot. Most times you would linger there and listen to all the random boasting and griping about women, work, and sports above the ubiquitous drone of docking and departing airboats. All the ticking that gives life around these parts a little pliability beyond the reek of diesel, fry grease, and marsh.

You'd plant your back to the wall directly across from the small wood-framed mirror Beau Shambly hung beside the door frame as a way to deter you should you ever feel the urge to mingle out front. Beau was Leland's son, a squat little toadstool with bratwurst arms and a smile that skewed left as if to balance the lazy eye drifting right. As a kind of subliminal backup, he'd hooked above the door a large walnut mallet he was fond of strutting around with as an affect—the high striker type used at carnies to test strength and win Kewpie dolls for sweethearts by pinging a bell.

When the beloved-by-all Leland died the same day *Star Wars* opened, Beau swooped in, mallet in hand, and sprayed the place with all his pent-up bile and umbrage, booting his doubters and raising prices. He only kept you around so he wouldn't have to train anyone new on the workings of the place, though you were still banned from the bar proper on account of your facial scars, which he once told a new server could pinch off a squirting bronco on the spot. She of course had to look. She was young and it was late and the place was closing down, and you happened to meet her eye when hers crept through the rift in the curtains. Her sudden intake of breath varied little from the sound you once heard a man make when he was stabbed in the back during a bar fight in Terrebonne Parish, and she never returned to work.

Sometimes, when the room was jumping and most alive, and the gator po' boys dressed with Creole mustard were flying out of the kitchen like dealt cards, Beau would scrawl STAY! across the mirror with a red crayon, his crooked smirk reminding you how pleasure on certain faces can take on the glaze of disease.

It didn't bother you much by then. You weren't all too fond of your mug before the fact, and sometimes you'd squint into Beau's makeshift restraint just to see if you could spot the crooked nose or the pencil-thin lips through his letters and beneath all your knurled, medium rare meat.

Sometimes you'd even try to smile, never mind that those hinge points have been rigid spot welds for many years.

It's what you were doing when Liza walked in that day to hang her poster.

You only risked a peek through the curtains because you heard Freddy the barkeep—whose judgment towards the fairer sex was first rate—blow one of his understated wolf whistles from the other side.

When you first glimpsed her she was tip-toeing to pin a high corner on the corkboard by the bathroom doors:

3 WEEKS ONLY!
THE GOLDEN STARLING
&
THE RED LION MASTER!

Lord, was she a sight, with her peach sundress inching ever higher to expose taut calves. Even with an air that wagged between dour and blue as she gazed at the poster, and which you only noted in profile scribbled behind stringy bands of yellow-white hair, she was still a heart-stopper.

But as pretty as she was, it was her walk that sucked the rest of the air from your lungs. That familiar little hitch that was almost a strut, but not quite. Some old hurt that never healed proper. You recognized it right away. Didn't need Beau, his possum's grin loose and cold-blooded, to prance out of his office then to verify it. He brushed by you without acknowledgement and hopped up to slap the mallet's handle—his preferred good luck ritual—before bundling through the curtain with a kid's enthusiasm on Christmas morning.

Through the gap he left in the canvas you watched as he hooked an arm around her, then led her down the long hall and out the back door.

She didn't resist him, but neither was she gung ho. Often you thought of stopping him, but you needed your job and the freedom of seclusion it provided.

They were headed to his garage. It's where she would meet him once weekly during the four months the show was in town.

You gumshoe it across the gravel road and lurk against the bar's south wall, stepping in the spots Liza had ghosted moments earlier, hoping for a sense of her, yet grateful that you lack that thing animals have of picking up fear.

Reaching the corner, you stop where she'd stopped and creep your head forward till you see Beau's garage some ten yards down between a thicket of sumac. His makeshift studio. Whenever the icy blue light bleeds through the joints and knotholes of the pine-board siding you know he's at it, padding his income with a trunk full of secrets and a video camera borrowed from a reporter cousin of his—because really, everyone has to these days however they can.

Except that Liza is in there with him, and the lights are humming and tape spools are whirring, and like every occasion before, you're loath to venture closer, your old man's dogmatic warnings about divulging heroes cantering around your skull in ever reducing circles.

For extra money, you took work with the circus whenever it rotated into town, mainly shoeing horses and cleaning animal pens, which was ideal for all concerned as it kept you segregated. Mostly though, you did it because you'd always been fond of carnies and travelling shows, even though they weren't the draw they used to be before you shipped out from Parris Island in '68.

In those days, a featured act of some daring feat or talent

would headline each show. What you most relished about them was their mystery. Beyond just their stage monikers, marquee performers often veiled themselves behind masks or under makeup. Rarely did anyone know who these people really were in the flesh. Sometimes, not even the circus regulars knew. They'd keep to themselves, having learned long ago the paradoxical lure of anonymity, often showing up only minutes before their acts, always incognito, ready to execute miracles for their audiences.

To them, every day was Mardi Gras.

In the small swamp towns where you grew up, especially amongst the kids, they were living, breathing superheroes with secret identities, and you caught them every chance you could, often hitchhiking for hours up and down Highway 90.

In Raceland, you had *The Electrifying Basilisk*, who was a fire-eater and wore a dragon's mask.

Over in Charenton, you had *Antoine the Transcendent*, a magician who wore a different voodoo-inspired mask at every performance.

In later days, you had *The Stupendous Crane Sisters* in New Iberia, who walked the high wire and wore matching feather costumes with wings for arms.

Here in Bayou Vista, we had *The Red Lion Master*, a big-cat tamer who donned auguste clown paint with a Kabuki-styled, fiery-red underlayment.

And of course, *The Golden Starling*, a legendary aerialist under alabaster white face.

The first time you saw *The Golden Starling*—before you ever saw her as Liza—you had slipped under the bleachers so as not to spook the kids behind their cotton candy beards. Between a gangly scrim of legs and droopy socks, you watched her grand finale with the stunned wonder of youth, and for a little while at least, you felt the smile quickening beneath the rind of your skin. You weren't the burned man anymore. You weren't the adult who eventually cued into life's masquerades. Who learned how *The Electrifying Basilisk* was really a loan officer who once did time for embezzling. Learned how *Antoine the Transcendent* was really homeless and living out of his VW van by Grand Avoille Cove. Learned how *The Stupendous Crane Sisters* really weren't sisters at all, but a couple of strippers from Lafayette who belonged to a doomsday cult.

As to what you knew about *The Red Lion Master*, well, you tried not to brood over that hard tale.

And *The Golden Starling*? It was after her dismount from the net that first night that you noticed the slight hobble you would peg once more at Leland's a year later. You'd assumed it at the time to be some muscle tweak resulting from her act, but as you'd observed her in the intervening years from behind tents, kiosks, and wheelbarrows, you came to learn that her limp was as much a part of her as your scars were to you.

Sounds drum from the garage. Hefty sounds, as if they're hammering something of permanence into those brittle walls.

As your back peels from the tavern's rolled siding and you skulk to the grove just shy of the garage, you realize all this nighttime cloak-and-daggering is an echo of your public, day-lit world—how you exist solely in the long, thin snippets of light and movement between shadows, or parted doors, or windows, or drapes. At night, well after Leland's closes and under the interrogation of loon and barn owl calls, you'll heel-toe carefully down the stairs despite it being empty because, among other lessons, 'Nam drilled into you the virtues of stealth. You'll bypass the mirror without so much as a glance, though you'd make certain to slap the mallet over the door, and then sit in the open nursing a Blatz, forgetting for an hour that you attend AA twice weekly in a repossessed playhouse. You'll imagine yourself in deep, soulful tete-a-tetes about love and death with some lovely lady, mostly Liza, and you'll tell her about your Natchez roots, and she'll wonder about your face with only her eyes and restless fingers, and though your skin is stubborn to reveal it, you'll assure her that you're smiling. And she'll reply in kind that she knows what that's like, and you'll feel more at ease explaining the cagey morality of combat, and the persistence of white phosphorous—how it burns until you smother its oxygen, and even then it keeps on smoldering, which was why you and your buddy, Lee, referred to it as the "resentment" of ordnance. And you'll tell her about how sometimes you'll steal into the animal pens at night and listen to the nocturnal whimpers and moans of striped, tawny beasts so far removed from their homes as to almost sound human in their forlornness, and has she ever felt that same ache herself?

And as you consider how their musk and grievance always stalks you well beyond their cages, you shudder as, beyond a lattice of morning glory and across a narrow patch of lantana, and ultimately through the worm snake wide gaps in the garage wall, you glimpse a menagerie of shadows heaving in ways you can't define.

In a fluke moment mid-season, you and Liza ended up face-to-face for the first time without her makeup.

The night before, you'd heard her and Beau arguing outside the garage for a good half hour. Money matters from what you could make out. Vague issues of raising the stakes and opening new markets overseas and the like, whatever that all meant.

At one point you peeked around the ragged shade of your one window to watch them. It was only a few seconds, Liza standing askance of him, arms akimbo and hard eyes raking the garage walls for harder answers, and Beau gazing at her cock-headed in his bathrobe and Jesus sandals and perpetual shellac of flop sweat, dragging on a hand roll and sucking at the insides of his cheeks as though to taste his own simper. Testiness grizzled at the core of their relationship, ever since you'd first spied them at Leland's. They had a dance. Liza, with the practiced, exasperated fortitude motherhood had wrought. Beau, with his feeble indignations and always-pointed finger loaded with duds.

It explained somewhat her fugue state that following morning when, as you were pushing a gilly wagon of feed after shoeing the horses, you almost collided as she emerged suddenly from between a pair of flat-bed trucks, a bucket of feed in each hand.

You don't know for how long you both stood not four feet apart, you gaping stupidly, trying to push a grin to the surface of your blasted skin, and her looking right through you as if sidetracked by a waft of odor from her youth she couldn't right pinpoint. She was dressed in her performance leotard, which was odd since she wouldn't be up for another three hours. But she was makeup free. A fresh dapple of bruises tumbled from the base of her neck, past her shoulder and down to her elbows. An especially nasty indentation flared on her right shoulder—vague half crescents, like bite marks, only too large for the average mouth.

From her ear grew a single morning glory, which she'd certainly plucked the prior evening from the vines that grew wild against the east wall of Beau's garage.

Though clearly out to sea, she nonetheless reacted as if fully aware of your gawking at her welts. Or maybe she'd developed an enhanced sense over time—a protective reflex that showed through as a self-conscious rolling back of the shoulders, as if to spur along a dormant confidence.

But it wasn't you that reaction had been meant for, and maybe if you'd bothered to ask her, she might've told you that. The jade of her eyes brimmed with the kind of dread you only saw in troops thrown into their first firefight, and when she finally brushed past you towards the petting zoo with her lopsided stride, it was with the compressed tension of those same troops about to have their frontiers obliterated.

The limp merely confirmed her identity. It was the morning glory and the bruising that broke your heart and stoked a fire you thought you'd left seething in a Saigon hospital another life ago.

If you go another fifteen feet, you'll be able to peek through one of the knotholes straight into the garage.

The noises within are mounting. Primitive, rhythmic, muffled. An inverse to the root canal trill of tree frogs in heat.

You try to imagine her as you've watched her through the years—the version not of the garage, and not the one that rendezvous with odd men throughout town. Men who sate her purse while leaving the rest of her starved. Sometimes, after your AA on Mondays and Thursdays, as she walks home late after a show, you'll watch her stop by a neighbor's house to pick up her kids. Two girls and a boy, ages four through ten. Those are her best smiles, rivaled only by those in the heat of performance.

The ones she attempts when pausing at flower beds, or outside the arcade to listen to the hawkish play within, those curve and hold with the strain of arm wrestlers.

You edge forward, and at the closest you've ever been, the sounds are more brutish, more feral than ever.

In the mud, over by the garage's rolling door which you can now make out because of your advanced progress, maybe those aren't hoof prints that you see leading inside, but simply a trick of the light.

Beau's voice, low, guttural, coaxing, encouraging. The clink of metal, soft and pleasant, as how you remember it trailing from Santa's sleigh in the town square when you were a boy in Opelousas, and still unwise to the poor shell-shocked

D-Day vet under the beard and red hat who bagged your groceries at the A&P.

At the swelling snorts and whimpers, you turn from the garage and slink back to your apartment.

Maybe you've unmasked enough heroes for one lifetime.

Later in the night—this eve of the closing of *The Golden Starling* and *The Red Lion Master*—you stare at the ceiling long after the lights in the garage have snuffed out, and it's only the scarlet glare of Leland's sign to birth shadows.

Looking at your hands, you try to recall the shade of your skin as it once was, and not the waxy husk that sponges whatever cast happens to fall on them. Often you glance at your feet to remind you, as they were basically unscathed, and maybe that's what prompts you to kick them out of bed and get up.

Downstairs in the bar, and the obvious hits you as it tends to, in a series of endless postscripts: 'Nam was the last time you had hair and pigment. The last time you knew who you used to be. 'Nam was also the last time your unblemished fingers had built anything, and as you rustle around the storeroom you wonder if there's enough detergent left to mix with the few gallons of gasoline out back.

Beyond stealth, 'Nam taught you many lessons, including consequence. That if you're too cowardly to point blank a bullet into a double agent's head, and opt instead to set off a device of Semtex and white phosphorous, unpleasant results can happen if you're not far enough away.

That if you aimed to purge the world of traitorous villagers without the surgical precision it called for, their babies' screams will never let you forget that you failed to sweep for civilians beforehand.

Gazing out the tiny storeroom window, you realize that the sounds of the bayou differ little from that place, especially at night. The air is thick with verdancy and rot, and light fingers in from everywhere and nowhere at once, splayed by mist and the immortal aqueducts of bald cypress knees. It is light as perceived in a dream, and often you wonder if you're awake or asleep in this sultry womb. No wonder it's a place opulent in mysticism and death. Here you can cast your hurt into the bog. Here you can be your unalloyed self. Here you can confess sin and depravity, even if you're too chickenshit to do so. Don't worry—the swamp won't care. It won't ever tell a soul.

Using the clincher from your farrier's pouch to pry open a gas can, you're waylaid on the spot by new inspiration, and you scratch the torching scheme altogether. Love and desperation will do that you, especially when you realize they're virtually the same emotion, bordering on madness. The idea is so impeccable as to be ridiculous, but you don't have all night.

Should you do it? Beau's in New Orleans conducting his shady extracurriculars, but he'll be back. He always does some editing before dawn.

And of course, it'll require you entering that garage.

In the end, it all goes down fast.

You prepare Beau's mallet first, which takes all of three minutes. Then you slip into the neighboring barn and bridle the spryest looking colt of the bunch.

At Beau's garage five minutes later, you pick the padlock open and slip the horse in before relocking it and sweeping your footprints so Beau will be none the wiser, then using a ladder in back, climb through the eave vent and drop onto the garage's floor through the attic door. The lights are off, but the moon creeps through the siding gaps and blue washes the light stands, editing bay, steamer trunks, and bed. The other things you glimpse, you disregard immediately and will not describe here. You simply keep your eyes to the floor and melt into the shadows by the doors. The horse sniffs about, but remains otherwise calm and ignorant to mankind's darker proclivities.

A half hour later, someone fidgets with the lock, and Beau steps through. The horse snorts simultaneously with Beau pulling the light chain, whereupon he literally hops back a step and hiccups a high pitched *Fuck!* at the sight.

You don't waste a moment, muttering an "*Adieu,* Beau," before bringing the mallet down on his head with all your zeal the moment he turns to face you. Even as he crumples to the ground, you can see the perfectly outlined indentation of the horseshoe you hammered on the end of the mallet start to flower atop of his head—an impact angle that matches well what the rearing of a spooked horse would inflict.

Surprisingly—or maybe not at all—you feel no fear or anxiety throughout, and the rest is carried out with a smooth, quiet efficiency you can't help wonder might've accompanied your task back in 'Nam had you dredged up the stones to do it right. You'll wear the reminder of that for the rest of your days.

After reshoeing the horse with the killing instrument of record, you slap it loose and send it scampering, taking extra care to check the area thoroughly beforehand. You then drag Beau's body next to a studio light that you make sure is going good and hot before knocking it into a heap of swept up straw in the manner one might have with flailing arms.

Before the garage is fully engulfed, and before calling the fire department, you pluck for yourself a tiny clusters of violet, yellow, and red lantana flowers as a memento, so like miniature wedding bouquets for lost brides.

A knock at the door.

Your hands freeze while smearing the last of the red foundation on your cheeks. No one ever knocks on that door or ever tries to come in. The cat wagon is the last big-rig trailer on the lot, and the only one connected directly to the big top. This is for ease of bringing the big cats in and out of the arena, as well as corralling them should one manage to escape their pen within the trailer itself.

It also happens to double as your dressing room when you feature. Like tonight. The last night before Coolidge & Sons rotates out to another town for four months, and *The Red Lion Master* dispels into the wind for another season.

Back to Leland's paltry paycheck to tide you over till next spring—at least for as long as Freddy the barkeep can run it without Beau before new owners buy it, or it folds altogether.

Back to you without the foundation and the maquillage, and the glory of the tigers and lions, and crowds of children who still adore their heroes.

You wait a few seconds before stepping to the door, though you're made up enough to remain unknown, or so you think. Outside you hear the crunch of tanbark—the shuffle of uncertainty before it starts away, at which point you open the door.

The Golden Starling is halfway down the corridor when she stops. Again, that preparative rolling of the shoulders for baseline self-assurance before turning to face you. In her full performance costume, she's radiant. An effigy freshly stepped from a niche in the Pantheon. At a dozen feet away, you can't tell if she's smiling or not, only that something *Mona Lisa* sublime is sculpted in the greasepaint.

And this is how we speak for that first minute, you squinting for purchase in my blue irises which, against my alabaster makeup, are even more blue. An impossible glacial blue.

I raise a hand and give you a single wave. For some reason this prompts a pair of tears to rut down my foundation and stamp a parenthesis between my half-smile. My chin quivers, and slowly this gets transmuted into my hand which ultimately points at you, so like Beau's castigating finger—if Beau's finger ever had any caliber behind it.

That's when I see you notice it, because really, it's been right there before you the whole time. The morning glory, slipped into my ear, scorched and curled like Christmas wrapping tossed in a fireplace, only the inner fringes still bearing a hint of their original violet-blue.

You're probably telling yourself the fire that killed Beau had to be an accident, even as you're imagining the soot leaving a stem-imprint on my temple as the morning glory sloughs from my ear at my first aerial flip, and you only realize I'm already walking away by the fading scratch of my footsteps.

You want to follow me, but me knowing that you do is enough to lock your knees.

Blinking your eyes at where I stood, hoping I'll return on my own to refill the space so you can explain your side of things—perhaps finally confess your love—that's when you see it. The mirror. Beau's mirror. I'd hung it right across your door the way Beau would have, which is why you hadn't noticed it till after I'd walked away.

Oh, he told me all about it, and the rest I picked up from your AA meetings in that old theater I'd follow you to every time. Because I'm nothing if not at home high up in the fly rafters.

On the glass, in white grease paint, you read the two lines of four words I left for you. Like an aborted quatrain:

I HAVE THREE KIDS.
YOU HAD NO RIGHT.

Because I could use a little deniability. Stockholm Syndrome, I believe it's called? And like insanity, it can't be the case if you're aware of it, right? Either way, I'm sure the police won't have trouble doubting that of a supposedly abused against her will single mother.

But you? Well, are you even considering that possibility? I doubt it. The obvious always seems to elude you. You and your flights of fancy. I'm guessing that right about now the only thing you're imagining is the charred flower moldering from my ear as I step into the arena—flakes that you'll be stepping on later since you're scheduled to follow me tonight, and you've never felt less up to the task.

I'll walk away now, and it'll be back to the makeup mirror for you, where you'll pat on the rest of your mask and misgive and pine in silence, and keep on patting and misgiving and pining until you hear the crowd swell at the announcement of the penultimate act.

And I know you'll picture *The Golden Starling*, one hand extended in salutation as the other grips the trapeze, and surely you'll wonder if those in the audience below see her the way you do. Heroic or crazy? Controlled or reckless? Appreciative or ungrateful?

But will you ask yourself if they see the love? If they recognize the perfection that is the duo of *The Red Lion Master* and *The Golden Starling*?

Behind you, the big cats yawn and groan their collective torpor. Do you envy their indifference to our masks and makeup? Their ignorance to desperation and co-dependence?

And that's all you're gonna say about Liza.

The Boggy Bayou Caper
Terrie Farley Moran

For the better part of two hours, Zack and I were glued to a couple of rickety bar stools at Ivy's Road House just north of Tampa. Of course the time came when Ivy ran a rag over the vacant spot just to my right and suggested that we might want to leave seeing as how we were out of money. We'd been drinking no-name tap beer thanks to the change Zack stole from the ash trays of every unlocked car in the parking lot over to the SuperTarget. But now even the pennies were gone.

I could have used another beer or two but I was mostly glad we were done for the night. The more beers Zack hoisted, the more he moaned about losing the love of his life, Caroline. I heard all I could stand and heard it more times than I could count over the past couple of weeks.

Three sweet young things dressed in their Friday night uniform of white tank tops and skinny jeans took over the south corner of the bar and ordered shots of Patrón. We were about to miss our chance. We'd be leaving just as the tequila party was getting started.

Two of the girls, a tall blonde and a taller brunette, sashayed over to the jukebox and started pressing buttons. I closed my eyes and willed those gals to play anything, long as it wasn't being sung by Billy Billeaudreau. Ten seconds later, Billy's latest hit, "Finally Found You," was pulsing through the air and bouncing off the rough-hewed wooden walls, which started Zack punching the bar and hollering, "That sumbitch Billy Billeaudreau broke my heart." And he fell onto the bar top, head cradled in his folded arms.

The tall blonde flung her hair over her shoulder. "Sorry for your trouble, but didn't y'all know that Billy is straight? No way a hottie like Billy Billeaudreau would fall for you."

Perfect. If we'd ever had a shot with these young beauties, and I'm not saying we did, Zack just went and ruined it. I moved in hoping to make the recovery. "Billy broke Zack's heart by stealing his girlfriend."

The blonde motioned to the bottle of Patrón and said to Ivy, "Give these boys a couple of doubles. Sad stories make me generous."

If Zack's stupid fixation with Caro Adrieux was going to get us free tequila shots, well then I was in on the pity party.

A dimpled redhead sitting in the very corner of the bar said, "I been reading his fan website and Billy Billeaudreau bought himself a special made Gibson guitar. Cost around ten thousand dollars. Studded with sapphires to match his sexy blue eyes." She settled back in her chair with a satisfied smile although whether it was because she brought news to the conversation or piled more misery on Zack, it was hard to tell.

Zack's head snapped up. "Fancy guitar is window dressin'. Y'all know his real name is Otis Kammerer and for all he claims Cajun roots, he's from someplace in New Jersey. Ain't many Cajuns born up there."

The redhead threw Zack a look that said she was done with him. She slid off her bar stool and headed for the juke-box. I had a feeling we were going to hear a lot more music sung by Billy Billeaudreau.

I elbowed Zack and pointed to the two shot glasses lined up in front of him. He tossed one back and when he reached for the second, I grabbed his wrist. "Slow it down. That's your last drink. If we sit a while, who knows where this night could go?" And I rolled my eyes toward the sweeties in the corner of the bar.

"None of them could hold a candle to Caro," Zack said loud enough to be heard in Tallahassee.

Well that brought a mean blaze into the redhead's eye. She walked from the jukebox and stood directly behind Zack's chair, "Hey, sugar, want to know where your ex is tonight? She's up in Niceville, near Fort Walton Beach. 'Cause Billy is the main attraction at the Boggy Bayou Mullet Festival."

"He's getting a mullet haircut? Up on the stage? Ain't seen one of them since high school." Zack tousled his overgrown high fade and reached for his second tequila but I moved it just out of reach. "Don't act all stupid. Not the hair kind of mullet. It's the fish kind. Folks sit around for days, listening to fine country music and eating fresh mullet. Ain't I right?" I asked the redhead still hoping to get a little friendly talk with the girls.

The redhead nodded and pointed a thumb toward me. "Your friend totally gets it. Lots of fish, lots of crafts and lots of fine music provided by superstars like Billy."

Zack grabbed his glass, downed the tequila and said, "We'd best get going. I got an early morning tomorrow."

I was so relieved that he wasn't going to have a back and forth with the redhead that I never questioned what Saturday morning would bring.

I was sound asleep for what seemed like a minute and a half when I heard thunder rolling against my trailer door. Then Zack started yelling, "Wake up. Wake yourself up. Do I need to come in and dump a bucket of water on your head to get you out of that bed?"

I opened my eyes and looked out the window. Wasn't light yet. What was Zack going on about? Usually the sun was high in the sky before he so much as blinked.

I stumbled out of bed and pulled the door open. "What the hell?"

"Get dressed. We're going to claim my woman. Billy took her from me. I'm aiming to get her back." Zack looked more determined than I'd ever seen him.

Still, I decided to give him some push back. "Ain't my woman."

Zack picked up the green shirt I'd thrown over the back of a chair last night and threw it to me. "Yeah, but I need your truck. Mine'll never go the distance and I'm betting you ain't having me take your Dodge Ram four hundred miles there and another four hundred home again, so you need to come along."

Actually going off anywhere with Zack was the last thing I needed, but it wasn't like I had a long to-do list and if I did have one getting Zack to finally be rid of Caro would be at the very top. Maybe this trip would make that happen.

"What are we supposed to use for money? How you putting gas in my truck?"

Zack pulled a wrinkled stack of fives and singles out of his pocket. "I knew you'd be all anxious and stuff. I busted into my rainy day fund. Got forty-three dollars. Should pay for the gas and a burger or two."

"We been drinking no-name tap off stolen quarters and all this time you had money stashed away? Does that make sense?"

"Sure does. My momma said to always have a rainy day fund. Rain might come, roof might leak. Could need to buy a tarp."

I stuck my head out the front door. "Not a cloud in sight."

Zack shot me a look. "Petey, without Caro, it's raining in my heart."

I groaned. Here he's willing to spend his last dollar, money better spent on bottles of Rolling Rock, to go find a girl who ain't worth the trouble. This could take a while. I pushed my toothbrush, some clean underwear and a sweatshirt into a grungy backpack. I tucked it behind the driver's seat and we headed north.

We stopped for gas one time with Zack yelling at me, "Can't you pump faster." Like it was going to make a difference. We still had hours of driving in front of us.

We were starting to see signs advertising the festival when Zack pointed to my left. "Look at that. They call that a bayou? That there is more like a bay or a pond, although it is a little sluggish and does have all them long leaf pine trees growing, so I guess the name bayou might fit."

Sure enough a big green county sign shouted BOGGY BAYOU for all the world to see.

"Let them call it whatever. Watch the signs for the festival." I was losing patience, already sorry I ever agreed to this trip.

It was early afternoon when we pulled into public parking at the festival site. Place was mobbed. The only spot I could find for the truck was so far deep over tree roots that I knocked off a couple of feet of gray wispy Spanish moss from the branches when I slid in. Zack bought festival tickets and hustled me through the main gate. Row after row of vendor tables were lined up with every kind of art and craft. I walked a few feet and a hand-tooled leather vest on a table full of belts caught my eye. The vendor, a woman who had the same gray curly hair as my grandmother, was wearing a gray Stetson and a plaid shirt. She caught my eye and waved me over. I was inclined to look but Zack grabbed my arm and fluttered a piece of paper under my nose.

"We got to find the main stage. Says here Billy will be singing in a few...is that Caro? What has Billy done to her?"

Caro was standing by the entrance to the clown stage and handing out flyers trying to steer folks away from the clowns and over to the main stage to hear Billy. She had wide blonde streaks in her hair and was all tarted up in spangles and beads scattered on a low-cut tank top. Her Daisy Duke shorts left nothing to the imagination.

"Look at her. That ain't the girl I loved. Billy's dressing her like some sort of hoochie coochie to bring in his audience. That ain't right."

Before I could remind him that Billy had an audience long before he met Caro, Zack was at Caro's side trying to pull the flyers out of her hands.

"You don't need to do this. You can come on home. No need to be hawking for Billy."

Caro gave Zack a *hey look, my best friend is here* smile. "What y'all doing here? Billy will be thrilled to see you. Come on back. We got a few minutes before the show." She turned to me. "Hey, Petey, still hanging with Zack, I see," she said it like she thought I could do better. Guess because she figured she'd done better herself.

I threw her a howdy and followed along wherever she was leading Zack. We wound up behind the stage where an old Keystone Laredo fifth wheel trailer was hitched to a Silverado. Billy's name was painted on the side and the man himself was sitting in a canvas chair strumming on the showiest guitar I'd ever seen. There were so many baubles stuck to the front and along the sides that it outdid Caro's tank top for flash. I was wondering if the ten thousand dollars was actually a bribe Billy paid to the guitar maker to fix up the gaudiest six-string to ever hit a stage.

"Caro, darlin'," Billy whined. "Who's out front drumming up an audience if you're back here?" Then he saw me and Zack and took us for fans. "Aw, you brought company. That puts a different spin on it."

He splashed a big good ol' boy grin on his face. Then he recognized Zack. And that grin fell right off. "Hey, what are you doing bringing hometown boy back here right before my concert? What's he doing here at all?"

I grabbed a flyer from Zack's hands. "We don't mean no

trouble but being old friends of Caro's, well she said she would get you to sign one of these for me." That put me firmly back in the "fan" category in Billy's mind.

"Caro, get me a pen." What should have been a request sounded more like a command the way Billy barked it.

Caro scurried into the trailer and came out with a couple of pens. Sure enough the first one didn't work but Billy used the second to sign his name across my flyer with a flourish. He tossed the paper at me and said, "Hold on to that, boy. It'll be worth good money someday. Now you follow along with Caro and she'll get you at the front of the rope line for the show. I need to warm up my gee-tar." Billy gave Caro a slap on the butt just 'cause he could and then he went back to strumming.

Caro led us to a primo spot right in front of the stage and told the guard that we were special friends of Billy's. Then she blew air kisses at us and disappeared.

I turned to go and Zack said, "Not so fast. We're staying right here, clapping and cheering until Billy is sure we are his new best fans."

I sure didn't get it but I went along. I'll say this for Billy, his backup band was loud and energetic. Every time he looked our way, we cheered and fist pumped. When he sang "Finally Found You" he kept throwing steamy glances over to Caro who was standing behind the curtain to his left. Didn't seem to bother Zack at all.

When the show ended, Billy took a few too many bows and then hustled off the stage. Zack punched me in the arm. "C'mon, I'll buy you a Rolling Rock."

We got a couple of beers at the beverage booth and when we turned I had to squeeze between a cowboy carrying a guitar case and an old guy with a fiddle tucked under his arm. I muttered an "excuse me" and followed Zack as he wandered around the midway, listening to teenagers scream their fool heads off on a roller coaster while toddlers squealed with delight on a merry-go-round.

I was enjoying my beer and not really wondering what Zack was up to when he said. "Okay. It should be time."

"Time? For what?"

And I nearly choked on a gulp of beer when Zack answered, "Time to steal Billy's guitar."

"Whoa, partner..."

Zack put his arm around me, his mouth close to my ear. "Where do you think Billy is now? I mean right now. Show is over. Adrenalin spiked. What would you do?"

"You think he's in the Laredo doing what-all with Caro?"

"I do indeed. And I bet the guitar is the last thing on his mind. Bet he wasn't too careful putting it away while he was dragging Caro off to bed."

We snuck back to the trailer and sure enough the guitar case was leaning against the side of the chair where Billy had been sitting and strumming a while ago. Could it really be that simple?

I looked around. Not a soul in sight. Zack tiptoed closer to the chair. As soon as he lifted the guitar case I could tell it was empty. Zack opened it and placed it across the arms of the chair.

My heart darn near stopped when Zack opened the trailer door, first an inch, then a few more. He stopped to listen a time or two and then opened the door wide. There it was all dazzling with sunlight shining through the door and bouncing off the jewels—Billy's ten thousand dollar Gibson leaning against the driver's seat.

Zack slid the guitar out of the trailer and into the case. Then he shut the door and walked away with me on his six.

There were so many musicians wandering the festival that no one gave us or the guitar case a second glance. In the parking lot we jumped into the truck but saved the whooping and hollering until we were off the festival grounds.

Zack kept saying, "I wish we could see Billy's face when he finds his guitar's gone missing. But that's behind us now." I heard a little regret in his voice, like he was never going to do anything more spectacular that what he'd just done.

"Long as they don't figure out it was us took it, I can enjoy the ride." Although truth be told, I was a little nervous every time we passed a sheriff's car and believe me with all the traffic, there were plenty of green and whites riding around.

Then Zack went all silent. I figured he was planning his next move. Even I knew we sure couldn't sell the guitar. I was stumped but I hoped he had a plan.

"Stop the truck."

Not sure why I listened to him but I pulled up next to the big green BOGGY BAYOU sign and Zack got out. He dragged the guitar behind him and stood by the side of the road strumming a few pitiful chords.

I half thought he was going tell me to turn the truck around so we could give Billy back his guitar and be on our way, but instead he held the guitar over his head and flung it way out into Boggy Bayou. Then, calm as could be, he got back in the truck.

"I don't want his stupid 'gee-tar'," Zack imitated the way Billy had said it. "It just don't seem fittin' that Billy gets Caro and the guitar, too."

He slammed his door shut. "I still got some rainy day money in my pocket. We should make it to Ivy's before closing. Rolling Rock is on me."

I threw the truck in gear and we headed for home.

Three Rivers Voodoo
Liz Milliron

When I left the bayou for the 'Burgh, and traded the mighty Mississippi for the Three Rivers, I left a lot behind. Spanish moss. A bakery that made awesome beignets. Voodoo. The steel and glass skyline of Pittsburgh had nothing to do with the swamps of Louisiana. Sure, *Grandmere* insisted I take a *gris-gris* for luck, but that was just sentiment.

Right.

I sat in the conference room, nervous system on fire. Bernie Kaufman, our department manager, addressed us from the front of the room. He was immaculate, as always, in a dark-blue pinstriped suit, white shirt, and dark tie. The picture of modern financial business success.

"I'm pleased to announce the lead for the Adventus project will be...Kristy Gottschalk. Congratulations, Kristy."

My nerves stopped sizzling and I deflated. But I forced myself to smile and clap politely with the rest of the team.

Kristy beamed and flipped her hair. It wasn't the first time she'd beaten me to something I wanted. The premier parking spot reserved for the analyst of the month. The cute guy, Jake, who worked in legal. And now the lead for the Adventus project. It wasn't fair. I wanted to punch her in her perfect smile. Yank out hunks of her perfectly waved ash-blonde hair.

There's a better way and you know it, *Grandmere's* voice whispered in my mind.

Kristy leaned across the table and smirked. "Oh, too bad, Vi," she said. The layer of insincerity was as thick as water hyacinths on the bayou. "Better luck next time. Unless you're tired of losing and want to give up." She pushed herself out of her chair and strutted out of the room, accepting accolades as she went.

I gripped the edge of the table so hard my knuckles turned white. Tired of losing? Not a chance.

At home that night I dropped my keys, went to the kitchen, and did what I always did when under stress. I made gumbo. As I stirred the roux with the wooden spoon *Grandmere* had given me, I couldn't stop thinking. I'd worked my ass off these past four weeks to get the lead for the Adventus project. I wasn't going down without a fight. Not this time. But how to fight back? That was the question.

You know how, *Grandmere* whispered.

While the gumbo simmered away, I went to the table in my living room and picked up the *gris-gris*. I ran my fingers over the burgundy chamois bag. For luck, *Grandmere* had said. Good luck or bad? Had to be good. I was the oldest granddaughter. The one who'd graduated from LSU summa cum laude. *Grandmere* wouldn't wish me ill. But could you make a *gris-gris* for bad luck? One way to find out.

The smell of the gumbo filled my apartment, a soothing fragrance. I inhaled, then dialed *Grandmere's* number.

"Violette," she said. "What a pleasant surprise." A beat of silence. "You need something."

Trust *Grandmere's* uncanny sixth sense to ferret out the fact this wasn't a social call. "I have a question," I said. "Before I left home, you gave me a *gris-gris*. For luck, you said. I assume you meant good luck."

A pause. "Yes."

"I was wondering." I swallowed, but the aroma of home encouraged me to continue. "Can a *gris-gris* be for other things? Like bad luck?"

Another pause. "I thought you wanted to leave voodoo in Louisiana," *Grandmere* said.

"I did, but there's this woman at work. She's...awful. A *macaque*. The type who always has to show off. Get her own way. I thought maybe a bit of bad luck would bring her down a notch. Nothing serious. Just one time where things *don't* work out."

"Violette Marie." *Grandmere's* voice, rich and melodious, sobered. "When it comes to voodoo, everything is serious."

I'd always brushed off *Grandmere's* adherence to voodoo as superstition. Something unbecoming of a good Catholic girl. But nothing in my Catholic upbringing was appropriate for a response to Kristy Gottschalk. Voodoo was.

"Certainly, there are charms for bad luck as well as good. But, *cherie*, are you sure? You must be sure."

I turned off the heat and added the filé powder, watching as the green tinge spread over the surface of the gumbo. Was I sure? It only took a moment to decide. "Yes," I said.

"Very well." *Grandmere's* voice became crisp. "Write this down."

I followed *Grandmere's* instructions and made a little felt doll. It wouldn't win any art prizes, but that wasn't the point. I hesitated, holding the black-headed pin over its head. Last chance to turn back. I pictured Kristy's self-satisfied face and jammed the pin through the doll's head. Take that, Kristy Gottschalk.

The next day, I detoured past Kristy's desk on the way to my own. She was chatting up the mailroom guy, looking like the very picture of professional perfection. As always.

"What do you want?" she asked, twirling a strand of hair around her finger, not even bothering to look at me.

"To say congratulations and good luck," I said. "I was really disappointed at first, but you deserve everything that's coming to you."

She focused on me, brown eyes narrow. "I'm late for a

meeting. See you around, Vi." She batted her eyes at the mailroom guy and walked off, hips swaying.

He didn't even bother to say hi to me, just dropped some envelopes on Kristy's desk and left. I watched Kristy's back as she entered the elevator. A meeting about Adventus, no doubt. I clenched my teeth, forcing down my breakfast grits.

That morning, I'd given the black pin an extra shove. The voodoo was done. All I had to do was wait.

I waited longer than I expected. I watched Kristy for the next week, looking for bad luck to descend like an avalanche. But it didn't. She was commended for her work. She and Jake went on another date. Her new haircut was fabulous. Not a pimple marred her complexion. She didn't even break one of her manicured nails.

It was maddening.

Over the weekend, I baked beignets. I hadn't yet found a place in Pittsburgh for my favorite treat. Despite the fact it'd leave my desk a mess of powdered sugar, I took one into work Monday morning. I arrived to see groups of employees in hushed, frantic conversation.

My friend, Tina, pounced on me before I had time to unpack my beignet. "Did you hear?"

"Hear what?" From Tina's expression, I figured the entire market had flat-lined.

"Kristy's dead." Tina leaned into my cube lest anyone hear her. But judging from the whispers rushing through the office like a hurricane wind, everybody knew.

Except me. I'd spent the evening drowning my sorrows in a pint of fudge ice cream and the music of Joni Mitchell at full blast. I hadn't turned on the TV, radio, or my computer all night. I hadn't checked the paper this morning. And since I listened to satellite radio in the car, no hint of anything on my morning commute.

Maudit. I stared at Kristy's empty desk. "No way."

"Way," Tina said, worrying her bottom lip. "Worse, the cops are here. From the way they're asking questions, everyone figures she was murdered."

Murdered? *Merde.* I'd asked for bad luck. Okay, death was bad luck but a bit exTremé. I'd been thinking more along the lines of public humiliation. "Are...are you sure?" I could hear the waver in my voice. I hoped Tina would chalk it up to shock.

She nodded, bright red hair falling out of her headband and over her forehead. "Yes. Well, kind of. Not sure-sure, but why else would the cops be here?" She jerked her thumb over her shoulder.

Two men in suits that screamed "police officer" were talking to Bernie. My manager's face was drawn. He pointed toward Kristy's desk, and at several people in the room. Including me.

A string of curses ran through my head, some English, some Cajun-French. At least I hadn't brought the voodoo doll to work. I'd have a hell of a time explaining that one, considering no one else in the office hailed from Cajun country.

I sat at my desk and pretended to get to work, Tina forgotten. Maybe if I looked really busy, the cops would leave me alone.

"Violette Lemaire?" a deep male voice asked from above me.

I looked up. It was the cop I'd seen talking to Bernie. Calm down, Vi. Sound natural. Maybe he wants to know where the bathroom is. "That's me. May I help you?"

"Follow me."

I didn't move. "What's this about?"

"Detective Harry Blackwell, Pittsburgh Bureau of Police. Homicide. One of your co-workers was found dead this morning. We're talking to everyone in the office." He turned, expecting me to follow. It didn't occur to me to disobey. *Merde.*

Detective Blackwell led me to one of the conference rooms. Not the one where Bernie had made the Adventus announcement. This one was smaller and it felt positively claustrophobic.

"Sit." Blackwell waved at one of the leatherette chairs around the glossy black table. My shoe caught in the carpeting and I stumbled a little as I moved to the chair. Blackwell took the seat opposite me, back to the windows. Bright sunlight streamed through and I squinted. I didn't know what to say, so I opted for silence. But as Blackwell reviewed his notes, not speaking, I broke. Probably what he intended, but I couldn't help it. "What's this all about?"

He lifted his gaze, face unreadable. "As I said, we're talking to everybody in the office. At least this department. Routine. How long have you known Ms. Gottschalk?" he asked. He removed a cheap ballpoint from his pocket and uncapped it.

"Since I joined the firm. About nine months." I smoothed my hair, which was frizzing out of the knot I'd put it in this morning. Normally it only did that when it was humid. I clasped my hands to keep them from trembling.

"Did you know her well?"

"Not especially, no." Truth. Kristy and I didn't spend our free time together.

"Were you on good terms?"

Think. Blunt honesty and lying would both make me look guilty. "I guess. We didn't talk much."

"A few other people have said there was some animosity between the two of you." Blackwell stared at me. "Something about a project lead and a guy."

I tried not to wince. Of course others would talk. They

didn't want to look like suspects. And I was the new girl, the outsider. Tread carefully, Vi. "Yes, I was hoping for the lead on the Adventus project. I'd been about to ask Jake Cotterfield out. I waited too long and Kristy got there first."

Blackwell held his pen, but didn't write. "That make you angry?"

"Angry?" I hated the way my voice broke on the second syllable. Angry enough that I'd resorted to voodoo, but I wasn't going to say that to Detective Blackwell. "I was disappointed. Of course." I licked my lips, which were dry as dust.

"One of your co-workers said you threatened to stab Ms. Gottschalk's eyes out."

Maudit. Me and my big mouth. "I may have said some things in the heat of the moment, but I assure you they were just words. I didn't wish Kristy any harm." Maybe this all was because I'd stabbed the doll through the head. Was that wrong? Perhaps I should have targeted an arm.

Blackwell stared at me for eternity, the silence stretching on long enough to become torture. He probably heard this kind of story all the time. Right before he slapped on the cuffs.

"Is that all?" I asked when I could bear it no more. "I've got to get back to work. Deadlines." I winced at the word *dead.*

He paused. "You can go. We'll be in touch if we need to talk to you again." Without another word, he looked down and started writing notes.

I wanted to read them, but I couldn't. And I couldn't stay. I opened my mouth to say something else, but what more was there? I should shut up before I got myself arrested. I fled back to my desk. Never mind work. I needed to call *Grandmere.*

* * *

That night, I poured out my agony to *Grandmere* while I emptied my bottle of pinot noir. I didn't need more gumbo and I definitely didn't need more beignets. "What am I going to do?" I said, shaking the bottle to get to the last drops.

"I would think you've done enough," *Grandmere* said.

"I didn't kill her." I picked up my glass and wandered to the living room. "I only wanted her to have some bad luck."

"Dying isn't bad luck?"

"*Grandmere*! This is serious." I knew I should have stayed away from voodoo.

The sound of her sigh told me she was smiling at the same time. "*Cherie*, I told you. Voodoo is always serious."

I swirled my wine and muttered.

"The spirits' definition of bad luck and yours is not always the same. You wanted the misfortune to befall your friend."

"She wasn't my friend."

"And it did." *Grandmere* continued as though I hadn't spoken. "How did she die?"

"She was strangled." I'd looked up the account of Kristy's death in the paper. "Strangled and left behind some garbage cans. A block from my house. I didn't like her and I wasn't quiet about it. And the police know it." I gulped the wine. "Tell me honestly. Is this my fault?"

"You made the doll. You wished for her misfortune. The intent was in your heart and the spirits knew this." Her voice was serene. She might have been reading the weather forecast.

I needed more wine. "Is voodoo recognized as a murder weapon?" I should find that out. It would probably be important.

"What did you do with the doll?"

"I threw it out." Last thing I needed was the police to search my apartment and find a voodoo doll with a pin through its head. "Too late to reverse the wish, huh?"

"Indeed. I think there only one thing left to do," *Grandmere* said. "Pray to the Virgin."

"Pray? *Grandmere*, I don't think voodoo and Catholicism are compatible."

"My dear Violette." She laughed. "This world is big enough to include the spirits and *le Bon Dieu*. You've tried one. Perhaps you should try the other." She ended the call.

It took everything I had to go to work on Tuesday. As it was, I couldn't quite cover the purple smudges under my eyes and or tame my curls. And to top it all off, Jake was standing by my cube. My bad luck continued. Maybe the spirits thought that doll was supposed to be me, not Kristy.

"Morning, Vi," he said. He glanced at Kristy's desk, still adorned with yellow tape. "Hell of a thing, isn't it? Kristy."

"Yeah."

He tapped my cube wall. "They know anything? Besides what was in the paper?"

"Not that anyone's told me." I sat and rubbed my temples. I needed more coffee. I preferred my own, as close to what they served at Café Du Monde as I could get, but the office one-cup machine was going to have to do.

He leaned on my desk. "Want to go out for a drink after work?"

Today? He'd gone on dates with Kristy just last week. That was...disturbing. "Weren't you and Kristy a couple? Awfully fast to be moving on, isn't it?"

"It didn't go so well. She was a downer. Strangled the conversation, made it all about her. I couldn't shut her up." He looked at me. "What do you say?"

"I don't know." I straightened my desk calendar. Two weeks ago I'd have jumped at the invitation. But now, a day after Kristy's death, it felt wrong. First I'd wished for her misfortune and she died. Could I steal her boyfriend? Wouldn't people talk? The timing felt suspicious, but could Kristy have been a bad enough date for Jake to strangle her?

"Come on. A few beers, a few laughs. We could use them." He lifted an eyebrow.

Bernie walked up to my desk trailed by the man who was probably my least favorite person in Pittsburgh right now. "Violette, you're here. Detective Blackwell needs to talk to you. Use the small conference room." He started to walk away, then turned. "We need a new Adventus lead. You were our second choice. Project's yours." He walked off. Jake muttered something and hurried off, leaving me with Detective Blackwell.

The detective looked at me. There was a gleam in his eye I didn't quite like. Had he been close enough to hear Jake's invitation?

The guy I wanted. The project I wanted. With Kristy gone, they were both in my grasp. And Detective Blackwell knew it.

In the conference room, I felt the need to put the table between me and the detective, so I picked a chair against the windows. Let him squint. He took the seat opposite, but there was no squinting. He stared. I fidgeted, this time determined to let him speak first.

"I saw you talking to Jake Cotterfield," Blackwell said. "Wasn't he involved with Kristy Gottschalk?"

Blackwell had to know all about Kristy and Jake. He didn't need me to confirm.

"I heard him ask you out." Blackwell sat back and folded his hands on the table.

I bit my lip.

"Moving a bit fast, aren't you? Taking a dead woman's boyfriend?"

"He asked me," I said. I immediately wished I could take the words back.

"But you like him," Blackwell said.

I was sure any number of my co-workers would testify about my attraction to Jake. I nodded.

"And you've got the project lead you wanted, too." Blackwell leaned forward.

I knew it spelled motive. With the way my luck was running, the next thing Blackwell would drop on me would be that damn doll.

Blackwell took out his notepad and flipped through it. "Where were you between nine Sunday night and three Monday morning?"

"Home. Eating ice cream and listening to loud music." Even I knew it was a pathetic alibi.

"Can anyone confirm that?"

I tried for a note of levity. "Only if you count the stray cat who comes to my back door."

Blackwell didn't smile. Either he didn't like jokes or he didn't like cats. "You didn't go out for anything? More ice cream?"

"No, I swear." I felt the itch of hair sticking to my forehead and a droplet of sweat ran down between my shoulder blades. Did they turn off the A/C? "I know, pretty sad. But true."

"Where's home?" Blackwell's gaze pinned me in place, dark eyes not giving a hint of his thoughts. He had to know.

Could this get any worse? I couldn't not answer this time. "South Side. I rent a house on 19th." A block from where Kristy had been killed.

"Really."

Blood pounded in my ears. "If you're thinking I killed Kristy..."

"Did you?"

I thought of the doll. "*C'est fou*...I mean, that's crazy. Of course not."

"Lemaire. French?" He twirled his pen.

"Cajun," I said, surprised my voice still worked.

A wry grin twisted his lips. "Don't bother telling me you were pals. I've heard from other people you two didn't care for each other. Did you put a voodoo spell on her?"

My brain was racing. Me and my big mouth. No use backpedaling. My nature wouldn't let me do that anyway. But as much as I might have *wanted* to hurt Kristy, I hadn't killed her. I'd be damned if I'd go to jail for that without a struggle.

I fought to keep my voice calm. "No, I didn't like her. Yes, I like Jake. I wanted the Adventus lead. I was pissed that Kristy got both. But I didn't kill her." Not with my hands at least. "*C'est tout.* I'm done. If we're going to continue this conversation, I want a lawyer."

"You're not under arrest," Blackwell said. "You can leave this room whenever you want."

I stood with enough force that I knocked my chair over. "The next time you come see me, Detective, you'd better have a warrant or something."

He didn't say anything, just leaned back and looked at me.

I left the room and stalked to my desk. Once there, I found a hair band and used it to pull my curls into a ponytail. The only way I was going to get myself out of trouble was to figure out who really had killed Kristy. How the hell was I going to do that?

On the way home, I stopped at St. Paul's Cathedral in Oakland. I hadn't put a prayer corner in my apartment. Something I hadn't worried about, but that now seemed like a gross oversight. The last weekday Mass was long over, but there were a few folks kneeling in prayer. I found a pew near the statue of the Virgin Mary, knelt, and bowed my head. *Holy mother Mary, get me out of this and I promise I'll never touch voodoo again.*

Could you bargain with the mother of God? *Grandmere*

often said I was *tête dur*, stubborn as an old goat, but I wasn't above asking for help this time.

A soft footstep and the sense of someone standing by me made me raise my head. A middle-aged priest with a kindly expression on his round face was next to me. "Can I help you? I saw you come in. Perhaps you're looking for confession?" Take off the black robes and stick a pair of wings on this guy and he'd be positively cherubic.

"Uh, no. I need to think. A peaceful place to collect my thoughts."

He gazed at the white marble of the altar and the serene, pale face of Mary. "There are few more peaceful places. If you need someone to talk to, I'd be willing to listen."

Yes, I could just imagine the conversation. *Well, Father, I performed this voodoo ritual for a woman I don't like. I was going for bad luck, but instead she's dead and I think I might have done it.* Even in my head it sounded ridiculous. "Thank you, Father. Just need some quiet time."

"Very well." His face might be cherubic, but the dark blue eyes were piercing. Like they could see my soul. "As you think, remember. Nothing is beyond God's forgiveness. Listen with your heart and you will know what to do." He smiled and walked down the aisle.

The sound of his footsteps faded. I stared at the statue. I knew what I had to do. Tell the police about the doll. What I'd tried to do. Trust that being honest would keep me out of trouble. I had motive. I had no alibi. Kristy had been killed yards from my house.

I might well get arrested. I already looked guilty as sin. Hiding only exaggerated my guilt. I didn't care. Cajuns never backed down from a fight.

A fresh bottle of pinot noir had not helped me last night. Well, it had helped me to a wild headache, but not to a solution. There was only one. Find the culprit. But how?

I'd barely sat down when Jake's voice pulled me out of daydreams to the present. "You thought any more about that drink?"

I looked at him. He could have stepped off the pages of *GQ*, all perfect dark hair, immaculate suit, and probably a nice build underneath, judging from how the clothes fit. Why the sudden transfer of affection? Unless...

"I don't think I'd be great company," I said, fidgeting with my calendar.

He leaned against the cube wall. "It's not like you and Kristy were buds."

I pondered. "I heard the two of you were an item. Guess that wasn't true."

His shoulders twitched. "We went out for drinks. In fact we were out—" He straightened, adjusting his tie.

When? "The night she was killed?" I asked. Had to be. "Where?"

He flicked at his lapel. "Castaways."

Castaways was a bar on the South Side. And not a dive.

"She wasn't appreciative," he continued, voice a touch bitter. "Not like she should have been."

What had he said? Kristy had *strangled* the conversation. And that's how she'd died. I smelled a rat.

I started to ask another question when a ruckus drew my attention. People were popping out of cubes like prairie dogs. It wasn't hard to see the cause. Detective Blackwell and his partner were striding through the room. And they were headed straight for me.

I jumped up. I had to make them see it was a mistake. Jake may well have been the last person to see Kristy alive. How bad were those dates? How unappreciative had she been? They were going to drag me out before I could say anything.

As the detectives got closer, Jake edged away. Of course. He wouldn't want to be next to me when I was busted for murder. As the detectives approached, I tried to summon an effective defense. Something that would keep me out of prison. But the words wouldn't come. Instead, all I heard was *Grandmere's* voice. *Are you sure?*

Blackwell and his partner stopped by my cube. "You're under arrest for the murder of Kristy Gottschalk." He pulled cuffs from his belt.

And snapped them on Jake.

Jake's face went rigid. "I want a lawyer."

Blackwell shook his head. "We'll get to that part. Take him." The last was addressed to his partner, who grabbed Jake's upper arm and hustled him out through a sea of whispers, wind rustling through the trees on the bayou.

Blackwell turned to me. "Sorry to interrupt your conversation."

"That's...that's okay," I said, brushing back my hair. "I thought you were coming for me."

"Means, motive, opportunity. You figured you had them all, huh?" He gave a brief, humorless smile. "You did. But there were other details that led away from you."

"And you didn't bother to tell me?"

"Of course not. We don't tell suspects everything." He glanced at my nameplate. "Cajun, you said."

I crossed my arms. Mostly so Blackwell wouldn't see me shaking, but I suspected he saw it anyway.

"Well, Ms. Lemaire, let's just say there were facts we knew that indicated we were looking for a different killer. Unless you really were using voodoo, there was no way you were the guilty party. And what kind of judge and jury would buy death by voodoo?" He buttoned his jacket. "Have a nice day."

Blackwell walked off and I collapsed into my chair. What judge and jury indeed?

* * *

After work, I stopped at the cathedral. I lit a candle and said ten Hail Marys in front of the statue of the Virgin. Thanks for getting me out of a close call.

Once home, I rummaged in my drawers until I found *Grandmere's gris-gris*. I rubbed my thumb over the chamois. Then I opened the small safe I kept in my closet, put the *gris-gris* inside, and locked the door.

I wandered to the kitchen to open a fresh bottle of wine. Could I attribute my good fortune to the prayers to the Virgin Mary or the Cajun spiritualism of the *gris-gris*? *Grandmere* would say either. Or both. Me, I wasn't sure.

But I was certain of one thing. I would never mess with voodoo again.

Hell Hath No Fury
R. T. Lawton

Silver wisps of fog drifted across the restless black water of the bayou, twisting and moving on as if doomed spirits lost in a primeval marsh. A rising evening breeze rattled hollow reeds along the muddy bank, knocking the slender stalks against each other like the clacking of small dry bones suspended on strings. Higher up where the ground was solid, long tendrils of grey Spanish moss gently swayed from broad limbs of ancient trees.

This back country wasn't for city boys as far as Blue was concerned, and he didn't much like how he felt about this place. But, he'd come along with the other two and here they were.

Using a yellow nylon rope tied to the bow, he moored their skiff to one of the wharf posts and stepped up onto the sagging boards of the old boat dock. A long splinter at the edge of one board briefly tugged at the right cuff of his prison trousers before the denim stretched taut and finally broke free. Blue ignored the inconvenience and stared at the white antebellum mansion resting on the rise of ground well beyond the wharf. This wasn't where he expected to hide out, but there weren't that many choices given when he agreed to join the escape plan.

He took in the tall dark oaks forming a giant archway over the lane leading into a yard grown rank with weeds. The crushed shell pathway beneath the arch seemed to end at the foot of a wide verandah attached to the front of the old southern mansion. On the verandah stood several wooden pillars covered with peeling, white paint. They supported a second story balcony running the width of the house before the pillars continued upward to the lower edge of the roof.

Beyond the roofline, a dying sun leaked watery red through gaps in the straggling lines of heavy grey clouds.

"Night's coming fast," Blue said. "Best get our stuff out of the boat and inside that old house before the rain catches us in the open."

Tunk, big and black, moved silently up behind him. He spoke in a deep, low voice, "Don't think Mister Charles is gonna make it much longer. That bullet hole in his chest is hurting him some bad."

Turning his head toward the skiff, Blue tried to get a reading on how the injured man was doing.

"You get him up to the house," said Blue. "I'll unload the skiff and bring the gear."

Stepping back into the shallow boat, Blue started lifting sleeping bags, boxes of canned food, cases of bottled water, a .22 caliber gator rifle and other supplies onto the dock. When he finished, he calculated the number of trips it would take to move it all. There'd have been more in the pile, except the owner of the bait store near the boat launch surprised them by showing up after hours. Morning sun wasn't even up yet and here this guy come through the back door, gun in hand like he knew he was being burgled. With no forewarning, he'd popped a hole in Charlie and was looking for his next target. That's when Tunk stuck the owner with a shank he'd made in the prison machine shop.

The smell of gunpowder and fresh blood hurried them out of the bait shop with what they already had stacked in a pile. In the small marina out front, they quickly found an old skiff was the only boat not chained up or needing ignition keys. Slow travel, but they'd gotten away in the dark.

On his last trip lugging stuff up to the house, Blue took a closer look at the old mansion. The verandah sagged on one end where wood had decayed and fallen. Green moss grew out of a couple of weathered boards on the front siding and the left half of the front doors hung crosswise from a twisted top hinge. It spoke of sudden money and a quick leave taking.

Blue walked through the foyer and dumped his last load onto the floor inside the Grand Room. He took stock of the mansion's interior. There were open doors on both sides of the large room, while twin staircases at the rear led up to an interior balcony on the second floor. Charlie lay limp on a bedroll in front of a large brick fireplace set between the two curving staircases.

Tunk saw Blue and came over to stand close.

"Charles not getting any better," he said in a hushed voice. "Needs some help."

"He bleedin' out?"

"That and the man's having himself some hallucinations."

"Like what?"

"We was on that path between the oaks when the man happened to glance up at the house. Said he saw a woman's face in one of them second-story windows. Said she looked sad like she been crying or something."

"You see anything?"

"Myself? Nope. Ain't heard nothing either."

"Okay, get them gas lanterns lit and put one over by Charlie. I'll talk to him a bit, then you and me'll go search the house. See if anybody's home that shouldn't be."

Tunk rooted through the pile of camping gear, while Blue made his way over to Charlie's side.

The wounded man seemed to be staring up at one of the staircases as if he expected to see something coming down the steps. Over the right side of his chest, he held one hand pressed tightly against the spreading red stain on his denim shirt.

Blue noticed small pink bubbles leaking between Charlie's wide-spread fingers. Not much they could do out here for a sucking chest wound. And, going for a doctor was out of the question.

"How you doing there, bud?"

Charlie kept staring upward.

"Not so good. Doesn't look like I'm getting out of here alive."

Blue shrugged.

"We all die a little more each day. Some just go faster than others."

"No, Blue, that's not it. We shouldn't have disturbed the woman. She's going to make it personal."

"Who you talking about, Charlie? You said nobody was living here when you told us about this place. Said it was hidden back in the bayou so far nobody would ever find us."

Charlie's eyes darted to Blue's face for a brief moment, then back to the second-floor balcony.

"It is, Blue, it is. Nobody's come to this place in years. It's just that I'd forgotten about the stories. Always thought they were meant to frighten us kids a long time ago. Make us behave when we were acting up."

"What stories you talking about?"

"Doesn't make any difference now, Blue. Too late already. She's awake for true."

"Who's awake?"

"The woman upstairs. I saw her in the second-story window. She belonged to my great-grandfather. Was his mistress for a couple of years before he set her aside for another female."

"She's got to be pretty old then, if she belonged to him."

"Not so old. You'll see."

"So where do I find this not so old lady?"

A sudden spell of coughing delayed Charlie's response. The small pink bubbles darkened and grew larger between his splayed fingers. He pointed with the index finger of his other hand.

"Up there."

"Just don't be messin' with me, Charlie. You the one said this place was a good hideout. Night's coming on quick now and I'm not sleeping out in the dark with snakes and gators."

Charlie closed his eyes, took in a shallow breath and lay quiet.

Tunk set a lantern down by Charlie's side. The glow of light filled the space between the two staircases. He gave one lantern to Blue and kept one for himself.

"Let's go look, if we're going."

Blue retrieved the .22 rifle from the pile of goods in the foyer and started for the nearest room.

"Tunk, you stay with Charlie and keep watch while I search the main floor. Then we'll both go upstairs."

The big black nodded his assent and drew the bait shop owner's pistol from inside the waist of his prison denims. He looked to be ready for whatever was coming next.

"I be right here. Don't be long."

Fifteen minutes later, Blue had cleared all the rooms on both sides of the Grand Room. He returned to the other two men.

"Nothing alive on this floor, except spiders and mice. You set to go up?"

Tunk nodded again.

"Fine, you take the right staircase and I'll go up the left."

With the gas lantern held out front for light, Blue went slowly up the stairs, peering at the second floor landing, trying to see if anything waited for them at the top. Now, the glow of the lantern didn't appear to penetrate the darkness as far as it had down in the large room. It seemed as if the light was being repulsed by the heavy darkness inside the old mansion's upper floor.

For a brief moment, Blue thought he saw the face of a beautiful young female on the landing. His impression was of long raven black hair, sad eyes, high cheekbones and the smooth *café au lait* skin of a creole belle. He blinked and she was gone.

Blue hesitated for a step, cleared his mind, then continued up. Thick dust covered the stairs and landing.

They went through the upstairs rooms carefully, each man covering the other. Three rooms stood deserted of any human inhabitants. Nothing there but furniture old enough to be antiques. Rotted lace curtains hung over the large beds in each room and the seat cushions of straight back chairs had fallen through, leaving a litter of dirty brown stuffing beneath them. Lantern light on the floor boards showed only their own footprints, two dusty trails sliding from one bedroom to another.

The door to the fourth room was locked. Blue dropped to one knee and tried peering through the old-style keyhole in the door. Too dark inside to make out the interior.

"What do you think?"

"I think we check it out," replied Tunk. "This the room Charles said he saw the woman."

"Best be safe then." Blue stood, raised his right foot and kicked beside the lock. Wood cracked. He kicked again. The door splintered around the lock and swung open. Clouds of golden dust motes swirled through the air, sparkling in the lantern light like a living presence. Blue inhaled the slight stench of sweet decay, sneezed once and covered his nose.

Both men stepped in, one to the left, the other to the right. Their lanterns glowed less brightly in the darkness, but it was enough light for Blue to see the white bones of a skeleton in one corner of the room. The remains sat upright, held in place by the walls on either side.

"Damn. Tunk, come look at this."

Tunk came around the foot of a canopied bed where the moldy bedspread and top sheet were turned down as if someone had just risen. He stopped short.

"That thing's got a knife stuck in its chest."

"Looks more like an ivory handled stiletto, my friend. And, judging by the strands of long black hair and what's left of a red silk dress, I'd say them bones belonged to a woman."

Tunk gestured at the window near the skeleton.

"That the same one Charles said he saw the face of the sad lady."

"Bones don't get up and walk."

"Probably not."

Tunk moved closer to the skeleton and reached down for the stiletto.

"Leave it," said Blue.

"Don't think so," said Tunk. "Blade's corroded, but it's still better than my shank."

He grabbed the handle and pulled. The stiletto came loose with a grating noise as steel rasped across bone. At the same time, the skull toppled off the neck bones and rolled across the floor.

Blue watched the skull roll up against an old wooden travel chest now covered with scraps of a decaying cloth. When the skull stopped, he took a closer look at the wooden chest. Spread out on its top were small animal bones, a snake skeleton, strings of wood beads of red and green and yellow, some half-burnt candles and a gold locket and chain. Blue picked up the locket and opened it.

"Look at that," said Tunk over Blue's shoulder, "the photo on the left is a lot like you 'cept for them old-timey clothes the man's wearing. Reckon the picture of that female on the right is that pile of bones over there?"

Ignoring those thoughts, Blue picked up the skull and thrust it into Tunk's hands.

"Put it back on top of the skeleton and let's get out of here. I don't want anything to do with the woman or her room."

He tossed the locket back onto the chest and walked out into the hallway to wait for Tunk. As he left, he felt a tugging at his mind. Whispers he couldn't quite hear the words to. The voice in a lilting, velvet accent.

When Tunk came out, they went down the stairs and back into the Grand Room, each man wrapped in his own thoughts.

"Tell you what," Blue finally suggested, "I'll check on how Charlie's doing while you build us a fire. That'll give us some light and we can save on gas for the lanterns."

"Where am I gonna find wood for a fire?"

Blue gestured towards the rear of the house.

"There's some stacked up on the back porch where it's dry."

Tunk started for the back door, while Blue walked over to the bedroll and knelt by Charlie to speak a few words.

"Hey, bud, nothing up there but old bones."

Charlie opened his eyes. His chest wheezed with every breath. Using one bloody hand, he grasped the front of Blue's shirt and raised himself partway up.

"You saw her?"

"Just the bones."

"You found more than that. I see it in your face."

Blue started to pry Charlie's fingers out of the death grip on his shirt front. When he glanced up, Charlie was now staring over Blue's shoulder. Blue couldn't help himself. He craned his head around for a quick look.

"She's here," whispered Charlie.

Blue felt a chill in the air. His gaze darted back and forth across the room.

"I don't see nothing."

A strangled gurgle came from Charlie's throat. His fingers released their hold and he fell back on the bedroll. The wheezing stopped.

Blue snapped his attention back to Charlie and felt for a pulse. The man was gone.

It was on Blue's mind that they needed to bury Charlie, but

he wasn't in the mood to wander around in the dark night to find a suitable place. And, he was pretty sure he couldn't get Tunk to do it either. He also didn't figure to sleep in the same room as a dead man. Grabbing two corners of the sleeping bag where Charlie was stretched out, Blue walked backwards, dragging the bedroll across the floor, down the hallway and into a side room. He dropped both corners and hesitated for a moment.

From out in the darkness came the piercing squall of a trapped swamp rabbit. Blue felt a shiver between his shoulders. Predators roamed the bayou. He felt a desperate desire to get back to the lantern light in the Grand Room, and was almost there when he heard Tunk scream. Then a loud curse.

"Sonofabitch bit me."

Blue snatched up the gator rifle and faced towards the doorway leading to the back porch.

Tunk stumbled into the Grand Room, his left hand clutching his right forearm.

"What happened?" asked Blue.

"I was getting wood out of the stack when a damn snake bit me."

"What kind?"

"Looked to be a big copperhead. Thing hit me three times. Didn't want to let go."

"Let me see."

Tunk held out his forearm.

"Think he got me in the vein the last time. Arm's swelling up. Hurts like hell."

"Sit down against the wall and relax. It'll slow down the poison."

Tunk lowered himself to the floor and whipped out the ivory handled stiletto from his belt. With the point of the corroded blade, he started cutting X's over the puncture marks in his arm. Finished with that, he raised his right forearm to his lips and sucked on each X. Several times, he spat thinned-out blood onto the floor.

Blue chose a spot on the opposite side of the fireplace and kept an eye on the snake-bit man. In time, Tunk tied a tourniquet around his forearm and leaned back against the wall.

"Arm feels hot, but I feels chilled. Why don't *you* build us that fire now?"

Rising to his feet, Blue took two of the lanterns in hand and headed for the back door. Carefully, he placed one near the doorway and the second on the porch boards. At least with two light sources the area was well lit. He nudged some of the cut logs with the toe of his shoe. When nothing slithered out, he picked up a few sticks of firewood and carried them back to the fireplace. After several trips without incidence, he retrieved the lanterns, shut the back door and worked at arranging small pieces of wood in the fireplace.

Flames started small, then gradually grew as Blue added larger pieces of wood to the fire. Heat spread out into the room. Shadows danced against the other three walls.

Blue dug a sleeping bag for himself out of the pile and laid it on the floor away from where Tunk leaned against the wall. By now, the man's forearm had swollen to twice normal size and Tunk had moved the tourniquet to a place above his elbow. The stiletto stuck upright into one of the floorboards by his thigh. He kept his eyes on Blue.

"Where's Charles?"

"You were right; man didn't make it. I put him in the other room. We'll bury him tomorrow."

"You may be doing all the digging by yourself."

"So how you doing?" asked Blue.

"Wish I had me some whiskey."

"There was some in the bait shop, but guess we got in a hurry after you shanked the old man."

Tunk nodded.

"I tell you, Blue, we messed up, messed up a lot."

"How's that?"

"Everything. The bait shop. The old man showing up. Staying here." He paused. "That table we seen upstairs in the bedroom. Where that woman was."

"Yeah."

"Puts me in mind of some unnatural stuff I seen in backwoods places outside the French Quarter and over in Algiers. We shoulda let that woman upstairs be."

Blue put a grin on his face.

"Charlie spooked you with his talk about the woman. Just relax as best you can."

Tunk closed his eyes.

"Don't let nothing catch up with you, Blue, else we did all this for nothing."

"No worries, bud. Now I'm out a prison, I'm never going back."

"It's more than that. Me and Charles be seeing each other real soon now. You be on your own. Watch yourself. The picture in that locket makes me think that woman got an eye for somebody look a lot like you."

"We'll move on after daylight. You rest up."

Tunk slumped as though his body was collapsing in on itself. His limbs shuddered a couple of times and he seemed to slow his breathing.

Blue struggled to keep his eyes open. He wasn't sure it was safe to close them.

Coals from the fire glowed dark red as the flames eventually died down. Shadows lengthened.

Heavy-lidded, Blue's eyes were blinking shut when his brain told him there was movement in the room. He struggled to force his eyes halfway open.

There. Tunk's hand had twitched. Slowly, it moved towards his thigh. His fingers, one by one, wrapped themselves around the handle of the stiletto and pulled it out of the floor. Tunk's eyes opened.

Blue sat up on his bedroll and felt for the gator rifle. It was out of reach.

"Whatcha doing, Tunk?"

Wordlessly, the big man rose to his feet and shambled forward.

Blue glanced around. There didn't seem to be anything else in the room. He turned back to Tunk and saw a red gleam smoldering in his eyes. The man was staring straight at him and had the stiletto pointed his way.

Not waiting for an explanation, Blue rolled off the sleeping bag and came up with the rifle. He aimed the .22 and pulled the trigger. The slug hit center mass, just as the army had once taught him to shoot in close combat.

Tunk kept shambling forward.

Blue ejected the casing and slammed the bolt home. He raised his aim higher in the center of Tunk's chest and fired again and again until the magazine was empty.

Two feet away, Tunk's eyes flared to a blazing red, then grew pale until the fire winked out. His legs turned rubber, dropping him to the floor in a heap. A mournful wail escaped his lips.

Rolling the body over with his shoe tip, Blue studied his shot pattern. Other than the first shot, the rest of the holes could have been covered with a silver dollar. Right where the heart should have been. Either Tunk had a big heart, or something else was driving him.

Blue threw more logs on the fire, built it up until every corner of the room was lit. Then he dragged Tunk's body into the same room as Charlie's. Let them keep each other company.

Back in the Grand Room, Blue moved his sleeping bag closer to the fireplace and propped himself against the wall where he could watch the doorway to the room where the two corpses lay. Each time the flames died down, he threw a couple more logs into the fireplace.

Just a few more hours until daybreak, then he could leave this place. All he had to do was keep his eyes open.

Two hours from dawn, the warmth of the fire relaxed his body and numbed his brain into an almost somnambulant state. In his lazy, opened-eyed dreams he felt the creaks and groans of the ancient house. For a moment, he thought he heard the shuffling of skeletal remains on the upstairs landing. And, maybe the soft laughter of a woman in love.

Faint light glowed from the ash covered coals. Long shadows crept along the dusty walls. A chill covered the room.

By early morning, the sky had cleared and the breeze had died down. It had quit rattling the dried reeds out by the old wharf. And the tendrils of Spanish moss in the ancient trees along the path had stilled from any movement. Rays of sunlight shone through slats in the plantation shutters on the front windows, falling warmly onto floorboards in the Grand Room. One golden sunbeam slowly crawled across Blue stretched out on his sleeping bag, but Blue didn't move. The sunbeam hesitated at the ivory handled stiletto protruding from the center of Blue's chest and then moved on as if it had seen all it needed to know. It crossed over the long black strands of hair lying on Blue's shoulder and settled on the remains of a skeleton nestled in Blue's arm. A scrap of old red silk covered some of the stark white rib bones.

Written in charcoal letters on the hearth of the fireplace were the words: NEVER LEAVE ME.

The Odds
Gary Phillips

Visitors to the Ringtree Hotel often commented on the clever décor of its rooms. The owners, the Underwoods, Claire and Charlie, were a retired couple who spent half the year traveling or attending making money in real estate seminars in such locales as Honolulu. They'd been convinced to do the re-do post-Hurricane Katrina—where the hotel previously had a pleasant, preserved sort of Mayberry, as in the 1960's *The Andy Griffith Show*, look and feel to it. But now, with the help of FEMA funds and a finagled favorable loan from the bank, the rebuilt hotel had been extolled in travel blogs. The brick and slate façade was as before, but each floor of the three-story structure had a master theme. Western for the first floor, 1960's space station for the second, and pirate ship for the third. The redesign had been done at the suggestion of the day manager.

The destruction leveled by the hurricane in this part of Biloxi was not often mentioned compared to what had transpired across the gulf in New Orleans. To the nation, what happened more than a decade ago was recalled as a *Lord of the Flies* de-evolution of devastated citizenry huddled at the Super Dome. Or the infamous news report labeling a white man and woman fording hip deep water carrying canned goods as brave survivors, and black folks doing the same as looters. Wading while black.

Yet nonetheless the original quaint Ringtree Hotel, set a block and a half back from the water, was wracked in the climatic upheaval. The head chef lost his life that day carrying a large metal cooking pan filled with Cornish game hens.

He'd been busy trying to perfect a certain marinade for the birds and didn't want to see his work go for naught. In his chef whites he'd exited the rear door of his kitchen as brick first mortared in 1923 was ripped away in a funnel of wild wind. Trying to get to a perceived shelter, marinade sloshing over the sides of the tray as he went, Katrina swopped in under his cargo and Chef Raoul and his hens went airborne. He never once screamed or emitted a sound. His body was never found. But several of the hens would later be discovered impaled on branches or deposited on roofs many miles from the hotel.

"Ughhh," Janet Esparza grunted, the headboard gripped in her hands rocking and creaking. She grunted again and again as Joe Cully thrust himself in her from behind.

"Oh, damn, baby," he enthused as he vigorously continued.

"You sure apply yourself in whatever you do, Joe."

He responded with an animalistic growl. The two were making love in Room 314 in the Blackbeard suite. There was netting, of course, in keeping with the pirate-nautical theme of the floor, along with portholes offering a view of the water and a four-poster bed with a black flag-style canopy. Back during Katrina, Esparaza had been one of the part-time maids here. But she was bright and ambitious, had a facility with details, and over time had completed several courses in hotel management at Mississippi Gulf Coast Community College. Now she was the day manager at the Ringtree and planning a score with her lover that would mean she'd never have to deal with a cranky guest again. She could be the demanding guest at somebody else's hotel, a five-star one no less.

Cully's calloused workman's hands gripped Esparza's brown breasts as she urged him on like she'd seen those girls do in those porn clips they watched together online. "Harder, faster, deeper," she breathed hoarsely and he did his best to comply. Soon he had his hands clamped on either side of her well-proportioned butt. His fingers dug into her flesh as he shuddered to a climax. His squeezing hurt and it felt good to her. They both then collapsed onto the tangled bed covers

"Damn," Cully said, sweat dappling the center of his muscular chest. A build like one of those cover boys of a bodice-ripper romance novel Claire Underwood had noted to Esparza once. That was when Cully, a handyman in town with a solid client list, had wrestled a kaput water heater out of a tight space after uncoupling the connections. The Ringtree was one of his steady customers. Neither he nor Esparza could pinpoint who flirted with whom first, but they'd been having their thing going on two years running now. Funny, too, how the idea to pull off a robbery had taken root with the two—well, with her at least.

The Underwoods, currently in Denver at a symposium about investing in marijuana businesses, flipped houses and pursued other real estate interests. Claire, who liked to chat and enjoyed a white wine with Esparza now and then, had made mention of an interesting situation a several weeks ago as the two had a drink together in the hotel's small bar.

"We were looking to invest in this shopping complex over in N'awlins bordering the lower Ninth," Claire Underwood said, conversationally tipsy on her second full glass of Chardonnay.

"What happened?" Esparza asked, still on her first glass.

"Leland Haslip," the older woman sneered.

"The loud-mouthed billionaire."

"Bingo," Underwood said. "The reason that bastard's rich is not because he knows how to negotiate, make the deal like he boasts about in his books and on TV. Oh, no." She had more of her libation and leaned forward across the small table they were at. "He knows how to grease the goose. Buy off a community group that might be opposed to one of his developments or, you know, line a local politician's pockets."

"Bribes you mean."

"Exactly. Cash on the barrelhead. This project I'm talking about is peanuts to him but he has other plans for the land down the line you see. To him it's all about winning."

Esparza liked these talks with her boss. She'd been considering trying to buy a property to flip but now another money-making notion occurred to her. "So he spreads the wealth."

Underwood snorted. "He doesn't deign to dirty his own hands. Oh, no, he has underlings for that. Like this guy see, this guy that me and Charlie know about 'cause we been looking into Mister Dealmaker's doings on the sly." She leaned back, signaling for Emory the barman to bring her another wine. And before she had to go and take a nap after that third glass, Jan Esparza learned several other pertinent facts about how Haslip conducted his business.

"Let's go over it again," Cully said. He was a coffee with cream-colored black man of mixed ancestry with unblemished skin and arms toned like a wide receiver's. The handyman searched in the bed for his boxers.

Esparza took hold of him and slid her hand along his limp member. "Nervous? The odds are in our favor, you know."

He gave her an incredulous look as he dug out his dark blue underwear. "Neither one of us has ever done anything like this."

"Be bold in your decisions and you will be rewarded," she said, quoting Haslip from one of his books. Chuckling, she let him go and he slipped his boxers on. Esparaza lay naked on the bed on her back, her legs slightly apart. A shaft of late morning light painted part of her upper thighs in warm copper. The crossbones of the Jolly Roger gazed empty-eyed down at her. Cully stood, regarding her as well.

Too bad he didn't smoke, he lamented, it would give him something to do with his hands. It was always soothing to be working with his hands Cully long ago concluded. He could be wiring a juncture box, paying attention to the specifics, yet also be serene, be in the moment like he imagined pitchers were on the mound visualizing the knuckleball they were about to throw.

"Haslip's private jet arrives at Lakefront Airport at three-fifteen, or thereabouts," Esparza said. Claire Underwood had told her the cash run was made once a month. "The money is then handed off to the courier who will probably be traveling with another man, both ex-Army Ranger or some scary ass thing like that."

"The car they're driving is no doubt armored," Cully speculated.

"Yes, *mi amor*, but we're not hitting the car or them."

"I hear you, I just want to cover all the possibilities, ya know?" He sat on the edge of the bed, arms folded. "The variables."

"I got something else I need you to cover." Esparza opened her legs wider.

"Jan, shit, we got to get this right."

"Can I help it this makes me hot...and wet?" She smiled at him as she began fingering herself.

Cully shook his close-cropped head but could already feel his stamina returning as he got back into bed. The small digital clock-radio on the nightstand read 11:47.

Arching over the gulf ahead of schedule at 3:02, the Hawker 4000 private jet came in for a landing at Lakefront Airport in New Orleans. Touchdown was uneventful and the pilot taxied to a stop near the hanger maintained by a subsidiary of Leland Haslip's many enterprises. A black Navigator was waiting for the plane as well. Two sturdily built men, one with a bull neck, stood outside the vehicle. Their eyes were on swivel, hands clasped before them like bodyguards pretending to be hospitable at a Beyoncé concert just before going into action when a chump tries to rush the stage.

The half-shell door to the plane came down with its built-in stair steps. Out came a woman in a sensible skirt and shoes and a pressed light blue shirt. She carried an over-sized Geo Carbonate attaché case she handed to the one with the bull neck. He nodded slightly and accepted an identical case from the pilot, who handed that one over. The two got in the black vehicle and drove off. The travel time between the municipal airport and the Tremé section of the city was less than twenty minutes. Once in the area, reaching their destination took another three minutes. This the two thieves did not witness as each knew they did not have the skill to shadow the two professionals in the black car. They, or rather Esparza, knew where they would be going to deliver the seven hundred and thirty-five grand in the two cases—to Edmund Shoemaker, who operated in Haslip's interests in this part of the city.

That's why she and Cully were parked up the street from Shoemaker's Grocery after the ninety-minute drive from Biloxi. They were in a road weary Sentra they'd searched craigslist to find the right kind of motivated seller. They'd bought it for cash from an elderly widower who needed the rent money. They hadn't re-registered it yet and in fact were driving the vehicle on a stolen tag Cully had lifted from another car. The small store that served homemade po' boys on Tuesdays and the weekend was on a narrow street with a low curb, set at the corner and across the way from a three-story tool and die works.

"Ready?" Esparza said, grasping her breasts lovingly like Cully had earlier. But this time to adjust her cleavage in the lacy pushup bra, the edges of which were visible past the revealing scoop of her top.

"Hell, yeah," he answered, psyching himself up while swatting at a mosquito feasting on the back of his neck.

She gave him a peck and got out of the car, not bothering

to smooth down the short skirt with a slit up the side. On the roof of the tool and die a billboard was posted featuring Leland Haslip in a suit and tie, his arms held wide, face jovial as the words next to him stated: LET'S WORK TOGETHER FOR THE NEW, NEW ORLEANS. Part of his upper torso and head, topped with his signature confounding hairstyle, was cut out and rising out of the billboard.

Her back to this as she walked away, Esparza pointedly wasn't wearing heels as she expected to be hot-footing it as her Creole grandmother would say, any minute now. Along with her purse and the gun in it, she also had a wig on her head and a fake mole beside her ruby lips and owl-like sunglasses. The two in the SUV had delivered the money over two hours ago. The sun was setting as she pulled open a weathered wooden screen door and let it bang back in place after stepping across the store's threshold. She was surprised the place was well-stocked given the owner's underworld occupation. Esparza walked along an aisle of canned goods such as stewed gator and boxes of couche couche mix amid aromas of spices and coffees.

There was a lone customer being rung up at the counter, an elderly lady with one of those metal canes with a quad base. The kid behind the counter pushed down keys on an ancient cash register Esparza had only seen in old movies. The meshing of the thing's gears reverberated about the quiet store. Clearing the aisle, she was behind the customer and looked to her right at another sound, of food being consumed. She almost swore under her breath.

In the corner, at the juncture of the counter and a metal shelf with motor oil and dangling air fresheners rested a large dog languidly eating from a steel bowl. She was pretty sure the animal was a Rottweiler and there was a crunch as it ate. Mixed in with its dog food were corn chips she noted. She also estimated the beast was over a hundred pounds of muscle and fang.

"You got that, Mrs. Tibbadoe?" the young clerk said to the old woman as he loaded her two bags of grocers in an upright cart.

"Yes, thank you, Timothy." She wheeled her cart toward the door with one hand and clumped along with her cane in the other.

"What can I do for you, ma'am?" the young man asked, making sure to look into Esparza's face.

"Can I speak to Edmund?"

"Can I tell him what it's about?"

She put honey and smoke in her voice. "Just tell him I'm here to see him, sugah."

The kid, not more than nineteen she figured, smiled eagerly. "Okay."

What man, middle-aged or young for that matter, she reflected, married or single as long as they were hetero, was going to turn down an intro to a chick damn near spilling out of her clothes? Quickly she texted Cully as the kid walked toward a back room along a gloomy hallway behind the counter. From staking out the store, and the dog was a new factor, the couple knew that's where Shoemaker had his office and where he often napped.

Shoemaker was a late-fifties rotund individual, bald on top but with a ponytail. He moved in jeans with an elastic waistband and soft orthopedic shoes to sooth his diabetic foot pain. He made no pretense of not looking at Esparza's chest.

"What can I do for you, *mon cher*?"

Pleasantly she replied, "Don't say anything to have that beast attack and we won't put a hole in you, Mr. Shoemaker." She had the Dan Wesson revolver in her hand and low in front of her. She'd turned her body in such a way as to have her back partially to the dog which was laying on the floor, panting. Joining her in the store was Cully. He was supposed to have put on a ski mask but, after being warned about the dog, felt such might trigger a violent reaction from the animal. Instead he wore a baseball cap with a Saints logo on it pulled low and kept his head down. The couple knew the surveillance camera covering the counter hadn't worked in two years.

"Give them the money in the register, Tim," Shoemaker said evenly.

"That's not what we're here for," Esparza said.

Shoemaker remained calm. "Then if not money, why are you so brazenly invading my establishment?"

"Let's you and me go in your office and fetch that *mordida* you got there while my associate stays up front here with your young employee."

Shoemaker enunciated each of his next words. "If you know about the delivery, then you certainly must know who that property belongs to."

"You ain't simple, is you?" Cully placed the muzzle of his semi-auto against the storekeeper's temple. As rehearsed, he was talking in a manner he did not so normally. Playing into the stereotype of what was expected of a brother who was possibly a refuge from the previous incarnation of the rehabbed Iberville housing projects.

"In the back, now," Esparza declared.

Shoemaker pursed his lips but said no more. He headed toward the rear, Esparza behind him, the gun steady on the large man's back. Cully remained with the younger man. He'd also moved behind the counter, desirous of keeping a barrier between him and the still lounging Rottweiler.

The interior of the office was cool and warmly lit. On Shoemaker's messy desk was a stack of days-old editions of the *Times-Picayune,* a stuffed wooden in-and-out stacked tray, assorted loose papers and a push-button landline phone. Off to one side was a set-up of a free standing table like what a chef would have in their kitchen. There was a cutting board, mixing bowls, some with ingredients in them, cooking utensils and a heavy duty toaster oven on its own table. There was a current *Sports Illustrated* swimsuit model calendar tacked on the wood paneled wall. This was beneath a mounted octopus, its protruding writhing tentacles frozen in mid strike. The lacquer covering it glistened.

"Where's the money?" she said.

Shoemaker pointed. "Under the table."

Esparza made a face. "What's with that?" She indicated the cooking accessories with a shake of the gun's barrel.

"I'm working on a cookbook."

She crooked her head.

"Really."

"Come on," she said. Esparza stood close but not too close as they walked over to the table. Shoemaker put his hands along an edge and lifting, moved the table aside. Breathing heavily, the portly man got down on a knee and drew back the throw rug the table rested on revealing a square in the floor with a built-in latch.

Standing back Esparza said, "You know how this goes."

Shoemaker pulled the hatch open. She leaned forward and could see the attaché cases in there. The space was tight and if he did have a gun down there, it would have to be below the treasure she reasoned, an image of the Jolly Roger billowing in her head.

"Easy does it."

"*Oui, doucement.*" He got the first case out and set it on end next to the cavity. As he reached for the second one, a gunshot boomed from the front of the store, mixed with the barking and growling of the big dog.

"Dammit," Esparza seethed, temporarily distracted. "What's happening, C?" she called out. An impression of movement made her turn her head back towards Shoemaker, who blew a burnt-orange cloud of cayenne powder into her face.

"Motherfuck," she wailed, coughing, rearing back, her eyes searing and her lungs aflame. She squeezed the trigger but missed as the man was on her, his hand locked on the wrist of her gun hand. They stumbled about and Esparza fell back onto the wall, the gun skittering away as her hand went slack. The mounted octopus fell and, having forced one watering eye partly open, Esparza got a hold of the backing board and used it as a cudgel to club at the fat man. The stiffened tips of the tentacles poked and scraped bloody trails on Shoemaker's forearms as he grabbed at her and the stuffed mollusk.

"Greedy twist," Shoemaker swore, bringing his fist down like an axe, pounding her down. The wig went askew on her head. But the blow partially cleared her eyes and she scrambled forward on all fours, wrapping her arms around the shop owner's lower legs. She had him off-balance, but he fell forward, not on his back. He made a wheezing grunting sound landing hard on his stomach, the wind knocked out of him. She heard the dog's nails skitter along the worn linoleum of the hallway. Energized by fear, Esparza got unsteadily to her feet and took a shot at the doorway. She still couldn't see clearly and her bullet sang past the animal's flank. But having gotten her hand on the handle of the attaché case next to the hole, she swung and caught the Rottweiler alongside its snapping jaw.

The dog went sideways, woozy, blood dripping from its wound onto the floorboards. Esparza scrambled to the rear door. This in turn was fronted by a security screen door opened by depressing an inner latch. The Rottweiler was up and at the doorway too. His teeth took a piece of her skirt away and his claws raked her legs. She used the case again on the animal and he momentarily retreated, reflexively responding to his pain. Shaking, bloody but determined to control her panic, Esparza got the outer security door open and tumbled outside. She kicked the door closed just as the dog rushed at her again, slamming into the mesh. He barked at her through the screen mesh as she made for the getaway car in the front.

"Double fuck," she swore, realizing Cully had the keys. She sneezed orange mist, standing in the middle of the street, looking back at the grocery store, texting her lover and crime partner. The front door remained closed. Cully, who didn't respond to her text, wasn't in evidence. Was he dead, wounded? What about the kid? She should go check. But she only had half the money and splitting that up, well, where was the percentage in that she calculated. She was going to miss Cully, he'd been an attentive lover.

She righted the wig, and realized her over-sized sunglasses were missing. They'd been bought at a Dollar General so how traceable was that? If Cully was alive, now that was another matter. She hefted the pistol as she considered returning to the store to make sure he had expired. But that might mean shooting the dog first and who knew when the cops might roll on scene. Time to vamoose she concluded.

Her shirt as well had been torn, exposing more of the lacy brassiere. Therefore it wasn't too tough for a woman, even one with bleeding, scratched up legs, showing skin and a bra to flag down a ride—standing under a lit streetlamp. She then shoved the gun in the chump's surprised face, got him out of the car, and drove back to Biloxi in the jacked Malibu. Crossing over the bridge, she threw her wig out the window. Heading north, you didn't have to pay the toll, just the other way around. Esparza prayed that was a sign, that the police would concentrate on New Orleans, the city of desire, the city that counted, and not turn their attention to Biloxi, the forgotten city, until she got away.

She didn't go to the Ringtree, but circled her apartment a few times to check if it was being watched by the law. As far as she could tell at night, she wasn't and parked several blocks away. Esparza walked back to her place with the attaché case in one hand, the gun down at her side in the other. Inside, she quickly cleaned up, changing into jeans, and feeling fatigued, desperately wanting to lie down and nap before getting on the road. Yet she knew her luck had held so far and it was foolish to chance capture. Esparza used a screwdriver and hammer to force open the locked metal case and put the three hundred fifty thousand plus in hundreds in a larger soft bag along with some clothes. This she slung over her shoulder by its strap.

She sneezed again and closed the door to her apartment, never to see it again. Her plan was to drive her own car to the train station in Gulfport, leave the car, and get on the first thing heading west. Descending the outside steps from the second floor she could see clearly by the lights that were activated by motion sensors. But her vision began to blur and she wondered if there was still some cayenne in her eyes. She paused, her breathing now labored and her throat constricting.

"What the hell?" she croaked, fighting for air. Esparza wiped a hand across her sweaty forehead. She was dizzy and panicking. Had she been poisoned in some kind of way? It was if she were having a severe asthma attack but she didn't have asthma. She was light-headed and, taking a step, determined to make her getaway, terrified that if she went to the hospital the police would catch her. Esparza's foot went out from under her. Damned if there wasn't blood from the Rottweiler still slick on the sole, she queasily reckoned. She fell backward, the base of her head hitting the composition stone stairs. Dazed and bleeding, she flipped end over end down the stairs like a stuntwoman pretending to be drunk.

At the bottom, her leg was bent at an unnatural angle. Esparza passed out from the blow to her head and the fall. She died peacefully, unable to draw a breath due to her throat shuttering close. Later the police would put the pieces together. Timothy, who was watching Goliath the dog for an out-of-town girlfriend, had taken a chance and wrestled with Cully for the gun. He was pistol whipped for his effort, his skull cracked in two places. By then the dog had cleared the counter and was on Cully. Goliath bit his gun hand, nearly severing the tendons. As Cully attended to his wound, the Rottweiler charged into the rear of the store

While what caused Esparza's allergic reaction wasn't pinpointed in her autopsy, questioning Shoemaker about the cash had prompted a theory. Esparza being a Southern gal, it was felt she'd been exposed to cayenne before. But mixed in with that particular spice, Shoemaker had used a pepper-like spice related to ginger derived from a West African trumpet-shaped flower containing numerous small, reddish-brown seeds—the grains of paradise. It was concluded the grains of paradise must have been the source of triggering her anaphylactic shock.

A truly rare condition, but there it was.

What were the odds?

The Attitude Adjuster
David Morrell

A road-renovation crew. Trucks, grinders, rollers. Only one lane of traffic is open. As you drive toward the dust and noise, a man holds a pole with a sign at the top. The pole's bottom rests on the dirt so all he needs to do is turn the shaft to show you one side of the sign or the other. SLOW, you are directed, or else STOP.

The man is tall and scarecrow lanky, exuding the impression of sinewy strength. He wears battered work boots, faded jeans, and an old blue work shirt with the sleeves rolled up, revealing a rose tattoo above the hand with which he holds the pole. His shirt has sweat blotches. His face is narrow, sun-browned, and weather-creased. He wears a yellow vest and hardhat.

According to the radio's weather forecaster, the temperature on this Illinois August day is ninety degrees Fahrenheit, with eighty-seven percent humidity. But the sun radiates off the road, increasing the temperature to one hundred. Because the project is behind schedule, the man is required to work overtime. He holds that sign twelve hours a day—for the past three months. You've seen countless versions of him. Passing him, you never wonder what he thinks.

Stupid son of a bitch. Sits in his damned air-conditioned SUV, stares at my sign, speeds past, almost hits me, throws dust in my face. Can't you read, you moron? The sign says SLOW! One of these days, I'll whack this pole against a fender, hell, through a window. Teach these bastards to show respect. Everybody's got a snotty attitude. Here comes another guy barreling toward me. King of the road. Hey, see this sign I'm pointing at, dummy! SLOW! It says SLOW!

The man's name is Barry Pollard. He is thirty-nine, but years of working outdoors have made him look much older. His previous jobs involved strenuous physical labor, lifting, carrying, digging, hammering, which he never minded because he felt content when he had something to fill the time, to weary him and shut off his thoughts. But months of nothing to do except stand in the middle of the road, hold the sign, and watch motorists ignore it have given him plenty of opportunity to draw conclusions about the passing world.

Dodo, how'd you ever get a driver's license if you can't read? The sign says SLOW. For God's sake, you came so close, you almost knocked it out of my hand. You think you can do whatever you want? That's what's wrong these days. Nobody pays attention to the rules. When I was a kid, if I even thought about doing something my old man didn't like, he set down his beer can and punched me to the floor. Certainly taught me right from wrong. "You've got a bad attitude," he used to tell me. "We gotta correct it." From what I've seen the past three months, there's a lot of bad attitudes that need correcting.

A voice squawked from a walkie-talkie hooked to Barry's belt. "Okay, that's enough cars going north for a while. Stop 'em at your end while the cars on *my* side get a chance to go through."

"Roger," Barry said into the walkie-talkie, feeling a little like he was in the military. He swung his sign so the message now read STOP.

A guy in a van tried to go past.

"Hey!" Barry shouted and jerked his sign down in front of the windshield.

The guy barely stopped before the pole would have cracked the glass.

"Back up and get off the road!" Barry shouted. "There's a bunch of cars coming this way!"

Red-faced, the guy charged from the van. "You almost broke my windshield!"

"I could have, but I didn't!" Barry said. "Maybe next time!"

"You jerk, I ought to—"

Barry pointed the pole at the guy. "Oughta what? I told you to back up your van and get off the road. You're interfering with the project."

"You could have waited to stop traffic until I went past!"

"When the boss tells me to stop vehicles, I do it. You think you're more important than the guy in the car behind you. I should stop *him* but not *you*?"

"I've got a job I need to get to!"

"And *he* doesn't have some place to go? You think you're a big shot? A VIP? That stands for Very Important Prick. An attitude like yours, it's no wonder the country's going to hell. Here comes the other traffic, bozo! *Move your vehicle.*"

The guy spit on Barry's work boots, then stormed back to his van.

Barry stared down at the spit.

A sign on the van read MIDWEST CABLE AND HIGH-SPEED INTERNET INSTALLATION. A phone number was under it. As the guy got into the truck and backed from approaching traffic, Barry took his cell phone from his belt and pressed numbers.

"Midwest Cable," a female voice said.

"One of your installers was at my place today. He did such a good job, I thought I'd phone and tell you how impressed I am."

"What's his name?"

"Just a second. I've got his...Of all the...Dumb me, I lost the card he gave me. He's about forty-five. Kind of on the heavy side. Real short red hair."

"Yeah, that's Fred Harriman."

"He did a great job."

At seven, after the job shut down for the day, Barry drove into town, stopped at a convenience store, found Fred Harriman's name in the phone book, and made a note of his address. He waited a month, wanting to be certain that no one at the cable company would remember his phone call. At last, he drove to Fred's neighborhood, passed a white ranch house with two big flowerbeds, saw a pickup truck in the driveway, and stopped at a park down the street. With lots of other cars near him, no one paid attention as Barry watched the truck. Soon, the sun went down, and the people in the park went home, but Barry continued watching. Lights glowed through the front windows.

At nine-thirty, as Barry began to worry that a police car would cruise the area and wonder why he was sitting alone in a car in the dark, the front door opened. Fred came out, got in the truck, and drove away.

Barry followed him to a bar called the Seventh Inning Stretch, where Fred joined a couple of buddies at a table, drank a pitcher of beer, and watched the end of a baseball game. They cursed when the Cubs didn't win. Fred was such a putz, he didn't notice Barry watching among drinkers in the background. But Barry was gone when they paid for their beers.

In the shadowy parking lot, they made a couple of jokes. One of them burped. They went to their separate vehicles. Fred got to his about the same time the others got to theirs. He climbed into the truck, started to drive away, then felt something wrong, and got out. The shadows were so dense that he had to crouch to see the flat tire on the front passenger side. He cursed more seriously than when the Cubs lost. His pals were gone. As he straightened and turned toward the locked toolkit in back of his truck, he groaned from a two-by-four to the side of his jaw, although he never knew what hit him or saw who did it. Barry felt the satisfying crunch of flesh and crack of bone. To make it look like a mugging, Barry took all the cash from Fred's wallet.

Two weeks later, the roadwork was finished. With time on his hands, Barry unhappily discovered that everywhere he went, people had attitude problems. A guy in a sports car cut him off at an intersection and gave him the finger when Barry blared his horn. A woman pushed in front of him at Starbucks. A clerk at a convenience store made him wait while the clerk used the store's phone to gab with his girlfriend. A waiter at a diner brought him a bacon and tomato sandwich that had mayonnaise, even though Barry had distinctly told him he didn't want any mayo. When Barry complained, the waiter took the sandwich away and brought a replacement, but when Barry opened it, he saw traces of white. All the waiter had done was scrape some off.

Barry went to a movie theater, but people wouldn't stop talking.

"I wouldn't go into that warehouse," a woman said, pointing at the screen.

"Yeah, the cop should radio for backup," the man next to her said.

"He didn't radio for backup when he searched the abandoned house, either," the woman said.

"Well, if he did, the stupid writers wouldn't have a plot."

"Please, be quiet," Barry said behind them.

"And look at this. The lights don't work, and he doesn't have a flashlight, but he's going inside anyhow."

"Please, don't talk during the movie," Barry said.

"Yep, here's the vampire sneaking up on—"

"SHUT THE HELL UP!"

The man turned and glared. "Have you got a problem, buddy?"

"This isn't your living room! I'm trying to—"

"You want me to shut up?"

"That's what I've been trying to—"

"Make me."

Barry left the theater, waited outside, followed the couple home, put a ski mask over his head, and taught them to shut up by knocking their teeth out. Then he smashed all their TV sets and set fire to their car. Another job well done.

"There, your computer system's updated," the cable installer said.

"High-speed Internet." Barry marveled. "I figured it was time I joined the twenty-first century."

He found an online company that specialized in surveillance equipment.

Follow anybody anywhere, an ad announced. *Just hide this tiny radio transmitter on their clothes or in their briefcase or their purse. It gives off a silent beep that only you can hear through your matching radio receiver.*

But when Barry got the transmitter, it was the size of a walkie-talkie and the even-larger radio receiver needed to be no more than thirty feet from the transmitter or else Barry couldn't hear the beep.

He sent an email, asking for his money back, but never received an answer. He repeatedly phoned the number on the company's website, but all he ever heard was a recorded message, telling him that "every available technician is talking with another customer."

Barry drove four hours to St. Louis, where the company had its post-office box. From his car in the parking lot outside the post office, he stared through windows toward the company's PO box. After a rumpled guy took envelopes from the box, Barry followed him to an office above an escort service. When Barry finished teaching the guy the error of his ways, he had his money back, plus the guy's driver's license and his FOLLOW ANYWHERE business card, which allowed Barry to cash all the money orders in the envelopes (no checks accepted, the ad had warned).

Compensation for my time, Barry thought. *It's only fair.*

Back home after the long drive, he counted his money yet again, eight hundred dollars, and opened yet another beer. *Sure beats standing on the road, holding that damned sign.* He chased a shot of bourbon with a gulp of beer and told himself that he was actually performing a public service. Protecting people from jerks. You bet. Teaching bozos to mend their ways.

He slumped on his sofa, chuckling at the thought that some guys with attitude problems might even be thankful if Barry set them straight. *For all I know, they're ashamed of being dorks. Like my father said, everybody knows they need direction.*

Amused, Barry staggered to his computer. Alcohol made his fingers clumsy. He thanked God for the computer's spell-check program. After all, he needed to make the proper impression.

E-BENT
THE ADULT ALTERNATIVE TO EBAY
LOWER COMMISSION—FASTER SERVICE—MORE FUN
SELLERS ASSUME ALL RESPONSIBILITIES FOR LISTING ITEMS

I WILL ADJUST YOUR WAYS
ITEM 44735ABQE

High bidder receives an attitude adjustment. I am strong and tough from years of outdoor work. If you win this auction, I will teach you to walk the straight and narrow. I promise not to cripple or kill you. No weapons, just my boots and fists. Maybe a club, depending on how much your attitude needs adjusting.

Barry chuckled as he typed.

I will perform this service only if you promise not to resist and not to have me arrested afterward.

Clever point, Barry thought.

You will provide travel expenses and directions to your home and work. You will also provide motel expenses, but these should be low because I plan to do the job swiftly so that I can proceed to giving adjustments to other people. I will pick a time that you least expect. Perhaps while you're asleep or in the bathroom or going to work. During your adjustment, I may be forced to break windows or furniture. The costs for these are your responsibility. If you have a family or whatever, warn them to stay out of my way unless you want their attitudes adjusted also.

Ha! Barry thought.

No checks or PayPal. I accept only money orders made out to CASH. Good luck.

The next morning, Barry foggily remembered what he had done and cursed himself for wasting time when he could have continued drinking. E-bent was part of a porn site, for God's sake. The only reason he'd used it was that eBay wouldn't have allowed him to post his auction. For all he knew, nobody visited that section of the porn site. *Anyway, who's going to bid on getting beat up?* he asked himself. To prove his point, all week he didn't get a response.

Then, on Sunday, with a half-hour left in the auction, he received the following:

QUESTION TO SELLER
I thought about your auction quite a while: all week, every day and night. I have done something bad that makes me feel awful. I can't stop thinking about it. I need to be punished. How could I have done such a terrible thing? Are you serious that you won't kill

me? I'm a devout Roman Catholic, and if you kill me, God might see it as a kind of suicide. Then I'd go to Hell. I need to know that you won't endanger my soul, which is in danger enough already.

Dan Yates stuck the OPEN HOUSE sign into the lush lawn and walked past rose bushes toward the two-story Spanish Colonial Revival. Another sign was prominently displayed, YATES REALTY, under which was a phone number and a website address. Dan wore a navy sport coat, white shirt, and conservative striped tie. He paused on the porch and surveyed the handsome yard and pleasant neighborhood, nodding with confidence that someone would make an offer by the end of the afternoon. He left the front door open and proceeded to the kitchen, where he brewed coffee and arranged cookies next to bowls of peanuts and potato chips. He set out bottled water and canned sodas. He stacked brochures with eye-catching photographs of the house and information about it. $879,000. Two months ago, the price had been $939,000. With low mortgage rates and the housing market starting to return, he felt sure that it would sell for $859,000, close to what the sellers wanted.

His preparations completed, Dan gave his best smile to his first visitors, a man and a woman, who were obviously impressed by the marble-floored kitchen but tried not to show it. Thirty seconds later, another couple arrived, then another soon after, and the show was on.

"The house is three years old. This subdivision used to be the Huntington Beach airport. As you can see, there's no house behind you, only this low attractive wall beyond which is a Mormon church. Very quiet. Plenty of sky. You attend that church? The Latter Day Saints? My, this house would certainly be convenient for you. On Sundays, you could practically crawl over the wall and go to services. The subdivision has its own swimming pool and park. There's a golf course down the street as well as a shopping center three blocks away and a school three blocks in the other direction. You've heard the old saying about what makes property valuable? Location, location, location. Ten minutes to the beach. Honestly, this has it all."

And so it went, forty visitors, three promises to make offers and one firm offer for cash. *Not a bad afternoon's work*, Dan thought. "The owners are vacationing in Hawaii," he told the prospective buyers. "I'll fax the material to them. They have until noon tomorrow to respond. I'll let you know what they say as soon as possible." He escorted the couple to the door, checked his watch, saw that the hours for the open house were over, and allowed himself to relax. When the last visitors drove away, he went to the street and put the OPEN HOUSE sign in his SUV. He returned to the kitchen, where he cleaned the coffee maker and cups. He put all the empty cans and bottles into a garbage bag along with the coffee grounds and the remnants of the cookies, the peanuts, and the potato chips.

The Baxters are coming for dinner, he thought. *Laura's expecting me to bring home the steaks. I'd better hurry.* Giving the kitchen a final inspection, he saw movement to the right and turned toward a lanky man standing in the doorway to the living room. The guy had a creased, rugged face. He wore sneakers, jeans, and a pullover. His hair was scraggly.

"I'm sorry," Dan said. "The open house is over. I was just about to leave and lock up."

"I warned you I'd show up when you least expected," the man said.

"Excuse me?" Dan asked.

"You've been bad."

"What the hell are you talking about?"

"Your attitude adjustment."

"Adjustment?"

"The one you paid for. You're Dan Yates, correct?"

"That's my name, but—"

"Two-one-five Sunnyvale Lane?"

"How do you know my—"

"No sense in putting it off." The guy rolled up his long sleeves, as if getting ready for physical labor. He had a rose tattoo on his right forearm.

"Look, I don't get the joke. Now if you'll come with me, we'll just step outside and—"

"No joke. You bid on the attitude adjustment. You won the auction. Now you get what you paid for. I don't know what you did that was so terrible, but I swear I'll ease your conscience. You'll be sore, but you'll feel a whole lot better after I finish with you."

Dan reached for his cell phone. The man threw it against the wall, punched him in the stomach, kneed him in the face, whacked his cheek, struck his nose, then started beating him in earnest.

At five, when Dan didn't return home with the steaks for the dinner with the Baxters, his wife called his cell phone.

An electronic voice announced, "That number is out of service."

Out of service? Laura wondered. She called several more times, with the same response. The Baxters arrived at six. At seven, when Dan still hadn't arrived, Laura phoned the police, but no one named Dan Yates had been reported in a traffic accident. The Baxters agreed to watch the Yates's ten-year-old daughter while Laura went to where Dan had the open house.

The front door was unlocked. She found him unconscious on the kitchen's marble floor, lying in a pool of blood.

"Fractured arm, ribs, and clavicle," an emergency-ward doctor told her after an ambulance hurried Dan to the nearest hospital.

"Auction. Rose tattoo," Dan murmured as he drifted in and out of consciousness.

"Must be the pain killers. The poor guy's delirious," a police detective said.

* * *

Barry, who had never been to California, used the generous travel fee he'd demanded to stay a few extra days. He watched the surfers near Huntington Beach's famous pier. He planned to drive north to Los Angeles and cruise Hollywood Boulevard, then head up to Malibu. With luck, he'd cross paths with movie stars.

Those plans ended when he read the next morning's edition of the *Orange County Register*. With increasing anger, he learned that Dan Yates had attempted to identify him. *Auction. Rose tattoo. That wasn't the damned deal!* Barry thought as joggers passed him at the beach. *You weren't supposed to resist, and you weren't supposed to try to have me arrested afterward! Doesn't anybody keep his word? Didn't I adjust your attitude hard enough?*

In the hospital's lobby, he requested the number for Dan Yates's room.

"Are you a member of his family?" the receptionist asked.

"His brother. When I heard Dan was in the hospital—I still can't believe it—I drove all the way from Phoenix."

"Room eight forty-two."

One of many things Barry had learned while holding the sign for the road crew was that people got so absorbed in their affairs, they didn't pay attention to what was around them. They'd drive over you before they noticed you. Walking along the hospital corridor, a newspaper in one hand, a bunch of flowers in the other, just one of many visitors, he might as well have been invisible. The door to room eight forty-two was open. He passed it, glancing in at banged-up Dan lying in a bed, the only patient in the room. Dan's face looked like an uncooked beefsteak. Various monitors were attached to him. An IV tube led into his arm.

I'd almost feel sorry for you if you hadn't broken our deal, Barry thought.

A not-bad-looking woman sat next to Dan. Roughly Dan's age, she was pale with worry. *The wife*, Barry decided.

That was all he saw as he continued down the corridor. He went into a men's room, lingered, then came out, and returned along the corridor. Visiting hours were almost over. People emerged from various rooms and headed toward the elevators. The woman left Dan's room and did the same.

Barry went into Dan's room and used a knee to close the door so he wouldn't leave fingerprints. He set down the flowers and pulled his shirtsleeve over his hand, again so he wouldn't leave fingerprints. He turned off the monitors, grabbed a hospital gown from a table, shielded himself, pulled a section of garden hose from the newspaper he'd brought, and whacked Dan several times across the face. Blood flew. He set the crimson-soaked section of hose on Dan's chest, dropped the spattered gown on the floor, opened the door, and went down the corridor with the other departing visitors.

Twenty seconds, Barry thought. *Damned good.*

A nurse went into Dan's room. She was used to seeing blood in a hospital, but not this much. Screaming, she rang for an emergency team, then hurried to turn on the monitors, which immediately began wailing, the waves and numbers showing that at least Dan was still alive.

Keep our agreement, jerk, or the next time, you'll get an even worse adjustment, a typed note said, lying next to the flowers on Dan's chest.

When the police came, a detective asked, "Mrs. Yates, do you know anything about the agreement the note refers to?"

"I haven't the faintest idea." Laura trembled.

"Any idea what the reference to 'worse adjustment' means?"

"No." Laura wept.

* * *

From: Laura Yates
To: Jamie Travers
Subject: trouble, postpone visit

Jamie, I hate to do this at the last minute, but I've been so worried and tired that I haven't had the time or energy to send an email. I've got so much trouble. I need to withdraw my invitation for you and your husband to stay with us for a few days while you're in L.A. on business. Dan was nearly beaten to death on Sunday afternoon at an open house he was giving. Then he was beaten again in his hospital room. We have no idea who on earth did it or why. I spend so much time with him at the hospital that I won't be able to see you. Plus, I'm so sick with worry that I won't be very good company. Sorry. I was looking forward to meeting your husband and reminiscing about our sorority days. Life can sure change quickly. Laura.

From: Jamie Travers
To: Laura Yates
Subject: coming regardless

Laura, since we're in the area, we've decided to visit you anyhow. But you won't need to babysit us. This won't exactly be a social occasion. My husband's in a line of work that might be helpful to you. I'm pretty good at it myself. Apologies for sounding mysterious. It's too complicated to explain in an email. Kind of a secret life I have. All will be revealed tomorrow. What's the name and address of the hospital? Can we meet you there at noon? We'll see if we can sort this out. Don't despair. Love, Jamie.

Although Laura hadn't seen Jamie in five years, her former college roommate looked as radiant as ever. Five feet ten, with a jogger's slim build. A model's narrow chin and high cheek bones. Long brunette hair. Bright green eyes. She wore brown linen slacks, and a loose-fitting jacket over a beige blouse. But Laura processed these details only later, so distracted by her emotions that all she wanted to do was hug Jamie as she came into the room.

Laura wept again. She'd been doing a lot of it. "I'm so glad to see you."

"You couldn't have kept me away," Jamie assured her.

Laura's tear-blurred gaze drifted toward the man next to her.

"This is my husband," Jamie said proudly. "His name's Cavanaugh. And this is my good friend Laura," she told her husband. "She and I raised a lot of hell at Wellesley."

"Pleased to meet you," the man said.

Again, Laura paid attention to his appearance only later. He was around six feet tall, not muscular but somehow solid looking. Handsome, with a strong chin and forehead that some-how didn't intimidate. Hair that wasn't quite brown and not quite sandy, not long but not short. Alert eyes that were hazel and yet seemed to reflect the blue of his loose sports coat. He had an odd-looking black metal clip on the outside of a pants pocket. But all that mattered was his handshake, which was firm yet gentle and seemed to communicate a reassurance that as long as you were with him, you were secure.

"Cavanaugh?" she asked. "What's your first name?"

"Actually"—he grinned—"I've gotten in the habit of just being called 'Cavanaugh.'"

Laura looked at Jamie. "You call him by his last name?"

"It's sort of complicated," Jamie said.

"But it sounds kind of cold."

"Well, when I want to be friendly, I call him something else."

"What's that?"

"'Lover.'"

"Perhaps I should leave the room," Cavanaugh said.

"No, stick around," Jamie said. "We're finished talking about you. You're not the center of attention anymore."

Cavanaugh nodded. "Exactly. *He* is."

They turned toward Dan, who lay unconscious in a hospital bed, all sorts of equipment and tubes linked to him. His face was purple with bruises.

"Laura, the initials GPS on my website address stand for Global Protective Services," Jamie said. "My husband watches over people in trouble. He takes care of them. He's a protector."

Laura frowned, puzzled.

"Sometimes I help," Jamie said. "That's why we're here. To find out what happened."

"And make sure it doesn't happen again," Cavanaugh said.

"But I *don't know* what happened, only that Dan was attacked. *Twice.*" Laura's voice shook.

"Tell us what you can," Jamie said. "Tell us about Sunday."

Ten minutes later, wiping more tears from her cheeks, Laura finished explaining.

"'Agreement?'" Cavanaugh asked. "'Worse adjustment?'"

"That's what the note mentioned. I don't understand *any* of it." Laura raised her hands in a gesture of helplessness.

"Has Dan been able to say anything?" Jamie asked.

"Nothing that makes sense."

Unconscious, Dan fidgeted and groaned.

Cavanaugh studied the room and frowned. "Why isn't someone watching the door?"

"The police said they don't have the budget to keep an officer here."

"Jamie said you had a daughter."

"Yes. Bethany. She's ten years old."

"And where is she now?"

"At school. I need to pick her up at two forty-five. She's worried sick about her father."

Cavanaugh pulled out his cell phone and pressed numbers. "Vince," he said when someone answered, "can you bear it if you don't do any sightseeing in L.A.? I need you to come down to Huntington Beach." Cavanaugh mentioned the name of the hospital. "A patient needs watching. Dan Yates. Jamie went to college with his wife. That's right—this one's for friendship. I'll fill you in when you get here. If Gwen's available, bring her with you. A little girl needs watching also. Great. Thanks, my friend."

Cavanaugh put away his phone and told Laura, "They're a brother and sister team. We brought them with us on the Gulfstream for a job that starts two days from now."

"Gulfstream?" Laura looked more bewildered.

"Global Protective Services has a lot of resources," Jamie said. "That's why I married him."

It was a joke. Jamie, who sold a promising dot-com company during the Internet stock frenzy ten years earlier, owned plenty of resources of her own.

"Laura, we need to ask the obvious question," Jamie continued. "Does Dan have any enemies?"

"Enemies?" Laura made the word sound meaningless.

"Surely, the police asked you the same question."

"Yes, but...enemies? Dan's the nicest man in the world. Everybody likes him."

"From everything Jamie told me, he's kind and decent," Cavanaugh agreed.

"That's right."

"A loving husband. An attentive father."

Laura wiped her eyes. "Absolutely."

"Good-natured. Generous."

Laura frowned. "Where are you going with this?"

"In my experience, a certain type of person hates those virtues," Cavanaugh said. "Despises anyone who exhibits them. Takes for granted that someone who's kind and good-natured is weak. Assumes he or she is a mark to be exploited."

Laura looked at Jamie in confusion and then again at Cavanaugh. "That's awfully cynical, don't you think?"

"I work in a cynical profession," Cavanaugh said. "You'd be surprised how many kind, good-natured, generous people have enemies."

Laura, who'd been thinking a lot about the times she and Jamie shared at Wellesley, recalled an American fiction course they'd taken. "*Billy Budd?*" She referred to a work by Herman Melville, in which a ship's officer hates a kind-hearted sailor simply because he's kind-hearted.

"Something like that," Cavanaugh said. "Some people—sociopaths—get their kicks taking advantage of what they consider weakness."

"Then *anybody* could be Dan's enemy."

"It's just something to think about," Jamie said. "The point is, often the enemy isn't obvious."

"Often, it's someone who appears to be a close friend," Cavanaugh said. "You mentioned *Billy Budd*. Think about Iago in *Othello*."

Again Laura looked at Jamie. She might have been trying to change the subject. "I doubt many bodyguards know Shakespeare."

"Not a bodyguard," Jamie said. "A protector. As you'll see, there's a difference. We need to consider something else, Laura. Please, don't take this wrong. Don't be offended. Are you absolutely certain Dan's faithful to you?"

"*What?*" Laura's cheeks reddened.

"Stalkers tend to be motivated by sexual anger," Cavanaugh said. "If Dan were having an affair, if the woman were married, the husband might have been furious enough to attack Dan. Or if Dan tried to call off the affair, the woman might have hired someone to put him in the hospital. 'Keep our agreement, jerk, or you'll get an even worse adjustment.' The note can be interpreted to fit that scenario."

"I don't want to talk about this anymore."

"I understand," Cavanaugh said. "I'm a stranger, and suddenly I'm asking rude questions. I apologize. But I did need to ask, and now it's important for you to look at your world in a way you never imagined. Suppose someone thought Dan was making sexual overtures even when he was perfectly innocent. Did you ever have a fleeting suspicion that someone was needlessly jealous? If we're going to find who did this to your husband and stop it from happening again, we might need to suspect what seemingly couldn't be suspected."

Laura eased into a chair. "I don't feel well."

"I'm surprised you're holding up as strongly as you are," Cavanaugh said. "Why don't you let Jamie take you home? There's nothing you can do for Dan at the moment. Get some rest."

Laura looked at Dan, where he lay unconscious in the bed. "But..."

"I'll stay with him. Nothing's going to happen to him while I'm here. I promise."

Laura studied Cavanaugh for several long seconds. "Yes," she finally said. "I could use some rest."

Jamie helped her to stand. As they walked toward the door, Laura turned and studied him again. "What's that metal clip on the outside of your pants pocket?"

"This?" Cavanaugh pulled on the clip and withdrew a black folding knife from the pocket. With a flick of his thumb, he opened the blade. He touched his loose-fitting jacket. "I also carry a firearm that I have a permit for."

"So do I," Jamie said.

Bewildered but more certain of the reassurance they communicated, Laura let Jamie guide her from the room.

* * *

Cavanaugh identified himself to a nurse and doctor who came in. Although they frowned, they seemed relieved by his presence. Sitting next to the door, out of sight from the hallway, he performed the hardest, tensest activity in his professsion: waiting. Bodyguards might pass the time by reading, but protectors didn't distract themselves—they watched.

In a while, he sensed a change in Dan and glanced toward the bed, keeping most of his attention on the doorway.

Dan's bloodshot eyes were open, squinting. "Who..."

"I'm a friend."

Dan's eyes closed.

In a little while, a man walked into the room. Like Cavanaugh, he had strong-looking shoulders and wore a loose sport coat. He looked immediately toward Cavanaugh's sheltered position next to the door, as if that were the proper place for Cavanaugh to be.

"Vince, thanks for coming," Cavanaugh said.

"Well, you said the magic word 'friendship.'"

"Where's Gwen?" Cavanaugh asked.

"Jamie phoned and gave us directions to the house. Gwen's helping to pick up the little girl from school."

"That finally covers the bases," Cavanaugh said.

Again, Dan's eyes struggled open. "Who..." He squinted at Vince.

"Another friend," Cavanaugh said. "Isn't it nice to be popular?"

Dan's eyes drooped.

"Somebody sure worked him over," Vince said.

"Had a tattoo," Dan said a day later. His words were hard to understand because he spoke through mangled lips. "A rose. Here." Dan pointed toward his right forearm.

322

"Yes, you said that when you were unconscious," a police detective said. "Ever see him before?"

"No." Dan breathed and rested. "But he knew my address."

Cavanaugh leaned close.

"He claimed I paid him. For what he called an attitude adjustment," Dan murmured.

"What does *that* mean?" the detective asked.

"He said I won an auction."

"Yeah, you mentioned that, too. He must have been crazy. A crackhead who wandered into the house you were showing," the detective concluded.

"But then why would he go to the hospital and attack Dan a second time?" Jamie asked.

"That's the thing about crackheads. They don't make sense," the detective told her.

"He said I'd done something terrible." Dan forced out the words. "...Said he was easing my conscience."

"By beating you? Crazy for sure," the detective decided. "We'll check our files for crackheads who are religious fanatics."

A physician entered the room, examined Dan, and announced that there wasn't any reason for him to remain in the hospital. "I'll prescribe some pain medication. You'll probably get a quieter rest at home."

Helping to get Dan settled in the master bedroom, Cavanaugh asked, "Do you feel alert enough to answer more questions?"

"Anything to catch him." Dan took a painful breath. "To stop him."

"Do you have any enemies?"

Dan looked puzzled.

"Sweetheart, he asked me the same thing," Laura said. "I

told him I couldn't imagine anybody hating you."

"How big is your real-estate firm?" Jamie asked.

"Twenty brokers."

"One big happy family?"

"They're all a great team."

"No exceptions?" Cavanaugh asked.

"No." Dan's pain-ridden eyes clouded. "Except..."

"There's always an 'except,'" Jamie said.

"Now that I think about it..."

"Exactly. Now that you think about it...It's a great team because the ones that didn't fit got sent away."

"Six months ago. I had to tell a broker to leave the firm," Dan remembered.

"Why?"

"Sexual harassment. Sam Logan. He kept bothering a secretary."

"I remember now," Laura said. "But that's so long ago..."

"Wouldn't he have tried to get even with me earlier?"

"Not if he made himself wait until he hoped you'd forgotten him," Jamie said.

"But Sam wasn't the guy who attacked me."

"So he hired somebody," Jamie suggested.

"Auctioned somebody," Cavanaugh added. "He placed a winning bid at an auction."

"But *what* auction?" Dan winced from the pain of talking.

"Set that aside for the moment. Tell us more about your business. Is anything unusual or dramatic happening?"

"Just that this year was fabulous for us. Enough that Ed Malone made an offer."

"Ed Malone? Offer?"

"He's the best broker I have. He wants to buy a share of the firm and open a branch office close to the beach."

"You seriously considered his proposal?" Jamie asked.

"Not much. I told him I liked things the way they are."

"Do you suppose he wanted a share strongly enough that

he decided to put you on your back for a while?" Cavanaugh asked. "If business suffered, maybe he could buy a share of the firm for a lower amount."

"Ed?" Dan looked astonished. "Never in a million years. We get along perfectly."

"Tell us about the Baxters. Laura told Jamie you were supposed to have dinner with them the day you were beaten."

"Yes," Laura said. "They watched our daughter while I went to try to find Dan. They're close friends. They'd never do anything to hurt us."

"Because of the dinner invitation, they'd be the last people you'd suspect," Cavanaugh noted.

"You know," Dan said painfully, "I don't like the way you think."

"I don't blame you," Cavanaugh told him. "You're tired and sore, and we're badgering you with questions. We'll talk about this later. Meanwhile, arrangements need to be made. Jamie and I have an assignment in Los Angeles tomorrow. Vince and Gwen will go with us. But you need at least two protectors. Also, you need to tell your daughter's school to take precautions while she's there."

"Two protectors?" Laura asked.

"Three would be better," Jamie answered.

"We'd hire them?"

"Jamie and I were happy to do this for free," Cavanaugh said. "Vince and Gwen did it as a favor to us. But protectors who don't know you would certainly expect to be paid."

"How much?" Laura frowned.

"A reasonable rate would be three hundred dollars a day."

"Times *three*? Per *day*?" Laura shook her head in astonishment.

"Good God, for how long?" Dan wanted to know.

"Until you're recovered. Meanwhile, they'd teach you how to secure the house and to change your patterns and behavior when you're outside. We call it Condition Orange, a basic alertness that helps you anticipate trouble. You should read Gavin de Becker's *The Gift of Fear*. It teaches you to pay attention to your instincts when they warn you something's wrong."

"*The Gift of Fear?*" Dan asked. "Condition Orange? This is insane. You make it sound like we're living in a war zone."

"Not far from the truth. The world's a dangerous neighborhood," Jamie said.

Laura studied her. "You've certainly changed."

"Things happened that forced me to change," Jamie said. "I wouldn't be alive today if I hadn't started thinking this way. I'll explain it to you later."

"Meanwhile, think about this while you rest," Cavanaugh told Dan.

"I don't have time to rest." Dan shifted in the bed, wincing. "Not when I'm losing business. Laura, get me my laptop. I need to see the new listings and—"

"Do you really think that's a good idea?" Laura asked.

"The alternative is to let Ed try to replace me. That's how your friends have got me thinking."

"Sorry," Cavanaugh said, and started backing from the room.

Laura brought Dan his laptop and helped him sit up. Groaning, he opened it and used the hand on his unbroken arm to turn on the computer and try to type commands.

"We'll let you do your work." Jamie left the room with Laura.

"Please, close the door," Dan said.

Halfway down the stairs, Laura halted. She thought about something, then glanced up toward the bedroom. "Excuse me for a minute, Jamie." Laura climbed the stairs and, without knocking, opened the door. After a motionless moment, she stepped inside and closed the door. The back of her neck was red.

At the bottom of the stairs, Cavanaugh and Jamie looked at one another.

"Something's not what it seems," Cavanaugh said. "Laura was more upset about the expense of hiring protectors than Dan was. Do they have money problems?"

"Not if somebody's trying to buy into Dan's business and he keeps refusing."

"I'm bothered by something else. The police detective said Dan talked about an auction and a rose tattoo when he was unconscious, but Laura never mentioned a word about the auction and the tattoo when we met her," Cavanaugh said.

"Auction." Jamie thought about it. "What does that mean to you?"

"Christie's. Sotheby's. Paintings. Statues."

"Sure. But...Maybe it's because I used to be in the dot-com sector. Christie's and Sotheby's aren't what I immediately think of."

"I don't understand."

"I'll give you a hint. The auction's on the Internet."

"eBay?"

Jamie went into a study next to the living room and stared at a desktop computer. "Just out of the hospital, Dan was far too impatient to get on the Internet." Jamie turned on the computer, tapped a few keys, and pointed toward a list that appeared on the left side of the screen. "These are the ten sites that this computer accesses the most."

"No eBay," Cavanaugh said. "That hunch didn't work out."

"But what's *this* site? Dan visits it a lot. Let's see if this computer and the one upstairs are networked. Yep." Jamie tapped more keys. "Dan already signed off. Strange. He couldn't wait to get on, and now he couldn't wait to get off." Jamie typed keys. A prompt asked for a password. When she clicked on the empty box, a program automatically supplied the password. "Whoever uses this site wants to save time."

The image that popped up made Jamie tilt her head, trying to look at it upside down. "Gosh."

"Double gosh," Cavanaugh said.

"I didn't know that position was physically possible," Jamie decided.

"Just goes to show, we never stop learning. But I suspect they needed a chiropractor after doing it that way."

"A porn site," Jamie said.

"Chiropractor or not, would you mind if *we* tried that position?" Cavanaugh asked.

"I have no idea where we'd find the harness."

"Can't wait to see what *E-bent* is." Cavanaugh pointed toward a directory at the top.

After Jamie clicked on it, the new page made them motionless.

"Auctions," Cavanaugh finally said.

"Well, now we know where to get the harness. Also weird-shaped dildos, erotic creams, exotic vibrators, and inflatable dolls."

"Anatomically correct," Cavanaugh said. "Hey, the bid for that one is only up to twenty dollars. At that price, it's a steal. Maybe I should put in a bid."

A directory included the word "services."

"I wonder where *that* leads," Jamie said.

When she clicked on it and they read about the things that people were willing to be paid to do to one another, Cavanaugh said, "The road of lost souls."

"Seen enough?"

"To last a lifetime."

As they returned to the living room, Laura descended the stairs.

"Hey, Laura," Cavanaugh said, "remember, at the hospital, I told you we might need to suspect what seemingly couldn't be suspected?"

Laura frowned. "What's wrong?"

"How long has Dan been addicted to computer porn?"

"What kind of question..."

"Is that what he was looking at when you went back to the bedroom just now?" Cavanaugh asked. "Were you checking up on him? Even fresh out of the hospital after taking a beating, he couldn't resist taking a peak. Is he that far gone?"

"I have no idea what you're talking about."

"E-bent."

Laura's cheeks paled.

"We all agreed Dan was kind and decent. A loving husband. An attentive father. Good-natured. Generous," Cavanaugh said. "None of that's incompatible with a porn addiction. He's not hurting anybody, right? If he enjoys watching, what's the big deal?"

The room became silent.

"Unless he gets more turned on by fantasy than reality," Jamie said. "Then the expression 'loving husband' has a limited application."

"Jamie, you're supposed to be my friend."

"I couldn't understand why you were so concerned about the cost of the protectors. If you were worried about Dan, the price would have been cheap," Jamie said. "Unless you knew who'd attacked him and why. Unless you were fairly confident the guy who did it wouldn't return after the second attack."

"You hired the attacker," Cavanaugh added. "You used the auction directory of the porn site Dan's most addicted to. Poetic justice."

"Did he stop having sex with you?" Jamie asked. "Did he get all his satisfaction from the porn site?"

"Jamie, really, I'm begging you as a friend. Leave this alone."

"Did you resent the way he ignored you? Did you plead with him to stop going to the site? Did you promise he could indulge all his fantasies on you, but even *that* didn't tempt him to pay attention to you?"

Trembling, Laura hugged herself.

"I'm sorry," Jamie said.

"Damn him, he wouldn't stop. I wanted to punish him. I wanted to put him in a position where he needed me, where he'd appreciate that I took care of him."

"The second attack?" Cavanaugh asked.

"A mistake," Laura answered. "I contacted the man and made sure he knows not to come back."

"That's why the cost of the protectors bothered you. Because you knew they wouldn't be needed."

Laura's knees bent. She eased onto a chair. "I don't think I can bear going to jail. Being away from Bethany will kill me."

"We're the only ones who know," Cavanaugh said.

Jamie looked at him in surprise.

"Except for Dan," Cavanaugh added. "*Dan* has to know."

"You mean you're not going to tell the police about this?"

"It seems to me there's been enough suffering," Cavanaugh said.

Laura looked hopeless. "But you insist I tell Dan."

"Otherwise we won't stay quiet."

"When he finds out, he'll leave me."

"Possibly. But the way things were going, one of you would have left soon anyhow. So you're not exactly losing anything. Do you still love him?"

"Yes, Lord help me."

"And maybe, despite everything, he still loves you."

"Do you seriously expect me to believe Dan will forgive me? That's not going to happen."

"Perhaps if you can forgive *him*. There's no denying this is a mess," Jamie said. "But you won't know if this marriage can be saved until the two of you face the truth."

"I feel nauseous."

"I know." Jamie went over, crouched next to her, and held her hands.

No one moved for several minutes. Finally, Laura took a deep breath, freed her hands, and stood. "There's no sense waiting to tell him. It only hurts worse."

Gripping the banister, Laura slowly climbed the stairs.

"The attacker," Cavanaugh said.

"He called himself an 'attitude adjuster.'"

"What's the email address you used to get in touch with him?"

Laura paused at the top of the stairs. Her face was even paler.

"Don't worry. We won't tell the police," Cavanaugh said. "If we did, he'd implicate you. He wouldn't be the only one going to prison."

"But he needs to feel responsible for his actions," Jamie said. "*He* should do some soul searching the same as you and Dan are."

E-BENT
I WILL ADJUST YOUR WAYS
High bidder receives an attitude adjustment. I am strong and tough from years of outdoor work. If you win this auction...

QUESTION TO SELLER
I have been bad. Frightfully horribly bad. I have never felt so ashamed. I can't eat or sleep because I feel so god-awful guilty. I need to be punished as soon as possible. Please. I'm begging you to adjust my...

Barry put on his leather gloves. A refinement he was proud of, they protected his knuckles. At the same time, they guaranteed he wouldn't leave fingerprints. *I don't why I didn't get the idea earlier*, he told himself. The gloves were shiny black. Their thin leather fit snugly on his hands. He loved their smell.

Time to earn my pay, he thought.

He was in New Orleans, another interesting city he hadn't visited until his auctions led him in new directions. Streetcars. The Garden District. The French Quarter. Bourbon Street and Jackson Square, where Steve McQueen walked in one of Barry's favorite movies, *The Cincinnati Kid*. The food was terrific, although some of the restaurants were pricey, but adjusting attitudes was bringing in cash, especially when he robbed people after beating them senseless, making it look like a mugging. The world was purer by the day.

Almost midnight. A ship's horn blared on the river. Barry was outside a warehouse. At a corner of the building, a light glowed faintly in an office. He peered through a dusty window. A man sat at a desk. His head down, he sorted through documents. Crutches leaned against the wall behind him. Barry nodded. The man had sent him an email about a car accident in which his drunken driving had caused his Mercedes to veer toward a van full of high-school kids on their way to a party after their prom. Swerving to avoid him, the kids hit a concrete wall, the impact killing all of them. The man who caused it managed to drive home. Nobody witnessed the incident. Thus he avoided punishment, except that when he got out of his Mercedes at home, he was so drunk that he fell and broke his leg. *That's not enough punishment. I don't want to go to prison, but I can't bear feeling this guilty*, his email said.

You've come to the right person, Barry had replied. *I will make you feel better.*

Now Barry tried the door. As promised, it wasn't locked. He pushed it open, stepped into a dark corridor, and walked toward light seeping under a farther door. As promised, *it* wasn't locked, either. Barry swung it open, revealing the grief-stricken man hunched over his desk.

"You've been bad," Barry said.

"You have no idea," the man murmured, his face down.

"I'm here to adjust your attitude. You'll be sore afterward, but I swear I'll ease your conscience."

"Actually," the man said, "I planned on doing some adjustments of my own."

"What do you mean?"

The man looked up. His intense hazel eyes reflected some of the brown from the desk. His strong chin and forehead radiated the wrath of hell.

"I think I'm in the wrong place." Turning, Barry faltered at the sight of a gorgeous woman with searing green eyes and a pit bull on a leash.

"No, you're definitely in the right place," the woman said.

A noise made Barry pivot toward the man. The noise came from the chair scraping as the man stood and grabbed one of the crutches from the wall.

"Wait," Barry said.

"Why?" The man held the crutch as if it were a baseball bat.

"There's a mistake," Barry said.

"What'll it take to convince you the only attitude in need of adjustment is yours?" the man asked.

"Uh," Barry said.

"We'll keep track of you," the man said. "Believe me, we know how. If you ever harm anyone again, we'll come back."

The man swung the crutch with all his might. It slammed across the desk. With an ear-torturing crack, it split apart, one end flying across the roof, crashing against a cabinet.

"Uh," Barry said. Feeling something wet on his legs, he realized that his bladder had let go.

Growling, the dog bared its teeth as the woman urged it forward. Barry stumbled back and tripped over a chair, crashing into a corner. The man whacked the broken crutch against the wall above Barry's head. The impact sent plaster flying. It was so loud it made Barry's ears ring. The dog growled nearer.

A road-repair crew. A man holds a pole with a sign at the top. SLOW, it says on one side. STOP, it says on the other. The man holds it listlessly. Tall and scarecrow lanky, he looks even more weary than his dawn-to-dusk workday would explain. His cheeks are sunken. His shoulders sag. A chill November wind blows dust across his face. His coat and yellow vest hang on him. Cars speed past, ignoring the SLOW sign, almost hitting him.

You've seen countless versions of him without ever paying attention. As snow starts to fall, he looks so pathetic that you actually give him a sorrowful look. What kind of dismal life does he have? What on earth must he be thinking?

Is that them in that van? The light was so dim, I never got a good look at their faces. The pit bull. Jesus, all I really noticed was that pit bull. Growling. Foam spraying over my face. "We'll come back, Barry." *That's what the guy said after taking all of his money.* "We'll keep a close watch. We'll make sure you learned the error of your ways. If we find out you've been doing more adjusting, we'll put the fear of God into you, Barry."

The fear of God? They're the ones I'm afraid of, Barry thought. *I was never so shit-scared in my life. That van's gotta be doing sixty. Slow down! You almost hit me! But I don't dare shout. If that's them and I shake my sign at them, they'll wait for me after work. They'll—*

"Barry! What the hell's wrong with you?" a voice shouted.

"Huh?" As the snowflakes got larger, Barry turned toward his big-chested foreman stomping toward him. The man had angry red cheeks.

"Don't you listen to your walkie-talkie!" the foreman yelled. "I've been giving you orders for the last five minutes!"

"Orders?"

"To stop traffic from coming through! Turn the frigging sign! Make everybody stop!" As roaring traffic almost hit them, the foreman raised his beefy hands. "This has been going on too damned long. How many times do I have to tell you to do your job?"

"I'm sorry. I..."

"Look, I hate to do this. You're just not fit for the job anymore. Don't show up tomorrow."

"But—"

"Can't risk it. Somebody'll get hurt. Get your head straight, man. You need a better attitude."

Cavanaugh and Jamie are continuing characters in David Morrell's protective-agent series, which includes *The Protector* and *The Naked Edge.*

ABOUT THE CONTRIBUTORS

KAY WILKINSON BARLEY is the author of *Whimsey: A Novel*. She has had several short stories and memoir pieces published in magazines and anthologies. A recent short story was among the top-ten finalists for the *Southern Writers Magazine* annual short story contest. Kaye is the mistress of Meanderings and Muses (meanderingsandmuses.com), a blog which has everything from crime fiction author spotlights and interviews to recipes to political rants. She is a monthly contributor to the popular Jungle Red Writers blog. More about her work can be found at kayewilkinsonbarley.com.

ERIC BEETNER is the author of more than a dozen novels including *Rumrunners, The Devil Doesn't Want Me, Dig Two Graves, Run For The Money,* and *The Year I Died Seven Times*. His award-winning stories have appeared in over twenty anthologies including *Unloaded: Crime Writers Writing Without Guns*, which he created and edited. He lives in Los Angeles where he hosts the Noir At The Bar reading series. For more visit ericbeetner.com.

G. J. BROWN is the author of four crime thriller novels set in Scotland and the U.S. and is a co-founder and director of crime writing festival Bloody Scotland. He has also delivered pizzas in Toronto, compered a two-day music festival, floated a high tech company and was once booed by 49,000 people at a major football cup final. Gordon runs a creativity training business called Brain Juice and is a DJ on local radio. Gordon has been writing since his teens and has four crime and thriller novels to his name—*Falling* is now out in the U.S., published by Down & Out Books.

SHEILA CONNOLLY, Anthony and Agatha Award–nominated and *New York Times* bestselling author, writes three mystery series for Berkley Prime Crime, set in Philadelphia, rural Massachusetts, and the Wild West of Ireland. In addition, she writes the *Relatively Dead* paranormal romance series for Beyond the Page Publishing, as well as the occasional romantic suspense. Her short stories have appeared in multiple Level Best anthologies. She lives in Massachusetts, surrounded by a few hundred of her ancestors, and in her spare time she loves to travel and to excavate old trash heaps.

O'NEIL DE NOUX is a New Orleans writer with thirty-two books in print and over three hundred short story sales in multiple genres: crime fiction, historical fiction, children's fiction, mainstream fiction, sci-fi, suspense, fantasy, horror, western, literary, young adult, religious, romance, humor and erotica. His fiction has received several awards, including the Shamus Award for Best Short Story, the Derringer Award for Best Novelette and the 2011 Police Book of the Year. Two of his stories have appeared in the *Best American Mystery Stories* anthology (2013 and 2007) He is a past Vice President of the Private Eye Writers of America.

BARBARA FERRER'S writing career officially began with the 2006 publication of her first YA novel, *Adiós to My Old Life* (as Caridad Ferrer), although she'd been writing for a really long time before that. Not that anyone will ever see those efforts. She is, however, extremely glad to have readers see her effort for this anthology, "Way Down We Go." A native Floridian, she now makes her home in the Pacific Northwest, thriving amidst the rain and cooler weather, finding it the perfect environment for crafting slightly twisted tales.

JOHN M. FLOYD'S short stories have appeared in *The Strand Magazine, AHMM, EQMM, The Saturday Evening Post, Mississippi Noir,* and *The Best American Mystery Stories 2015.* A former Air Force captain and IBM systems engineer, John is also a three-time Derringer Award winner, an Edgar nominee, and the author of six books, including *Rainbow's End, Midnight, Clockwork, Deception, Fifty Mysteries,* and (coming in fall 2016) *Dreamland.* Visit him at www.johnmfloyd.com.

USA Today bestselling author **ALISON GAYLIN** has been nominated for the Edgar, Anthony, Thriller and RT awards and has won the Shamus award for her Brenna Spector suspense series. Her ninth book, the critically acclaimed standalone *What Remains of Me,* is out now in hardcover and paperback from William Morrow.

HEATHER GRAHAM is a best-selling American writer, who writes primarily romance novels. She also writes under the pen name **Shannon Drake**. She has written over a hundred and fifty novels and novellas, has been published in approximately twenty-five languages, and has had over seventy-five million books in print. Her most recent novels are *Flawless* and *Haunted Destiny,* from her Krewe of Hunters series.

GREG HERREN is the award-winning author of over thirty novels and fifty published short stories. The New Orleans *Times-Picayune* called his *Murder in the Rue Chartres* "The most honest story about post-Katrina New Orleans to date." He has also edited over twenty anthologies, including the award-winning *Love Bourbon Street: Reflections on New Orleans.* His most recent novel, *Garden District Gothic,* was released in September 2016.

DEBORAH LACY runs Mystery Playground, a blog about crime fiction and fun, and Storyteller Playground, a consulting firm that helps businesses tell their stories. Over the years, her clients have included the Bill & Melinda Gates Foundation, Intuit, and Google, among others. Jeffery Deaver once told her the secret to getting short stories published. It seems to be working.

Author, poet, and journalist **BV LAWSON'S** award-winning stories, poems and articles have appeared in dozens of publications and anthologies. A four-time Derringer Award finalist and 2012 winner for her short fiction, BV was also honored by the American Independent Writers and Maryland Writers Association for her Scott Drayco series, with the debut novel, *Played to Death*, named Best Mystery in the 2015 Next Generation Indie Book Awards and a Shamus Award finalist. BV currently lives in Virginia with her husband and enjoys flying above the Chesapeake Bay in a little Cessna. Visit her website at bvlawson.com. No ticket required.

R.T. LAWTON is a retired federal law enforcement agent, a past member of the Mystery Writers of America board of directors and a two-time Derringer nominee with over 100 short stories in various publications, to include *The Mystery Box* (2013 MWA anthology), *And All Our Yesterdays* anthology, *Who Died in Here?* anthology, *West Coast Crime Wave* anthology, *Deadwood Magazine*, *Easyriders*, *Outlaw Biker*, *Woman's World* magazine, and thirty-five sold to *Alfred Hitchcock Mystery Magazine*. He also has four ebooks at Amazon.com and at Smashwords for other e-readers. You may have attended one of his Surveillance Workshops at various mystery conferences.

EDITH MAXWELL writes the Quaker Midwife Mysteries and the Local Foods Mysteries, the Country Store Mysteries (as Maddie Day), and the Lauren Rousseau Mysteries (as Tace Baker), as well as award-winning short crime fiction. Maxwell, a former technical writer, farmer, and doula, is Vice President of Sisters in Crime New England. She lives north of Boston with her beau and three cats, and blogs with the other Wicked Cozy Authors (wickedcozyauthors.com). You can find her on Facebook, twitter, Pinterest, and at her web site, edithmaxwell.com.

LIZ MILLIRON has been making up stories, and creating her own endings for other people's stories, for as long as she can remember. She's worked for fifteen years in the corporate world, but finds making things up is far more satisfying than writing software manuals. A lifelong mystery fan, her short fiction has been published at Uppagus, Mysterical-e, and in *Lucky Charms: 12 Crime Tales,* an anthology from the Pittsburgh chapter of Sisters in Crime. Visit her on the web at marysuttonauthor.com, find her on Facebook, or follow her on Twitter (@mary_sutton73).

TERRIE FARLEY MORAN is the best-selling author of the Read 'Em and Eat cozy mystery series including *Well Read, Then Dead,* winner of the Agatha Award for Best First Novel, *Caught Read-Handed* and *Read to Death.* Terrie's short mystery fiction has been published in *Ellery Queen Mystery Magazine, Alfred Hitchcock Mystery Magazine* and numerous anthologies. Her Read 'Em and Eat prequel, *A Killing at the Beasoleil,* was an Agatha Award nominee for Best Short Story. Terrie co-writes Laura Childs's Scrapbooking Mystery series. Together they have written *Parchment and Old Lace* and *Crepe Factor.* terriefarleymoran.com.

DAVID MORRELL is the award-winning author of *First Blood,* the novel in which Rambo was created. Morrell is an Edgar and Anthony finalist, a Nero and Macavity winner, and a three-time recipient of the distinguished Bram Stoker Award from the Horror Writers Association. The International Thriller Writers organization gave him its prestigious career-achievement Thriller Master Award. He also received an RT Book Reviews "Thriller Pioneer" award and a Comic-Con Inkpot award for "outstanding achievement in action/adventure." His short stories have appeared in numerous *Year's Best* collections. With eighteen million copies in print, his work has been translated into twenty-six languages. Morrell's latest novels, *Murder as a Fine Art* and *Inspector of the Dead,* are Victorian mystery/thrillers that explore the fascinating world of 1850s London.

When not scribbling twisted musings into spiral notebooks, photographing the odd puddle or junk pile, or building classy furniture, **DINO PARENTI** earns a little scratch drawing buildings. His work can be found in a several anthologies, as well as the following journals: *Pithead Chapel, Menacing Hedge, Pantheon Magazine, Cease-Cows,* and the *Lascaux Review,* where he won their first annual flash fiction contest.

MIKE PENN'S story, "The Cost of Doing Business," originally appeared in *Thuglit,* Issue 24 won the Derringer Award for best mystery. One of his stories, "The Converts" was recently filmed as a short movie. Another story, "The Landlord," was recently translated into a play. Fiction of his can be found in over ninety magazines and anthologies from six countries such as *Alfred Hitchcock Mystery Magazine* in the U.S., *Here and Now* in England, *Crime Factory* in Australia. Comic book publishers include IDW and JKOR Graphics. He has been an Associate Editor for *Space and Time* Magazine as well as the Editor of the horror/suspense anthology, *Tales From a Darker State.* Organizational Affiliations include The Mystery Writers of America and the International Thriller Writers.

GARY PHILLIPS draws on his experiences ranging from community organizer, teaching incarcerated youth, running a nonprofit to better race relations begun in the wake the Rodney King riots, director of a shadowy political action committee to delivering dog cages in penning his tales of chicanery and malfeasance. He has written online serials, comic books, radio plays, screenplays, novels, novellas, short stories and anything else he can get away with. Currently he is president of the Private Eye Writers of America.

THOMAS PLUCK is the author of *Bad Boy Boogie*, a Jay Desmarteaux crime thriller coming from Down & Out Books in 2017, and *Blade of Dishonor*, which *MysteryPeople* called "the Raiders of the Lost Ark of pulp paperbacks." He has slung hash, worked on the docks, and even swept the Guggenheim museum (but not as part of a clever heist). He hails from Nutley, New Jersey, home to criminal masterminds Martha Stewart and Richard Blake, but has so far evaded capture. He shares his hideout with his sassy Louisiana wife and their two felines. You can find him at thomaspluck.com and on Twitter as @thomaspluck.

PAULA PUMPHREY is a former newspaper reporter and staff writer. Her short story, "Sweet Murder," appears in *Lucky Charms: 12 Crime Tales* (December, 2013). Several of her Pittsburgh profiles were published in *Pittsburgh Legends and Visions, An Illustrated History* by Eliza Smith Brown from Heritage Media Corporation and Pittsburgh History & Landmarks Foundation (2002). She has provided book reviews, articles for magazines and online publications locally and abroad. Currently, she is a correspondent for a newspaper. She is a member of Pennwriters, Pittsburgh Sisters in Crime and serves on the board, Religion Newswriters Association and the Society of Professional Journalists.

Bestselling mystery writer **ELAINE VIETS** has written thirty mysteries in four series. In *Brain Storm,* the first Angela Richman Death Investigator mystery, she returned to her hardboiled roots. Elaine passed the MedicoLegal Death Investigators Course for forensic professionals to research the series. She's written short stories for *Alfred Hitchcock's Mystery Magazine* and anthologies edited by Charlaine Harris and Lawrence Block. *The Art of Murder,* featuring South Florida PIs Helen Hawthorne and her husband, Phil Sagemont, is Elaine's fifteenth Dead-End Job mystery. She's won the Anthony, Agatha, and Lefty Awards. Elaine is director at large of the Mystery Writers of America. elaineviets.com.

OTHER TITLES FROM DOWN AND OUT BOOKS

See www.DownAndOutBooks.com for complete list

By J.L. Abramo
Catching Water in a Net
Clutching at Straws
Counting to Infinity
Gravesend
Chasing Charlie Chan
Circling the Runway
Brooklyn Justice

By Trey R. Barker
2,000 Miles to Open Road
Road Gig: A Novella
Exit Blood
Death is Not Forever
No Harder Prison

By Richard Barre
The Innocents
Bearing Secrets
Christmas Stories
The Ghosts of Morning
Blackheart Highway
Burning Moon
Echo Bay
Lost

By Eric Beetner (editor)
Unloaded

By Eric Beetner and
JB Kohl
Over Their Heads

By Eric Beetner and
Frank Scalise
The Backlist
The Short List

By G.J. Brown
Falling

By Rob Brunet
Stinking Rich

By Dana Cameron (editor)
Murder at the Beach: Bouchercon Anthology 2014

By Mark Coggins
No Hard Feelings

By Tom Crowley
Vipers Tail
Murder in the Slaughterhouse

By Frank De Blase
Pine Box for a Pin-Up
Busted Valentines and Other Dark Delights
A Cougar's Kiss

By Les Edgerton
The Genuine, Imitation, Plastic Kidnapping

By A.C. Frieden
Tranquility Denied
The Serpent's Game
The Pyongyang Option (*)

By Jack Getze
Big Numbers
Big Money
Big Mojo
Big Shoes

(*)—*Coming Soon*